ON THE NICKEL

ON THE NICKEL

A Jack Liffey Mystery

John Shannon

This first world edition published 2010
in Great Britain and in the USA by
SEVERN HOUSE PUBLISHERS LTD of
9–15 High Street, Sutton, Surrey, England, SM1 1DF.
Trade paperback edition published
in Great Britain and the USA 2010 by
SEVERN HOUSE PUBLISHERS LTD

Copyright © 2010 by John Shannon.

All rights reserved.
The moral right of the author has been asserted.

British Library Cataloguing in Publication Data

Shannon, John, 1943–
    On the Nickel. – (A Jack Liffey mystery)
    1. Liffey, Jack (Fictitious character) – Fiction.
    2. Private investigators – Family relationships –
    California – Los Angeles – Fiction. 3. Missing persons –
    Investigation – Fiction. 4. Los Angeles (Calif.). Police
    Dept. – Fiction. 5. Detective and mystery stories.
    I. Title II. Series
    813.5'4-dc22

ISBN-13: 978-0-7278-6903-6   (cased)
ISBN-13: 978-1-84751-247-5   (trade paper)

Except where actual historical events and characters are being
described for the storyline of this novel, all situations in this
publication are fictitious and any resemblance to living persons
is purely coincidental.

All Severn House titles are printed on acid-free paper.

Severn House Publishers support The Forest Stewardship Council [FSC],
the leading international forest certification organisation. All our titles that
are printed on Greenpeace-approved FSC-certified paper carry the FSC logo.

 **Mixed Sources**
Product group from well-managed
forests and other controlled sources
www.fsc.org Cert no. SA-COC-1565
FSC © 1996 Forest Stewardship Council

Typeset by Palimpsest Book Production Ltd.,
Grangemouth, Stirlingshire, Scotland.
Printed and bound in Great Britain by
MPG Books Ltd., Bodmin, Cornwall.

For the novelist and critic Michael Harris:
dependable friend, ambitious writer, big soul.

Acknowledgements

Deepest acknowledgements to the wonderful suggestions offered by my friend Mark Jonathan Harris and for the insights culled, with his permission, from his lovely and moving 1989 young adult novel about Skid Row, *Come the Morning*.

Also to the inspiring work of *L.A. Times* columnist Steve Lopez, whose 2005 and later articles about the remarkable homeless cellist Nathaniel Anthony Ayers grew exponentially from a series of poignant newspaper columns to a book and then a movie, both called *The Soloist*, while I was working on this novel.

And finally, to the great social historian, friend and writer Mike Davis, his son Jack, and the rest of the family. They have graciously served as archetypes for the malleable and fictional Mike Lewis family through twelve Jack Liffey novels, and counting. In addition, I have been deeply influenced by Mike's groundbreaking books such as *City of Quartz* and *Ecology of Fear*, along with his other books and articles, which have suggested new and fruitful ways of looking at this strange phenomenon of Los Angeles. He has enriched my books immeasurably.

And if the city falls but a single man escapes
He will carry the City within himself on the roads
of exile
He will be the City . . .
  – Zbigniew Herbert, 'Report from the Besieged City'

On thinking about Hell, I gather
My brother Shelley found it was a place
Much like the city of London. I
Who live in Los Angeles and not in London
Find, on thinking about Hell, that it must be
Still more like Los Angeles.
                              – Bertolt Brecht, *Poems*

ONE
The Raging Homeless

'I'll be your Archie Goodwin,' Maeve offered.

Jack Liffey's brow furrowed, and it was clear he didn't know what she was talking about.

'Nero Wolfe's right-hand man. Ironside had a legman, too. But I've only seen a few old reruns. Mark something. OK, I'll be your Doctor Watson, you fuddy-duddy.'

He got it. He rattled the arms of his wheelchair angrily, a tiny charade of a tantrum, one of the few ways he had of expressing annoyance, or expressing much of anything.

She gave him the zucchini and ginger curry sandwich she'd been withholding and stuck out her tongue. 'You're in my power, decrepit dad-o-mine. Better get used to it. I can play Ornette Coleman real loud. I'll dance in seven veils. I'm trying to make life a little more interesting for you. Get you a job to do.' There, she'd said it. 'Give your mind a task to fasten on like a leech.'

He'd been unable to use his legs or his voice for more than a month now, since he and Maeve had been trapped under an immense slumping hillside of mud and debris, having taken desperate refuge in a bathtub when they glanced out the window and saw the brown wall coming. The mudslide had ripped open the walls of the house and pressed a brute thumb down on his spine, disturbing something within. He had lain atop her, trying to protect her, as he always did, for forty-five minutes. It had been no fun for her either, as most of that time he'd been unconscious because of a claustrophobic panic that she knew he'd been carrying around like a secret charm since falling down a well as a child. The doctors had since prodded him and spinal tapped and X-rayed and CT-scanned him no end, spoken in a mumbo jumbo of T9 and L6, but always ended up shrugging and saying that his problems were probably only psychological.

That invariably set Maeve off. 'Is that what they told Hemingway when he was desperate for help? Why *only* psychological? The mind can be everything!' Doctors were pretty useless.

Her dad was scribbling furiously on his yellow pad now.

<u>NO</u> TO NERO WOLFE. HATE ORCHIDS. AGREE WITH GEN.
STERNWOOD. TOO MUCH LIKE FLESH OF MEN.

'Well, I like orchids,' Maeve insisted. 'They're weird and beautiful.'
They'd watched a DVD of *The Big Sleep* together the week
before – just wonderful! – so she knew his referents, knew about
the old general out in his hothouse who was trying to hire Philip
Marlowe. Unfortunately, she hadn't been speaking theoretically, but
her father remained purposely obtuse to all her hints about helping
him get back on track as an investigator. His old friend Mike Lewis
had called just that morning with a possible job for him – not
knowing how badly off he was. It didn't look like she was going
to get away with nudging him into it, and her program wasn't all
altruism. She had her mind set on playing Dr. Watson. Maeve was
in her last semester of high school and still unsure of a college or
even a major, and a break from all that annoying future-anxiety –
and a few other personal problems – would have been delightful.

Her father took a bite and nodded a reluctant appreciation of the
odd sandwich. She refused to make him anything even vaguely
reminiscent of animal. He opened his mouth to say something –
old habits die hard – and emitted a kind of tortured squawk.
GINGER ALE. He tapped his finger on the words on the second
pad he kept in his saddlebag, which contained whole pages of alpha-
betized requisites:

BATHROOM	HOW ARE YOU	SWEATER
BED	HUNGRY	TAKE LOCO AWAY
BAD IDEA	KILL THE TV	THIRSTY
BRING LOCO	KILL THE RADIO	TO BACK YARD
BRING MY BOOK	KLEENEX	TO BED
COFFEE	MAKE CALL FOR ME	WAKE ME IN _____
COLDER	MAKE HOTTER	WHATS ON TV TONIGHT
DOCTOR!	NEED CHECKBOOK	WHEN
GET MAIL	NEED MY MEDS	WHERE'S GLORIA
GINGER ALE	NEW PENCIL	WHERE'S MAEVE
GOOD IDEA	NEED READING GLASSES	WHO CALLED
HATE THAT MUSIC	PUT TV ON	WHO VISITED

If his mute condition kept up, they'd have to get him one of those talking machines like that physicist guy, she thought. Are-we-a-lone-in-the-un-i-verse? She mimicked the affectless robot voice in her head.

But her dad still had use of his hands, so he could write. She kissed the top of his head. Maeve loved her father to death and would have given up her own future and stood by his side translating for him forever if he'd have allowed it, but she knew he wouldn't.

When he nodded off in the wheelchair after lunch, she went into the living room of Gloria's house, out of his hearing, and called Mike Lewis back at his home in northern San Diego County.

'Mike, this is Maeve Liffey. You know, my dad got hurt pretty bad in the PV landslide. He has to sleep a lot these days, and he just went off into noddy-ville. But he asked me to call you back and get some details about the job.'

'I'm sorry, Maeve, I didn't know he was so bad. My own Prager-Sjöman's is getting worse too, I hate to say. I had to give up teaching.'

She made a horrified face that he, of course, couldn't see. Her father had never told her about this, but Mike Lewis made it sound like she should have known. And if she was to be her dad's Dr. Watson, she should know everything.

'I'm sorry, Mr Lewis. Dad told me, of course, but I've been in a null zone for a while. What is it you want him to do?'

'I know he's a damn good child-finder. Even if he's on half speed, I'd trust him ahead of just about anyone up there. My son Conor has run off, and I think he's in L.A. I usually trust Conor's judgment, pretty much, but he's still only sixteen and there's too many ways a boy can get hurt at that age. I'd like Jack to make contact if he can. Have him call.'

She knew those dangers only too well. She herself had fallen madly in love/lust with a gangbanger a year earlier and got herself beaten to a pulp joining his Latino gang, and then got herself pregnant and for quite a while had felt that she was truly lost in an alien world and would never get back.

'Dad would want me to get whatever background you can give him,' she said.

'OK. Conor's quite an idealist, in all the senses. A Platonist – and the ordinary political meaning, too.'

She'd have to look up Platonist, she thought. Best to pretend she had a grasp on it right now. She wished he would give her something practical.

'He was in a rock group, like all kids his age, but it was based on pretty erroneous affinities. The other kids were rebellious and defiant but really just suburban assholes who didn't want to learn anything. He was a lot smarter and more curious.'

'What was it called? It might help.'

'You do take after Jack. The Raging Homeless.' She could hear him laugh softly. 'As if there were any homeless within fifty miles of here. As if the completely demoralized go on rages. He named it, probably acting out some version of the politics he's heard all his life, from me and Sinéad and Soledad.' He sighed audibly. 'I think what might have upset him this time was my condition – I know it's tough to watch a parent decline – plus a nasty argument I had one night with Soledad. Then he had some kind of dust-up at high school. I couldn't get it out of him. Jack can check on that. Fallbrook High.'

'What makes you think he came to L.A.?'

'Other than L.A. being the great magnet for everything loose in the U.S.A.? The music business, I suppose. As far as I know, he has no friends there.'

'Anything else my dad should know? Is he gay, is he an anarchist, has he broken up with a girl, does he drive a chopped 'fifty-eight Chevy with a supercharger?'

'You must have interesting friends, Maeve. Conor is not gay, as far as we know; he loves soccer but he was too short and slow to be much good at it; I think his girlfriends are all still casual, and he drives our old Prius when he can borrow it. Let me think. The concept of not harming the weak and innocent is so powerful to him that he says he can't read Dickens. It hurts him physically. For a while in junior high he called himself Commie Boy and founded a collective whose only other members were a couple of disturbed twins. Their parents sent them away to a military school and phoned us in a rage, screaming that Soledad and I were an evil influence. His band is the only thing that's endured.'

'Was their music any good?'

'Not really. It was a garage band run on the old punk-rock ethos that you really shouldn't be proficient. They did pay to cut a couple of CDs and sold them on the web.'

'Would you send a picture of Conor to my e-mail? Dad still

won't get a computer of his own.' *Even now*, she thought, *when it could be his lifeline*. But she didn't want Mike to know any of that. 'You know what a Luddite he is. And e-mail the names and phone numbers of some of Conor's friends.'

'Will do. I've got your address.'

'Can I tell Dad how you're doing, healthwise?'

She heard Gloria's car in the driveway and knew she had to make this quick.

'We're hoping it's stabilized, but to put it simply, my autoimmune system is eating me up. I had to give up teaching because I can barely walk. I suppose it's just the American experience – the long slow decline in expectations. Tell Jack I miss him and to call me when he can.'

'Thanks, Mr Lewis. I've got to go now.'

'And tell Jack we love Conor a lot and want him home.'

'I sure will.'

Notes for a New Music

Day Zero

One shouldn't make a fetish of caring for its own sake, but maybe for the sake of the world. Is there anything more powerful in the world than the loneliness of a simple soul who cares? (Whoa! – I'm getting sentimental.) I will probably never lose a girl as important to me as Tessie, but we didn't belong together, and I know it.

I wonder if I've already written the best songs I'll ever write. Dad warned me not to feel that way, that the future would always open up like a mountain vista, but he's trying so hard to hide the slow collapse of his health. The grace – the grace that man has. He is a man that I will never equal. Are sons always less than their fathers?

This is not the first day of the rest of my life. Today was just a bus trip, all numbnuts, burgers and suburbs, and an empty chat with a sad seatmate who got off at Oceanside to join the Marines. (I didn't say what I felt. Fuck that!) Maybe tomorrow will be the first day of the rest my life. I think I can pick whenever tomorrow starts.

I've been in a coma for years, all through school, something so horribly common in America. I guess I've chosen trouble now. Disruption. Instead of continuity. I'm sorry, Mom and Dad, but I had to make a run for it. You two are all about language and words and your obsession with reason, and you'll never understand that all those things get in the way of meaning for me.

Jack Liffey was trying to work out how to send a message to the legs that he could see down there, enclosed in chinos that were a bit wrinkled, with black postal walkers on his feet, resting like stones on the foot flaps of the wheelchair. In body sensation, most of the time he was a floating torso, though with a little buzz in his butt and even his feet now and then when he ran the chair over a rough surface. It was the strangest sensation he'd ever had, being so obviously connected to the outlying provinces of his body but the messages from out there were so weak and ineffectual. Provinces of the body in revolt. What was that poem? Auden. *In Memory of W. B. Yeats.*

He ran his wheelchair carefully down the makeshift plywood ramp to the back lawn where Loco was sunning in the weak winter light. His rump felt the unevenness of the crabgrass as a vibration, faintly. Loco hadn't really adjusted either. Somehow the dog knew it all, and the beast tended to treat his immobile legs as alien objects, sometimes even barking frantically at them, as if to protect his master from them. Jack Liffey encouraged it with gesture, figuring the dog's wide-open outrage might just help somehow, loosen his own expression of . . . what? A kind of bewildered resentment that seemed to hold him caged in his muteness, baffling and without physical cause. Or so he'd been told.

The paraplegia – that was different, somehow. A more straightforward kind of shirking that his body had taken on, in the face of the panic of claustrophobia. Being literally buried alive, entombed. Even now he had chills thinking of it. Some part of his psyche was probably still cowering in a deep inner cave, down inside himself where he had crushed and hidden away all the other things in his life that he'd fucked up.

'It's in your mind,' the docs said. 'Work on it.' But he'd be damned if he'd go back to the shrink of a few years ago who'd kept wanting him to 'take ownership' of a collapsed lung and the

intermittent weeping that had been described as his 'breakdown.'
Enough. He'd already passed the saturation point of thinking about
his rebellious body. *I fought the mutiny*, he thought, *and the mutiny
won.*

He listened to the silence of his legs, their absolute heavy stillness. It had a different quality than other silences. An aggressive
hush, like a belligerent drunk in a bar preparing to bludgeon
someone. He swore that his legs had become smug with their new
power to immobilize him. *Just one nerve impulse, legs, and I will
get you back. I swear to God, when I do, I'll hurt you for this.*

They laughed at him. *We give the ultimatums here*, they told him.
*When you've separated all that rage from your soul, you may begin
to live your life again.*

He wondered if he was going mad. Imagining voices talking at
him from his own body, for Chrissake.

Loco half-rose and glared at the immobile legs. Jack Liffey was
maybe thirty feet away from the half-coyote who'd been his pet for
ten years now, and the dog approached cautiously across the lawn,
a bit sideways and gnarring softly.

Good boy, he thought. Bite those motherfuckers and let's see
who feels it! Too bad Loco couldn't read: Jack Liffey couldn't give
the order out loud.

Find a way to surrender to your weakness, his legs told him.
It'll be your renewal and your survival. Stop your pointless raging.

His mind was awash in inane counsel, and he felt the need to
punch someone.

Obviously you're not really ready for the struggle, the voice said.

The dog yelped once and ran off, as if cuffed.

I'm in charge here, Jack Liffey thought. *Whatever you say, I'm
still in love with living. I will talk again and I will walk again.*

It seemed that his legs heard and laughed at him, as if he'd made
a grand joke.

Gloria beckoned her out on to the front porch with one urgent flap
of her hand. Out of her dad's hearing, presumably. Maeve didn't
see her very often in her formal navy blue on-duty skirt-dress, the
bulge of her pistol not so well concealed at her hip. She looked a
lot more formidable this way, like she could take down a couple
of nasty muggers without breaking a sweat, tell them their rights,
bang their heads together and cuff them to a parking meter.

'Hi, Glor. You look pretty rough and tough like that.'

'I am tough, kid. You'll never know. Any change?'

She meant in Jack, of course. They'd been checking in regularly for some time.

'He forgot and tried to talk a while ago.' Maeve shook her head. She knew she shouldn't say it, but she couldn't help herself. 'He sounded like Daffy Duck.'

Gloria put a hand on her shoulder and looked hard into her face. 'Don't try to be some *macha* girl if it's hurting you.'

She nodded a kind of thanks. 'I'm used to Dad like this now, just like you are, but I *do* want him to get better.'

'He will. I feel it. Jack's not a quitter. I only wish I knew what he needs.'

Maeve decided she must have been crazy to go on, but you have to trust sometimes. 'What if we gave him some simple job? Not directly, but if he was just the overseer. Get his mind back in the saddle, so to speak.'

Gloria's broad brown Indio face took on all the expressive suspicion any human face could possibly display. 'You're not going Nancy Drew on us? Not again?'

'Of course not. It's just an idea.'

The frown did not let up for the longest time, and Maeve wasn't sure she could wait it out. That was one of the tricks cops learned, she knew.

'If he needs cases, let's get him some Ross Macdonalds to read; there's lots of them,' Gloria said. 'I read them all in one bad patch in my life. The guy's a nice diversion until you realize it's all the same story – the sins of the parents descending on the children.'

'Is that my fate?' Maeve asked. 'Something Oedipal?'

'Honey, you're already as Oedipal as it gets. Except I think they call it something else for girls.'

'You're right. I idolize Dad. And I'm soooo dying to hear his voice again.'

'Me, too, believe me. But not enough to let you put yourself in danger. How are you doing out there in the cold world these days?'

Maeve guessed that was probably some kind of code for her recent and still unassimilated lesbian affair, or even the pregnancy and abortion that preceded it. 'Do you know about Ruthie?' She watched Gloria's expression, but couldn't read it, of course. It was just too oppressive, this whole confusion of sorrows that oozed through her life like lava. The abortion, yes, but Beto himself, the wicked charmer and how she had flown straight to the flame.

'Jack still communicates,' Gloria said. 'And he's worried about you.'

'*He's* worried about *me*? Give me a break. I can walk and talk like a normal person, and I'm perfectly tuned to my own channels, thank you. I'm in the real world, Gloria. It's just taking me a little time to adjust to a few things, maybe a few mistakes.' *Fumbling my way through an eventful life, to say the least.*

'OK. Come to me if you need to, hon, any time. I mean it.'

Thunder crashed and rumbled suddenly across East L.A., and they both looked up at the vermillion sky, darkening with rain-clouds. A month earlier, it had been the first hard rains after years of drought that had touched off the dread mudslides that had hit her and her dad. And had touched off this interval of tragic strangeness.

Generally they said L.A. had a true Mediterranean climate and the big rains came in winter from an onshore flow of moist air, trapped over the basin by an inversion. In that particular dread downpour, however, the mudslide had been touched off by a crazy man with dynamite who was in jail now.

'C'mon, Gloria, have a beer and offer me one. You look beat.'

'Thanks, I am.'

For just an instant, the weak three-quarter moon shone through a rent in the clouds, exotic, brushing their immediate world with silver. The glide on the porch and the tall lilac bushes in the yard stood out like photo-negatives. The old-fashioned domed street lamps on the block seemed to dim in the moonlight and then blazed up again as the dark cloud healed.

'Is it really supposed to rain?' Gloria asked.

'Global warming,' Maeve said. 'It'll either rain forever or never rain again.'

'Anything along the spectrum from a nice view of city lights to exposed brick walls to the promised return of Jesus will sell these lofts fast.'

'Can I quote you?' she asked, holding out the little digital recorder.

'Sure,' Eddie Wolverton said. The westward view out the tall steel-rimmed industrial windows of the top-floor loft was really terrific. All of L.A.'s downtown with the centerpiece being the

Library Tower (now renamed for its third change – the U.S. Bank Tower) rising above them at seventy-three stories and 1017 feet, the tallest building west of the Mississippi. Downtown lights were picking out the underside of the low dark cloudbank to give it an eerie lumpy purple-to-chocolate glow. Wolverton had been a partner in rebuilding several of the retro deco buildings he could see out there. The Blue Pacific. The old Wilton Department Store. The only real problem with this building was its location about two blocks too far east, which meant plenty of homeless folk on the sidewalk.

The architect-builder-preservationist Eddie Wolverton was leading a gorgeous young woman from the magazine *L.A. Loft Living* around a $3.6 million loft on top of the First Finance Building on South Main. He knew he had nothing to lose from a little Jesus irreverence, if it was witty enough. Very few loft buyers listened to Pat Robertson or any other TV Christian.

'What about that piss smell just outside, and the homeless camping on your doorstep?'

She was trying to ambush him, as writers always did. 'You're exaggerating. We're just outside the boundaries of Skid Row. And floors three through five are guarded parking so nobody's going to panhandle you when you park your Maserati.'

She had long silver-blonde peek-a-boo hair, à la Veronica Lake, his father's favorite actress whom he only vaguely remembered from old films, and a split-up-the-hip blue dress that invited glances toward the Promised Land, but he was careful not to let that distract him from selling himself.

'You may be just across the street from The Nickel, but that's all,' she said. 'What do you say to the criticism that by buying and converting these old banks and hotels, you make it impossible for the homeless organizations to set up any more SROs?'

SROs were single-room-occupancy hotels – what others called flophouses. Eddie Wolverton was a Kennedy Democrat and self-righteous about what he was doing. He insisted that anybody he partnered with support mixed use in his buildings, with shops and affordable apartments downstairs, and he even donated heavily to Sister Mary Rose's HFA organization six blocks away – the Catholic shelter she called a Home For All.

'If you really want sound-bites, this building isn't suited for an SRO, and in the long run, I don't really think the answer to the homeless problem is to warehouse all the schizophrenics and crack-addicts and shell-shocked veterans in tiny filing cabinet rooms downtown so the area becomes unusable for everybody else. Homelessness is a social problem that belongs to the whole city. L.A. should be setting up homeless centers all over the suburbs, not attracting every single lost soul into one big cesspool.'

An aura of wealth and power was indeed an aphrodisiac, Francie Lusk thought, her legs going a little rubbery as she listened to his confident voice. The woman turned and set her hands on her hips. 'Mr Wolverton, do you want to fuck me, right here in this empty loft?' She gathered up her dress to reveal a blue thong panty and a lot of undyed black pubic hair.

'You're not being very professional, Ms Lusk,' he said. 'My soul is weak, like most men, but it doesn't change what I believe.'

She snapped off the recorder ostentatiously. 'Screw what you *believe*, man. I'm in heat. Hurt me a little and call me a slut, and I'll write you up in *Loft Living* like you've never been written up. You'll be a humanist hero of the whole housing world.'

Gloria wheeled Jack Liffey toward the bedroom. 'It wasn't a terribly bad day for me, as they go,' she explained. 'The Jackson murder investigation is as stalled as ever, and they dumped a new burglary on me that's probably the guy from the Rancho that we call the Black Shadow. You know, the guy I've been after for weeks. I think Davis Davis has finally decided I'm good enough to risk being my partner for a while, and he's stopped asking every ten minutes if I'm on the rag. He's a lot less of a woman-hater than Ante Bratos, that's for sure.'

She pushed open the bedroom door and horsed the wheelchair around in the narrow hallway. 'Elbows.'

He gave her a thumbs-up and she knew he was with her. But it wasn't enough. She had to admit to herself that she desperately wanted the old Jack back; she wanted to hear his voice and his jokes. He could always make her laugh.

'I'm a little worried about Maeve,' Gloria said as she sealed the door behind them. 'I have a feeling she's going Nancy Drew again. And, of course, pretending it's all for your sake.'

He waggled a hand in mid-air and made a gargling sound. *This was all so intolerable*, she thought. He'd better recover soon or one day she'd drive him out past Barstow and drop him in the middle

of the Mojave. But, of course, she wouldn't. Any more than she'd
dump him on The Nickel, the way several hospitals had been caught
dumping their indigent patients.

Before she could begin undressing him, he held up his notebook.
WHAT'S THIS NANCY DREW!!!

'Oh, Jack. Don't press it right now. Maeve is just trying to help
you, I think. I really don't know anything much, but I'll stay on
top of it. You've got my word.'

He nodded and gave the thumbs-up again.

'I can give you a blow-job tonight,' she said, but it must not have
been very convincing, because he just shook his head. It was never
very satisfying because nothing much worked at a hundred per cent
these days. And then he pointed at her crotch and gave a questioning smile. She thought about it and decided, why the hell not?
It would do them both good.

'Yeah, Jack, I want you to eat me, but only if you really feel
like it.'

The Greyhound station was on Seventh, a fairly new but battered
and evil-smelling place with cordoned-off areas meant for nothing
recognizably human. Several men were sleeping slumped forward
on plastic chairs or on benches with humps that were meant to
make it hard for sleepers. Conor claimed his backpack off the bus
and headed out into the darkly overcast evening. A lot of obviously
poor people were out and about, pushing shopping carts, chatting
and laughing, trading cigarettes or selling something more furtive.
Most of the people he saw seemed to be African-Americans. He
found himself drawn toward the bright skyscrapers maybe a mile
or more away. West? All the other directions looked dark and semi-
abandoned.

All at once as he walked a bell began to clang, and he halted to
see a half-dozen black men in sweat shirts and assorted jackets,
who'd been reclining amongst tents and cardboard shelters, leap to
their feet and form up in a precise line blocking the sidewalk, their
backs to him. A wide garage door trundled open mechanically, and
a Fire Department ambulance rolled out, winding up its siren. Conor
was astonished to see the rag-tag squad along the sidewalk snap to
attention and salute the vehicle. A fire truck followed the ambulance out of the station and the salute was repeated.

Both vehicles passed him and he was astonished to read the

words on their doors. They said *Los Angeles City Fire Department Station No. 9,* but underneath, each one added: *Skid Row.*[1] Whoa, he thought. A real place, not a myth, and somebody was actually proud of it. The ragged squad who had saluted the firemen were just settling back down against their shelters as he approached.

'Do you guys do that every time the fire trucks go out?' Conor asked.

'Say what?' A hard-looking man down at the end of the platoon glanced at him, from under one of those shiny black do-rags.

'Just off the bus,' his neighbor said.

'Everybody loves firemen, kid. They're the true good guys in this world.' This second man looked and acted like their leader, with an unruly grizzled beard. He wore an old army camo jacket and a green beret with a patch that had diagonal red and yellow stripes. Conor didn't dare ask if he'd actually been Special Forces. Normally, people didn't intimidate him, but he knew he was almost comically out of his depth, a suburban boy facing a half-dozen older homeless black men down here where things were bound to be a bit raw.

'Ever since Nine-Eleven,' Conor agreed.

'True dat. Where you from, son?' It was almost kindly.

'North San Diego.'

'Sure you shouldn't go on home now?' another man said. 'After dark somebody here boil you down for the small change.'

'Rat do a mambo on you ass,' Do-rag said. 'What are you, sixteen and cherry ass?'

'I'm not afraid.'

'Kid, ain't a question of 'fraid. You're just the fucking new guy for the whole world. Ain't no TV movies here. You fell down the hole to the lan' of crack and bad-lucks and psychos.'

For some reason, Conor was determined not to seem to turn tail. 'Can you tell me a good place to spend the night?'

The man with the beret thought for a moment. He obviously lived in the blue tent pitched against the fence, standing amongst a jumble of possessions that spilled out of it. 'Fortnum ain't so bad,

---

[1] This inscription has recently been changed to 'Central City East,' by roughly the same people who invented the expression 'differently abled.'

if you got cash money. It's up San Julian, that corner there. Some of us won't be trapped nowhere inside at night. Too much incoming.'

'A truth-tellin' man.'

'Thank you, sir, for the advice. What's your name?'

'Carl. Carl Roosevelt. Son, you tell Dusty at the Fortnum that I sent you. He'll find you something.'

'Then I owe you a favor, Mr Roosevelt. My name is Conor Lewis.' He almost let slip the name of his band. They'd actually distributed two CDs and a lot of downloads, but all of a sudden the name Raging Homeless seemed obscene.

Roosevelt smiled briefly. 'Nobody don't owe nothin', Conor. We're a community here, and we're all doing our damn best.' He waved his hand down the row of tents and cardboard shanties. 'Federal do his best, and Cubic, and the General, and even Felix the Cat. We're proud men, but we all know, no matter how hard you try, you can't shine shit. This is just The Nickel. This ain't the way to live if you got a choice, son.'

'I thank you again, sir.'

'Protect yourself out here. Try the Fortnum.'

The guy at the end of the row with the do-rag, possibly Felix the Cat, said, 'Try not to scuff up our street with those nice Chuck Taylor All-Stars, boy. It was important back in the day.'

Deep in his self-respect, Conor felt it was OK to wander on now, probably to the Fortnum.

Los Angeles County has approximately **73,000** homeless human beings looking for shelter on any given night, far more than any other county in the United States. That number is twice the population of Beverly Hills. In L.A. County the price of an average home is over half a million dollars.

[See endnotes for the sources of these statistics.]

TWO
The Overture

'He was dialing into some mysterious frequencies,' Turtle said. 'Uh, what does that mean?' Maeve asked on the phone. As soon as she'd got out of bed and got the information she needed in Mike Lewis's e-mail, she'd started contacting Conor's friends.

'Yeah, I know. Say what? I think we could feel him detaching, you know, like the capsule coming off the mothership to go into descent to the alien world. He still gave his guitar hand to the band when we was practicing but not his head no more. There was a plain vanilla weird faraway shit in him. I hate to say it – he was acting like he felt he'd just totally used us up, and we weren't worth shit anymore. It hurt.'

'Was he good in school?'

'Absolute-a-mente. But I know school was boring him to death. He was carrying around these weird French writers. Lacan?' The boy pronounced it Lake-un. 'I don't know who the shit they are.'

'Did he have a girlfriend?'

'F. said Conor was getting buggy with her, too. Francine Matkinov. She's big time in women's beach volleyball,' he added, almost apologetically.

'Did they break up?'

'I don't know. I'll find out, if you want. But it looked like he was cutting himself off from all his friends. I mean, like, on purpose. He used to be really tight with Mr Peters, the Social Studies teacher, and in the hall I heard Con tell the guy to go fuck himself.'

'Where do you think he'd run away to?' Maeve asked.

'There's only two places to go – aren't there? New York and L.A. *Maybe* Frisco.'

'Anything make you think it might be L.A.?'

'His dad wrote a bunch of books about L.A.' The boy was starting to punctuate his words with a terrible sound, like a cough from deep in his chest. The guy named Turtle was either crying or bumping coke and it seemed a little early for that.

She'd read some of Mike Lewis's books about L.A. They were really interesting, but hard to read sometimes with jargon. 'Thanks, Turtle. If you hear anything at all, would you call me?' She gave him Gloria's number and her own cell.

'Sure. I love the guy to death, honest. The band means the world to me. If you find him, I bet you'll like him, too. He always made me feel super alive. Even if he went and killed himself in one universe, I know he's still alive in the next universe over.'

She didn't want to ask about that, and the voice was getting worse, breaking up somehow. 'Stay in touch, Turtle. I mean it.'

The connection cut off.

With her twelve-hour straight, three-day-on, four-off schedule – the normal LAPD shift for now – Gloria got to lie in on odd mornings that Jack Liffey could never keep straight, and she snuggled against him now in her silky silver gown. It was very arousing, at least theoretically – he was having a bit of trouble in that department. Sensation and command more or less trailed off at the equator, but right now he'd trade the whole southern hemisphere for having his voice back.

You had no idea how much you relied on quick replies, or on inflection, modulation and nuance, until you lost voice itself. Irony in particular was important to him, and underlining words or putting quotes on a written phrase just didn't cut it – though he and Maeve had joked for years about the unintended irony in 'fresh' fish on menus and signs saying that everyone is 'welcome.'

Gloria had always had excess body heat, at least to his touch, and he had to toss back some of the covers to stay next to her. He studied her sleeping face, so much calmer than when she was awake, so much more at peace, lacking that habitual ferocious suspicion. He wished there was some way he could give her this kind of relaxation in her waking life, but he'd been around enough to know that people at their age rarely changed the basic baggage very much. She was always so tense and tormented, and yet, as she insisted and he believed implicitly, talking to a recognized shrink about anything at all would be the beginning of the end of one's career in the police department.

Not that he was doing so well himself, right now, he thought. At least two doctors had pronounced his handicaps 'psycho-physiologic' phenomena. A fancier word for what they had once called psychosomatic.

But it all felt very real to him and very *non*-psycho-anything. More like a deliberate revolt of part of his body – as if something else had taken up residence inside him, grabbed the controls, and was forcing him to live in a much smaller portion of the old hulk. It was a fucking annoyance, whatever it was called.

He sensed the initiation of Gloria's commotion of waking and backed away slightly to allow her to thrash a bit. The first step would be one of her sleep-talking jags. Though it would be too rapid and too angry, or just too plain incoherent, for him to follow.

'Never don't you you! I'm not – dubba-dubba-dubba,' or whatever. She lashed over on to her stomach, and he set a hand gently against her shoulder, trying to calm her.

'What's that?!' She thrust herself upward in a powerful push-up, her eyes coming open, as feral as a prodded wildcat. He couldn't help watching her large breasts droop and sway within the silvery gown.

'Ak-ak!' He tried desperately to tell her that everything was OK, as he had so often. All he could do was move closer and hold her to comfort her, and her dream-manager chose that moment to thrust him away hard. She sat up.

'Giant heads are talking,' she said. She was only half back. He moved close again, and she sucked in a few deep breaths and seemed to calm as he held her hard. But there was a post-nightmare gravity now that he'd never been able to do much about.

'Bad dreams,' she said sluggishly. 'Half-breed. Oh, man, evil pearls strung on my confusion.'

Jesus, where did *that* come from? he thought. It was almost poetry but it would take him too long to write out a query. He grabbed his pre-figured pad from the night table and pointed to the big question mark.

She shook her head and let things settle. 'Yeah, bad dream. Could be Paiute. From my old Tia Eduviges. I think I said "evil pearls." Hell, maybe it's from that knucklehead Harmony who works the phones at Harbor and does Tarot cards and covers herself with costume jewelry.'

'Ak-ak.'

'Yeah, I agree. But don't give yourself a hernia, Jack. I'm coming around. You look a little peaked.'

YOU WERE TORMENTED. LOUD.

She nodded deliberately. 'I can usually tell. What time is it?

Seven? On the loud nights I wake up feeling it's about time to go
to bed.' She shook her head like a dog throwing off water. 'You
gotta stop worrying non-stop about me, Jackie. I'll be OK. Think
of yourself a little these days.'

He nodded, but there was not a thing he could think of to do
about himself. Drugs did nothing, and talk therapy was out of the
question, from the therapists he knew.

'Well, let's get up and see if Maeve has launched some new
crusade against evil.'

Jack Liffey wondered if life would ever offer him an hour's peace
with Gloria. He wished it with all his heart.

Moses Vartabedian waited by the hump bridge in the Japanese
garden that somebody had once lovingly built in the space behind
the Japanese Community Center and then let decay to ruin. Vagaries
of funding, he thought. It was only a five-minute walk from his
office at the top of the Golden West building on Broadway, and
he figured this site had just about the least probability of being
bugged or cop-visited of any location in the whole downtown
area, though it was only two blocks from the new central police
station. The vegetation had overgrown, two broken bricks and a
short length of rotting 2-by-4 had been abandoned in the burbling
stream, and he'd bet no one had visited to meditate here in years.
It was one of several Japanese gardens in the downtown area, all
in hideaways in Little Tokyo, and it was easily the least patron-
ized because they made you go through a very inauspicious
building lobby, announce what you wanted to see, endure the
incredulous stare of the Latino rent-a-guard at the desk, and then
take the elevator down to the basement to get out to the sunken
garden.

Moses Vartabedian leaned against the tall cement retaining wall
that separated the garden from the alley up at street level and lit a
cigar. He was a man with a problem and, like many men of his
occupation, he had a number of resourceful types on call to deal
with problems. The local alternative paper had called him a slumlord, and he resented that deeply. He thought of himself as a man
who provided a valuable service to the city – he took virtually unin-
habitable rundown hotels and long-abandoned office buildings, with
swaybacked and rat-infested floors, and with the help of his architect partner Eddie Wolverton, he fixed them up to decent residences

for the arty middle class. The homeless had their own shelters and SROs – which weren't palatial but they kept the poor out of the weather and the room doors could be locked. And they all accepted the Los Angeles Homeless Services Authority's certificates. He tried never to cross swords with the HSA when they wanted or needed a building, but once in a while it happened.

The door from the elevator opened abruptly and Steve McCall pushed into the garden. The man was the size of a small island off the coast, wearing an *Ignore Previous Hat* baseball cap pulled down over long gold ringlets that made him look like a chubby General Custer. He was followed discreetly by his partner, the much shorter but more volatile Rice Thibodeaux, his eyes almost always as wild as a small prey-animal startled by a predator.

Vartabedian wondered, not for the first time, about the fates that had brought the two of them together with him, but whenever he needed a potentially profitable building cleared of its recalcitrant last few tenants, Custer and Psycho were the go-to guys, and he made sure they could not be tracked back to him.

'Hey, Mose!' McCall called. 'Why don't you take over this here place and fix up the shitty garden? And fire that Spic at the desk. I'm tired of watching him roll his eyes at me like I'm nuts to wanna see a Japanese garden.'

The other one, Rice Thibodeaux, didn't greet Vartabedian. Instead he brought out a switchblade, for no apparent reason, popped it open startlingly as he walked behind McCall and then stopped beside the hump bridge and cut a three-inch-long swipe straight down his forearm. He waited, letting the blood run down his arm to drip off the webs of his fingers on to the clay path. 'Say the word,' Thibodueax announced. 'Anyone is history.'

Vartabedian needed to keep his spirits up, and the way to do that right then was not to acknowledge to himself the weirdness of these characters in his employ.

'Be cool, guys. Forget this place. I do not want it. Sit with me on the bench. I have a job. You want to do something about that cut, man.'

'What cut?' Thibodeaux said.

Around them downtown went on honking and making the noises of its tires over a loose manhole cover and boiling off the other white noise that permeated the Japanese garden like a fog of unease. The derelict garden had obviously been designed at one time to bring peace, but it was losing the battle – maybe that's why they'd given up tending it, Vartabedian thought.

McCall sat down, but Thibodeaux never would. The short man stood in front of them, dripping blood on to the path as if it were of no consequence. 'Mexicans,' Thibodeuax said, for no apparent purpose. 'They either work on their cars or piss against walls.'

'Forget that,' Vartabedian said. 'I've taken an option on the Fortnum Hotel over on San Julian, by Sixth, but there's a half-dozen tenants still residing on SRO chits, and I've got to get them out in order to rebuild.'

'Do we get to fuck them up?' Thibodeaux asked quickly.

'Jesus, man, *no*. It makes things too complicated. Listen to McCall. Just convince them it's better for all of us if they move out voluntarily. A little tiny threat is OK, but that's it. I'll pay them twice the vacate costs, and I'll even find them other hotels nearby. Good ones, and if I have to, I'll subsidize the SRO rent that they have to pay in the new place.'

'This is just like the last job at the Globe,' McCall said. 'No sweateroo, V. We huff and we puff and we tell them the wolf is at the door. But the wolf is not you; you're just the wolf's friend, or maybe not at all.'

'Stephen, I *am* the friend of the tenants. You're a genius. No violence, please, gents. I mean that.' Vartabedian gave them each a wad of twenties – a thousand dollars for what McCall had called their green-'em-up money.

Vartabedian knew that the building could be cleared out expeditiously with a little discretion – he'd done it a dozen times. The elevators became unusable. The heating system failed. The water became unreliable. Toilets overflowed with human shit. Everyone knew they lived in some relationship to bad luck, whatever they chose to call it, and it didn't take much to remind them of that fact. He always offered a painless and perfectly reasonable alternative.

A fire truck siren went off nearby and Vartabedian thought of his beaten-down old man in Erciş, in eastern Turkey, all five-foot-one of him, and wondered if anybody had ever offered him a painless and reasonable alternative. He doubted anyone ever had. The elder Hagop Vartabedian had insisted that his family had lived right there on Lake Van for 3,000 years, within sight of Mount Ararat, where he told his kids that he had once found a chip of the Ark. But nothing could be painless and reasonable in eastern Turkey, not for a Christian infidel, hated by all the Turks, part of the tiny remnant population of Armenians after the genocide, hiding out now amongst the Kurds.

The old man had played at staying invisible most of his life, evaporating before insults, until he'd finally had too much and abandoned his fifty generations in Erciş and taken his family to Fresno, California, to work amongst the second-rate grapes of his cousin Aram.

'Boss,' Thibodeaux said from the far end of the bench. The blood had congealed over his cut and no longer ran down his arm. 'When can I use Diane?' The small man seemed to mean his switchblade.

Jesus Christ. Anybody who'd name a knife should be dropped by parachute into Turkey wearing a big sign saying how much he hates Mohammed. Just on general principles – to keep the gene pool uncluttered.

It was the golden-haired McCall that Vartabedian had hired, and he wasn't sure why the man kept this little loose cannon around. 'No, Rice, not now. Maybe later.'

Rice Thibodeaux snicked the clasp with a sigh, and then flipped the blade back into its housing with one of those great show-off flourishes that with a little bad luck would one day see him slicing off his own ear.

'Baby, I only put you in da linen closet 'cause we full up wit wheezers las' PM. There a room now. A guy passed last night, pray his soul be save. You wanna sleep where some guy pass? Wasn't no blood.' The man's odd pink eyes went wide.

'People die everywhere. I don't believe in ghosts.' He wasn't sure the man remembered. 'Carl Roosevelt sent me.' As far as Conor could tell the hotel was nearly empty so all this talk about lack of space was a genuine mystery.

'You done tol' me. Carl he pretty bad impair, baby. Don't take nothin' for granite roun' here. You don' wanna lean on jus' every swingin' dick on The Nickel says he kin help.' Dusty Phillips was the only albino human being that Conor had ever seen in person, though he had always revered Johnny Winter and Piano Red. He thought Dusty was probably an African-American, but it was hard to tell. He tried not to stare at the pink blinking eyes, or the tightly curled bleachy hair on the old man.

'And git yo'self out of the Fort as quick as you can. Ain' fit for a nice clean boy like you, whatever your reason.'

The manager sat in a cage with a good view of the four dilapidated and unoccupied sofas in the lobby and the TV that was
murmuring away on some good-morning show.

'You've been good to me, sir. San Diego thanks you.'

'San D.? You know Harborside?'

'I know where it is, but it's not my territory. Mostly Latino, isn't
it?'

'Now I guess. Not back in the day. People still talk about Alonzo
Horton blow into town and buy him a big chunk of the place for
$260?'

'I might've heard that.'

'I can't really decide who you is, boy. Whether you a curveball
coming off a lefty.' Dusty cocked his head, as if judging Conor on
some invisible scale. 'Hell, OK, I don't care.' The albino handed
him an old-fashioned skeleton key on a paddle that said C-20.

'I'm not sure who I am either,' Conor said. 'But I pay.'

'They's two black plastic bags inside the do'. Take what you
want, it all dead man stuff. Toss 'em in the hall when you done.'

Coming out of the master bedroom, they'd caught Maeve on the
phone to somebody she obviously didn't want them to know about
because she'd hung up immediately. 'Gottagobye. Good morning,
Dad. Glor.'

'You've got the most transparent guilty look in North America,'
Gloria said.

SPANK HER AND THROW HER OUT, Jack Liffey wrote and
showed it to Maeve instead of Gloria.

'Dad! I'm almost of age. You can't be spanking me unless you
get me to Saudi Arabia first.'

Gloria tipped the pad back with one finger to read it and laughed.
'I'm not in a spanking or a cooking mood here, but I'll set out
some tortillas and leftovers, and there's the usual cereals. In your
honor, hon, we actually bought some Pop-Tarts.'

It was the one junk food that Maeve seemed to have brought
with her from her childhood.

Jack Liffey pointed to WHO CALLED on his master list.

'Nothing important, Dad,' Maeve said. 'You gotta get over
thinking I'm always up to something.'

It took him a while to scribble WHEN DID THE POPE STOP
WEARING A DRESS.

'Hon,' Gloria said to Maeve. 'Whatever you're doing, what's the worst thing that could happen? Just tell us that.'

'I could fail completely and feel like an idiot, I suppose.'

'If you succeed, will somebody dynamite the house?' It wasn't an empty joke. Maeve's bedroom in her mother's house had been dynamited two months earlier by an aging disaffected surfer whom Maeve had inadvertently poked with the sharp stick of her curiosity, trying as usual to help.

She tore open the foil packet and dropped two frosted raspberry Pop-Tarts into the vintage Toastmaster, and pressed the deco handle down. 'How did you know I love this flavor?'

'Somebody's definitely changing the subject here. You promise that there's no risk at all of catastrophe in what you're up to?'

'Oh, no. Of course not.'

SHE HAS NO NOTION OF RISK. Jack Liffey showed this to Gloria.

'Oh, I know.' Gloria rested her hand tenderly on his shoulder in the wheelchair for a moment. 'Not everything blows up, Jack. Damn few things, in my experience. Possibly she'll get lucky this time and just fall out of a tree. Let's all calm down and have breakfast.'

Conor peered briefly into the big black trash bags but the old-man clothing and possessions looked so filthy and unpleasant that he twisted the bag necks and swung them both out into the hallway. His needs were few, in any case, and a dying old man would have little of interest to him. He needed a bed, some food, a place out of the cold and some time to think things over. Some time to write songs.

He looked around. He had the bed he needed, a metal frame single bed with what looked like fresh institutional sheets and a prickly horse blanket, tucked with military tightness. There was a washbasin with only one tap and some serious rust stains. He'd already seen the tiny cookroom for the whole floor three doors along the hallway, with a beat-up microwave, a double electric hotplate and an old round-top fridge. A cockroach appeared to peek over the rim of the basin at him but insects had never bothered him.

There was one wood chair tucked under a desk the size of a big handkerchief, parked in front of a window that looked out on a brick wall. An angle of old pipe was screwed into one corner of

the room and had five wire hangers depended from it. Nothing
about the room struck him as unacceptable or offensive. Just another
place. The asceticism actually appealed to him.

He extracted his current notebook from his duffle.

NOTES FOR A NEW MUSIC

Day 1

**OK, it's now. Right now is Day 1 after the break in my normal
drift. That big gillotine (spell?) blade fell across my life, maybe
to make it into Before and After.**

**I wonder if I'm being too obstinate about breaking with my
parents. I have no permanent dispute with them, but I need
them to forsake me for a while to whoever I am inside. Or who
I am becoming. Like a rocket dropping the first stage, I'm in
some trajectory now that I have to follow without all the old
baggage. Hi Mom, hi Pop, oh nothing special just a sense of total
desperation. In this very basic place, among basic people, I can
sleep alone for a while and write and practice alone and maybe
have some of my fantasy life released. I brought my old Martin
acoustic guitar to work on, even though it's a drag to carry
around. We'll see how well things work out. I eagerly await the
conclusion of the overture.**

After breakfast Jack Liffey wanted to visit a little with Loco, who
had been a steadfast pal for more than a decade. The aging yellow
half-coyote mutt had seemingly made a full recovery from
Osteosarcoma, or doggie bone cancer, after an expensive surgery
and a lot of chemo that had involved some fantastically expensive
drug containing platinum. But they couldn't promise how long the
remission would hold. The vets gave you near meaningless percent-
ages. They were even more offhand about that than the doctors
specializing in human cancer.

Jack Liffey had had to sell off his old condo in Culver City to
put a big chunk of his only capital into the save-Loco fund. The
rest was ardently earmarked for Maeve's college scholarship, if she
ever made up her mind where to go. Or to go at all.

Once again he recognized all of a sudden how life threw curves at the handicapped. The hastily built plywood ramp into the back-yard had broken its back somehow the night before, and though there were only three steps down, maybe two-and-a-half feet, it was as definitive a barrier for him as a 100-foot cliff. Loco wasn't in any hurry to give up lying on the grass in a lozenge of the weak sun, especially since Jack Liffey couldn't call him with more than a rapping on the frame of the screen porch, which the dog was choosing perversely to ignore.

Eventually Gloria noticed it all and came out to stand beside him. 'Loco, shame on you, get up here!' she shouted. 'Loco! Move your ass *now*!'

His muzzle rolled in their direction languidly, and he staggered to his feet, as if much put-upon.

Jack Liffey rubbed his head against Gloria as thanks. 'Ak.'

He refused to think about having the ramp rebuilt. If the doctors were right, he would damn well beat this thing by pure will power long before he would become another Ironside, and a mute one at that. He couldn't let anything permanently deny him his own body, for Chrissake. Loco approached across the browning crabgrass in a painful toddle and boosted himself up the broken ramp to growl once at the dead legs and then change his mind and rub against them a little. Jack Liffey warmed with affection, reaching down to pet the dog's wiry shoulder hair.

Gloria mussed Jack Liffey's hair in turn. 'You are, sir, the soul of this house, and I will tend you in whatever form I have to. Including a crate in my closet.'

He laughed silently at the dark humor, and she rested her hand on his head as he rested his on the dog, as sensual a physical experience as he'd had in quite some time.

Gloria went off to work apologetically and left him with Loco. *Dude*, Jack Liffey thought, *whatever you might believe, I think I'm in love with living. How about you give me the best you've got. They say I'm a T-9 or something like that, but that's mech-anistic shit. And you don't care about that, anyway. You don't care that I have to stuff a new plastic tube up my dick every two days. You're a goddam Carboplatin miracle – and to prove it the condo's gone, my only refuge in dire trouble – so it's you and me once again. If Gloria throws us out, we're just fucking doomed. No more take-out meals from El Tepeyac, no more comfortable house on Greenwood. We get to live in my old pickup truck on*

some backwater street, like so many of those sad destitute divorcees
out there.
  Stay with me, pal, even if it comes to that. I stayed with you
through your troubles. I think all I have to do to walk and talk
again is find my cape and save the world from tyranny. OK, I'm
kidding, you know that. What I'd really like to know is how on earth
you recognize that my legs are such a dubious part of me at the
moment, appendages to be snarled at. It might help me figure it all
out if you could just tell me that, laddie.

Maeve figured Conor would probably end up in old Hollywood –
that's where all the music hopefuls converged like locusts, ending
up living or just crashing somewhere within eyesight of the vertical
cylinder of the thirteen-story Capitol Records building, which had
allegedly been built in 1954 to resemble a stack of 45-RPM records
with the pinnacle on the roof as the needle. According to legend
the shape had been suggested by Nat King Cole. It had been the
first round high-rise in the world.
  Maeve was one of the few people in L.A., other than her father,
who knew that the blinking red light atop the pinnacle spelled out
H-O-L-L-Y-W-O-O-D in Morse Code. She'd read it somewhere
trustworthy and passed it on as part of her long-running contest
with her dad to trump one another's L.A. oddities – a competition
that was pretty much suspended for the moment.
  She also knew that her dad's old friend Art Castro, along with
the whole Rosewood Detective Agency he worked for, now had a
primo office right on Hollywood Boulevard. The agency had been
forced out of the magnificent old Bradbury building downtown
during a recent upgrading and, ironically, had moved to an even
cooler location, though they probably didn't know it. The six-story
Pacific Security Bank building on Hollywood Boulevard near Ivar
had been the model for the mythical 'Cahuenga Building,' home
office of Philip Marlowe – call GL(enview) 7537. Amazingly, Castro
was on the sixth floor just where Marlowe had supposedly inhab-
ited his ratty office, but Castro's room number was off a bit, 644
instead of 615. And Castro would never be half as cool as Humphrey
Bogart, hiding the Four Roses in the bottom drawer of the filing
cabinet.
  She'd had a bit of trouble parking since everything around here
was metered or forbidden now, though the graying secretary smiled

tightly, recognizing her, buzzed and let her go on into Castro's office right away.

'Maeve, it's all good. How's Jacky doing?'

He stood up. The room was pretty small and she wondered about his status within Rosewood. Her father had always said the man had gone up and down in the huge detective company like a yoyo, but that he always held some mysterious hold over old Leonard R., the founder's nephew, and apparently couldn't be fired.

When she stepped closer, he leaned over the desk to take her small hand between both of his, one of which was weirdly much colder than the other.

'He's not so great. Can I call you Art?'

'Course, kid. Sit down.' There was only one possibility, a lopsided divan that looked like it had come right off the set of a movie about Napoleon. Somewhere she'd heard that ski-jump-like sofa called a fainting couch. She either had to lounge sideways like the Naked Maja or prop her back against the wall. She chose the wall.

'Dad's still having trouble with his legs and his voice, but the doctors say it's only a matter of time.'

Castro sighed. 'That little nugget of wisdom from their profession always makes me want to say, "Up yours sideways, docs." Excuse my French. Time is not a goddam limitless Artesian well. We all know it can conk out pretty fast.'

'Wow, I really hit a nerve.'

'Sorry. I'm not really going off on you, Maevie. What would you do if your doc told you you had only six minutes to live?'

'Did *yours*?' She sat up straight.

'No no no. Death is just present to me these days,' he said. 'I mean, think about six minutes.'

'Well, I know about six *months*,' Maeve said, getting angry and self-righteous. 'I met a boy with active AIDS and Carposi's, and the drugs aren't working, and that's what they say he's got – *maybe* six months. To be a friend, I go see him when I can and try to help him through it. He's like a kicked puppy, and all these jerks keep telling him there's something comforting not far off. I'm trying to learn what hospice people know so I can help the comfort along. Be good for me, too, I'm sure.'

'Well, bless you, hon. That's better than I did when my nephew kicked last month. I couldn't face it. Let's not talk about that. It's well past the *Dia de Los Muertos*. What is it you want for Jack? You wouldn't be here otherwise.'

'Don't be mean, Art,' Maeve said.

'Or not. What's worse in life, the stuff you done, or the stuff that ain't done?'

'I can't help you, Art. Really. Do you know Dad's friend Mike Lewis?'

He settled back, apparently giving up the idea of getting any wisdom out of her. 'I've heard of him. The writer.'

'His son Conor is a runaway, maybe up here from San Diego. He's into rock music, so I thought Hollywood.'

'Smart guess.'

'Don't be sarcastic. Here's copies of all I know about Conor. I want to keep the case warm for Dad, if you could find out anything at all.'

'I can't remember if I owe Jack one or vice-versa – but it would be a little lame, me claiming overdues on him right now, wouldn't it? I'll look into it for you. And, Maeve, I'm sorry if I've been rough-and-ready.' He sighed. 'I had a bad week. One of these days I'll get me into a booze-haze and nobody will be able to reach me.'

Maeve stood up and took his hand again. 'Dad always speaks great of you.'

He shook his head. 'Your papi is a real *mensch*. And, yeah, I know what that word means.'

L.A.'s Skid Row is known locally as The Nickel because its east–west axis is Fifth Street. It's a roughly fifty-block area of warehouses, missions and nondescript brick buildings that in the late afternoon finds itself literally in the shadow of the modern glass-and-steel eighty-story skyline on Bunker Hill half a mile west. The Nickel has the largest concentration of homeless people in the United States: between 8,000 and 11,000 souls live here, many of them scrambling nightly for charity shelters, single-room-occupancy hotels or makeshift tents, plastic lean-tos and refrigerator boxes.

CALGARY
PUBLIC
LIBRARY

August 28, 2019 05:46

39065157518489   18/Sep/2019
Adult magazine - Fish Creek - 2018
(CheckOut)

39065157528041   18/Sep/2019
Adult magazine - Fish Creek - 2018
(CheckOut)

39065157526367   18/Sep/2019
Adult magazine - Fish Creek - 2018
(CheckOut)

39065157524800   18/Sep/2019
Adult magazine - Fish Creek - 2018
(CheckOut)

39065156033696   18/Sep/2019
Adult Magazine - Fish Creek, 2019
(CheckOut)

39065157522564   18/Sep/2019
Adult magazine - Fish Creek - 2018
(CheckOut)

39065139772048   18/Sep/2019
Extreme prey : a Lucas Davenport mystery
(CheckOut)

39065119168514   18/Sep/2019
The sentry : [a Joe Pike novel] (CheckOut)

39065106066598   18/Sep/2019
On the nickel : a Jack Liffey mystery
(CheckOut)

Total   **9 Item(s)**

Register for the Ultimate Summer
Challenge
Starts on May 15
http://calgarylibrary.ca/summer

THREE
Free Despair Test

'You ever remember your dreams, Rice?' McCall asked. Thibodeaux cranked his neck around to stare at his partner across the tall buckets and the padded console of the big black RAM-3500 as if McCall were some nutcase in the funny farm.

'What the fuck for?'

'So you can get a look at what's inside you, man. Just last night I was back in my home town in Carey, Ohio, but I was lost in a neighborhood with golden domes and fancy monuments much more interesting than they ever was in that one-Edsel town. All there is is a pilgrimage place for mackerel-snappers, but it's just a big ugly church with a lot of crutches in the basement. In my dream, the town was full of stuff like Baghdad – minarets and shit. I guess it's hard to get past Eyc-raq.'

'Fuck Iraq.'

'Well, yeah, sure. But you went there for Blackwood, and you had real hotel rooms and good food with all the knobs on.'

'At least I didn't have to do no jumping jacks in the morning and salute no assholes.'

'You kill anybody?'

He glared again. 'That's how you know you're all grown-up, guy. Second gas-o-line convoy I went out on, I lit up a old Buick full of pop in his man-jammies and mommie and the kiddies in back. They got too close to our tailend truck so I cook off the M-60 and put a death blossom in that ol' Buick, and they're all swerving into a hooch. We couldn't stop but they could of been hajis, easy.'

'Course.'

'You know, shit. It was so boring over there, mostly I slept, except when I had to ride shotgun on the convoys or cure cancer.'

McCall laughed. 'I preferred Fort Living Room and Camp Couch. It wasn't really jumping jacks for us, not after basic. We saw some shit too, all of it messed up bad. Here's the Fortnum. What a fuckin' dump.'

The place was brick, the side walls scarred regularly between the floors by earthquake plates, which were common enough in old downtown. It was seven stories tall and obviously on the down-swing of its life story. The front door was chickenwire glass in a wood frame, and one big lobby window in front had been covered by plywood that was starting to delaminate. Red spray paint on the plywood window pretty much announced it as completely outside the system – neither a mission-type shelter nor an SRO – just a true flophouse:

> American owned. No drugs or whores. Will the last American
> to leave bring the flag.

'Luckily we both got all kinds of good sense, Rice. Let's gear up and move out.'
'I want to be the hard guy.'
McCall could see him fingering the knife in his pocket.
'You *are* the hard guy, shitbag. But keep it dialed down.'

Maeve had found a disturbing international postcard in the basket with her mail that morning, from an old boyfriend – in fact, from Beto, the next-door neighbor who'd been hiding out in Mexico ever since he'd attracted her like a butterfly-to-a-flame, had her pounded into his gang and then got her pregnant. Gloria had half hidden the card inside a PennySaver, as if unable to overcome her scruples about ditching it completely, but obviously hoping Maeve would miss it.

She picked it up gingerly. At first Maeve had thought Beto would mean nothing to her at all, but in fact his clumsy card had trou-bled her deeply. I'll BE BACK SOON had been written in painstaking child's capitals (he was almost thirty). QUERIDA. WELL SEE IF OUR EYES ARE OPEN WHEN YOUR 18. ¿STIL LOVE ME? B.

She'd thrust it immediately into the wet garbage. It didn't bear thinking about. Beto didn't even know about her pregnancy and the abortion. Enough of that. His whole universe had been fading out of her life for some time, but apparently not fast enough.

Maeve gassed up at an ARCO and headed for Hollywood on the off chance that she might recognize Conor Lewis' face amongst the scores of sad-sack runaways and rock wannabes who hung out at the fairly predictable places. Plummer Park, the Guitar Center, Gower Gulch – which was now a mildly slummy mini-mall with a cowboy theme, but back in the day, the day of the silents according to her dad, a place where hundreds of real cowboys from Wyoming and Texas had hung out in spectacular desperation, trying for jobs as extras and stunt men. The gulch had a Starbucks now, a sushi bar and a doughnut shop, and was often wall-to-wall with freaks, as was the supermarket two miles west at Sunset and Fuller that everybody called the Rock'n'Roll Ralphs, where the street kids hung out and shoplifted twenty-four hours a day, which would be her next stop.

The drive to Hollywood was a lot different than she was used to, starting out now in East L.A. instead of her mom's place in Redondo in the south. She stayed on the road that was named Cesar Chavez Avenue at the east end, formerly Brooklyn Avenue, but became Sunset Boulevard once it passed the Harbor Freeway. She seemed to have inherited her dad's luck with oddities as the first thing she saw at the Soto Street intersection, still on Chavez, was a tall nude man in the middle of the intersection clasping a wooden lance to challenge cars to a joust, first north–south, then wheeling around as the lights changed to east–west. His other lance was pretty flaccid, and his eyes looked droopy, too. Meth tweaker, she guessed, or angel dust. So sad – the cops were obviously on their way. *OK, Dad, I'll remember this one for you. A peewee league Don Quixote.*

Sunset Boulevard passed in sequence through precincts of China, Central America, Korea, Thailand and possibly a bit of Armenia, though she didn't know for certain that the signs on several shops in a row – with letters looking like rows of humpy chairs – were in the Armenian alphabet or the Thai.

Somewhere near here, up on Hollywood Boulevard, there was a small Thai eatery that her dad used to bring her to, and the cheerful owner had always greeted them with a big toothy grin and an offer of some appetizer or dish for free, returning some old favor because of something her dad had done for him. She couldn't even remember why he had stopped bringing her – maybe the place had gone out of business. So much about her dad was starting to seem lost, or tragic, or just enfeebled. Even without his new problems (such a euphemism!), he was beginning to have an old-man way about him, the way he woke up so stiff and full of mucous, and the way he sat forward attentively to people he might once have scorned, with his hands on his knees. Most of her friends had parents in their forties, still pretty vigorous, but hers had started late.

She'd always thought she and her dad had a bond that was stronger than other fathers and daughters, something that would endure forever, but most of it resided a beat or two back in her memory now, and she wondered, very much against her will, if she was drifting away from him and would eventually end up forsaking his comforts, despite all his shrewdness and kindness and compassion. What an awful thought – an absolutely insupportable thought, she decided. She focused hard on her drive down Sunset to keep from bursting into tears. *OK*, she told herself, *some of this emotion is from that damn Beto postcard, sneaking up on me. Get it together, girl.*

She pulled to the curb on a red zone on Sunset and killed the engine to spy on Gower Gulch. A girl with green hair, wearing a blanket like a cape that kept flapping open to reveal that she wore no clothes at all, was striding along in the wake of a basketball-tall hippie in fringed buckskin. They didn't speak a word to each other as they crossed Sunset right in front of her and headed for the Starbucks in the Gulch, like fur-trader and squaw. If you could speak of a bright-green-haired squaw. A handful of other kids sat around on low walls, accepting and then discarding leaflets that were being distributed dutifully by a wino with a heavy canvas bag over his neck. Nothing here, she thought after a careful examination.

The Rock'n'Roll Ralphs a little farther along drew her inside, but was little better, with only a handful of what might be runaways who were watched over by eagle-eyed security men. Then down to Pink's, the hotdog place on La Brea, then the kid-shelters on Vine, the McDonald's and Jack in the Boxes in the area, the warren of streets above Yucca that led up Ivar Hill to a nest of fleabag apartments. Few kids were out and about. It had been the dumbest of ideas, she chided herself, to come here in the light of day. She should have known. Most of the town's freaks and dopers and Goths vanished like roaches into the baseboards by the light of day, awaiting the sulky urban night to prowl.

Before she could stop him, a leafletter had tucked some wordy flyer under her wiper.

FREE DESPAIR TEST.

Wow, just what she needed.

Beyond Despair is human growth, she read through the windshield. Beyond bad pain maybe, she thought, but not despair. The only thing she'd ever found beyond despair was more despair.

All streams of life flow onward side by side until a time comes when one of the wise and loving ones who have chosen to stay behind to help others crosses into your immediate zone to help guide your evolution on to a higher plane.

Oh, yeah, she knew these folks: the Theodelphian Elect, who had bought a huge old hospital in the middle of Hollywood and painted it yellow and attracted lost kids from all over the country with the promise of solving all the problems of adolescence and loneliness and then some, with a little abracadabra. But she didn't think any of this was Conor's kind of vulnerability.

Remarkable that such a highly evolved elect would choose homeless alcoholics as their paid apostles. She wondered if the Theodelphians paid in small bottles of Thunderbird or Night Train.

Answer Honestly. (You only have your soul to lose.)

1. Do I feel empty and lost sometimes? Yes. Never. (Circle.)

She opened the door enough to reach around and grab the quiz off her windshield, and then she violated her principles by crumpling it and littering the gutter with it. She couldn't get the loathesome thing away from herself far enough and fast enough.

There wasn't anyone at the desk. The albino was probably dozing in back, as long as you didn't ring the little desk-bell to disturb his sleep, or maybe he'd fled after seeing Rice's switchblade. The elevator had an *Out of Order* sign, starving out anyone who couldn't hobble down the staircase to the little store up the road. *We're going to save them the trouble of all that,* McCall thought.

They went up the urinacious and unlit stairwell, Rice making a slight face. McCall knew there were only three tenants left to worry about now, all old-timers Vartabedian had inherited when he'd bought the Fortnum, the only three who clung to long-term leases as if the hotel were somewhere over in Santa Monica with a nice view of the ocean, or maybe about to rebound from years of skunk-time. The last three could probably be chased out in a week, but the old farts had banded together and talked to the Joe-goody Tim Voorhis about a pro bono suit – a high-profile lefty lawyer who loved getting his picture in the paper. That had to be discouraged toot-sweet.

Door 322 looked like it had been painted every week for years to cover the graffiti most of the others displayed. McCall gestured and Thibodeaux hammered his fist on the wood, as if trying to squash a bug.

'Look alive, Greengelb! Talk to us.'

Eventually the door came open two inches on a new chain that looked like it would hold the *Queen Mary*.

'You can tell Vartabedian to fuck his own ass,' the short man said.

'That's not very nice, sir.'

'And fix the elevator or we'll have the city on him.'

'Mr Vartabedian wants to pay you far more than it's worth to move into a nicer place out on the Westside,' McCall said reasonably. 'We'll find you a big comfortable apartment. I swear it'll be near a deli and a synagogue.'

'What do you know from delis, *putz*? Mr Moses can go take a flying leap into his tax deductions.'

'You're a genius, man,' McCall said. 'Don't you know the really big guys always win? I mean, *always*. Why don't you let him buy you out while you still got the first-class offers? You get twice what the city requires.'

'What happens meantime, with me and my friends? Mysterious fires? Stairs collapse? Serial killers in the lobby?'

'Sudden death is always a bitty inch away, Hebe,' Thibodeaux put in.

'Ahh! I heard that! I will go on with my arrangements in the law, and you can go on with your arrangement with Mr Strongarm here. We'll see who got the moxie.'

'Do you remember your dreams?' McCall asked mildly.

'I want you to know this is the United States of America, under law.'

He was still in a good mood. 'Dreams interest me, Mr Greengelb. Especially the bad ones we all have. The way people fight off their coward self with some kind of show-off stuff. They shout into the darkness. They still try to run when they're stuck in the glue.'

'Go away. Enough of the *mishigas*.'

'Then I can't help you a bit with your dreams, friend.'

'Contact Tim Voorhis, *gonif*.'

'He's just another goat-fucking lawyer, man. V. got him in the bag, too.'

The door slammed and Thibodeaux looked at McCall as if for permission to pound again or break it down.

'He's doomed and he knows it. Let's hunt up that albino, see if he's run off yet.'

It was only an eight-block jaunt to the park but the nuisance of oddity had found Jack Liffey nevertheless, as he stared out the side window of the rented van, strapped this way and that against sudden momentums. Gloria, at the wheel, had undoubtedly missed it entirely and he had no way to call her attention to it, in any case.

A woman wearing only a white bra and panties and an old flying-nun nurse cap carried a gigantic mock-up of a syringe under her arm and stepped quickly from street tree to tree (mostly stunted Chinese elms) pretending to inject them with the blunt needle, then giving cach tree a genuine pat of condolence.

I'll have a little of that, Jack Liffey thought, *whatever it is. It must be good to escape contingency for a while.*

Gloria held the control lever down to send the power-lift of the van grumbling down to the curb, and when it stopped Jack Liffey unhooked all the shock cords and wheeled himself off the shelf. She carried the bags of food and he fought his rubber wheels across the ragged Bermuda grass of Greenwood Park toward a picnic table that didn't look too hacked up with carved graffiti. Across the way, young wannabe gangsters were sitting in the baseball bleachers passing around a slim dark Sherman, probably laced with something, and punching shoulders playfully.

'You know, I could get used to doing all the talking,' Gloria said as she started to dig into the food bags for their picnic. 'It's a little creepy sometimes when you nod and smile like crazy, but I think I could just go on yakking for years – it suits me well. When I run out of cop stories, I'll tell you all those yarns from my aunt up in Owens. Paiute nonsense about how the gods hide themselves inside animals and rocks and trees. I wonder if there's some shaggy little god hiding out in Loco?' She laughed.

REALLY WORRIED ABOUT MV SORRY.

He smiled tightly and showed her the notepad.

'Aw, shit, Jack. Give it a break, please.'

He shook his head as she started to set out burritos and chips and salsa.

'Remember that bushido guy? It was when we first met? The guy that killed Ken Steelyard and almost killed us. I never forget that he said the secret to being a great warrior was deciding you were already dead. I don't mean Maeve's dead, but there's something to just relaxing into what's inevitable, OK? What she's doing she's doing. It's already a happening thing. And your fatherly concern ain't going to undo a bit of it. You got to decide she's running with the native sense you taught her and won't do stuff too stupid. And I promise I'll do what I can to watch over her.'

He nodded his thanks, but he was obviously still fretful.

'I probably shouldn't tell you this. I caught her with those business cards off her computer again: *Liffey and Liffey, Investigations*, with the big stupid eyeball from some old black-and-white movie.' She smiled. 'But I really think she's safer than if she was trying to protect herself in a suit of armor. I got a cop on her – though I know it worries you.'

EXPLODING WITH FRUSTRATION.

She reached over to press a strong hand on his arm. 'I get it, Jack. You're the original guard-all-the-gates dad, but I think that time's probably about over. Get with the new program. For right now, you get to park in the gimp spaces and let others help you out.'

'Ak, ak!'

'Come on, lighten up. The salsa is the fresca kind you like. I made it with lime juice. You can still enjoy your senses.'

He ate a few chips, scooping up the terrific homemade salsa, and then gave in to his worried nature again and wrote painstakingly.

WHAT'S UP WITH MIKE LEWIS' SON? I KNOW MIKE CALLED IS MV LOOKING FOR HIM?

'So you know about that. You've got a sixth and a seventh sense, don't you, Jackie? Like Loco.' They both looked over at the rented van, but despite the front door standing open, Loco was sound asleep on the front floor mat. He usually went pretty far under when he slept these days, either still recovering from the last of the chemo – or dying. Damn, he'd thought it.

ARGH! HAVE TO PROTECT MV.

'And we will, Jack. I promise. But your love is kind of a one-note fortune-teller of loss, it's so gloomy. You know that?'

There was an outcry from the bleachers, but it didn't seem serious, and when they looked over, nothing seemed amiss.

IS THAT THE GREENWOOD KLIKA?

Greenwood was the gang Maeve had been involved with.

'Jack, Jack, use your eyes, not your fears. The oldest kid over there is about fourteen. They're taggers, wannabes. Bangers don't sit out here in the afternoon.' She knew he was thinking of Beto, the Greenwoods' leader and Maeve's Svengali.

I'M SORRY, IT'S LIKE ALL THE AIR'S BEEN SUCKED OUT OF MY BRAIN.

He wrote fast.

'It can't be easy to lose your voice, I know. Right now, you've got to learn to lean on me,' Gloria said. 'Lean as hard as you have to.' All she could see in his face was shadings of desperation, and it made her sad. 'I don't have your expertise with your daughter, but I'm off shift today and tomorrow, and I'll track her for you, wherever she goes. I'm good at that.'

GOD BLESS YOU. I BLESS YOU, GL.

'In my mind, you and that god guy are just about equally doofus. Maybe equally demanding. But there ain't no philosophers going around claiming Jack is dead.' She laughed. 'Just don't impose any of those giant losses on me.'

He thought he saw her touch the pistol in its waistband holster at her skirt, just a brush as if for reassurance. 'Jack, I can deal with the real world. It's my profession. I think I can even change your goddam luck for you. But don't make me deal with you losing heart. The way your fading dad does. It's too much like my own relatives.'

I HAVEN'T GOT ANY GODS FOR YOU – DARK OR LIGHT.

'I know that. But I got a few Paiute gods left over and I may call on them. You're too fragile now to call on anybody. That's why I'm here for you.'

He almost smiled.

ONCE IN A GREAT WHILE I STILL BUY THE CATHOLIC LIBERATION NEWSPAPER. JUST TO SEE IF I CAN STILL BE TOUCHED BY PEOPLE SO DEVOTED TO THE POOR.

'Don't do it. Leave all that touching of shit to me.'

He tried to enjoy being out in the park with Gloria in the after-noon – the wind, the noises of the kids across the way, traffic, passersby, sensations of life going on willy-nilly to punctuate his involuntary silence. It had been a strong bright day and should have filled him with self-awareness, the way that clarity tended to do, but he found he was watching what was happening around him as if it was all on TV, most of the feeling missing, his participation totally missing, except a faint rasp that he could sense now and then as air rushed through his airways. He tried to remember if tomorrow was the day the physical therapist came to give his legs and feet their range-of-motion exercises, a humiliating series of twists and tugs punctuated by such expressions as, 'Now let's do our best to flex that pinkie – oink, oink, oink, on the way to market.' He desperately wanted his voice back, if only to bellow an insult.

Yet Gloria was a nourishing presence, he never doubted it, and after watching the physiotherapist once, she reproduced many of the same exercises, with a lot less of the boiled twaddle. Gloria was certainly trying hard for him. He wished he could turn a page and recover some sense of hope in himself. Turn to challenge that dark ogre that he felt pushing him down deep into his own body, away from the surface, away from life. He knew he needed to do something about the rage that had taken him over so completely.

A bird cried joyously overhead, and he took it for a sign. But a sign for what? Give life another try? He put everything he had into the will to move his right leg, and he may have managed a millimeter of a twitch, maybe not. He knew his attempts were not currently part of the clinical picture. If any sensation and movement returned – *if* – he had been told, it would be a glacial process, the beginnings of his real counter-revolt against the rebellious provinces, gaining a tiny tremor or a centimeter of attentive skin a day. The trench warfare of his Great War.

Gloria told him that their neighbors were reporting in now and then that they were praying for Jack, lighting candles for him at Our Lady of the Assumption. He was in no position to refuse their spiritual ministrations, and he decided to dedicate each prayer, if he heard about it, to a specific body part. Old Señora Mendoza's candles were for his left ankle. Señora Preciado's rosaries could fly into his butt where he occasionally felt a throb of sensation from the chair. If Gloria only knew a Paiute shaman, he would offer up his vocal cords to a meso-American god. A Ghost Dance – that was what he needed. To bring back his buffalo and all the dead warriors.

NOTES FOR A NEW MUSIC

Day 2

I met a very black man today on the street outside my hotel who held a fiddle on his lap on his wheelchair. We talked for a while and when I asked him to play something he liked for me, expecting 'Turkey in the Straw,' he played Liszt. It was not great but it was good enough to alarm me for some reason. In fact, I found myself crying. But, really, I wept secretly only after he had stopped playing and told me in a flat voice, 'I'm sorry, kid, I just wet myself.'

What kind of country treats a journeyman musician like this? I took him to a public toilet and then bought him a lunch of shrimp and scallops at a place he asked me to push him to, Fisherman's Outlet, at the huge produce market between Central and Alameda at the east end of Fifth where the truckers all eat. I had wonderful tilapia, from one of those busy ordinary counters where the food was better than you'd believe and everybody was elbowing everybody, and where Latinos did all the cooking and most of the eating, too. We ate outside on a city block of concrete that was filled with picnic tables, and then I had to wheel him back down Fifth to the middle of The Nickel.

He warned me to watch out as we went. That guy, or _that_ guy maybe, might tip him over and try to run off with his wheelchair. Not everybody who's got one down here needs it. The chairs have a perceived value – unlike their occupants, I guess. His name was Eddie Monk. Eddie Coltrane Monk. He suggested I get the hell out as soon as I could, but I wanted to stay, and then he suggested the Fortnum Hotel. There was some kind of mischief in his eyes when he did.

Surprised, I told him I was already staying there, and I went home for a while and tried to write a song. He'd mentioned hunger as a muted drumming in his belly. Human contact was terribly precious. Simple courtesy in life. The dignity of the docile. The wonder of eating a great filet of fish. Fearing what is odd and unexpected about poor people and disliking yourself for it.

This one was purely my observation: how hard it is living beyond the borders of what you know. These observations deserved to be a song but it wouldn't come together, no matter how hard I tried. Maybe with a backbeat like reggae.

Maeve had had a horrible evening, frightened now and again once things got dark, despite herself. Old Hollywood was full of really dangerous people who could overtake you faster than fate. Guys with Mohawks and knives, guys with tattoos on their necks saying *Vainglory* who could hurry up behind you and tap you on the shoulder and say 'Your turn to bend down, ho' bitch!'

She'd avoided them all – the green-haired beanpole at Hollywood and Vine and the little insinuating Asian guy at the Highland Center and even the smooth-talking business suit who'd promised her a 'dead-easy' part in a reality TV show if she'd only have a drink with him. Nobody had even looked very closely at the photo of Conor Lewis that she held up, and she was getting a bit crestfallen about her own delusions of being a detective. It was a city of way too many millions of people – ten million or more, if you counted out to the far boundaries of habitation. What did one person matter in all that? Who could care about one sad story in that immensity of sorrow?

In shop windows she saw dozens of homemade missing person signs and thought of making one for Conor and Xeroxing up several hundred copies, but nobody seemed to be looking at the other sad pleas, either. The signs seemed about as effective as the lost-cat posters on telephone poles, or the famous milk carton photos.

Maybe the new version of these was the ubiquitous sign she had started seeing at every Freeway offramp. *Lose your accent. Speak English like a native.* She wondered who on earth those were meant for. Would-be actors? Or just Mexican laborers tired of being treated like shit?

A bare-chested man with big rings in his nipples strode toward her, muttering something that sounded like the blood of the lamb. Just as he reached her, his head snapped around to glare, and she smiled as unthreateningly as possible. 'I *do* fear you,' he challenged. 'It was all slick before *you* came.' And he hurried on.

An old black woman in a flowery print dress had her back to the traffic, apparently staring in the window of a T-shirt shop that specialized in Draculas and rock stars. At first Maeve was about to approach her, and then she noticed that the bulky woman was ranting softly into her fist as if it were a microphone. 'And if thy foot offend thee, cut it off: it is better for thee to enter halt into life, than having *two* feet to be cast into hell, into the fire that never shall be quenched.'

Maeve gave her a wide berth and was just about ready to give up the search on Hollywood Boulevard for the evening when she felt a tug on a fold of her shirt. It was a little girl who couldn't have been much more than nine, skinny and dirty looking, barefoot, her thin dress ragged. In her free hand she dangled a naked pink plastic doll that dragged one foot on the sidewalk.

'Hi, honey. Can I help you?'

'Millie needs to eat.'

'Are you Millie?'

'Huh-uh.' She picked up the doll, utterly without a hint of affection for it, as if it were something she had just found in the gutter.

'Hello, Millie,' Maeve said to the doll. 'Is your mommy hungry, too?'

'Don't be a pill, girl. There's a place to eat right over there.' She pointed across the street to a shabby-looking diner, narrow as a shotgun shack, which was named Old-Time Movies Cafe. It was at the corner and on the side street just off Hollywood Boulevard the brick was painted with big portraits of W.C. Fields, Marilyn Monroe, James Dean and John Wayne. Somebody, undoubtedly after the original artist, had painted a cartoon talk balloon out of John Wayne's sneer. It said: 'So I walk funny. What's it to you, Pilgrim?'

'OK. Who else is eating tonight?' Maeve had a credit card that would cover it.

The girl glared at her for a moment as if Maeve had just taken something away from her. 'My mommy. That better be OK or I scream.'

The belligerence was breathtaking, and even sadder than the hunger. 'Of course it's OK, honey. Go get your mother. We can all eat whatever we want.'

A woman appeared almost immediately out of a dark alcove, looking like a stretched version of the little girl, barefoot, ragged and skinny, with stringy blond hair.

'Hi,' Maeve said cheerfully, offering her hand. 'I'm Maeve.'

'Hi, Maeve. My name is Felice. We're from San Antonio and we're lookin' for my old man name Clarence. You know him?'

Maeve suppressed a laugh and shook her head. The woman

showed her a tattered photo of a cocky-looking, lanky man in a Stetson. It was becoming a whole town of photo-displayers, Maeve thought. It was like after the Twin Towers, with everybody posting photos on a wall, looking for so many loved ones. She thought of showing the woman Conor Lewis, but decided there was no point. The only thing that made sense was posting it where hundreds of passersby would see it every day.

'Clarence drove off one day after he was outta work long past the county checks, but he sent us money from a address in Los Angeles that don't exist. This is awful embarrassing.'

'No, it isn't,' Maeve said. 'Please think of me as your friend. Let's have dinner. I'm very hungry.' She didn't ask how long the husband had been gone, because it was obviously quite a while for them to have wended their way as far as L.A.

The little girl stabbed the button for the WALK signal over and over, and then they trooped across to the Old-Time Movies Cafe, which had several plastic booths along the blank wall, mostly free. It didn't look like a gourmet hangout.

'This is all on me,' Maeve said, as if there might be any question. 'I mean it. Let me treat you guys. I believe everything friendly that you do comes back to you a hundred times over.'

'You're too good,' the woman said shamefully, but quickly she had the big plastic menu open.

'Forget it. Where are you staying? Please tell me the truth.'

'I *can't*,' Felice said. 'It ain't a good place. It ain't even really a place.'

'Aw, I can get you to a shelter,' Maeve said impulsively. She was imagining the two living in a refrigerator box in an alley, and she wondered how close she might be to a fate like that herself if things changed just a little in her life and she found herself all of a sudden dead broke in a strange city where she had no friends. 'You may not know about shelters, but they exist, and they're for people like you – good people with a sudden need for a place to stay.'

'God made the earth for the poor just as much as the rich,' Felice said adamantly. 'We mayhap look pigpen, but we ain't unclean folk at heart.'

'Of course not, I know that. You need some food and hot water and a little helping hand, that's all.'

'Rice Thibodeaux, you get away from our women!'

He turned to glare. It was Sister Mary Rose, though she sure didn't look much like the nuns he'd known in N'Orleans, always whacking his knuckles and his shoulder with their rulers. Those nuns wore blue serge habits in all weather and white cotton wimples over their heads. Actually, this woman reminded him more of a whippet out at the dog track at Gentilly, skinny and nervous and fast, with freckles and a lot of limp reddish hair going gray. She had an unruly energy about her that he found very disturbing in a woman. He wasn't even sure he'd want to fuck her.

'It's a free country, sister,' he insisted.

'We have a restraining order against all John Does, and you're definitely John Doe – Rice Thibodeaux.'

Catholic Liberation Women's Shelter was on the Little Tokyo side of Skid Row – that is, the north side – and it had a little lawn in front where the women and their kids could sit outside protected by tall chain link with a hoop of razor wire at the top.

There were sometimes good pickings there, to get laid on the cheap or even free, and Rice Thibodeaux liked to drop by and look them over, chat up the likely ones a bit, the ones maybe not so good looking, maybe a little fat or plain. You knew they weren't getting any inside there, and he could offer his services.

The nun was smoking like a firestack, which was becoming odd in L.A. for almost anyone, let alone a nun. He knew by experience this nun never backed down on a challenge. Some day he'd carve her up a bit, show her what a little pain could make you do.

'Gotta run,' he said. 'Gotta see a man about a walrus.'

'Well, if you get hard up again, Monsieur T., you just take up with that walrus. We're not interested here.'

A couple of the women chuckled, and he stored that away in the get-even bin, too.

Six distinct groups reside in The Nickel. In the outer circle are mostly women: the temporary homeless, having lost a job or a husband or a home. They often bring children along with them. Then there are 'wino' panhandlers who are still able to collect a few dollars in the business district several blocks away to pay for a small bottle of Night Train or Thunderbird. In the next circle, there are the drug addicted, particularly those caught up by the cheaper forms of crack and meth and PCP. There are the schizo-phrenics who carry on a lively intercourse with many people they think live here but are invisible to the rest of us. There are the parolees and hospital releases dumped on The Nickel. And finally there are the drug-dealers and criminals who prey on all these inner circles of hell.

FOUR
Sister Mary Rose

'**B**uzzard's luck,' Art Castro murmured to himself. This would probably waste the last fragile string he had left to yank at the LAPD. On what was probably no more than a fool's errand for Jack Liffey and his daughter. He sighed and picked up the telephone. He hadn't really noticed the sorry state of his relations with the LAPD until a few months earlier when his contacts were almost all gone. One by one they'd taken themselves off the job or moved to other departments in Duarte or San Bernardino – or just gone off him, for some reason. Sergeant Javier Guzman was seemingly still taking Art's calls, but he didn't sound very happy about it. In the end, he agreed to check Missing Persons for him.

'This is a favor I'm doing, Javi,' Art Castro said. 'It's not a money case. I'd like to find the kid before he's peddling his ass to all the *gabachos* in Bentleys at Heartbreak and Vine.'

'Don't play no *raza* card on me, Ar-tur-o. Not since your buddy there at Rosewood flaked on us and testified and hurried on to the White Guy Fortress up in Idaho.'

'No buddy of mine, if you mean Marty Hansen. He just worked down the hall.'

'Hansen, yeah, that's the puddle of filth I mean. The guy testified he never ever talked shit like "spic" and "greasers" to anybody, oh, no, he loved Mexes like his own wife and kids, and the defense produces a tape with a hundred fifteen "spics" and "beaners" on it. Blew our case against the Garzas to hell.'

'Shit, man, you got plenty of problem guys in the department, too, that nobody brown will deal with; still think the only trouble with this city is too many blacks and Mexicans.'

'I hear you. But we're evens after this, A.'

'I don't know why you want to be that way. I do you specials all the time.'

'It's tough these days,' Javier Guzman said. 'This new chief is all bad news on favors. I don't want to look up some day and see some rat squad sticking a piece of paper in my hand, OK? I swear I'll light that Shoes up. And you, too, if it tracks to you.'

'I'll keep you in my good mind, Javi, I mean it. *Gracias*. Never no bad shit.'

'Code four, *ese*. Be good now. I'll get your info-nympho.'

The mother and daughter had devoured their Old-Time Movie meals at warp speed – Felice's spaghetti on side-by-side burger patties (called the Sophia Loren Special, which she didn't want to think about) and Millie had the ham steak with a pineapple ring on top (Princess Grace's Wedding), while Maeve had picked a little at a godawful salad of near-frozen iceberg lettuce dolloped with something sweet and lumpy and pink. Everybody had refused seconds or desert, and Maeve phoned Gloria to ask about a shelter. Maeve was certain they existed, but she had no practical knowledge of their whereabouts.

'So you picked up some strays?' Gloria said evenly on the cell.

'That's not how I'd put it.'

'Of course not. Mother Theresa and how many kids?'

'One daughter. They really need a nice place to stay, Glor.'

'You got the Beverly Hilton not too far from you.'

'Be serious, please. You can point us.'

'I don't know Hollywood, hon. I was never on the job there. San Pedro I could tell you three places off the top of my head. Harbor City . . . Wilmington. OK, how 'bout this. I heard Catholic Liberation opened a women's shelter downtown last year. I think it's on Third or Fourth a little west of Alameda.'

'Do the women have to be Catholic?'

'No way. Nobody does that stuff.'

'That's a pretty rough area, isn't it?'

'Where are you calling from?'

'OK, I get it, Mom.' The 'mom' was as gently ironic as she could make it.

'They'll be in good hands with Liberation, believe me. Those women are so clean and good they frown if you make a joke.'

'Thanks a bunch, Glor.' She cut off before Gloria could get in another snide dig about picking up strays.

'We got a place to stay,' Maeve announced. She realized she should probably call ahead, but she had an inkling they might be much better off this late at night just showing up and throwing themselves on the mercy of the nuns, or whoever ran the place.

'Thank you,' Felice said gravely. 'I wish I could give you something.' The little girl looked very guarded, as she had all evening.

'That's OK. Let's get your stuff.'

'We'll go fetch it and meet you right back here,' the woman said.

Maeve realized immediately that the woman didn't want her to see where they were staying, but it could have meant a long walk with their possessions. 'I have a car around the corner. Look, I promise I won't watch where you go. I'll wait anywhere you say and you can go out of sight.'

Millie squeezed her mother's arm with some message Maeve couldn't read.

'Your daughter's tired,' Maeve said.

'Why you be so nice to us?' the woman asked. 'We ain't had nothing but busted luck since we got to this awful city. People so mean here, the eating places they soak they throwouts in bleach so can't nobody eat it outta the dumpster.'

'Aw, I didn't know that. That's *terrible*. My parents taught me to be nice to folks. Don't you think people should help other people?'

Maeve thought she could just see tears in the woman's eyes. The little girl, who'd obviously had her share of busted luck too, remained hard and suspicious.

'Some day, when you're back on your feet, you'll remember this and help somebody else. That's the way it comes around. OK?'

The woman nodded, and the little girl thrust out the doll toward Maeve. 'Here.'

'Will you let me hold her, just for a minute or two?' Maeve said.

Millie nodded grimly.

That evening, Conor had started getting used to his utterly plain room at the Fortnum. Austerity normalized, like everything else. It was a strange thing, he thought, but any resting place that didn't devour you or call down the dogs of hell, you pretty quickly come to feel safe, even a bit homey. His only problem really was the squashed roaches on the walls, almost like a wallpaper pattern. Before him, somebody had had a contest with himself to see how many he could crush every night, and nobody had ever cleaned up. It was hard to imagine a hotel that didn't even scrape off the dead roaches between guests, but some things were getting easier to imagine every day.

All Conor's life, his father had written about the poor, the working poor in America and the dirt poor in Mexico, and he really admired his father for doing that, but he realized how abstract it had all remained for him. It hadn't really penetrated his personal reality out in suburbia, not in any meaningful way. He remembered the joke he'd heard at school about the kid at Beverly Hills High who'd written an essay about poverty. *Everybody was poor, the maid was poor, the cook was poor, the butler was poor . . .*

He went out at night, braving the busy murmuring darkness all around, along Sixth Street and then San Julian, to Mike's Market two blocks away and bought a sponge and some 409. He retraced his course and started wiping off the insect remains and depositing them in the plastic bag he'd been given for his purchases. *Thrift*, he thought. Never in his life had the reuse of a plastic bag meant anything at all to him. *I'm learning a few new things here. I'm learning how other people have to live.* He tried to think of rhyming lines for a song about extreme forms of thrift, but nothing would come. Bag. Tin can. Need-feed. Plastic.

Even the roaches were poor, he thought.

They were very careful to make her park around the corner at Cherokee Avenue, but Maeve could see the dark alley toward which Felice and Millie walked hand-in-hand. Aw, *no*, she thought, when they confirmed her suspicion by turning abruptly down the alley. They'd actually been living in a cardboard box, or under a hedge, living rough. It was inconceivable, though she had certainly tried to conceive it. No wonder they'd seemed so unwashed. She glanced down at the naked doll beside her, left in her temporary custody and nearly wept.

'Sorry, dollie. I'll get you some clothes. I promise. And your owner. My little sister.'

They came back with a dilapidated pair of those red plaid hardboard suitcases from Kress or Newberrys that you never saw any more. She'd had a tiny one herself as a child, for weekends with her dad, before her mom had replaced it with a Gore-tex wheelie from some catalogue.

'Your dollie was almost crying, she missed you so much,' Maeve said.

The little girl glanced at Maeve as if she were nuts, then sat in the back seat and withdrew into herself.

'It's not far,' Maeve said reassuringly, though she was a bit nervous herself about driving into Skid Row after dark.

She headed back along Sunset Boulevard, past gentrifying Silverlake and Echo Park, and just as she approached the cheery overlit and counterfeit Mexican tourist trap of Olvera Street, she headed south into Downtown on Main. She motored slowly east along Third Street through a stretch of abandoned buildings that grew darker and more forbidding. No center to be seen. She came back along Fourth, hoping Gloria hadn't got it wrong.

But eventually the shelter stood out like a radiant island on the street, with even a bit of lawn protected by a high wire fence. She stopped right in front.

'You guys wait.'

Maeve plucked up her courage and walked to the gate and called to a large black woman who was sitting on a beach chair on the lawn, smoking. 'Ma'am. I have a mother and child who need a shelter bad.'

'We full up.'

'Please.'

'Wait there, girl.' The black woman frugally scraped the burning tip off her cigarette, tucked it into the grass beside the leg of her chair, and went inside.

Eventually a thin woman with graying red hair came out into the puddle of brighter light by the door. She looked vaguely familiar to Maeve.

'Hello, there, I'm Sister Mary Rose.'

It was the voice that did it, and the nervous energy that the woman gave off. *Omigod!* Maeve thought. But she betrayed no sign, because the woman obviously didn't recognize her. After all, she was almost ten years older now and Maeve's jump from nine to eighteen was much bigger than this woman's forty-five to fifty-four.

'I have a mother and young girl in the car who really need shelter.'

The woman sucked her teeth an instant. 'We're always full by this time.'

'They need a place really really bad, ma'am.'

'Don't get in a tizz. We'll set up cots or something until we have room.' She used a key from a chain around her neck and unlocked the gate. 'Bring them in. Let's see what we can do.'

The woman hurried away into the building. Eleanor Ong was her name – whatever her nun name had been before and probably was again, Maeve thought. Her father had been madly in love with her then – yes, it was almost ten years ago, not too long after he'd left her own mother. Eleanor had already quit some convent, but apparently she'd gone back, or she'd gone back to work with her order on some dispensation. The coincidence was just too great, but life was like that.

Maeve vaguely remembered that her dad and Eleanor had been tied together and thrown down a storm drain during a heavy rain by a couple of Mafia thugs, and the relationship had turned out badly after that. The poor woman couldn't handle her dad's life, she had said, like several other women had said later. But why not? Her dad had never been a Sunday School picnic, but he always gritted his teeth and set off up that sad lonely honorable road that everybody else just talked about. It was why she loved him so desperately, and Eleanor Ong should have, too.

Maeve brought Felice and Millie out of the car, clutching their string-wrapped suitcases. Once they were into the yard, Maeve closed the gate behind them so it at least appeared to be locked. 'That woman said she'll find you a place to sleep. I gotta go.' She felt terribly vulnerable out there on the street alone but she didn't want to get mixed up with the nun.

'Thank you, Maeve,' Felice called through the fence. 'You been a prayer's answer. We won't forget you.'

'I won't let you. I'll come tomorrow and find out how you're doing. I want to get the doll some clothes.' Though she had a ton of second thoughts about coming back here. She was afraid Eleanor would recognize her in some way. But that was a pretty long shot. Eleanor reappeared as they were still talking, and she decided she'd better disguise her voice a little.

The nun greeted Felice and Millie warmly where they waited patiently. 'You'll have to be on fold-a-beds for a few days, but they're pretty comfortable. I use one of them myself. You'll have a private space and you can lock the door. We'll get you some food tonight if you haven't eaten.'

'Oh, no, we ate up a storm thanks to this kind young lady.'

Eleanor turned to look at her, and Maeve decided it was past time to split. 'Gotta go,' she called in an unnaturally deep voice.

That only drew Eleanor's attention. 'The Lady Lone Ranger rides off. Hi-yo, Silver.'

'That's sexist,' Maeve said automatically, then fought to unlock her car.

'I think I knew a girl like you once,' Sister Mary Rose called wistfully. 'I have a memory for faces.'

'No way. No no. I'm from Kansas.'

'Give my regards to the others in your family back in Kansas.'

All the hair on the back of Maeve's neck stood on end.

There was a soft rap on Conor's door, and he guessed, by its volume if nothing else, that it probably wasn't anybody dangerous. He opened on a very short old man wearing one of those Jewish skull-caps, navy blue with a white pattern around the rim – what were they called? He felt bad he didn't remember. The man also wore a thick wool suit and white shirt but no tie.

'Hello, sir.'

'You're new here. I'm your neighbor, Samuel Greengelb. I bet Vartabedian's *gonifs* haven't had a chance to threaten you yet. *Feh*, the room smells of carbolic.'

'It's just 409. I was spraying to clean up the cockroaches.'

'With all due respect, *nu*, you should spray the *gonifs* the first time you see them. That will take the smell away. Listen, have we met?'

'No, sir, I don't think so.'

The old man sighed. 'I have to check these days. I sometimes forget things.'

'Come in, sir, please. Mr Greengelb. My name is Conor Lewis.'

'An interesting name. Of the Irish, no?' He took a step inside the room.

Conor shrugged. 'The last name is Welsh really, but my mom was real Irish, from Cork – Brigid Glanchy. That where-you're-from stuff doesn't mean anything to me. I'm a mongrel American.'

'Heritage should mean to you, my son. Look, there are three of us who live here for many years, and we're fighting back against the new landlord. We joke we are the three Musketeers. The new owner of this hole is Armenian and he should know better. They were once victims, too. But the thugs he hires are the true mongrels – they're of the lost ones, men with no family, no roots. They're from the army or worse – just guys sent to places of much killing for money. Fighting dogs, you point them and take off the muzzle.' He shrugged.

The man came in stiffly and Conor realized again just how short he was, barely to his chin. A selfish thought occurred to him – that there were interesting songs to be found in this man, and then less selfishly, there was obviously a real drama playing itself out here. Something his father might admire. And he liked the man's abrupt manner, almost rude. He'd never seen anything like it. 'Sir, please sit on my chair. I can't offer you coffee or anything yet.' Conor sat opposite him on the bed.

'You look like a smart boy. You play chess?'

'I'm afraid not, sir. My friends at school always said they preferred games with more chance of cheating.'

Greengelb laughed. 'I been playing chess with a dead Russian Jew for many years, name of Boris Shpilman – forty years dead but in all the books. Real problems he posed, all the time. The Shpilman Gambit. The Shpilman Knight Opening. *Oy.*' He tapped his forehead with three fingers. 'Very hard to outthink this man.'

Chess didn't interest Conor, but the rest of the story did. 'Sir, can you tell me about these thugs who come around?'

'The *akhzers* pound on our doors late at night and yell at us for the owner, Vartabedian. The elevator they have already *kiboshed*. They are heartless men who have no brain of their own. You watch – soon they will cut off the heat or the water or some new atrocity. I curse them and say they should lose all the ill-gotten money they are paid to painful and bungling doctors. Let them suffer and remember.'

Conor couldn't help laughing at the colorful curse. 'If I stay at the Fortnum a while, do you think they'll threaten me?'

'*Nu*, probably not.' He gave an elaborate shrug. 'You they can throw out any time. You don't have a lease from the old owners. Bless the souls of 4-G Property Management, who that was. They were good to us for fifteen years, paid a Jamaican super named Bevan who kept the place up, painted the halls, changed the bulbs, fixed stuff. The 4-G stood for four guys from the Valley, but we knew them as the four *goy* dentists. When all this loft insanity started, sadly the four dentists saw a chance to make big money. The four *shmos* is all they are now. Vartabedian will probably throw us out in the end, and he'll bring in cheap labor to rebuild the place and sell his "artist lofts" for millions.'

'How can you stop him?'

Greengelb shrugged. 'He's got the bigshot lawyers. And we're at the end of our rope, but we don't give up easy. Morty Lipman is my *nexdoorekeh*, room 324. We're D'Artagnan and Athos. And Joel Wineglass upstairs is with us, too. Maybe Porthos. But those *gonifs* of Vartabedian's never even heard of all-for-one or Milady. They're ignorant as bricks. They never read nothing but Donald Duck.'

Conor was a bit chagrined that he'd never read Dumas either, though he'd seen the movies.

'These thugs,' Greengelb said with a smirk. 'I watched them one day in the coffee shop over on Broadway arguing about what side the jellied toast falls on. Amazing shmucks, truly. As if this is science.

'The little one, always clinging to a knife, he says, "The jelly side up, it's got more air resistance." Strange that he's the optimist. He's the really evil one.

'So the big one holds the toast out and drops it with a flip, and it falls on the dry side just like the *meshuggenah* says.

'"My mistake," the big thug says.

'"What you mean?" the knife guy says, very suspicious.

'"I jellied the wrong effin' side."' Greengelb cackled at his own joke, real or apocryphal.

Conor did his best to laugh anyway.

'You sure I don't know you?'

'You do now.'

Maeve came home pretty late – on a school night, too – and parked as quietly as she could on Greenwood Street. She'd had just a single twinge as she'd passed the street sign at the corner. She could never completely forget that the street, and its namesake *klika*, were burned into her life now, an Old English G tattooed on her left breast that neither her dad nor Gloria had seen. She tiptoed up the walk. Her dad was somewhere deep inside, but she was shocked to find Gloria waiting on the glide on the front porch, nursing a beer.

'No sneaking home here, hon. Stakeouts are my game.'

'I knew I should have gone back to Redondo.' That was her mom's house where she could always sneak in, a half-dozen ways. 'So, you do a lot of stakeouts?'

Gloria frowned. 'Sit.'

Maeve sat on the rickety Adirondack chair that tended to throw you back hard if you weren't careful. She was avoiding the glide where Gloria sat. Gloria creaked the glide a little with a kick. Maeve wondered if the balky glide had been there since Boyle Heights had been the first Jewish suburb of L.A. a century ago, before the Jews had moved on west.

'You don't ask the questions. *I* ask questions. That's the deal with cops.'

'It wasn't really a question.'

Gloria gave her the fish eye, and Maeve subsided to neutral. 'Anything. Ask.'

'You know perfectly well that your dad is helpless right now. I know you're trying to do some work as his stand-in, but it might end up involving him in some way. Don't get skittery now and start denying things right and left. I know you picked up a couple of sad sacks in Hollywood because you called me about it. Good for you.'

'Should I have just left them in that awful alley where they were living?'

'Remember, *I* ask the questions.'

OK, Maeve thought. *I'll play it your way – hardball all the way. I won't tell you that the woman who runs that shelter is Eleanor Ong, dad's staggering Really Big Love from long ago – and this torch-bearer, this beautiful skinny woman with all the freckles, might have recognized me. Put that in your pipe and smoke it, Ms Hard-Nose Cop. Except you can't because you won't deign to meet me on equal terms.*

'I just want to protect you and your dad, hon. You can understand that. Is there anything I need to know about all this? Jack has enough trouble worrying about his condition and his damn dog recovering from the cancer – and, I admit it, worrying about me, too. I'm not so easy to live with. He sometimes worries himself sick about this hard case and all her problems.'

'I love you, Glor.'

'Thank you very much, Maeve. Love is not always relevant or sufficient, but it always matters. And I'm glad you care.'

'Do you think I'm hurting Dad? Honestly? I'd rather die than hurt Dad.'

'I have no reason to think so. But can you stay in touch with me about what's going on?' Gloria was studying the empty beer bottle in her hand, as if she couldn't meet Maeve's eyes. 'For his sake. You don't have to find me civil or fair or motherly – just truly fierce in defense of your father.'

Sure. But trust was already a lost game, Maeve thought, since she was still feeling a bit angry and wasn't going to tell Gloria about Eleanor Ong. 'Of course,' she said, feeling a bit sick inside.

NOTES FOR A NEW MUSIC

Day 3

Met some wonderful old Jewish men who somebody's trying to throw out of this hotel. My neighbor Mr Samuel Greengelb visited me for a long time. He even taught me some Yiddish, which he speaks fluently. (I didn't know anybody spoke it anymore.) It's very sad, too; he's very afraid that he's starting to lose his memory. More to come on this. I'm exhausted now.

It was about nine at night, and Maeve's father sat in his wheelchair in the kitchen reading a book, with Loco lying across his feet. He'd lifted the foot-pads up to rest his feet on the floor beside Loco – either to gain comfort for himself or to comfort the dog.

'What you reading, Dad?'

He nodded a greeting to her and held up the book, a Cormac McCarthy that she didn't know.

'You like it?'

He made a noncommittal face and then retrieved a notebook to write.

VERY DARK

'That's like saying Groucho Marx is funny.'

He smiled and nodded. Then at Maeve's urging they had a discussion – if you could call it that – about divorce. Maeve got around to asking him which of the women he'd known in his life, excluding Gloria and his first wife – her own mother, of course – had meant the most to him.

YOU LEARN SOMETHING ABOUT YOURSELF FROM EVERYONE YOU LOVE

He quickly inserted the word 'IMPORTANT' with a caret after 'SOMETHING.'

That was terribly diplomatic, she thought, but not what she wanted.

'Sure, I learned a lot from Beto, too,' she said. *And I hope you never see the tattoo*, she thought. 'But, really, Mr Loved-Each-One-in-Her-Own Way. If you *had* to say . . .'

PROBABLY ELEANOR. DO YOU REMEMBER HER? LONG AGO.

'A little bit. I was very young. What was it about her?'

LOST. LOVELY. TRYING DESPERATELY TO DO GOOD IN THE WORLD. BUT NEEDY.

He smiled warmly and laughed.

AND SOME SEX STUFF I WON'T TOUCH ON.

'Were you her first lover? I know she'd been a nun.'

YES BUT IT'S COMPLEX.

'You always say something like that to avoid explaining. One of these days you've got to start talking again.'

'Ack,' he said desperately.

'Sorry, Dad. That wasn't fair. I'd better go home to bed. This is a school night.'

When she finally got home to Redondo at about ten, she called Art Castro on his cell.

'It's not a complete report yet, kid, but I know your boy is in town. He accessed an ATM at a Skid Row mini-mart called Mike's. He's either staying at one of the flops nearby, or he's got a pal in one of the fancy new lofts. They're asking a small fortune for those places. Of course he could be camping out on the street with the schizos and winos. You didn't say if he brought any gear.'

'Thanks, Art. I'll tell Dad when he's ready to go on the hunt.'

'Sure, kid. You're just keeping his spot on the bench warm.' He sounded skeptical, but basically not all that interested.

'That's the deal.' If she'd learned one thing from her dad it was to keep her mouth shut and resist the temptation to amplify, justify, explain. 'He owes you one.'

'Oh, a lot more than one.'

She hung up and thought immediately about her father. Did she really expect him to join the hunt at some point, become reanimated all at once by the challenge, or some other impetus? *Good work, Maeve, now you go back to school and I'll take over.*

It was terrifying to her that he seemed so small and powerless now. He had once been big enough to blot out the sun, and now he seemed just shriveled and weak – not so much in his wheel-chair, but in her head. This silence, when his voice had once filled a whole house, had once perfectly filled her longing for company, for someone to joke with and ask questions and always, always back her up. *Dad, oh, I still need you.*

She wasn't even sure if she'd said any of it aloud, but there was an addendum in her head that she knew she hadn't said out loud. *Don't go yet, please.* She hurried downstairs and threw her arms around her mother, who was sitting on a kitchen stool raising and lowering a teabag in a cup.

'Your dad?' Kathleen Liffey said.

'Yeah. I can't stand it. He keeps getting smaller and it makes me smaller, too. I want him to talk to me.'

Her mother tipped the cup to study the color of the liquid, then kept dipping. 'Being brave never feels brave, does it? When Jack and I split up – God, that was so long ago – I kept wanting to find him somewhere in the house to tell him what I was feeling.'

'Oh, Mom!'

'But I have hopes. For something in life. I don't know what. I'm sure I've had enough of sorrow.'

So much for running to her mother for comfort – her mother, deep in her own misery.

'I'm not so terrible, am I?' her mother asked.

One problem with positive thinking, Jack Liffey thought, was that adopting an expectant attitude predisposed you to a sense of failure.

'We must be very patient now, Mr Liffey. We'll start getting it, any time now. I've seen it happen many times. Try to press our nice soft foot against my hand.'

Of course, the alternative was moping. It was important to count your blessings, even as a cripple. It got you a close parking place in most lots, a good spot for your chair at the movies. And once you could accept it, most people offered you help, a push over a big hump, a quick fetch of something you needed. After they got over the terror of meeting your eyes.

What *was* that, anyway? People mostly glanced away quickly as if you were a schizophrenic who was about to sit beside them on a bus and tell them all about the tinfoil hat that kept out the rays from space. While children stared hard at you, sizing up a freak for the entertainment value, for tales to pals. The life of Cain.

But another advantage: he now had the opportunity of experiencing two different lives in a single lifetime, learning something to convey to the remains of the normal one from the new one. Able

and disabled. Conventional and challenged. Pre-crippled and crip-
pled. Normal and lame. John Doe and Gimp. Like everyone else,
he had pushed the thought of what it meant to be 'like that' aside
for most of his life. Now there was no choice. He *was* like that.
Exiled to this lesser world and deprived of so many simple things,
left a kind of intelligent jellyfish to be moved out of the way of
those who were doing real things. But still loved, he thought, still
with Gloria's fingers running through his hair. *Yes, count your bless-*
ings, Jack Liffey. Keep me in a crate in your closet, you great big
unsentimental woman.

Despite occasional claims by Los Angeles homeless authorities that
'most' of the homeless who want a bed are sheltered every night,
at least 83 per cent of the homeless in L.A. sleep the night behind
bus benches, under overpasses, in business doorways, in alleys, in
unlocked autos, against houses with wide eaves and under park
trees.

FIVE
The Fighting Musketeers

'He be fiddlin' his fiddle with the symph-harmonic at that Disney Hall,' a skinny bearded man said in a screechy voice that was like lawn furniture dragged across cement. Then he guffawed to give his declaration the lie. 'Whyfor you wantin' Eddie?'

'I like his music.' Conor had run into Eddie Coltrane Monk the day before and then earlier today in Pershing Square, serenading the pigeons and one or two tourists. Liszt both times – pretty good but not that great. Still, passable Liszt.

'Say what?' the man said from his post just outside the hotel.

'I want to talk to him about music,' Conor said.

'Well, Eddie can't be disturb.'

'What do you mean? Do you know where he is?'

'Worth a buck to you?' A long scar stood out in ashy gray on the length of the man's cheek. He wore very short floodpants, his hair hung in dreadlocks, and all he really needed was a parrot to look like Long John Silver, Conor thought, almost laughing aloud. Somehow, in the daylight, he was less frightened by this unreasonably tormented universe of abject poverty.

'It's worth a quarter,' Conor said. 'That's all I got.' He figured he'd have to start drawing lines in the sand sooner or later. He dug out a quarter and held it up to show he was serious, not talking about imaginary quarters.

'Shit. Take that and rub it wid' two more you still ain't can buy nothing a man would want.'

'It's better than a poke with a stick, isn't it?'

'Gimme.'

'Where's Eddie?' Conor retracted his hand with the quarter.

He'd set out to hear Eddie play again because his own recollection of the playing worried him, and he wanted to give the man another shot, and anyway he'd liked him as a person. Conor wondered if he might have judged him wrong – expecting only mediocrity and then hearing a false mediocrity in his head. Who was he to judge? Anyway, he'd bought Eddie lunch yesterday and they'd got on well.

'Suck my Johnson, kid. Eddie's in San Julian Park, where he always be, serenading the bums. Gimme.'

Conor flipped the quarter softly, and the man bobbled it a few times with swollen dirty bandage-wrapped hands before corralling it against his chest.

'Thank you, sir,' Conor said politely.

Another man down the road told him for free where San Julian Park was, and he set out westward on Fifth, a street where much of the curbing and even some of the sidewalk itself had crumbled away, and nobody had bothered to repair it, as nobody had bothered to sweep up the mounds of rotting vegetable-and-piss-smelly cardboard that had collected in the gutters. Small knots of black men lounged against brick buildings or sat on what was left of the curb like basking cats trying to stay in the lozenges of winter sunlight that squeezed down between the tall buildings.

McCall and Thibodeaux had watched the young kid exit the building and talk to a couple of the bums before even thinking of getting out of their jacked-up truck. McCall had no idea what a teenager was doing there, but there was no sense stirring up somebody who was dressed so well, might have influential connections, and obviously didn't have any legal tenure in the Fortnum. The friendless old Jews, they were the target, and McCall was having trouble keeping his strongarm confederate from yanking out the Mexican switchblade at every opportunity. The guy could still be held down with a combination of reason and pure energy.

'S'up, professor?' Thibodeaux said.

'We got to run an R.F. here. That means a rat-fuck, if you Orleanies don't follow the idiom. The Big V says to use some tricks to get the Yids out.'

Thibodeaux slowly nurtured a private grin that made McCall uncomfortable.

'Not *that* way.'

'I wish you wouldn't. You keep spoiling mah doldrums.'

McCall wondered if he meant *daydreams*. 'What's that, pard?' He knew better than to provide an opening, but he asked anyway as they stepped out of the truck.

'Know thyself,' Thibodeaux announced as they reached the

Fortnum's plywood window. 'Consult Nietzsche. The righteous man don't never run out of well-honed proposals.'

Thibodeaux lingered a moment on the empty sidewalk behind, forcing McCall to stop and look back. Thibodeaux flicked open his switchblade, and swiped a big T in imitation of Zorro's Z into the plywood covering the Fortnum window. Then he grinned and slammed the blade closed against his leg. The gesture left a small cut in his jeans and blood began to run down the well-worn pants. They both watched it trickle for a moment, irresistible to the eye.

'Blood is my captain,' the little man said nervelessly.

'Jesus fucking Christ,' McCall said, disturbed to his core. 'Forget it, man. No way. We got orders to screw up the doorlocks, to ruin the elevator for good, to kill the heat and tell the night manager to fuck off forever. That's the program. Get with the program. Do you hear me?'

'Oh, sure. I'm a lifelong pacifist, jus' like yo' dead mama.'

'I don't need a comedian for a partner. Straighten up and fly right, Waldo.'

Maeve found Mike's Market and parked about a block north of it, where things looked a little more like part of the world that she was used to. The market was an oblong of eroded brick with an iron security gate set into a jumble of abandoned warehouses and blank walls. Even the sign over the door had been hand lettered by an amateur, with wobbly letters. The whole aspect suggested tiny packets of offbrand foodstuffs past their expiration dates.

She didn't often play hooky from high school, but today she was a practicing truant, and maybe she'd forge a note from her mom in time for tomorrow. Maybe she'd do it like the old joke, just for the hell of it: *Maeve was sick yesterday – My Mom.* What could they do to her? Send her back to middle school?

She had waited until rush hour traffic cleared out, about ten, then headed straight over to the Harbor Freeway on Redondo Beach Boulevard. On the way there was a big furniture store that for years had flown a really big barrage balloon shaped like a sofa as a come-on. Weirdly, five or six men were clinging to the sofa's mooring cable now, being towed eastward along the street by the onshore wind and calling out to others for help. She didn't know whether she should root for the men or the sofa, but it was definitely a tale to save for her dad.

She got off the Harbor at Sixth Street downtown, and drove right past the south end of what had long ago been the city's main park, Pershing Square. Recently it had been paved over with multi-colored concrete slabs and filled with giant concrete shapes to make it distinctly unpleasant for anyone to hang out – particularly, of course, the homeless.

As she stepped into the gloomy interior of Mike's Market, a tall African-American security guard watched her with a hawkeye. The Asian clerk (could he be Mike?) was protected by a wall of thick woven wire and sheets of bulletproof glass at the counter, where the access porthole was surrounded by racks of tiny bottles of Thunderbird, Night Train, Big Dog, Fairbanks Cream Sherry and several other wino wines she'd never heard of. She saw the free-standing ATM that Conor had probably used, looking like a solid steel pillar anchored to the floor by bolts that would have stopped a bus dead in its tracks.

In order to buy herself a right to be there, she looked around and found a rack of small potato chip bags. It wasn't her particular weakness, but she knew her dad loved them so in his honor she picked up a bag of plain chips and took them to the small orifice. At least they had no animal content, she thought.

'Hello, sir. Could I ask you a question?'

'Missy?'

She slipped him the photo of Conor. 'This boy used your ATM. Have you seen him?'

'No know, sorry.' The reply was almost automatic.

'*Please*, sir. Look at the picture. He's a good friend.' She wondered if her lie sounded as obvious to others as it did to her.

Reluctantly the clerk actually took a look and grumbled something indistinguishable.

'Is there a problem here, Tan?' The African-American security guard had come up behind Maeve, and his intimidating presence was sucking up all the air within several feet.

'Come on, man,' Maeve said to the guard. 'I'm just looking for my friend. You know what this city can be like for a lost kid.'

'We're just a mini-mart, ma'am. We ain't a lost-and-found for bad boys.'

'Please – just be human for a minute, sirs.'

The black man studied her peculiarly, wrinkling up his eyes, and then turned to the clerk. 'You seen this kid, Tan?'

'I seen. He come that way one time. Buy 409. No more.'

The clerk had pointed to the door and then to the left, and she passed him a dollar for the potato chip bag.

'One-sixty-nine,' he said.

It was an outrageous overcharge, but she dropped three quarters into his pass-under tray and then started away. 'Thank you, sir,' she said as she passed the guard.

He chuckled in a conspiratorial way. 'I think I'd rather go back to re-poing Cadillacs. But in this job I get to get shot closer to home.'

Young men were playing a quick and aggressive three-on-three basketball game at several courts, with a lot of arm-hacking and trashtalk. None of the hoops had nets, but the balls looked firm if thoroughly scuffed raw.

The whole park was only about a tenth of a city block, but it had some grass and benches and was surrounded by a forbidding spiky ten-foot fence. Not many of the parks he knew in northern San Diego County looked like this, but not many of those parks were dense with homeless black men either. Eddie might be here somewhere, or at a similar one called Gladys six blocks away – or even at Pershing Square near the Biltmore a half mile west, where Conor had seen him the day before playing Liszt for tourists under Beethoven's statue.

'Why not Beethoven?' he'd asked the man.

'Hell, kid, he's damn hard.'

Conor wondered why any city agency had bothered to build a park at all for people who didn't pay taxes and didn't vote. Some weird kind of civic guilt about poverty, maybe – like building them a miniature carwash that they could push their shopping carts through. A big passenger jet rumbled overhead, surprisingly low as it came in to LAX ten miles west, and something about the contrast of worlds struck him. How many tens of thousands of tourists and business people passed directly over Skid Row every day without even knowing it was there? While the poor down here knew perfectly well that the rich were up there, sitting in rank after rank in the silver birds.

Near the entrance to San Julian Park there was a small group of men with long straight black hair who appeared to be American

Indians, but they were all asleep or passed out beside small bottles in brown bags. This group was patrolled by bobbing pigeons, hunting for something edible. Beyond, he could see card games at fixed cement tables, some chess matches, and even an obvious drug deal, men passing a little baggy, but no one anywhere playing violin.

There were lines at each of the port-a-potties along the fence, and he wondered if Eddie had just taken a pee break, but a five-minute wait outside the one marked for wheelchairs produced a forbidding-looking woman on a walker, definitely not Eddie. These were ordinary port-a-potties, like the ones at construction sites, not the strange new ones that some civic power had scattered here and there around Skid Row. The new ones were just too weird to try. They looked like art deco escape pods from some old science fiction movie. In between each user they seemed to lock themselves up and roar and groan, almost rocking with the effort, spraying themselves clean according to one old man who sat watching.

A very light-skinned black man on wooden crutches waited alone just outside the park, staring into space, and Conor approached him on the dubious theory that the handicapped might know one another.

'Sir, do you know Eddie Monk?'

The man's eyes focused gradually on Conor without seeming to see anything that interested him. 'Jus' saw da man hisownself. Stan' up in a dumpster over on Seventh.' He gave a shudder of horror. 'Same ol' same ol'. Dis hoojy man had him a big coat, jus' be stan' dere in da greenie. Stare at me, you know? King Jesus. He don' move no muscle atall. You friend of dis guy?'

'Don't know him, sir. I haven't been over on Seventh.'

The man shook his head, as if sorry for Conor's deficiency. 'Learn the greenies, boy. You think about it. Metal proteck you from alla rays.'

'Thanks for the advice.'

'You don't believe me, do you?'

But Conor was already walking away, as politely as he could, with a nod and a smile back to the man. He had no real reason to fear the man, but something told him that somebody that far gone could suddenly stick a knife in you, for no reason. Watching his back, he was startled by a voice ahead.

'Game, kid?' A tall man in sweats with a basketball resting on his hip.

'You'd skin me alive, sir.'

'Two on three. You with the three. We make it fun.'

Conor raised his leg. 'Bad ankle, sorry.' He'd expected a blast of scorn but got only commiseration in return.

'You take care of that ankle. You don't get none but two of them in this life. Though one day you got to give them both up.'

'I guess.'

'Dudley – it the absolute truth.'

Conor backtracked along Sixth to Gladys, a smaller version of San Julian Park, but Eddie wasn't there either, and then he headed for Pershing Square, an altogether different version of parkland surrounded by ritzy hotels and office buildings. You could see it coming for a long way by a twenty-story tower of purple cement with a huge red ball stuck into a window cut out of it at the top. This park was a full city block but most of it was cemented up and very strange. He headed for the side where he'd met Monk before, where he found the statues of a striding Beethoven, plus a general on a horse and some other soldier from one of the black-and-white wars. He wondered what these three figures had in common, but they were meeting now with a ten-foot orange concrete pingpong ball, a canon, a dozen vertical pink cylinders and several palm trees in a cat's litterbox. It was the kind of sight his mom and dad used to say you needed to take dope to appreciate. He had a feeling all this stuff was just left over from other parks that had been closed. The area around this strange assembly was paved to a hot griddle, and there was a distinct smell of human shit on the air.

Sure enough, just past Beethoven like the day before, Eddie Coltrane Monk was bowing away at his violin, and mostly being ignored by the handful of people who had drifted into the park, a few obviously well-heeled Asian tourists and some people who probably worked nearby. *Eddie, Eddie!* he wanted to say, *they aren't worth it. I bet they don't even know you're working so hard at the Violin Concerto in D, Opus 61. You're no Perlman, but you* are *better than I remember. Maybe you really worked at this piece once. You did say that Beethoven was hard.*

He watched as Monk seemed to give up in mid-bar, let his violin slump and cranked his neck up at the powder-blue sky. The man looked like he was going to howl like a coyote, but he didn't. He merely sighed and leaned forward to pick up the violin case that had been at his feet. He studied it to see what it contained in change, and then rolled his wheelchair a few feet toward the cannon. The

only place to sit was a wall with a rounded top that was clearly
built to discourage sitting.

'Mr Monk, sir, your Concerto in D was very nice.'

'You know it, huh?' As if nothing could surprise him. When he
looked over, he seemed to recognize Conor vaguely.

Conor boosted himself onto the barrel of the cannon. 'Of course
I know it. Doesn't it hurt you having all those people walk past
when you're giving it your whole soul? You really were going at
it.'

The man raised his graying eyebrows. 'Son, you gotta just let
that stuff sink into the general burden. You can't use no kind of
feeling of resentment for nothing.'

'You're a wise man.'

'Well. Didn't nobody tell you that sometime the wise men end
up playing for dimes in the park. Cormer?'

'Conor. Do you ever do popular music?'

'Not so much. To my ear, the violin don't sound right squalling
at "Barndance Polka." You want to play with me some time? Guitar
and violin go together like harp and kazoo.'

He *did* remember. Conor laughed. 'I'm trying to write some
songs, and I could use your help with the music.'

'Can you buy me dinner?'

His father would have said, *does a goose go barefoot?* or something like that, but he just said, 'I'd be honored, sir. At the finest
restaurant on this square.'

They both studied the upscale eateries across at the Biltmore,
the forbidding look of them, the valets in uniform out front.

'Well . . . you and me,' Eddie Monk said, 'we can play bold
when my tuxedo comes back from the cleaners. But there's a taco
wagon very soon gonna park itself over that way that wouldn't do
me no druthers.'

'You got their best filet mignon sandwich.' He hopped down
from the cannon. 'What went wrong with your career, Mr Monk?
I can tell you've got fine hands.'

'Oooh, where *did* that pot of gold at the end of the rainbow get
off to?'

'Sirs! Hello.'

Maeve had seen the two white men emerge from the Fortnum
Hotel and they obviously weren't the kind of men who lived there.

They looked more like desk men or security guards who might be able to give her a coherent answer about Conor.

'What you doing down here in the deep shit, kid?'

The one in front was really big-shouldered, like a TV wrestler, and had ringlets of golden curls cascading from under a baseball cap that said *Ignore Previous Hat*. The other was shorter even than she was, and his eyes were all over the place. She began to doubt her judgment about approaching them at all. There was something distinctly hostile and dangerous about them.

'I'm looking for an old friend,' she said. 'Have you seen this boy?' She held out the photo of Conor at arm's length. But they barely looked at it.

'Get a new boyfriend, Sugar,' the little one said. 'If he's living down here, he won't never do you right.'

'He's a nice young man, a musician.'

'Poverty and death are all you'll find here,' the big man said, and she backed a step involuntarily at the harshness of his voice. He shooed her away with a backhand gesture just as three very old men emerged from the hotel door carrying aluminum baseball bats. One of them wore a *yarmulke*, and it was one of the oddest confrontations she'd ever witnessed. Maeve ducked down behind a trash dumpster near the curb.

The little man with the wild eyes turned to his pal. 'Can I take them down?'

'Not now, Rice.'

'Did you just cut the steam pipe for our heat?' one of the old men demanded.

'Don't know what you're talking about, Fructose.'

'We're calling the cops and the city inspector immediately. You're not welcome in this building any more. Tell Vartabedian that we'll move out of here when he gargles in the toilet.'

'Tell who?' the big guy said.

'Just tell the prick you work for he's *farcockt*,' another of the old men said.

The little man with the strange eyes was trembling, his right hand digging around in his pocket, and the big man encircled Rice's shoulder gently but forcefully and walked him away hard.

'It ain't but one thing to know,' the big man called back at them. 'One thing. Clear out real soon, darlin's.'

The two men climbed into their high SUV and drove off, and

Maeve cautiously came out from behind the dumpster where she'd been hunkered down.

'Sirs!' she called as the three old man headed back toward the hotel.

'Young lady. What are you doing in this den of iniquity?' The man who seemed like their leader lingered while the others waited for him by the doorway.

'I'm looking for a friend who might be here,' Maeve said. 'Is this place so terrible?'

'I'm afraid it's a war zone, daughter, and we're a bunch of dainty cowards,' the old man said. 'Thank you, Musketeers,' he said to the two other old men as they chose to ignore Maeve, shoulder their baseball bats and slip inside.

She wanted to ask immediately about Conor, but she was too intrigued by the confrontation she'd just witnessed. When she kept talking, the man waited outside with her and told her his name was Samuel Greengelb, and then he insisted they go into the lobby. 'Please, child. It's safer for all in here. Have I met you?'

'No, sir. I don't think so.'

All but two of the overstuffed chairs had been slashed to shreds, and she settled primly near a dead TV. He told her about their fight with the landlord over expelling them in order to expedite the conversion of the Fortnum into high-priced lofts.

'But we have long-term leases from an old owner. We're the three Musketeers – pardon me – the Resistance. We got nowhere to go but some public-assistance *dreck*. Those thugs of Mr Vartabedian are playing every dirty trick in the book to get us to leave. They kill the elevator so Joel in his rheumatism can't hardly get down to the store. They paint the halls with curses and they even deposit human excrement on the floors. They bang on our doors at three a.m., yelling anti-Semitism. They break our door locks when we go out, so we got to use wood bars and chairs to be safe. Tonight they cut the steam pipe. It's the only heat we got in winter. We talked to a lawyer, *pro bono* like, but he says it's very hard to beat guys with the big money.' Greengelb was so obsessed by his story that he hadn't even asked her name or why she was there.

'My name is Maeve Liffey, sir,' she said, when he finally ran himself down. 'My father is a detective, and I'm helping him look for this boy.'

She didn't expect much from showing Conor's photo. The old man studied it for some time. 'Yes, I think this little *pisher* is staying here. He's on floor three near me, but he's usually out all day. He really should be home with his *mamele* and *tate*, if you ask me – he's a very nice boy. If he's the same one.'

'I'm glad to hear it.'

'Maybe this boy is too nice. This is a rough place here – it's so much worse now trying to live on The Nickel, and I don't think this boy really knows about the bite of the snakes out there.'

'Thank you for the information, sir. Please tell Conor I'll come back to see him tonight. I'm Jack Liffey's daughter, a friend of his father. Remember Jack Liffey.'

He nodded gravely. 'Better you write a note. I forget names. And if your father has any power in this city, don't forget us, the Fighting Musketeers.'

'One for all, all for one!' Maeve said.

'That's it!' He almost shouted. 'Kibosh the mothers, in the idiom,' he responded with an arm pump, like a tennis player taking down his opponent.

NOTES FOR A NEW MUSIC

Day 4

What a wonderful day! Eddie Monk introduced me to musicians all over The Nickel, and we spent so much of the day talking eagerly! These people are every bit as interesting as any people at home – much more really – and I'm a little hoarse from talking so much through all the excitement. But not too hoarse to try hard to work out a song.

After a while, he glared at the notebook that was mostly chicken-scratches and inserts, but he finally crossed out all his mistaken attempts and copied over his semi-final version, with only a few more amendments.

The Knowers

He lies on his face to drink from the Concrete River
Brushing away the rainbow slick of oil

That has leaked from the factories and the gutters
Of a city that once knew his name
But what does he know now?
He lives in a box that contained a stove.

It made Maeve edgy to return to the Catholic Liberation shelter, but she'd finally convinced herself that she'd really only imagined that Eleanor Ong had recognized her. There was no way, not after so long – nobody had that kind of memory. So she'd come back to mollify her sense of duty and see how Felice and Millie were doing. She was a bit chagrined that she hadn't thought of buying any dollie clothes yet. Finding Conor was still at the top of her agenda, but she'd checked the Fortnum again, and he wasn't back, even though evening was gathering.

A skinny woman with a strawberry mark on her cheek, who was either taking the last of the sun or discreetly on guard, sat on a folding chair in the unlocked yard. The strawberry woman told her Felice and Millie had gone out looking for the missing husband. They'd had a second-hand report of a man much like him staying at a nearby flop a few days earlier. It seemed so sad to Maeve, all of it – suggesting a whole post-apocalyptic world of people who were out on their own in the hard rain, hunting for someone they had lost or a job they desperately needed or just the big lottery ticket. Felice looking for her husband, Maeve herself looking for Conor Lewis, her mother looking for a new boyfriend, her father looking for the secret to his legs and voice – everybody else in The Nickel probably looking for a smoke or a drink or just a generous soul to pass a few hours with.

'Is your husband lost, too?' Maeve asked.

The woman on the chair roared with laughter. 'Girl, I be runnin' *from*. If that cheatin' motherfucker ever find me, we both dead and buried. D'Sean – the dog, the whoremonger, man of a hunnert per cent lie . . .' She seemed to run down. 'He say he gonna hit me with his big whoopin' karate swing when I lef', but I know he just gonna die stupid. This nun's got a place of peace here, what I call my temp'ry high tower of retreat. That what Reverend Lonald C. King back in Michigan say we all need, ever' one of us. Thereafter shall ye live in stillness, delivered from the hand of the wicked.'

Maeve wondered if she might need a high tower of retreat herself.

She could see how it would be nice to think something like that was out there for her, waiting for the day when her father was truly gone and buried and there was nobody else she could lean on in that particular way. The way that had probably spawned the idea of god for millions in the first place. Thinking of her dad made her choke up a little.

'What's the name of that nun who runs your high tower of retreat?' Maeve managed to ask.

'Sister Mary Rose. I tell you – that woman got one great big soul on her.'

It was strange that nuns changed their names so radically, but Maeve decided not to say anything more about her for fear of arousing suspicion – plus the fear that her voice might break.

'Please tell Felice that I'll come back later. My name is Maeve.'

'I mos' surely will, Miss Maeve.'

Maeve slipped outside the gate into the abrupt piss-smells of the ruined street. What an unpleasant place, she thought. Then, standing not twenty feet away like an evil crow watching her, she noticed the short white man with the funny eyes that she'd met coming out of the Fortnum. He was watching her like a predator. She remembered the way he and his pal had challenged the old men at the hotel, and a chill clutched her spine as she walked deliberately toward her car, which meant diagonally past him, trying to ignore him.

'Don't be no Runaway Sue,' the man said gently.

She wondered why something inside her required her to face up to moments like this rather than just sprinting away as fast as she could. She stopped on the crumbling street and turned back to meet the little man's crazed powder-blue eyes.

'You rich kids hang down here, get you a big kick out of it. Mostly at Thanksgiving. You serve turkey dinner an' shit to the winos. Ever'body tell you how terrific and sanctified you are. That right, waspie?'

'I'm not rich.' She saw his hands moving restlessly in odd patterns. She had a feeling that this man had risen from a trap door from somewhere deep down below, and his simple presence could taint any place on earth that he happened to stand, even a great cathedral.

'Mebbe, girl. But you ain' no poorhead. I *know* you. I saw your picture of your boyfriend. What you think is worse? The things you do in this here life or the things you go and neglect to do?'

His whole body moved fretfully now, foot to foot. All she could think was that this was some poor puppy who'd been kicked badly when he was little. And for some reason she still had an urge to try to save even the worst of the lost ones. 'I don't know what you want me to say, sir. Your manner is scaring me.'

'I want you to say the truth. Your very own dumb ideas of the truth.' He brought a switchblade knife out of his pants pocket and her neck prickled as he held it up between them and snicked it open. 'This is my truth.'

It made her too terrified to move, and then angry that he'd do this to her. 'Why is a weapon the truth to you? If I had a gun, I could hurt you even more, and it wouldn't change anything about me or you.' For the first time in her life, she actually considered the idea of getting a little gun. Just for men like this.

He grinned and let the knife sag. 'Oh, it wouldn't change anything, you say?' he said. 'How you forget about Indiana Jones pulling out his big pistol against all them waving swords on the bridge. Life is all about relations of power, sugar. Having the most pow'ful weapon is what wins ever' time.'

'No!' she said with determination. She grasped for an idea that had come to her but was so easily dispelled she almost couldn't hold onto it. 'Life is about holding out a hand of help. Good people do it for anyone who needs it. You need it, too.' She didn't actually hold out a hand – wouldn't that be insane? – but it made her wonder how sincere she was. The idea made him cock his head in a strange way.

'They tell me I'm a sociopath, missy,' he said. 'Psychopath, they used to call it. My juvie counselor said so over and overtimes. That means they should have strangled me at birth.'

'No,' Maeve insisted. 'No one on earth is hopeless.'

'Get away from that girl, you Satan!' The strawberry woman at the shelter had come out the gate, and she began yelling back toward the shelter for help.

The man's eyes went to the woman for just a moment, as if to fix her in memory for the future, and then back to Maeve. Something strange happened within his eyes, and then he laughed and drove the knife hard an inch or two into his upper thigh.

Maeve gasped.

'We decide what hurts us,' he said. 'And what doesn't.' He yanked the knife out and walked away without delay, not even limping.

African-Americans make up 9 per cent of Los Angeles County's population, but constitute a full 41 per cent of the homeless, and seemingly 90 per cent if one takes even a cursory drive through The Nickel. Latinos and Anglos make up 77 per cent of the county's population, but represent only about 50 per cent of the homeless, spread through many other impoverished pockets in the city.

At least 20 per cent of the homeless are war veterans, largely from the Viet Nam War, men and a few women who've been forgotten by the government that sent them as cannon fodder into that misbegotten war.

SIX

A Slow-Down Theory

It's lucky you're not a horse, Jack Liffey thought, looking down at Loco basking in a trapezoid of winter sun in the back yard. They shoot horses, so they say. The dog had worn one of those plastic lampshades for a while to keep him from gnawing at his leg stitches, but that was before the chemo had killed his appetite, even for chomping on himself. Now the ordeal was over, and he was getting his relish for some foods back, even sampling dry food, which he would never touch before.

Staring at the dog lying there lazily, experiencing a pang of affection, Jack Liffey had what he knew was a meaningless premonition that Loco would die in the near future, despite all of the – what did they call it? – heroic measures. Cancer. It seemed like half the women he'd ever met had either died of it or were fighting it. Gloria had had her own bout with breast cancer just before they'd met. Breast cancer was the plague of our time, he thought. Aside from AIDS, of course. He was a gimp now himself. When you got stuck in disability thinking, everything in the world seemed to suggest disease.

The phone rang in the house and brought him alert as he heard Gloria answer it. Your other senses were supposed to sharpen to make up for the missing ones, and he was doing his best to listen for nuance these days. But the voice was coming through too many walls where his chair sat above the top step of the porch. Before long she brought the cordless out with her, pressing the speaking end to her thigh to suggest confidentiality.

'I think it's time you know about this, Jack.'

No worry about nuance here, he thought, as he nodded pensively. Maeve was eloping? The police were sending Gloria to New York? His health insurance had been canceled?

'It's your old friend Mike Lewis. Get out your pad and I'll translate.' She brought the phone up to her ear. 'Mike, I'll let you talk directly to Jack, then he'll give me a signal, and I'll read you what he writes back. It'll take some patience. Does that dog hunt for you?'

Jack Liffey could just hear the reply, the voice of a tiny man in a bottle. 'Of course. I love Jack. Don't tell me this has all been Maeve's doing?'

'Jack hasn't been in the picture, I'm afraid. You get to start from Go.'

She handed him the phone, and he listened, as Mike Lewis told him that his sixteen-year-old son Conor had been missing for about five days now, presumed headed for Hollywood, a bit peeved and rebellious, to try his chances at the music business. A few days ago, Mike said, he'd thought he was relaying this message to Jack through Maeve, but apparently that wasn't quite the case. He should have suspected.

'Ack-ack!'

Gloria grabbed the phone away. 'Write, *pendejo*. Stop that *acking*. Mike, I'll tell you in a minute what he's scribbling furiously right now, but you can probably guess some of it. She's a headstrong girl and I'm sure she meant well, trying to spur Jack into action.'

'There really shouldn't be any danger,' Mike said. 'It's not like Conor stole the family Porsche, or joined some death cult out in the desert. He's a pretty sensible guy, but he does have an empathy overload that tends to draw him to three-legged cats.'

'Then he'll get along fine with Maeve.'

GLOR – YOU DIDN'T TELL ME THIS!
MIKE – PLEASE TELL ME <u>EVERYTHING</u> YOU TOLD MAEVE.
ALL OF IT. AND WHAT SHE SAID TO YOU.

'Incoming,' Gloria announced on the phone. She pursed her lips as she read over the reproach in the first sentence, directed at herself, then read out the rest, word-for-word. 'Over,' she said evenly.

'Jack, I'm really sorry,' Mike said. Jack had the receiver, but she could hear the tiny voice clearly. 'She said she was going to tell you about it and you couldn't really talk right then, but she said you were getting better and you'd love an easy job to get you going again.' Mike Lewis told him as much as he could remember, including the fact that he'd faxed Maeve the photo and other information about Conor.

Jack Liffey rapped the phone on his forehead in frustration, then handed it back to Gloria and went off into scribbling at a white heat again.

'Me again, Mike. How's your wife taking it?'

'Pretty hard. She's his stepmom and that's more hurtful, somehow, but I cooked up my own wild oats when I was his age, and I think he's going to be fine. His aren't really that wild at all, if I'm right.'

'It's a rougher world than ours was,' Gloria said. 'The city parks where I ran barefoot long into the dark, you'll stab yourself to death on used syringes now.'

'Yeah, somewhere deep in the funhouse they're making the children give up their innocence. I think we had a window of about fifteen years after World War Two that were different from everything that came before or after. That whole cohort of dads came home hating what they'd seen in the Depression and the war and wanting to make a protected world for their kids. And they damn well did their best – as long as you weren't black, of course, or some other kind of outsider. It was a model railroad and Erector Set kind of world for a long time, the Fifties and most of the early Sixties.'

She couldn't help thinking of her first lover, the cop Ken Steelyard, and the huge model train layout he'd worked on for thirty years in his basement in San Pedro. He never acknowledged it, but part of his pleasure had obviously been playing God over that tiny little world that he could still control, the Twin Peaks and Western Railroad in imaginary Colorado.

She felt a tug at her skirt.

BOTH OF YOU, I NEED TO KNOW ANY TIME M CONTACTS YOU AND <u>EXACTLY</u> WHAT SHE SAYS AND <u>DONT</u> LET ON THAT I KNOW ANYTHING. OBVIOUSLY I CANT TRUST HER ANY MORE. FIND OUT ALL YOU CAN ABOUT WHERE SHES BEEN AND WHATS HAPPENED. SHED JUST CLAM UP OR GET CLEVER IF I GOT MAD AT HER. PLEASE – BOTH OF YOU!

Gloria read it off, and Mike talked to him once more, mainly apologizing for not guessing what was going on. Jack Liffey just handed her the phone and nodded, and she talked to Mike a little – she'd never met him in person but what she'd heard she liked – and she said goodbye for Jack and then endured his angry glare for a while.

'I was about to check up on her, Jack. I think Mike is right. There's no real danger, and she's got to try this business on her own for a while. She idolizes you so much that if she doesn't find out how boring and shitty your job is, she'll never even go away to college.'

He wrote three words: CHECK UP NOW!

She thought for a moment about how exhausted she was but then nodded. For the first time, she felt a bit of remorse. 'OK, I should have rode her harder. Let's make a trade. Can I get a psych therapist in to start working on you?'

He shook his head angrily. They both knew that getting him to accept mental help was like pulling teeth without anesthetic.

WATCH OVER MAEVE. LET IT BE THE XMAS GIFT YOU GIVE ME.

Jack Liffey thought he detected a hint of amusement on Gloria's face, and he felt overwhelmed by things, unable to check up on them, exiled to his customary inner prison, paralyzed and mute. He was deprived of so many simple faculties, basically reduced to a jellyfish in a chair. Maybe it was time to treat it all as a joke, he thought. Nothing more tragic and existential than that.

'Ak-ak.'

'Oh, Jackie. I do love you.' Gloria ruffled his hair.

I'm not a cat, he thought. *Though I shouldn't mind, I guess.* A cat was a remarkable being, a castaway from some other world – bred down over millennia to be something quite unlike its hunter-killer species-being, yet still disdainful, still authentic in some way. Proud and fierce – despite being relegated to a fondle-object and stuck with some ludicrous name. Mieumieu, Booties, Annie Oakley, Griddlebone, and so much worse.

Art Castro was the only person he'd ever let use the revolting nickname Jackie (except Gloria, now), and he'd had to grit his teeth at it sometimes. Something about them both demanded indulgence to their foibles. Perhaps a general sense of desolation about them – a life interrupted by something and never properly restarted.

Which led him to tell himself to stop whining. He still had his sight, his hearing, his touch, some of the function of his dick, and all his taste buds. To assuage the other losses he began to hanker after spicy sausage, an old indulgence. A gift to his body. He'd

have to get Gloria to buy some dry Genoa salami, some German
liverwurst, Argentine Chorizo, Chinese *lap cheong*, even that South
African stuff, *boerewors*. His mouth was watering already. Was this
the way the devil worked to distract you?

It was only a few blocks to the big downtown library with its pointy
tile tower where scores of the homeless – fairly smelly, having
splash-washed in the public bathrooms – snoozed over the comfy
chairs. Maeve spent several hours there, killing time by looking at
a huge photo exhibit of street pictures of Broadway, which was
now a part of Latin America, with all its old-time department stores
and movie palaces turned into Swap Meets, a term that had just
come to mean a collection of small shops. Then she did some
research on G-8 summits for her International Relations class so
she didn't feel like a total truant, and she helped an incredibly timid
Japanese tourist find the section of Japanese books. He bowed and
thanked her profusely in words she couldn't understand.

In late afternoon she emerged to find two helicopters circling
low overhead with their blinding searchlights illuminating the block
where she'd parked. She waited back in the shadows as sirens wailed
and police cars came on so fast from so many directions that they
almost collided. At the far end of the block a dark-skinned man
wearing the top of a pink bunny suit was waving a shotgun in the
air and shouting.

A cop came up from behind Maeve, unnoticed, and shoved her
face hard against a building, then pushed her into an alcove.

'That wasn't necessary,' she complained. Why did they always
need to hurt?

'Shut up. Stay there.'

She clearly heard her dad's voice in her head, insisting that there
was almost never a point to antagonizing a policeman. She decided,
for once, to follow the advice she seemed to carry around now that
she didn't have his real voice in her life any more. The cop had
his pistol out, but there were plenty of officers down near the pink
bunny so this one seemed to take it as his primary responsibility
to bully Maeve.

'Don't move!'

She had yanked her head around to see.

'The children! The children!' the bunny man seemed to be
howling.

She could see one officer near the bunny man go down on a
knee with a strange gadget like a salad shooter in his hand. The
device jerked upward a little, and the pink bunny screamed and
fired his shotgun high into the air. Maeve winced, expecting return
fire, but miraculously they all held off as the shotgun fell to the
ground, and the man in the bunny suit collapsed like a sack of old
bricks.

'Moke is down and clear,' her cop said, touching a microphone
pinned to his chest.

Squawk.

Maeve sat down in the alcove and encircled her knees to suggest
she was no danger to anybody, and he finally wagged a finger once
at her and moved off toward the ruckus to get his share of whatever glory was going. Luckily her car was parked nearby. She waited
a minute or two, then walked very slowly toward it and then very
slowly drove away in the opposite direction. She wondered if she'd
just seen a Taser in action. They said it was better than getting shot,
but they also said it had killed more than 150 people. It disturbed
her personally ever since she'd found out her dad had been water-
boarded six months back, another sort of high-concept demonstra-
tion of official bullying. All legal, apparently, under the Patriot Act.

She felt a little trembly – that kind of treatment disturbed her
deep down – but drove back to the Catholic Liberation shelter in
the waning light, past scores of men drifting along the roadway or
sitting on the curbs. A different black woman let her in the gate,
the heavyset woman she'd seen at night when she'd dropped off
Felice and Milie. She settled back down on to her folding chair,
breathing a little hard, as if just getting up had been a chore.

'Your friends done came back.'

'Felice and Millie?'

'Yeah. They be pretty upset. The little squirrelly cat with the
N'awlins voice, he be hittin' on Felice most all they whole walk
home.'

'You know him?'

'I seen him some. He seem to think the shelter his personal ho'
junction.'

'Can't you do anything?'

'Sister dimed him once, but you know the cops, they make a
face and take down your words – maybe – but they don't stay round.
We need a really tough armed guard.'

'You look pretty tough. I'm sorry, I don't know your name.'

'Kenisha Duncan.'

'Mrs. Duncan, I'll bet you scare that little funny-eyed man more than you think.'

She smiled. 'He scare *me*, girl. He best scare you. They's long ho' trains in this world dead and gone to hell 'cause of men like that. He got the awful power of violence. You know that, don't you?'

'I don't believe in hell but I believe in sociopaths. I guess that man likes to hurt women. And he probably only fears somebody who can hurt him.'

'Say amen. Girl, do me a favor real quick.' Kenisha Duncan looked around furtively and saw no one at the wired windows of the shelter.

'Course.'

'Slip yo'self out the gate. They's a small sack on the ground just by the twisty wheel of that honey-bin.'

It couldn't be anything positive, but Maeve undertook to do it anyway. Everybody had needs that should be honored. The sun was low in the west, blocked by the wall of downtown's high-rises, but the sky was still light enough out not to be too frightening. She found the paper sack right away behind the overstuffed dumpster and could tell by feel that it contained one of those flat bottles of booze. She didn't look, feeling it would violate the woman's trust. Kenisha had two long slugs of whatever it was, and then she had Maeve put the bag back at the front caster of the dumpster.

'That medicine not 'lowed in here, but a body's got to have a taste now and then to stay well.'

'I understand, I do. Can I go in and see Felice?'

'Why sure, chile. They either in the TV room or up in 202.'

'Thanks, Mrs. Duncan. Next time I'll have a sip with you.'

The woman chuckled. 'You most welcome. You the onliest person here to understand what a body got to do to keep her ol' carcass goin'.'

Maeve wanted to tell her she understood hardship and compromise and weakness, maybe better than the woman thought, but there was no need.

'Bless you,' Maeve said.

'Keep it real, baby girl,' the woman said. And Maeve felt an electric jolt as she walked away. That was what Beto and his bangers had called her.

'You can do this to any building down here,' Vartabedian said.

'Well, not *any* building. It would be tough to build lofts in the Disney Music Center.' Eddie Wolverton had his forehead to the tall glass windows that he'd had his guys put into the two luxury penthouses of the Driscoll Building. The view west was worth it all. He wouldn't mind one of them himself, but living up Corrigan Canyon ovelooking Hollywood in a famous Lautner house was hard to beat. He hadn't even thrown his housewarming party yet.

'You know what I mean. What you've done here is just gorgeous, Eddie. This was a shithole. I saw it. A brick rectangle full of sweatshops. Though one was a pretty good cigar-rolling sweatshop, somebody who'd got himself run out of Havana.'

'Yeah, I had one of his *Yamilet Robustos* myself.'

'Where did the shop go?'

Eddie just shook his head. 'Who knows? It was Puerto Rican leaf. You can't shine shit, V. Fuck it. They're gone now.'

'That's a bit harsh.'

'There isn't room in life for second rate. Look at me; I stood beside Bobby Kennedy up in Delano in 'Sixty-Six. Me. If Bobby hadn't been shot, you know, I'd probably be designing big monuments to César Chávez on the Mall in D.C., and you'd still be selling used cars out in Glendale. We all move on, and life gets funny when you watch the Current disappear from Events. OK, the Driscoll's over now. What's next?'

'The Fortnum Hotel,' Vartabedian said. 'I almost got it cleared.'

Wolverton turned and his forehead wrinkled up. 'That's right on the edge of The Nickel, uh-huh?'

'Sure. Skid Row is doomed, Eddie. We're gonna see it put to rest in a few more years.'

'I hear there's some guys in the Fortnum who want to stay. Jewish gentlemen with gentlemen's agreements – or maybe even real leases from the old owner. Am I right? The press is going to love this, kicking out a bunch of old Jews. You better hope none of 'em are Holocaust survivors.'

'I'm going to pay enough so they want to clear out.'

'A horse head in the bed?' Wolverton said with a grin.

'Real money,' Vartabedian countered. 'To them anyway. It's worth a little premium to keep the process moving.'

'Ah, the code of gentrification,' Wolverton said with a big grin. 'I guess it's our very own kind of global warming, isn't it?'

Conor came back to the Fortnum a bit jittery, anxious to write down the tales he'd been told by the homeless men he'd met around Eddie Monk. These men were more fascinating than anyone he'd have met in a thousand years around Fallbrook. He was writing furiously in his diary when a knock interrupted him.

'Hi there, Mr Greengelb.' Conor was on the very cusp of saying he was busy just then. In comparison to his diary, he couldn't help thinking of Greengelb as interesting but not quite as memorable. Nothing to do with music. But some quirk of ingrained courtesy held his reply. 'What's happening, sir?'

'The Musketeers are meeting. Vartabedian's hooligans sabotaged our heat today. I thought you might like to be with us. You get just as cold as we do.' There was something else Greengelb was supposed to tell the boy, but he couldn't remember. His anger made it all worse, more confused.

'I tremble like a leaf.'

'Come to my room in ten minutes. We can't let this go unanswered.'

'Count on me, sir. I'll just be a minute or two.'

Felice and Millie weren't in the TV room, which was full of women sprawling with their children on threadbare sofas and old bean bag chairs watching something — a TV surely — around a corner that flashed light over their faces and emitted unnatural laughter too often to be anything but a sitcom. She went on up the stairs, past posters for The Year of the Woman from Mozambique, and some bearded man named Paolo Friere under a big quote: 'Washing one's hands of the conflict between the powerful and the powerless means to side with the powerful.'

As she already knew, Eleanor was not part of an organization that worried too much about what the Pope thought. And this was not a place that would have a lot of use for wry humor either, she thought. Though the women here, like Kenisha Duncan with her hidden booze, might have appreciated a little mischief now and again.

She found the room number and knocked softly.

'Felice! Millie! It's Maeve.'

Felice opened the door and smiled a strangely cool recognition as she beckoned her inside. Maeve almost froze in her tracks when she saw the slim form of Sister Mary Rose/Ms Eleanor Ong propped placidly on the windowsill watching her neutrally.

'I just wanted to know if you were OK,' Maeve said to Felice. She noticed the little girl moving slowly toward her.

'We had a bad scare jus' half a thumb-twiddle ago,' Felice said. 'That little shitass! Oop, I think I'm losing my religion. He snatched hard at my nipples when I told him to go away.'

'I bet I know who you mean,' Maeve said. 'He tried to shake me up by stabbing his own leg. What a creepy guy.'

At that moment Millie took Maeve's hand hard. 'Hi, Millie,' Maeve said. 'I'm sure you'll be OK here.'

'I got to go out sometimes, look for Clarence,' Felice said. 'I know he's here somewhere, I feel it in my heart. That drip-nose with his knife seem to be ever'place, like a used Kleenex. He said I remind him of Marilyn Monroe.' She made a contemptuous noise.

Maeve looked up at Eleanor, who hadn't said a word. Her eyes were watching her thoughtfully, almost disinterestedly. 'He's what's called a sociopath,' Maeve said to Felice. Eleanor didn't move a muscle. 'He even said it himself. That means he's got no conscience.' She studied Felice, dowdy and drawn and plain, but she decided a lot of that was worry and lack of taking care of herself. 'You know, you could be really pretty with a little fixing up,' Maeve told her. 'I'll bet some of the women here would help.'

'I don't care about that. I just want to find Clarence and go home where things is normal.'

'I'm looking for somebody, too, a missing boy. I showed you his picture. But when I get through finding him I can help you.' She wondered if tasks and missions had multiplied unpredictably like this for her dad.

'Could I talk to you outside, Maeve?' That was Eleanor, speaking at last and smiling now, though barely, like the Mona Lisa.

It turned out to be impossible to separate her hand from Millie's, who had fastened on like a sucker fish, so the three of them stepped into the hallway. 'We'll just be a second, Felice,' Eleanor said. 'We'll do something about that rotten man. I promise.'

All of a sudden, Maeve was tense as a small wild animal caught out in the open. Eleanor shut the door behind her.

'You know who I am, so please let's not belabor it,' she said pleasantly. 'How's Jack these days?'

Maeve wouldn't give the woman an inch. Whatever she did, she had to keep this woman away from her father. She knew he'd had such an overwhelming infatuation with her that he could never again be trusted to keep his pants zipped around her. After her own bout of love madness, she would never underestimate the tug of infatuation. 'Should I call you Sister Whatever, or Eleanor?'

'Whichever name makes you comfortable, Maeve. I don't mind.'

'I thought you'd gone back into one of those silent convents. That's the family legend – after Dad's life turned out to be a bit too technicolor for you.' She couldn't think of a nastier way to put it.

Eleanor laughed softly for a moment. 'I tried. It turns out I'm better at serving than silent prayer. I can't really keep my mouth shut, they tell me. Speaking of legends – have you ever heard the age-old convent tale?'

Maeve shook her head.

'This isn't strictly true – but take it as an analogue of the truth, possibly said about another nun centuries ago. The Mother Superior allows us to speak two words out loud every fifth year. My first two words were "hard bed." So they got me a better bed. Then, just last year, after ten cloistered years, I said, "lousy food."

'"OK, it's going to be best if you leave us," the Mother Superior said. "You've done nothing but complain since you got here."'

Maeve smiled but did her best not to laugh. 'Dad has a permanent woman now. He's very committed to her.'

'And I have what we call a vocation. I'm still a nun, Maeve, a bride of Christ.' She displayed the plain gold ring on her marriage finger. 'My order is St Procopius, of the Benedictines, the same as Dorothy Day. If you don't know her, look her up. She's a wonderful hero. "Bride of Christ" works much the same way as marriage.'

'Not exactly,' Maeve said. 'Gloria isn't imaginary and Jesus is.' She was trying to be hard as a rock to remain loyal – insulting and untouchable – but she realized she'd just revealed Gloria's name. Was that a mistake?

'Gloria,' the woman mused. 'A Latina? How interesting.'

'A Paiute Indian, in fact. She's strong as an ox, hard as nails, smart as a really good shrink. A very good cop. And possessive as all get-out.'

The half-smile came and went. 'Don't worry, Maeve. I don't covet Jack. I just wanted to know how he's cooking along these days. I was worried. When I knew him long ago, things were a bit ragged.'

No way on earth Maeve would tell her about Jack's problems. 'He's fine. Just perfect, in fact.' She felt Millie's hand tighten twice on hers, like some kind of weird lie detector going off.

'You should go back to your mom now,' Eleanor said to the little girl, as if there was something more she wanted to say to Maeve.

'I have to go find a runaway boy now,' Maeve said quickly.

NOTES FOR A NEW MUSIC

Day 5

Make a song of that afternoon, Conor. It was like being caught up in a wildlife special on PBS. But that's a mean thought. Eddie introduced me to an old friend Macedonio Perez, who looked as shriveled as a prune though something told me he wasn't really very old at all. Eddie said PAIR-ez, I remember that. 'I just took a bad blast,' Perez said. 'Sorry, old man. But my brother died yesterday at MacArthur Park.'

'Of what?' I said. Pretty naive, I guess.

He squinted one eye at me. 'TB maybe. No T-Cells left, septicemia, diabetes, hearing voices, not feeling a thing from the knees down. Pick your favorite.'

'I'm so sorry,' I said.

'It's OK, kid. You didn't know him. He had seizures, same as me.'

And not ten minutes later, after Macedonio and Eddie had talked at random in a slang I had difficulty following, Macedonio was lying on the sidewalk near Mike's Market, throwing his arms around, and Eddie was fighting to get a balled-up corner of his shirt into the man's mouth. I did my best to help. After a while, he went limp and passed out peacefully, and Eddie took his violin gently out of its padded case and offered the man a little solo – Brahms, to lull him far away. Eddie just seems to get better and better at the instrument as I stay near him.

'They swallow their tongue and strangle if you don't keep the teeth apart,' Eddie explained.

'I've heard about that. We had a kid in school.'

'Mac spent all his life with high windows, from eleven or so in juvie, then the old L.A. jail north of the I-10, then prison up in Corcoran. He never learned to read, and he's sensitive about it. He pretends he needs glasses and asks you to read letters to him. But there's lots of Mex words in his letters that kind of mess up my steez. I never learned much Mex.'

'I know it pretty good,' I said. 'I'll help you if he gets another letter.'

Eddie seemed surprised. 'That's a mind-blow, kid. They teaching Mex to white kids in the 'burbs now?'

'Only if you want it. Most of my friends took French or German.'

'They oughta teach you coon talk, too,' he said, grinning. 'Strivin' my duns be dollar and coin.'

'What's that?'

'Nothin' you wanna know, son. You really gotta have a coon-life, you wanna unnerstan' coon talk.'

'That's not fair,' I said. 'I'm doing my best . . .'

Uh-oh. He broke off writing at the knock on his door, thinking it was the Musketeers again, then he tried to ignore the interruption and finish the sentence, but he'd lost his train of thought. So he sighed and got up and opened the door. Surprisingly, he found a girl there, freckled and aged about eighteen. She was slim and big-breasted and looked pretty good, even though she was trying to be fierce-looking, for some reason. You didn't really have to guess about self-protection on Skid Row.

'Wow, you're Conor,' the girl said.

'Whoa – who told you that?'

'Your dad, Mike Lewis.'

'Ah, shit. Tracked down to my hideout. Who are you?'

'Come on, man, let me in. I'm not screwing with you, and I'm not your enemy.'

'How do I know that?'

She shrugged. 'Maybe I made it all up. I'm Jack Liffey's daughter.'

He smiled. 'Amazing. Another generation torments the new one.'

'Come on, come on. There's no torment here.'

He waved her in at last. 'You've got the hospitality of everything

going, believe me. But it's not much. Hard surfaces, cold looks
and schizophrenics. Hey, that could be a song. 'Hard surfaces,
cold looks and schizophrenics,' he sang. 'And nobody sleeps like a
baby.'

She stepped in and saw his guitar leaning against the rickety
table at the window. Her focus bored in on an open journal book
with a pen beside it on the table. She sidestepped, surreptitiously
she thought, to try to get a glimpse of a little of what must have
been a diary, but he hurried over and slapped it closed.

'That's private, friend.'

'I was looking for you in Hollywood – that was your dad's best
guess,' Maeve said. 'My name is Maeve. Hollywood is the usual
destination in this town for music-heads on the lam.'

'I don't think I want to explain myself to you. I came here
because I came here.'

'Cool. You picked The Nickel because it's the utter bottoming-
out of America's moral abandonment of its poorest and weakest.'

His eyes widened. 'Well said, Maeve.'

'I'm sure I could have said it better.' She sat in his only chair,
beside the closed diary that drew her eye from time to time. 'I was
scared at first walking around out there,' she admitted. 'I bet you
were, too. There's still a few guys out there who scare me, but
mostly they're just people, aren't they?'

'Yeah,' he said. 'Lost people who drink too much and bad-luck
people and some really really crazy people. They may be strange,
but nobody wants to be here. I think so, anyway.' He plopped down
on the edge of the bed, the only other seat.

Maeve folded her arms. 'I think we were actually talking about
different things, if you listen really close,' Maeve said. 'I was really
talking about myself and my own fears, wasn't I? You were talking
about the people who live out there.'

'Maybe.' He screwed up his face and looked even younger for
a moment. 'Back in high school, I gave up trying to cure my really
angry friends. Goths and punks. They were so angry they were like
chained dogs who were straining out at the end of the chain, and
you couldn't do a thing for them. Seeing it that way helped me see
them better.'

'Were you part of the garage-band tribe?'

'Uh-huh, and a little Goth, too.'

'I think I'm still in the movies-and-books tribe.'

'I don't think we have to be so extreme any more,' he said. 'Maybe we're all a little bit of everything, even soch and dweeb. You know, I heard a homeless man play a Beethoven concerto this morning. Not perfect, but pretty damn good. Jeez, let's give credit.'

She noticed that there was a delay before he spoke, and almost everything he said was considered first, measured out, trying so very hard to be fair – or just not quite trusting her. He didn't have that pop-off-at-the-mouth quality that she knew she had. 'You seem to stay very slow and thoughtful. That's a compliment, Conor. My foot's been stuck on the accelerator for years.'

He smiled, also delayed. 'That's where the prestige is, isn't it? The fastest mind, the quickest wit. But you can slow down, too, I'll bet. And without drugs.'

'I don't do drugs. Have you got a slow-down theory? I'd like to hear about that.'

'I think so. But right now, all I can think about is the Musketeers. These old guys are fighting the pirates who want to take over this building. They asked me to meet with them tonight to make plans.'

'I met the chief, I think,' Maeve said. 'I'd love to sit in, if I could.'

Like a signal in some spooky dream, her voice drew a knock at the door.

'That must be them,' Conor said. He got up and opened the door, but seemed to be knocked back by an invisible shove.

'You don't deserve this palace, kid!' the tall one with the golden curls barked at him. The short one already had his switchblade open and was waving it at Conor.

'Come back to me, sport,' Gold-head said.

The short man took three quick paces inside and wrapped his arm around Conor's neck, holding the knife point up, just poking a little into the soft underbelly of his chin.

'You guys are really fucked up,' Maeve said.

'Mouth *shut*,' the tall man demanded. 'But *real* shut. It's this one we wanted, sweetie. But maybe we're going to take both of you because you seem to be hitched now.'

'I don't give a damn about this guy,' Maeve said, taking a leaf from one of her dad's stratagems. 'I don't even know his name.'

'You keep your version. We'll keep ours. Start for the door now, girlie, or my pardner sinks his knife right up through your boyfriend's tongue.'

'Don't! I'm there.'

In 2005, police cars from various jurisdictions and ambulances from several nearby hospitals were observed dumping their unwanted mentally ill and homeless on The Nickel (one was even on an I.V. drip). This discovery provoked a furore in the press and L.A. City Hall for a while, and the courts ordered a stop to the dumping. But very little changed. The Nickel is still very often the designated last stop.

SEVEN
Words are Worth a Thousand Pictures

Gloria began to worry when she called the school, using the police codeword for the week – Frosting – to establish her bona fides, and the attendance clerk at Redondo High told her Maeve Liffey hadn't responded in home room and was presumed to be out sick for the day. A discreet call revealed that she wasn't at her mother's, and by dark she hadn't shown up home at Boyle Heights.

Maeve Liffey was presumably at it again, the scourge of evil-doers, answering some Bat-Sign that only Maeve could see in the sky. Well, strictly speaking, it wasn't that great a mystery, Gloria thought. She knew Maeve was out looking for Conor Lewis. She had total recall of both sides of the phone conversation with Mike Lewis, between Jack's scribbles and the boy's dad responding. And she'd also gone out of her way to find out for Maeve the address of the ATM that was Conor's last cash-out the day before – Mike's Market on the edge of Skid Row. Jesus! Gloria thought. She didn't look forward to spending her evening after a twelve-hour shift down on The Nickel, fending off horny old men, trying to make sense of mushmouth ravings and avoiding the body sores that would give her a methicillin-resistant staph infection in a blink.

She heard a pounding behind her and turned to see Jack Liffey glowering from his chair and hitting the side of the stove. When he saw that he'd got her attention, he started to write.

YOUR WORRIED LOOK SAYS TROUBLE. MAEVE ISNT HERE. QED.

She didn't know what the hell QED meant, but she got the gist of the message all right.

'Yeah, Jack, Maeve didn't come home. I'm off to look for her, right now.'

TAKE YOUR PIECE.

'You want me to shoot her when I find her? Don't worry, *querido*. Going into the world armed is department policy. I'm an officer of the law even in my down time. I can't go to a Sunday picnic without my sidearm.'

Loco limped in and rubbed against her legs in an ingratiating way before plopping down beside Jack. *Thanks for that*, she thought. *I did contribute quite a bit to your cancer fund, old man.*

SORRY IF IM A BIT RATTY, Jack scrawled.

'It's OK, Jack. I know worrying about Maeve always does it to you. You're damn good at finding runaway kids, but I'm better at ordinary police work, and you know it. This *should* be ordinary. We know she's looking for Conor Lewis.'

NOTHING ABOUT MAEVE IS EVER ORDINARY.

They both smiled at that, and she crossed the kitchen, hugged him awkwardly and kissed his forehead. Every time she was about to step out of the house, she had an intuition that one of them was about to be struck dead, shot in the back by a teenage killer with an AK – such a nice boy, everybody said! – or blasted in the heart by a sudden blood clot stuck sideways. She always made sure her last communication was a moment of affection.

'Love you, civilian,' she said.

She detoured to the bedroom to get the small photo of Maeve they kept in a silver frame by the bed. She already had a surreptitious copy of the faxed photo of the Lewis boy.

They lay uneasily on either side of the super-high pickup truck bed, locked down under the camper shell. They were handcuffed and footcuffed to tie-downs that the men had pried out of recesses in the sides of the bed, and both of them had been duct-taped around the mouth and then around again. Maeve wondered what raw nerve in the world's underpinnings she had touched to set all this off. She assumed it was her doing. She just couldn't believe they were after Conor.

Maeve had recognized the one with the knife all right, but the fact that he'd brought yet another thug along, and a thug who didn't seem to approve 100 per cent of the whole venture, probably meant she wasn't destined for a night of someone's perverse sexual pleasure. That helped, but nothing really made sense.

It was possible that Conor was trying to tell her something with his facial expressions, but she'd always found that words – clear, direct, unambiguous – were worth a thousand pictures as well as a thousand passionate and desperate gestures. By turns he seemed to be miming fear, idiocy, nonchalance – he could have been signifying anything in some twisted game of charades. Who could tell?

It wasn't a long journey in the truck, and she wished she'd been counting turns the way real detectives always did. She was pretty sure they were still downtown somewhere. The abrupt stop and then the tailgate *skreeking* open and the little crazy creep unfastening their cuffs and hauling them out into a pitch darkness outside meant only uncertainty. He shoved them both under a steel roll-up door that looked like it led into an abandoned warehouse. She tried to look around for landmarks, but he pushed them on too fast, using his knife to poke her painfully in her butt. All she'd seen was one sign, a badly painted *Hsun's Toys* on a back door. She knew that the commercial toy district was against the northwest corner of Skid Row. She'd read that the Korean and Chinese toy merchants had begun hosing down their sidewalks day and night, trying hard to discourage street people.

The roll-up door clanged down hard behind them, leaving them in a big echoey room, with half collapsed cubicle partitions on one side and lots of pipes and ducts from overhead dangling cut wires. One old sewing machine hung from an electrical conduit pipe like a public notice of what the place had once been. It was so close to her that she could read its brand, Juki, which she'd never even heard of. Whatever became of Singer and Pfaff? Maeve and Conor, both with steel handcuffs snapped down on their ankles, were frog-marched into the remains of nearby cubicles. Maeve was recuffed out of sight of Conor to a pipe that rose straight out of the floor all the way to the ceiling. The knife-man took delight in ripping the duct tape around once and then off her face hard.

'Owww! Damn you! That hurt.'

'It was meant to. Pain is good for the soul, girl.'

'Give me the knife and I'll help your soul,' Maeve snapped.

'I only use my own pain when I don't have someone else.'

She didn't like the smirk she saw and decided to shut up. The big guy leaned against her cubicle wall as the little one went off to attend to Conor.

'Owww!' she heard. Undoubtedly that was Conor's tape coming off.

'No sympathy from me,' said the big one. 'We plucked you out of that human landfill.' For the first time she noticed with surprise that he was wearing a red Rutgers sweatshirt. She didn't really believe he'd gone there.

'You went to Rutgers?'

'Lousy football team. In a dipshit league,' he added. 'Everybody in Jersey would rather play for the Mafia.'

'Why did you pick me up? I'm nobody.'

He made a contemptuous flap of his lips. 'Your boyfriend means something to the old Jews that we got to move out of that place real quick to make room for progress. Consider yourself collateral damage, precious. Nobody nowhere gives a flying-A shit about a couple of runaways.'

She figured she should have left it there, but she couldn't help herself. 'I'm no runaway, you idiot. My mom's an L.A. cop. You've screwed up big time.'

He pursed his lips and seemed to think about it for a few moments and then disappeared into the darkness. A minute later it was the little psycho sauntering in, snapping open his switch-blade with a happy flourish and slicing open the back pocket of her jeans like gutting a fish to retrieve her cheap wallet. It wasn't her normal wallet. She'd taken a cue from her dad and assem-bled a 'city wallet' for expeditions that maximized the possibility of losing it to a pickpocket. This plastic one contained a photo-graph of George Clooney, one working credit card among several dead ones, a little cash, and a doorkey known only to god – but one of the stuffings had unfortunately had to be her real driver's license that she knew listed her mom's address. She wasn't sure what her mom would make of these jerks, but she wished the address had been Gloria's, who could certainly defend herself with more elan.

'Don't bullshit me on this,' Gloria said. 'I'll bet your name's not Mike neither.' She'd clapped her badge against the thick plexiglass window, and now she had her finger on the photo of Maeve, holding it in the metal slide-under tray that was the only physical access to the market's inner cage.

'I see girl,' the Vietnamese man told her, nodding obligingly. 'She here look for boy. Polite all mothahfuck. Is your girl?'

'What did you tell her?'

'I say I see boy. I very helpful. I say he come for ATM. Then he go that way.' He pointed left, which was the truth.

Gloria held up the photo to the black security guard, who was keeping a respectful distance from her.

'Mr Minh no speak with forked tongue, ma'am.'

She bristled and almost went for him. 'Is that supposed to be hilarious?'

'Sorry, sorry, sorry. Not at all. I love everyone.'

She realized the guard had no way of knowing she was a Paiute Indian, so the comment was relatively innocent. 'Do you know anything else?'

'The Fortnum Hotel two doors down,' he said. 'It's an SRO. And remember me in your prayers.'

'You're better off if I don't. The Great Spirit and I don't see eye-to-eye much. Here, split this with Mike.' She handed him a twenty. She'd never get it back from the sweetener slush fund in her own division, because she was off duty, but she was feeling generous.

'Thank you, ma'am. I wanted to be a police officer myself. Very very much once.' Gloria stood beside the waist-high freestanding steel ATM a few moments, noting there was no camera attached and no overhead camera focused upon it, and she debated her feelings, and then she turned back and tucked her business card into the rent-a-cop's shirt pocket. 'Call me if you still want in.' He was young enough if he was motivated, and clean. He just had to be free of serious felonies.

'Bless you, ma'am.'

She nodded and stepped out into the rancid shit-smelling aroma that emanated off the trashy pools of water at the curb. The Nickel – everybody's idea of a great evening stroll.

At heart I am profoundly melancholy, Gloria thought, *and that may never be something that the Great Spirit will forgive. But maybe Jack will. Oh, I need him whole again.*

She looked left. The Fortnum's sign up the block had seen better days, to say the least. One long squiggle of cursive neon tube, which would say NUM HOT if it could light up, had swung down to dangle vertically from the metal sign. She couldn't believe the gentrifiers were snapping these places up. But it was all location, location, location, as somebody had said. Or was it just cheap, cheap, cheap?

'So, the *nudnik* is back.' Samuel Greengelb had unwisely opened his door, holding on to his aluminum baseball bat, but he had a sense the golden-haired man could just reach out and take it away from him like an infant's lollipop if he wanted to. 'We want our heat back on.'

'Shutup, kike. Learn something.'

'Don't be a *nudzh*.'

'I said *shut up*! Your benefactor, the generous owner of this building, has just sweetened his offer to all of you. It's now twenty thousand dollars. For each of you fighting kikes. But only if you're out of here in three days. This fantastic offer will not be repeated.'

'Puh.' It was an exhalation through Greengelb's clenched lips, like steam from a pot lid. 'We should trust a *putz* like Vartabedian? We who know about real Brownshirts? Ira was three months in Mauthausen-Gusen. You go look that up. He's so upset he won't come out of his room.'

'Ancient history, Grandad. We got that pretty boy from room 205 that I know you like and we're holding him till you get out. You know my partner is a little crazy about playing games with his knife.' He showed the old man the high school photo of Conor that he'd taken away from the girl. 'If you want this dippy kid as a big stack of bone-in sirloins, just let me know. My pal can wrap and deliver.'

'Who is this boy? You leave children alone.'

'Play it your own way, gramps. But I have a lot of trouble restraining my friend. He used to be a butcher way over there in N'awlins before that Katrina, you know, and he's dying to try out his skills on a fresh bag o' meat. Twenty thousand clams for each of you.'

'I have to talk to my friends.'

'Sure. You'll find your benefactor is a true gentleman. You got twenty-four hours for your answer. Give or take half a second. It's not like you deadbeat fucks got to go off to work tomorrow. Find time to talk it over quick.' The big thug looked at his watch. 'I'll be right back here at eight at night. My advice is not to think of yourselves as anything special. You don't get to be no Jew heroes. You're just old men who won the lottery.'

'I'm not the boss of anything, but we'll talk.'

'Do that, Granddad. I'd hate to have to throw all you Christ-killers out a window.'

'Can we at least have the heat back tonight?'

'Wear a couple coats. You start asking for favors and benefactors aren't so nice.'

*   *   *

'Maeve, are you over there?' Conor hadn't spoken for a while, though the thugs seemed to have left the area some time ago. The night was going to be cold, and the cement floor was already damned uncomfortable on her hip, as well as her breath wicking dust up into her nose at every stirring.

'Where would I go?' Maeve called. Her hands were well and truly manacled around the pipe. 'Disneyland?'

There was a long silence, while the building groaned and popped in the dying of the day. 'Wasn't there some sports thing about saying Disneyland on TV?'

She decided to keep it light. He seemed given to panics. 'I heard winners got a free trip if they said they were going to D.'

'People sell themselves awfully cheap,' he said.

For a lot less than that sometimes, Maeve thought, but it wasn't something she particularly wanted to talk about. 'How are you tied up? Is there any way to get loose?'

'I don't think so,' he said. 'My arms are handcuffed around a big cast-iron sewer pipe that goes up from the floor about ten feet. It looks like it's been here for a hundred years.' She heard a rattle. 'It's pretty strong.'

'Don't knock yourself out. Did they take your wallet?'

'Yeah.'

She began to worry about her folks back home. Her mom in particular, but she remembered that she also had a university notice in the wallet, just an acknowledgement that they'd received her application, and she thought it had Gloria's address on it, so she thought of her helpless dad opening the door to the payphon and cringed. Why hadn't she purged the damn city wallet?

'Maeve?'

'Yes, Conor.'

'I think I want to sing something for you if you don't mind. Singing it aloud helps me remember. I've been writing new songs. I don't know what it'll be like *a capella*.'

'Did you think I'd say no?'

'Well, I'm still tentative enough to think it's an imposition to make somebody listen to me.'

'Go for it. I was supposed to save you, you know, and I seem to have failed miserably, so the least I can do is listen to you.'

She heard him laugh once, then he tried to beat out a slow rhythm on the floor.

'It's blues,' he called. 'I got the tune in my head.'
'Go on, dude. I'm here.'

> '*I just come up here from Fallbrook way,*
> *Ridin' the bus past the sea and the sailor bars*
> *Yes, I'm new here from Fallbrook town,*
> *From where the cars all shine like a million stars*
> *And the mothers lock the doors both up and down.*'

There were six verses like that. Wow, she thought, that was real white-boy blues, rich-boy blues. 'That was good,' she said.

'Come on, Maeve. You can be critical.'

'Well . . . I think I need to hear the music to get the feel of it.'

'Yeah, but there's something you don't like in the song, isn't there?'

'It starts to get pretty bitter, doesn't it? I don't know if blues is like that. It's usually more sad and resigned. You got some pretty strong up-front anger going.'

There was a moment that dragged on a while, in which he wasn't responding, and Maeve worried she'd offended him.

'You know, I wonder why I get so angry,' he said. 'My parents are wonderful, progressive people. I went to a good school. I didn't lack a thing I needed. What is it? I *was* angry. Is it adolescence? Is it all just make-believe?'

Maeve could feel a stir of cold air and the floor was starting to get chillier, as if a number of windows were open or broken to the winter air outside. 'There's plenty of real things in the world to be angry about. Stupid wars and homeless people right here, and women getting beat up.'

'Thanks for that, Maeve. But there's some kind of feverish personal anger I'm working out, isn't there? I think I'm so unused to anger – I have trouble dealing with it. I've listened to blues all my life. Real blues are redemptive – I read that somewhere – and I have this feeling my blues are just plain howling at the sky.'

'Don't be so dismissive of yourself, Conor. Maybe you'll find a positive energy in your anger. Your folks were always dreaming of a better world, weren't they? To do that you've got to have another source of energy. You don't seem to me cynical at all.'

'Wow, I could fall in love with you.'

'Not right now, please. We need to get out of here.'

'Practical to the end. You're the best, Maeve.'

'And don't give up hope. I know a damn good cop who's definitely looking for us right this minute,' she said.

She tried two other flophouses, probably only for hoodoo reasons, before she went into the most likely one all the way up at the corner, the Fortnum, where Gloria finally managed to galvanize a startling-looking albino behind a wire screen into acknowledging the boy's photo, though he didn't react to Maeve's picture, and he gave her a room number and thumbed up a dank stairway.

No one answered at the number, and the next two room doors were standing open strangely, like rat cages with the rats having fled some terrible fate. She glanced into the barren rooms with unsheeted beds, a three-legged chair. The place definitely wasn't the Biltmore.

A tiny dapper old man with a tonsure of grey hair opened a nearby door at her footstep. 'Good evening. Before you speak, madam, I must perform a minute adjustment to my hearing aid.'

'Go for it.'

He extracted a tiny device from his ear and fussed with what looked like a miniature hatpin for a moment before re-inserting it.

'Forgive me, I was napping,' he said. 'A greater and greater necessity, I find. I have so little juice of energy left. And, to be honest, the memory is not so good.'

Gloria showed him her badge and the faxed photo of Conor and then the one of Maeve.

He smiled at the boy's photo. 'Yes, I think this is the boy. He and his guitar reside in that room there. He's a good boy and very healthy. Good health has become so important. Are you healthy, Detective?'

'I can't complain.'

'You know, there is something I'm supposed to remember about this boy. I took a nap and that interferes. My memory is so terrible. He is gone away for a time, I think. I was supposed to call a meeting.'

She showed him Maeve's picture again.

He tried hard to recognize her. 'I may have seen them together somewhere, I'm not sure. I haven't been polite. Please come inside, Officer . . .?' His rising intonation appealed for her name.

'Ramirez. Thank you. Sergeant Ramirez.' She was in no hurry, and it was such a treat to interview someone who was polite, and mildly helpful at that. What was this sweet sane man doing on Skid Row? She could see what seemed to be a real oil painting of some romanticized cottage on the wall over his shoulder and a small bookcase jammed with foreign-looking hardback books. 'I will make some tea, madam, and you may join me or not, as you wish.'

'They said in the academy I shouldn't. A suspect could slip me a knockout drug and escape, you see.'

'Woe is me. So many rules. *Nu*, so I'm a suspect?'

'A manner of speaking, sir. No, you're not.'

'My name is Samuel Greengelb. For forty years I was a diamond-cutter for the commercial jewelers who come and go like shooting stars in the Jewelry District over on Hill Street. You'd think with all that wealth passing through my fingers, some of it would have stuck, but no. A wife and three children I raised, first in Boyle Heights, then in MacArthur Park.' He sighed. 'Almost all have become nogoodniks and want nothing to do with a useless old man. It's beyond sorrow. Many years ago I decided to leave Ruthie the house and stay here until I found a good place. Hah. You know, about this boy. Something is bothering me.'

He fussed with the teapot and a box of loose tea leaves. In his fussing, he knocked a note off the shelf, which fell to the floor. Probably just an old shopping list. He kept many of them. Greengelb set the kettle on an electric ring and ground the kettle hard against the device for some reason. 'Detective, now is the time in your life to plan for the future and save your money. Poverty is not a puzzle, I assure you. And it's not an accident. It's a simple consequence of bad decisions.'

'Thank you. I'll revisit my retirement plans. But the police have pretty good benefits.'

'Good, good. My children tell me I could always go to live on Mars if I want, but I hear the space program doesn't take too many old Jews.'

She laughed.

Just as the kettle began to whistle, there was an angry pounding at the door. Greengelb looked like he might know who it was, and he picked up an aluminum baseball bat, but then he glanced at her and took on a secret air of mischief. 'Let me work on the tea,' he said, 'and you can see to the *putz* who's banging on my door.'

'I'm here to make you happy tonight, Yid!' a voice called through the door.

She yanked it open to see a short furious man wearing a gray hoodie. His eyes went wide when he saw her, and he backed a half step. 'Whoa, this is fucked up!'

'You want to make somebody happy?' she snapped. 'That would be a real fucking challenge, little man.'

'Not *you*. I'm a messenger. My boss says the offer is fifty grand now. Take or leave tonight. All the Jew gentlemen get the same deal. You create your own luck, the man says, and that's real straight, cupcakes – it's great good luck that their own stubbornness has created. Gravity to you.' He swept back the hood and doffed a non-existent cap at Gloria. 'Good evening, miss.'

'Hold it right there. I mean hold it, dickhead.' She badged him – some days it gave her such great pleasure to use the power of her badge thrusting out of its own well-worn black leather wallet. Then she offered him Conor's photo. 'Have you seen this boy? Be very careful.'

He barely looked. 'Nah. I'm not very observant.'

'You're not very observant. Then do it because you're scared, little man. What's your name?'

'Friedrich Nietzsche.'

'Let's see some I.D., Nietzsche. *Now.*'

Instantly the strange little man pounded away along the hallway, a miraculously fast take-off like a dash-runner, and then he almost reflected himself down the stairwell. What a quick little fucker, she thought. Her choices right then had been to shoot him, for no particular reason, or be badly outrun and humiliated, or let him go.

'I bet you know who that was,' Gloria said, still staring at the space at the top of the stairwell that the man had just vacated.

'I'm not sure of the name. It's something French or Cajun. Thoreau, maybe, but I know who he works for, and that's a lot more important.' He poured out tea for both of them and told her about the plans for turning the old single-room-occupancy hotel into pricey lofts, and the three old-time residents who had tenure there and were trying to stay put, the bitter-enders of a much bigger crew who had had leases from the previous owner.

'You're the leader of this group,' she said.

'We all are.'

He studied the depth of color in the teapot and then poured their tea. 'The boy, I'm sure there's something.'

He gave a half-smile, but there was no humor in it. 'I do my best to keep things light these days and be a good neighbor to all. Like your friend, that boy. A place is only blessed if it has good neighbors. Conor is the boy's name, I remember. But there's more . . . '

In 2006, L.A. Police Chief William Bratton together with L.A. Mayor Antonio Villaraigosa, announced their 'safer cities initiative,' with significant input from right-wing think tanks back east. For some bizarre reason, they added fifty cops to The Nickel and decided to deal with the homeless by arresting and jailing them for every minor infraction, from littering, to public urination, to sleeping on the sidewalks. The estimated cost of the fifty new 'Safer Cities' police officers was about $6 million per year.

EIGHT
A Benefactor of the City

Maeve was beginning to feel seriously uncomfortable on the concrete floor, an ache so widespread and deep in her hip that she knew it was in the boy's, too. She could imagine him twisting this way and that, as well, to the limits of his handcuffs hunting for marginally more bearable positions. And the cubicles were getting colder and darker. In a few minutes she would no longer be able to read the **Seek Ye The Lord** that someone had spray-painted on the wall with a big-mouth enraged devil beneath. To admit the truth to herself, the devil frightened her a little, suggesting a mind she never wanted to confront. She wondered if the small man had painted it. 'Ow!' she cried out involuntarily, twisting one time two many.

'I can't get comfortable, either,' he called. 'It goes on and on. It's like a song that's stuck in the wrong key.'

'No, it's not *like* anything,' she said irritably. There was a hair in her mouth, too, and she couldn't pluck it out because her hands were impossibly far away. She could only move it around with her tongue and sputter at it ineffectually. 'It *is* being tied up on a hard floor and it hurts. Do you have any idea why they grabbed us?'

'I know they're hassling the old guys in that hotel. I think they want them to move out so they can rebuild. Maybe they thought we would be leverage against the old guys.'

Abruptly Maeve became aware of a scampering along the nearest wall, and two fingers of ice clamped against her neck. She flopped her head over quickly to look but no matter how intensely she stared, she could see only confused shadows at the foot of the cubicle – perhaps a mouse, a feral cat, something worse? What could be worse? A pit bull that would eat her face off?

'There's an animal in here! I hate it all!'

'Can you see it?' he called.

'No. But I heard something slinky. I know I sound girlish, but it's just so abhorrent. I need some other sound. Would you talk, please? Sing if you want.'

'It's better if we both sing. Do you know any folk songs?'

'Oh, God. I can't sing worth a damn. The only song I know is "Jeremiah was a bullfrog."'

'It's actually called "Joy to the World,"' Conor explained. 'Hoyt Axton wrote the nonsense verse just so he could demonstrate a tune he liked.'

'Spare me the musicology. That damn animal just skrittered again.'

'OK,' he said. 'Let's go . . .'

> *'Jeremiah was a bullfrog,*
> *He was a good friend of mine.'*

Maeve took a deep breath and joined in.

> *'I never understood a single word he said*
> *But I helped him drink his wine.*
> *He always had some mighty fine wine.'*

Jack Liffey heard the phone ring and debated answering it. How could he? But some fate drove him to lift the receiver.

'Is that Jack? This is Art Castro. Whack the phone a few times so I know.'

He hit the receiver on the plastic arm of his wheelchair. If only he had one of those talking machines.

'OK, listen up, man. You might as well know your daughter's been playing Nancy Drew, keeping the bench warm for you. Now, don't go ballistic, I only got a rumor and I hear she's basically OK. But the minute Gloria gets home you tell her this scuttlebutt. I hear that girl has upset a couple of low-lifes down on The Nickel.'

'Ack! Ack!'

'Be cool, Jack. Gloria can handle it in two seconds flat.' He told him the address. 'You write that down and tell Gloria to go there when she comes in.' But before Castro could finish speaking, Jack Liffey was pounding the phone against everything nearby as hard as he could until it came apart and no longer seemed to be working.

He willed his legs to move, but that only made his arms hurt with displaced energy. Everything had gone red around him. Maeve! NO! The feeling of wrists so fragile you could snap them like a carrot! He knew she had a sassy mouth that could piss off any hooligan in ten words flat.

He wheeled to his study and got out his Ballester-Molina, an Argentine copy of the military .45 auto that he'd bought years ago, and tucked it into his waist, then plucked his car keys off the tiny desk. The car hadn't budged in weeks.

He left the front door open behind him, and there was a painful drop where the makeshift ramp off the porch had slipped a bit, but he got to the old pickup across the lawn without tipping over. He had chosen an amazing lull in the busy life of Greenwood Avenue, and no one was there at all to help him mount the car.

First he opened the tailgate then tipped himself out on the driveway. From the ground, he folded up the wheelchair and hurled it into the bed. No way to close the tail now. He found he couldn't even crawl and had to arm-drag himself to the driver door. This was going to be tough! The keyhole was immeasurably far above him.

Gathering a little hand purchase on the metal and leaning, he finally boosted himself up enough to insert the key and open the door. Thank God his arms were strong and still worked fine. The steering wheel was a wonderful grab-bar to get his dead weight inside. He adjusted his legs into a normal driving position, still in such a panic about Maeve that only now did he realize there were foot pedals that had to be worked.

His eye caught on the sturdy black cane that Gloria, in a fit of hopefulness, had bought him and then left in the truck. Pressing the rubber-tipped cane on to the accelerator pedal, he started the truck without trouble. This was going to work – astounding! – but it would demand whole new feats of co-ordination. Luckily, Chris Johnson, from whom he'd inherited the wreck, had for some reason bought a 1991 with automatic transmission. A clutch pedal would have been a real stretch.

Shift into drive and then a panicky switch of the cane to the brake pedal as the truck lunged a foot. If he'd had a third hand, he could have used the handbrake, but this was going to be all cane and steering wheel. He attempted to steer with his teeth for a moment, but rejected the idea. Luckily it was late evening, long past rush hour, and there was no traffic as he rolled out slowly on to Greenwood and turned south one-handed. Going south on Greenwood would take him to a T-intersection at Fourth and a very cautious right turn would take him straight west into The Nickel and the address Arturo had given him.

He hardly noticed the deco triumphal arches on both sides of the old Fourth Street bridge over the L.A. River as he wove slowly and unsteadily toward his goal, having a little trouble keeping the cane from slipping off the accelerator.

So far, so good. He was calming down enough to wonder what came next. The address Art had told him, burned into his memory, was in the Toy District just north of the sorriest part of The Nickel, and it turned out to mark a big steel roll-up door on a dead dark street. The door next to it was marked Hsun's Toys.

He parked at an angle and managed to liberate his wheelchair from the back, expand it and climb inside so he felt normalized again – at least back to a recent kind of normality.

He banged hard on the roll-up door with his pistol. He'd have fired away at a lock if one had been visible.

When no-one came, he wrote GIVE ME MY DAUGHTER NOW! on one of his pads to have ready. He could feel his heart pounding away in his chest.

He banged again and again, as hard as he could, if only to let Maeve know someone was here. Of course, he didn't know for sure she was there. He was about to give up and think about a plan B when there was a *thunk* and the roll-up door trundled up about six feet.

He was facing two men, one tall and bulky, with long gold ringlets like the old photos of the foppish General Custer, and the other shorter, with spooky eyes like someone waiting for a long-distance bus that would take him back into a war zone.

Jack Liffey flashed his notepad at them, and pointed his big square pistol for reinforcement.

The smaller one just laughed. 'Don't know about you, Stevie, but I feel lucky. I don't think life works out for this funny guy.'

Gloria finally shook herself out of the reverie that had held her in this old man's apartment for so long – over the last half-hour mostly yammering to him about herself and him worrying about his memory.

She wasn't sure why she liked Samuel Greengelb so much, but it didn't happen to her often and she did. Maybe it was the kindly grandfatherly manner – with all the times she'd been fostered out, she'd never had anyone even close to the role of kindly grandfather – or maybe it was the sadness of his failing faculties. Finally she offered her regrets to Greengelb and left.

He had told her Moses Vartabedian's name, and it was no problem to call in and get his office address and maybe a bit more from the research people as long as you knew the voice code. It turned out that Vartabedian's main office was in a beautifully restored art deco mini-skyscraper a few miles west on Wilshire, on the seventh and top floor above a former grand movie palace with the unlikely name of The Glamorous Algerian that had now become a venue for big-name baby-boomer music events. The old blue tile marquee announced upcoming dates for Joni Mitchell and Ry Cooder and Airborne Toxic Event, which she certainly hoped was a music group. After a quick inspection of the building, she bypassed the main entrance and went inside an unlocked staircase door on the west side that she guessed would take her somehow to the tower.

Restored rosewood wainscoting lined the stairwell up one floor to a small elevator lobby where the fancy wood gave way to equally fancy marble, but she ignored the elevators and found a stairwell door and decided to hoof it the rest of the way up, partly for her health but mostly for the element of surprise.

Gloria was gasping a little when the top of the stairs gave out on a tiny foyer and she pushed the glass door open to what said V and L Enterprises and offered another tiny lobby. A gorgeous young receptionist with very large breasts was hunt-and-pecking something on a state-of-the-art Mac, all HD screen, apparently copying from a handwritten document that she was craning her neck at. The woman looked up, startled, and for some reason started typing really fast and blindly with two fingers until Gloria said, 'Cool it, honey. I'm not from the job agency.'

'Wow, you read my mind,' the woman said. 'I bet you can tell I can't really type. My skills just don't run in that track.'

Gloria didn't want to enquire what the skill track might actually be. 'Don't ask, don't tell, hon. Is Mr V in?'

'I ain't supposed to say.'

'That's terrific,' Gloria said. She resisted badging her, for some reason. There were two unmarked inner doors, one on either side of the reception desk. 'Don't say a word. Just point at the door. We'll give each other a break here.'

Sheepishly, the woman gritted her teeth and then nodded once at the door on her left, as if the quick nod didn't constitute 'pointing.'

Gloria gave the woman an OK circle with her fingers, for what that was worth, and went straight in.

Startling herself with the astounding full-wall view in the dark, she stalled for a moment in the doorway. It was a large office with a breathtaking panorama of the billion-light spectacle that stretched west along Wilshire toward the ocean fifteen miles away. Off to the right there was even a ghostly floating Hollywood sign in the invisible hills, a view that always contained a sense of tragedy for her, for no real reason she knew except for all the crap and abuse that the name had always represented.

At the desk in front of her was a paunchy dark-skinned man, his head cocked back as he puffed contentedly at a cigar, and who quickly ripped his feet off the fancy granite desk that looked like a mountain boulder that had been miraculously sawn in half.

'Jesus, who are you?' he burst out.

Once again she enjoyed the tacit pleasure of showing her badge. It established such an immediate relationship of power, which she loved to use on big men.

'Sergeant Ramirez, LAPD,' she said. She let him settle a bit. 'I want you to tell me about your boys McCall and Theroux or Thibodeaux or whatever. Don't pause to think about it. Just tell me.'

Funny things happened behind his eyes for a few moments, but he finally made his decision. 'Never heard of them, Sergeant.'

'Bad guess. I know they work for you, clearing buildings.'

'Those names mean nothing to me. As God is my witness. Or maybe the mayor.'

She noticed some music going fairly softly in the office, a kind of bleating bebop jazz that she knew Jack would've liked.

'You like that stuff?' She nodded toward his hi-tech mini-stereo.

He seemed puzzled for a moment. 'The music?'

'Yeah.'

'I usually like what's new, on principle. But this is such a mediocre time in history. The best you can do is rehabilitate what used to be great. That's my vocation. What's eating you, Sergeant?'

'Almost everything. Call it off, whatever game you're running. I'm sure you're one of those slumlords who's driving off the tenants so you can rebuild. Call it off and I'll give you a Get Out of Jail Free card.'

He puffed hard to keep his cigar going, which annoyed Gloria no end. 'You look really worked up about something, Sergeant. Honest, you should calm down. I promise you I'm well known as a benefactor of the city. I renovate landmarks, I save them. This fantastic Algerian from 1927 was about to be knocked down for an insipid Korean mini-mall. You know, a piece of crap where they sell doughnuts and acrylic fingernails. I saved this place. Everyone says it's glorious now. Come on, Sergeant, look out that window. What do you see?'

He pressed something that turned off the room lights and nodded to the vast spark-dotted black velvet nightscape, with the other-worldly HOLLYWOOD floating above it all. Involuntarily she glanced for a moment. You never accepted the terms a suspect offered.

'That's *my* city,' he said. 'Everything is accelerating, and you have to make a few compromises to keep what's valuable.'

'That's your dream? Leaving your mark on a bunch of half-assed old buildings?'

'Where's your name gonna be, ma'am? In tiny print on a brass plaque at the Police Academy up in Elysian Park?'

'Those are the cops killed on duty. Are you threatening me?'

'Jesus, no, ma'am. As God sees my soul, no. Look. They say that's the great town of illusions out there. But that was long ago, the Forties, maybe. That time is over. I just want to save what I can of the best stuff they built back then. My intentions are good.'

He had to relight his cigar and Gloria waited.

'I swear to god, man, if those two dickheads work for you and they hurt anyone I'll fuck you up. I'll fuck you up good. I just want you to know that. By tomorrow, I'll know everything there is to know.'

He seemed to pause again to give it all some thought. 'You don't really know how important I am in this town, do you, Sergeant? Look me up, ask about me. It's a cultural fact. I got the mayor and your own chief on speed dial.' He tapped a gold contraption that looked vaguely like a telephone and puffed hard. The reek in the room was awful.

'I could get you fired tomorrow,' he said. 'Or at least transferred to a job you wouldn't like very much out in the desert.'

The short man with the crazy eyes had worked himself around to the side of Jack Liffey while golden curls approached from the front. They had no weapons threatening him, and there was never a moment that justified shooting one of them. All he could do was pound a bit and wave the pistol around. It was hopeless. Again he willed his legs to move so he could rise but got only a twinge in his jaw from gritting his teeth.

The little guy was fast as a snake, and surprisingly strong, and he ripped the pistol out of Jack Liffey's hand.

'Well, Mr Special-de-dee, who the fuck are you now?'

They found the little pouch of business cards and had fun trying different pronunciations of his name and sarcastic renditions of his listed occupation: *I Find Missing Children.*

'If that girl or boy are yours, we ain't gonna hurt them none so don't give yourself a hernia, old man,' the curly one said. 'The kids are just leverage to get some old geezers to move out. But you, nobody cares about you. Hold on to your balls.'

The curly one kicked the chair over, and Jack Liffey went down hard and banged his head on the cement forecourt so his vision went pink. The little one had a switchblade out now and was waving it in figure-eights in front of his eyes.

'Ack!'

The knife-man made an odd sound, maybe mimicking his own helpless cry. 'We don't even got to cut his tongue out. Some fuckin' child-finder. Find this, wheelie!' And he swung a hard kick at Jack Liffey's thigh on the ground. He wore steel-toed cowboy boots and the pointy tip hurt like hell. Then the two tormentors took turns kicking and shoving him around with their feet until he ended in the damp gutter. He used his arms to protect his face from the blows, but they kicked his elbows and forearms away. Most of it was just desultory punishment, without much object, but the little one hauled off with a blow to his head and he probably passed out for a few moments.

'This is no fun, Stevie. Let me cut him up.'

'You should see yourself, old man. You really bleed easy. Give us all a break and just expire. On the average, you're nearer dead than not. No, don't cut him! Jesus, Rice, it'll be raining cops. Let's put him back in his chair and roll him down into the heart of The Nickel. Nature will take its course.'

They boosted him into the wheelchair, only half conscious, and had fun giving big pushes and then riding along, boosted on to the back, as the chair bumped over rubbish and cracked asphalt.

Eventually they kicked the chair over again, and his cheek lay in something soggy, a stink of decay and piss that announced another gutter, and not a gutter in Beverly Hills. The power of smell, Jack Liffey thought, retreating into his own head. People lived deeply in smells, auras of this and that, long habits of cosmetics and foods and spices that they shored up around themselves. These smells were Other.

His tormentors seemed to depart. From where he lay, eyes clamped shut, he could hear the wet noises of men hawking and spitting all around the compass, confiding things to one another, then conspiratorial murmurs like the visiting room of a psych ward. Far away somewhere there was traffic noise. When he opened an eye, all he could see was brick buildings with grilled-up windows across the street, a hurricane fence enclosing an empty lot, and, nearer, heaps of wet trash that he was not used to seeing in a street.

His chair jolted, and a voice demanded, 'Leggo, you fucker!'

A tennis shoe was on his neck all at once, and he couldn't turn his head to see who was speaking. He felt the wheelchair ripped away from him, inch by inch.

'Ak-Ak!' The chair! It was his last connection to a life that was still under some kind of control. It had his notebooks, a water bottle, several felt pens, and a snack bag of potato chips.

'Man, ain't this *cold*!' a voice exulted, already diminishing, and his newly sensitive ear detected the grindy bearings of his wheelchair, with no weight on the wheels, receding.

'Worth a Benjamin, I bet!'

Hell, Jack Liffey thought, not sure whether he was cursing or describing where he'd been deposited. Not so long ago there'd been something like a wall of affection surrounding and protecting him – Gloria, Maeve, friends, a house that he'd been able to maneuver around, a safe back yard, a dog, neighbors who knew him or at least knew about him and would come to his aid. But now he was alone in the dark somewhere, vulnerable and overwhelmed, without strategies. A small helplessness sinking into the void. Are you still home in there, Mr Jack Liffey? Honest to God, I don't know. There's so little left of who I was. There was one positive point, and he clung hard to it; he actually believed the claim that they wouldn't hurt Maeve and Conor. They had no cause to.

The docs insisted his disabilities were all psychosomatic – actually they'd used some fancy new word to that effect – but he tried his damnedest now to lever himself up under his own power. Maybe he'd just forgotten how. He did feel a bit of buzz in his legs, but he couldn't budge them. Even his arms seemed to have lost much of their strength. *It's just panic, self. Calm down.*

He thought of Loco for some reason, and the semi-crippled wreck that his poor dog had become. Or was he getting himself and the dog mixed up? Tears of self-pity pooled on his upward cheek, then dripped off the bridge of his nose. Loco, this is me, Jack. Sell your condo, sell your favorite pet-bed and buy me out of this situation, *please*, he thought. He could tell he wasn't thinking very clearly.

'Ma'am, could I have a word?' Gloria called through the tall chain-link at Catholic Liberation House. Sitting on a folding chair on the strangely idyllic lawn in front of the facility, a powerful-looking black woman was apparently guarding the place, but also imbibing from a small bottle she seemed to think was hidden in a paper bag.

'What up?' Her tone told Gloria that the woman resented this interruption of her righteous sundowner.

'I just want to know if you've taken in a new girl recently, about eighteen.' She held Maeve's photo up to the fence.

'A girl alone? We only take mothers and families, Officer.'

Officer. Some day she'd learn all the clues that made it that obvious to the rest of the world. Gloria was about to insist that the woman come over and take a good look at the photo anyway. Half your leads on the job came through pure doggedness, against all reason and inertia, but her energy was flagging badly after the twelve-hour shift that had started at 6 a.m. and now the dozens of random inquiries she'd made at shelters and SROs and foundations across the whole west side of The Nickel. She wasn't as indefatigable as she'd once been, she realized. She wondered if she was losing her edge. It was a bad sign for a cop, one reason so many cops retired early.

'Forget it, ma'am.' Gloria saw the woman go alert, the brown bag do a vanishing act in the grass, and then she heard the front door come open. Sensitive radar, the woman had.

'Is there a problem?' a soft-spoken voice called out the door.

A thin woman with graying red hair came slowly out of the backlight, and down along the walk, approaching Gloria. She seemed tense, not in a mannered way, maybe just a rabbity kind of energy that Gloria had noticed before in a number of women who'd worked their way up in charge of institutions – orphanages, shelters, schools – always a little more to handle than they'd bargained for. Or maybe it was simpler than that, she thought. Maybe that nervy alertness was just a mark of the ones who lasted, people with a strong sense of responsibility.

'I'm Sergeant Ramirez, LAPD Have you seen this girl in the last few days?'

She saw recognition immediately in the woman's green eyes, probably before she realized she was broadcasting it. She had a mobile freckled face with a kind of tenderness in the aging eye wrinkles.

'I'm Sister Mary Rose. I'm in charge here. May I ask you, Sergeant, why you're looking for this girl?'

She saw no reason to withhold. 'She's my daughter. Stepdaughter, and I think she's hunting for a boy who's gone missing around here somewhere. She should have been home long ago, and she didn't go to school today. I'm afraid she may have got mixed up with some of the toughs that hang out down here.'

Gloria could see the woman study her with an unusual curiosity, even a little amusement, as if Gloria had just grown a second nose, and she knew something was going on between them that she wasn't aware of. The thin woman took out a key on a chain around her neck and unlocked the gate.

'Come in, Sergeant. Yes, I've seen your daughter. I was pretty sure I recognized her. I won't keep you in suspense – a long time ago, almost ten years now, I knew Jack, too.'

'Knew?' Gloria felt herself stiffen. Only police training had kept her from coming to an abrupt halt and bellowing: KNEW?!

'Please have some coffee with me, Sergeant. Please. I am not a problem. Maeve is probably on her way home right now.'

She hadn't used Maeve's name. Reluctantly Gloria followed her in through the nondescript entry, past several militant posters in the hall, all featuring women of color looking competent and composed, and into what looked like a cramped staff room with cubby-hole mailboxes and a small fridge and coffee-brewer.

'Yes, a *long* time ago, Jack and I were intimate, Sergeant. I'm sorry. Is that a word that anyone uses any longer?' The nun explained that she'd left a convent back then, only a year before she'd met Jack, and she'd been running a different shelter and art center in south L.A., in the town of Cahuenga. She'd had almost no experience of men up to then, and Jack Liffey had shown up one day, a knight errant looking for the missing mother of a Latino boy, and he'd just bowled her right over, as she put it. She hadn't been prepared at all for how his attentions would 'sweep her off her feet.' Gloria noticed the old-fashioned turns of phrase in her speech, as if she'd slept soundly through a couple of decades.

The nun sighed and shook her head at her own tale. Jack Liffey's slam-bang life had turned out to be much too overwhelming for her, and after a particularly rough experience, she'd found she needed her old sense of vocation back, but maybe in reality, she'd needed the security of the large safe family that she'd left behind in the cloister. She confessed that there was probably a tendency for all that convent security and earnestness to infantilize the nuns a little.

Holy orders rarely took anyone back, on any terms, after they'd laicized, she explained, but her order, like most of them these days, was quite desperate for warm bodies and had been willing to make an exception. In many of the nuns' retirement homes, she said sadly, the women – unlike old priests – had been pretty much abandoned by the Mother Church. The declining eighty-year-old nuns were now left to tend the ninety- and ninety-five-year-olds. It should have been a terrible scandal but nobody took notice.

She fussed ineffectually with a coffee filter as if her mind were elsewhere.

'I'd actually prefer a beer,' Gloria said.

'I'm afraid we don't allow alcohol here . . . except for that inexpensive port you undoubtedly noticed Kenisha Duncan drinking. She thinks I don't know about it, of course. We could borrow it from her, but I have a feeling sweet port wouldn't suit you.'

'Uh, no. How long would you say you and Jack were intimate?'

'Really not long at all. A few weeks. Just long enough so we
were both almost killed by some terrible hooligans who came after
him. I had compound fractures in both my legs. We were thrown
about thirty feet straight down a storm drain. Unfortunately it was
raining in the hills that day, and the whole pipe soon flooded. I've
never been so physically frightened in all my life.'[2]

Gloria wondered if there was another kind of frightened that
mattered. *Be generous*, she thought. 'Jack's life does tend to attract
trouble. I've learned that, too. It's lucky my job leaves me used to
it.' Gloria thought of telling her about Jack's condition now, but for
some reason she held back, put off, or annoyed (jealous?) by this
competent middle-class white woman. She hadn't realized that she
had this jealousy in her. Even when she'd been with her first big
love, her police mentor Ken Steelyard, his flirtations with others
hadn't bothered her too much – though he'd never been much of
a ladies' man.

'I'll bet Maeve's grown up to be quite a bright girl,' the nun said.

Nice shift of topic, Gloria thought. 'Sometimes too clever for
her own good.'

'I suppose. Why don't you call her?' She nodded toward a telephone in the corner.

Gloria held up her own cell. 'I've been trying. She either means
to be out of touch or she's in trouble.'

'Of course.' The nun seemed amused at herself. 'I'm sorry, Gloria,
I completely forget about these mobile telephones that everyone
has, even the children. You know, I've never driven a car, never
watched television. I suppose I'm the true Luddite. I was cloistered
and silent for many years, but I think I've learned that claustral
adoration of God isn't really my vocation, even a second time, no
matter how hard I tried. I need to be more active, and I guess I
need to feel I'm being of use.'

'You were *silent* all that time! Sweet Jesus. That would kill me.
I need to chew people out now and then. I need to bang against
them.'

The nun laughed softly. 'I think Jack's found someone who's
really good for him.'

'You'd have to ask him that. It hasn't been all roses and fire-
cracker sex.'

[2] See *The Concrete River*, 1996.

She'd said that on purpose and saw the woman blush a little. 'I'd like to give you something,' the nun said, looking away.

'Uh-huh,' Gloria said, as neutrally as she could. The woman finally gave up her distracted, half-hearted attempt at making coffee and left the room. Gloria brooded for a moment and then studied the poster that faced her, above the desk. She liked the look of the woman on the poster and rose a little, leaning forward, to read that it depicted someone named Dorothy Day (1897–1980). Across the bottom was a quote that was presumably from the pensive-looking cleft-chinned woman: 'I firmly believe that our salvation depends on the poor.' She'd never heard the woman's name before and would have to ask Jack if he'd heard of her.

Why such a big deal? Gloria thought. Why the fuck not care about the poor? It's supposed to be the deal.

She finally decided that watching what powerful people kept doing to the poor was part of what was killing her. She liked the look of the woman on the poster. As a cop, she was supposed to be observant, but she wasn't sure she'd ever looked as closely at a photograph as she looked now at this plain-looking dead woman in black and white with the transparent plastic eyeglass frames, the vertical worry furrows over her nose and the squared-off jaw.

The nun came back into the room with a large loose-leaf notebook in black pebbled covers, fat with celluloid-encased pages, like somebody's memory book. She flipped through them rapidly and finally stopped with a closed-off unreadable look. She handed the open book to Gloria.

Each page seemed to contain a photograph of an oil painting, back-to-back. But that wasn't what caught Gloria's attention. The book was open to a startling oil portrait of Jack Liffey, a whole lot younger and more full of vigor than she'd ever seen. He was hiking one leg of his trousers to sit on the edge of a table. The painter was pretty good – probably this annoying nun herself, ex-nun, nun-again – and Jack Liffey looked back at the painter as if captivated by some ambiguous emotion, a little full of himself as usual, curious, almost smiling. Oh, it was Jack, all right.

'I want you to have it,' the woman said.

'Did he pose for you?'

'No, I did it from memory.'

'Where's the original?'

'Who knows? They were probably all thrown in the trash down in Cahuenga after I left. I want you to know I have no designs on your man, Gloria. This is all I have of him and I give him back. Jack is all yours now. I'm married to Jesus. Please take it.'

Gloria studied the woman for any nuance of irony or spite and saw nothing. 'In another universe I might have liked you.'

'I find I'm stuck in this one,' the nun said. 'If we ever started competing, God knows where we'd end up. Just take care of Jack. Jesus and Mary watch over you.'

'It's getting really dark over here,' Conor announced.

'No shit, Sherlock.' Maeve was so frightened and so intent on watching a faint line of gray at the foot of the cubicle wall that she'd almost forgotten who it was talking inanely at her from nearby. That was unfair – but still. She was preoccupied with her own fear. The animal noises had gone on skritching, now and again, along that disappearing line of gray. Catbox sounds, holding her full and utter attention.

Somewhere deep in the funhouse, somebody had decided to test one of her worst fears: it was Room 101, if she'd got the number right, from Orwell's *1984*. The room that held everybody's worst nightmare. Winston Smith's had been rats. And rats would do for her, too, *absolutely*, she thought. Oh, yes, rats eating at you when you're helpless. 'I wish you could save me,' she called. She figured she'd always wanted somebody to save her. Mostly her father, of course, who was incapacitated now and so self-obsessed by it all that he was impossibly far beyond saving anyone.

'I'm not very good at saving,' the boy called. 'I can't see myself as anything but myself – a guy who's a bit wretched at anything useful. I can't saw a board the right length, and I can't hammer a nail straight. But I *do* feel risk in the air right now, and it scares me. I'd sure like to be one of those people who always knows what he's doing, but I'm not.'

'Thank you, Conor. For your honesty. Let's try to help each other through this terrible night.'

'Yes,' he said. 'I don't know what options we've got. I've been trying to get my wrists out of these handcuffs for hours.'

'Well, I'll be honest,' Maeve said. 'I'm so terrified by these

animal sounds that I've almost gone into another state of being and
I'm surprised when I notice I'm still the same person I used to be.
I'm almost catatonic.' It seemed more like a nightmare than an
event, and she wished she could wake up in a cold sweat with the
danger over.

Just then she saw it, saw its vague ovoid shape scurrying along
the base of the cubicle wall. She screamed as she'd only screamed
in dreams – all her terror pouring out at once as if she'd unstop-
pered a big vat of fright.

'*What is it?*'

She brought her knees up to protect her face, assuming a fetal
mania of denial.

'Maeve, please! Tell me!'

Nothing bit her, nothing brushed against her, and after a while,
after increasingly desperate pleas from Conor, she forced herself
to breathe slowly and deeply, to imagine the rat somebody's scien-
tific subject – a harmless furry creature that could be set to hunting
through a maze, at the whim of some geeky psychologist. Then fed
to a boa. *Yes.*

'Just a rat,' she snapped.

'I'm so sorry.'

'So am I. My scream probably scared the poor thing spitless.'

'I don't know about the rat, but my mouth is pretty dry.'

Jack Liffey dragged himself along the gutter with what strength
he still had in his arms and found he was long past worrying
about the smells or the muck that he was accumulating on his
clothing as he plowed through the unmentionably squishy heaps.
Eventually he did navigate his body a few feet away from the
curb, away from the worst filth as he moved toward light. Up
ahead – either impossibly far or only a short walk, depending
on your condition – he could see an old-fashioned streetlamp
that was still functioning, spilling a yellow pool across a crumbling curb. Oh, yes, light. Better to be visible and to be able to
see.

He felt a bit detached from his fear now, but maybe that was
just a sign of coming unglued. He was doing his very best not
to worry about Maeve; there was nothing he could do for her
right now. The last true memory he nurtured of being able to
use his muscles with competence, he had twisted himself around

to embrace her but avoid pressing himself against her breasts as a mammoth mudslide headed for them. He had been told quite a lot about that event, but he had no memory of being buried alive. The idea alone was enough to bring back a brain-freezing horror.[3]

Needing a powerful image to push away the shuddering, he thought of his father, across town. A wizened old man down in San Pedro harbor, hunkered down in a bungalow that was surrounded now by the Latino families whom he loathed as he wrote his bizarrely scholarly, obsessively footnoted articles for the racist eugenics magazines that they still published for some indescribable purpose in Denmark and Sweden and now Middle Europe. *The Aryan Comeback. Nord Ren. En Framtid för Våra Vito Barn* (A Future for our White Kids). *Tsar Lazar* – a compilation of racist screeds named for the ancient hero of Serbia who'd fought the Ottoman Turks.

Jack Liffey had received these articles in the mail for years, and some superstition had made him tuck them away in a closet rather than burn them immediately. *Don't try to explain any of that to yourself*, he insisted.

A siren sounded, then died. *You explain too much as it is*, he thought. *Just get yourself into the light right now and plan from there.* A big truck rumbled past him, and its headlights couldn't have missed picking him out, but the truck made no effort to stop and help a prostrate human form in the street. *Thanks a lot, guys. I must look terribly threatening down here – a cripple who's arm-crawling along the gutter.* Of course, this was the borderlands of Skid Row and he was probably no more unusual than a lot of other sights down here.

He could imagine driving on past just such a person himself. *What a sad case*, he would think. Probably drunk as a skunk. Don't want to get caught up in *that*, for sure. Everyone knew that the chances of saving a booze-martyr were almost negligible.

Within a short walking distance southwest of The Nickel – about seven minutes on foot nearer the ocean from where Jack Liffey crawled – near the fancy new sports arena known as Staples

[3] See *Palos Verdes Blue*, 2009.

Center, $1.5 billion has been committed for an elaborate development that included a $400 million luxury hotel financed, in critical part, by city funds. Far more than the city has ever spent on the homeless.

NINE
Armor Geddon

Two black boys squatted beside him, then rolled him over. 'You ridin' on candy, old man? Juiced? Maybe you take some dust.'

'Ack!'

'Don't be talkin' no chop suey now.' One young man, maybe sixteen years old, patted down Jack Liffey's jacket pockets. At the same time, he felt an exploring hand testing his pants. He knew the wallet was already gone. What was left? A Chapstick maybe. A pocket knife. Loose change.

A drawling caution came into the boy's voice. 'Waal, you don' move now, old man.' A hand dug and found something, a Chapstick that the boy studied for an instant and contemptuously flung away. Then he found the penknife, an expensive Swiss Army model. 'Hey, a uptick in life. Old woman promise some Freddy got a gift for me. Not much of a gift, but I guess you can't never want stuff too bad or the stuff end up lightweight.'

'Ack.'

'Don't blow no gaskets. I be get to like this new lingo you got the ack ack talk.' The boy stood up. 'Ack to you, dad. Ack-ack-ack.'

'This guy my favorite flavor. Bye, sucker.'

The boys walked away laughing, tossing his penknife back and forth between them, the one shouting 'Ack-ack!' every time he caught it, and 'Ack, my niggah!' when he tossed it back.

Jack Liffey was so addled that he addressed a kind of secular prayer to the fates who might or might not be watching over him. *Protect me with a plastic bubble, please. And protect Maeve, too.*

This was probably the worst spot in the city to find yourself lying defenseless and immobile in the street, even if there was a tickle in his legs now. Maybe they'd strip you even faster in Beverly Hills, he thought. No, that was sentimental nonsense. In Beverly Hills a man lying in the gutter would be ignored, as long as possible, but nobody would ever fish in a derelict's filthy pocket. Over there, the stealing was all done with a pen and a bogus smile.

He glanced around, looking for further danger. The human need was so desperate that almost anything had value – even a beat-up wheelchair. He was surprised they'd discarded the Chapstick.

He heard a truck engine approaching up the road, saw its head-lights flood the pavement, then heard the engine gun hard as if trying to get up the speed to run him over. He closed his eyes tight but the roaring missed him by several feet. The drizzle had dimin-ished to a slow sprinkling, a mist. He rolled and lay face up, the front of his clothing soaked through, and he felt the fresh prickling on his cheeks.

How ridiculously frail I am now, he thought. A few angry tots, still in their Pampers, could finish him off with their rattles, hammering away in some maddened infant frenzy. Imagining just that, he lay there laughing for a few moments, wondering if he was descending into a hysteria.

Were the gods of neurology laughing *with* him or *at* him? He rolled back to his stomach and tried to drag himself toward the curb with his arms. He made some progress but ran out of steam after three determined crawl-strokes. There were hints, just hints, of feeling in his legs. But something had drained all his energy. When he opened his eyes, an emaciated gray cat was stalking toward him to investigate.

'Ack!'

The hungry-looking wet cat halted and tried to fluff up to appear larger than life, but then a car approached, flooding light past him and sending the cat fleeing along the gutter, tail low.

Sorry, kitty, but I'm probably not edible, not without some chop-ping.

The car diverted by a wide margin, audibly squishing through gunk in the far gutter. He wondered who but cops would be driving down here now in this menacing dark. Maybe a Korean importer on his way home from the toy district. Maybe a lost tourist trying to find his way back to the Biltmore. A carload of high school thrillseekers.

'*Hombre*, you need a big hit of tequila.' A powerful-looking teenager, holding a long brown cigarette, knelt to stare at Jack Liffey's face, grasping his chin and twisting to get a better view. 'You my own Idaho. Not so bad. If we in jail, I make you my bitch.' He massaged Jack Liffey's ass. '*Bienvenidos*, cherry, eh, sweetie? I guess you lucky. Too cold tonight, way too wet, too *swami*.'

Swami? Jack Liffey thought.

'Good shoes. They worth something.'

He felt the comfy Rockports wrenched off his feet and was surprised he felt it at all. Maybe some sensation was returning.

'What the big nobs say? Walk a mile in my shoe, uh-huh. Maybe I will. But *El Chibo* always give full value. *Aqui, esse*.'

Jack Liffey tried to turn his head away from the cigarette – he hadn't smoked in over ten years – but the kid wrenched his jaw back.

'Don' be no *pendejo*. You suck on my Sherm or you suck somethin' else, eh? This a real gift – me to you.'

Jack Liffey inhaled and knew immediately the cigarette was laced with something. The skinny Shermans were notorious as conduits for angel dust. Shit! Just what he needed.

'Yeah, take a big one, man. I gotta give fair for you Rockafella shoes. They hardly use at all.'

Fingers pressed Jack Liffey's lips closed over the cigarette.

'Go, *hombre*. You a real man.'

He drew in a mouthful, trying not to inhale.

'No, no.'

The boy pounded on his back and Jack Liffey was jolted into inhaling, watching this all happen from far away. He began to feel the high, whatever it was, needle points dancing on his cheeks.

'Aole!' He exhaled and closed his teeth tight.

'Wan' more, *hombre*? Jus' so I be you tycoon tonight.'

He gave in and inhaled. He held it, like his last memory of working on a joint, maybe fifteen years back, his world starting to spin now. Why the hell not?

'Love you, man. You got pretty eyes. Bye-bye.'

He heard the footsteps recede as the spinning carried on and on. Christ – but maybe this was just what he needed to get through the night. Relax and accept it. You're just a piece of useless meat anyway. A siren sounded not far away, and he heard fire engines speeding out of a station, one tire squealing in a turn, but nothing came his way, not even a hint of their light.

Alone now, he thought. *Lying on my stomach and going dopey. OK, I am a fortress. Of all that I have done and known. It's all got to protect me now.* His spine tingled as the sounds of something small and living scrabbled along the gutter nearby. He turned his head. Rats. A running parade of big fat rats hustled past only a foot or two from his face. They leapt small piles of wet garbage, one after another, like children at follow-the-leader. Then they were gone, and he realized his jaw was clenched so hard it hurt.

Something like sheet lightning flashed above him, revealing his entire universe for an instant. Oddly, there was no sound to the lightning, only the urban rumbles and grumbles far away. He was dizzy and euphoric. For a moment he felt he could float upward, if he only willed it hard enough, let himself detach from the earth. Stay focused, he thought. This was the damn Sherm acting on him. Fight for control. The sleep of reason produces . . . what was it? Giant flying bats?

'Hey, Lonnie's it!' The voice of a child cut through his thoughts, and he wondered if he was hallucinating. Maybe the sheet lightning, too. Even the rats. But his shoes were truly gone.

'Ollie-ollie-oxen-free!'

A small hand pressed his shoulder and released. He screwed his neck around and saw four pairs of dirty sneakers, attached to four children, maybe eight or nine years old.

'Ack.'

'This guy's home base. Guess what?'

'No "guess what," fucker.'

'I say we playin'. I'll go to a hunnert by fives. Step off, fools!'

'I'm there!' Foot-sounds scattered.

'Five, ten, fifteen, twenty-five . . .'

Jack Liffey gave up and resigned himself to being home base for a while. And why not? His immobile lump of a body would serve a useful purpose, and it pleased the kids. The cruelty of the irony was almost perfect.

'Here I come, ready or not!'

How little things change, he thought. The same words he had cried out in hide-and-seek so many years ago, and now, in an irresistibly circular logic, he had become the big forked tree at the south end of the bridge in Averill Park, San Pedro. At least he could look forward to human touch in the near future – touch with no ulterior motive. *Lord, make me useful. I'm all raw perception now. I'm the done-to, the object, the sheer modesty of a person so without deceit he's only thing.* At least he was out in the open, not trapped in a dark hole that would stir up his gravest fears like the panic of claustrophobia.

Two sets of footsteps churned toward him, and almost simultaneously hands slapped his shoulder.

'Home free!'

'Jammie's it – ah, fuck it. Least y'all didn't have no time to oxen-free.'

'Brah, De-shayla hidin' behind the pottie. Bet you can go injun up and kiss her.'

'You the best, my shizzle.'

The soft plop of tennis shoes receded, and one of the small black boys sat down cross-legged to study Jack Liffey's face, like a Zen monk contemplating a candle flame. Jack Liffey wanted desperately to speak to the boy, ask about his life down here on The Nickel, where his mother was, if he was able to go to school. Anything.

'Ack.'

'You funny, man. Why you lay there?'

'Ack.'

'Ain' no answer. You a boozehound? But I ain' smell no booze.'

Jack Liffey shook his head as best he could, if only to try to put the boy's mind at rest.

The boy edged closer and patted his pockets, but finding nothing at all gave up. 'You be clowned on, ain't you? Not even no shoes. Hope I never be a sucka like dat.'

The streetlights, none too close anyway, went out for a few seconds, and it was as if everything in the city was holding its breath. It gave him the creeps – but the lights came back on and, weirdly, traffic sound seemed to resume at the same moment. More hallucination? A pause as he drifted downward into an even more malign universe?

'How you gone take a whizz, man? You in a bad way. You need all yo' shit together to do things right down here.'

A car approached and the boy jumped to his feet to wave the car away to guard his new charge.

Thank you, my friend, Jack Liffey thought.

'Fucker got to be careful.' He turned back to Jack Liffey. 'I born Cuba, man. Moms come on the boat a *long* time, when I little baby. She say she from some place call Sen-fway-gos, but the Cubans here all rich white mothahfuckas – they don' like they own niggahs. She say Fidel her man.'

Jack Liffey nodded.

'You like him, too?' The boy appeared surprised. 'I don't got much Cuba-talk, but I know who I is. My name Oswado.'

'Ack!' The frustration was reaching breaking point – he wanted badly to reach out to this boy.

'OK, you be Mister Ak. I be Oswald. That what they say here, but Moms say Oswado.'

Small running feet were on their way back, and, amazingly, Jack Liffey looked forward to the human touches.

Several tiny hands hit his shoulders, and he warmed up with a rush of sympathy for them all.

'Ollie-ollie-oxen-free-free-free!'

'Ah, fuck you, ho'. Cause I don' be kissing you ass an' be nice, you bus' my balls.'

'Hey, you kids! Leave that old man alone!' It was a deep woman's voice from somewhere toward the sidewalk. The children cursed her and stomped and objected but eventually scattered when she yelled several more times. In a few moments, a very large black woman peered at his face and then tugged him forcefully toward the curb in fits and starts.

'Dear heart, I see you in some trouble. Gonna get ran down out there. I save your butt.'

'Ack.'

She grabbed him by the jacket and pulled, and as he moved, he could see the mounds of wet filth approaching. He closed his eyes as he squished over them. Ah, Christ, what was it he was doing penance for? He knew this woman wasn't a hallucination. Powerful black women were always real.

'You some fall-down wino, Freddy?' She laughed a little. 'Sorry I laughin'. I know *you* ain' laughin' cuz you ain' laughin'. It all strike me funny, tho. Your hair gettin' thin on top, I can see you scabby head.'

Woman, male pattern baldness is the least of my problems, he thought.

'You got boojie-lookin' clotheses. You been take off and lef' here. Kin you nod, Freddy?'

He nodded, as she sucked in a big breath and yanked his face and chest over the curbing and up on to the sidewalk. She sat down with a sigh, duty done, and put his head on her ample lap.

'You can call me Precious, Fred. Problems jus' keep comin', ain' it the truff. I jus' hope you ain' no crack-head. I hates swiffers.'

He had no idea where she'd got the name. He'd never heard whites called Freds or Freddies.

'How you soul doin'?' she said, as she patted his head the way you'd pet a dog.

'Ack.'

'Myself I'm poetical in my soul,' she said. 'I have a story for you. I surely love a man who gots to listen.'

All the lights downtown went out again. He just happened to have a view of the skyscrapers a mile away, and it was a shock – like a nuclear attack. After a few seconds, there was a chorus of groans and cries in every direction.

'Whooo-wee,' his rescuer said. 'End of de worl'.'

Then the lights flickered back on, area by area, one of those unexplained power interruptions that happened about half the time that it rained anywhere in the city.

Then she told him a long, long tale about marrying a Pentecostal from her hometown in Arkansas, a childhood sweetheart, who'd joined the army and called himself, improbably, Armor Gedden. He'd been posted to Germany with the Second Armored 'Hell on Wheels' Division, but when she wouldn't join his church and bark out gibberish with him to attract the End Times, he eventually went AWOL and abandoned her in their military billet in Heidelberg.

She got herself to Frankfurt but fell through the Army's cracks and spent days and days knocking on doors in the immense Creighten Abrams Complex there, the center of all things American on Hansa Alee, always being sent on to some other building.

His attention was drifting a little, worrying about Maeve and fascinated by a new tingle in his leg. Jack Liffey did his best to keep his spirits up, but the tale went on and on, full of men acting like dogs and demanding her favors, with technicolor descriptions, and every chance to get home evaporating at the last minute. She told him she was finally forced to offer her fanciest favors to a colonel who got her home on compassionate something.

A police siren stiffened them both and the black-and-white car roared past, but headed for something that was well away.

Two old men shuffled past them on Sixth Street and she fell silent, caressing his forehead absent-mindedly. Next, next, he thought. That was the essence of story. *Tell me.*

Abruptly there were more footsteps. She set his head down on
the curb, a bit too hard, and got up to run toward them.

'Man, all I know is the spread,' a man said.

'Shawn! Is that you, lover? I be your true one, it Precious.' She
was almost bellowing, but there was a desperation in her voice that
Jack Liffey hated to hear. He had a feeling he'd never see her again,
and never hear the bitter end of her tale. He waited, but only silence
and faraway city noise answered.

He realized he'd never even got a proper name. What a shame,
he thought. Don't we all want to come back some day and shower
our affection on those who helped us when we were in need?

'Shawn!' he heard her desperate voice in the distance. 'My Titan
missile!'

After careful consideration, he started to crawl generally westward with terrible effort, maybe toward civilization. The sidewalk
was cracked and heaved up here and there, impeding him. After
little more than a block, and one perilous street crossing, the attempt
had just about drained him dry, when he heard a man's voice.

'Man, s'up wit' you? Look like you went an' felled pretty hard.'

'Ack-ack.' The voice was friendly and sympathetic, but he was
tired of saviors who ripped him off or absconded. Jack Liffey rolled
on to his shoulder, to where he could see the middle-aged black
man squatting a few feet away. He wore a sweatshirt, ragged camo
pants and an L.A. baseball cap. Dodger blue.

'You hurt?'

What to answer to that, even if he could?

The man got up and patted his pockets. 'You got some niceside
clothes. Like you be dipped in butter sauce. But you got nothin' in
here. You been robbed bad, ain't it? Cain't you talk, man?'

He shook his head hard.

'Cain't talk, cain't walk. You a sad case. Don't you worry now
– Chopper ain't gonna leave no one to rot in no street, not now and
not never. And not some genna'man be turnin' up at dinnertime.'

The man got his hand in Jack Liffey's armpit and, surprisingly
strong, he dragged him away from the curb, toward two refrigerator boxes, abutting and attached, tented over with blue plastic.
Beside the doorway, an old food can was steaming on a grille set
on bricks over a can of Sterno. He realized how much he hurt all
over from the beating. And then he squeezed his eyes shut, morti-
fied, because he could do nothing at all for Maeve.

'You get the guest room, friend. My name Chopper Tyrus, and don't let that name worry you none. I don' be choppin' nothin' but cotton. That all ancient history.' Jack Liffey felt himself lugged by stages closer to the doorway. 'I think I call you Richard, my genna'man. I always partial to that name. And I hope you got a taste for ham 'n' motha-fuckahs for dinner.' He laughed. 'Tha's beans an' franks to you this wet night, for real. Just jokin' 'bout what we call that whack C-ration that ever'body hate back in Nam – the ham 'n' limas. Shit, and always just four fuckin' cigarettes. Seem I always got Kools.'

Jack Liffey remembered it clearly, indeed, even from his posting in the radar trailer in Thailand. They hadn't been called C-rations any more, not officially, but everybody still did, anyway, and ham-and-limas was the one that you could never trade away, especially for the prized spaghetti and meatballs or the steak and potatoes.

'You been in the big Nam, Richard? You look 'bout the right age.'

He'd actually been in Thailand most of his tour, but he was part of the whole fucked-up event, and he'd been over to Nam often enough on R-and-R to nod now without feeling bad about it.

'No money an' no voice. You don' got much to contribute tonight, do you, Richard?'

My luggage is coming along later, Jack Liffey thought.

Los Angeles has approximately 85,000 homeless people. It may not seem much for a city of four million, but New York City, with almost twice the population, has only about 40,000 homeless people. Chicago has less than 10,000 and San Francisco about the same. What does distinguish homelessness in Los Angeles is how few of its homeless are sheltered – approximately 21 per cent compared to 57 per cent in San Francisco and more than 90 per cent in Philadelphia, Denver, or New York City. These cities have made the political decision to try to house anyone who needs and wants a roof. Los Angeles has not.

TEN
Reality is a Hardship for the Prissy

I t was only a ten-minute drive home from The Nickel so Gloria headed east on Fourth Street to see if Maeve had just fallen dead asleep at home and was ignoring her cell. It was a cinch Jack wasn't going to answer anything. She stopped illegally on the long and narrow 1930s' viaduct that spanned riverbed and rail yards, just after the weird triumphal arch rising weirdly out of its side rails. She stepped out of the car, stared downward for a moment at the chemical-tainted rainbow-slick on the water flowing south in the channel, maybe twenty feet wide, that ran off-center in the broader concrete river. A car pulled out to pass her, honked as if annoyed, and she turned and gave it the finger. Then she slowly tore up the photograph of the nun's painting of Jack Liffey, doubled and tore again, letting pieces flutter away into the shadows far down below.

The nerve of that bitch. Trying to saddle her with a memento of her own love for Jack. Naïve only went so far, Miss Nun. *It's out of your control, woman. I may have had my doubts about the guy, but he belongs to me now, even if he is a basket case.*

She stewed over it the rest of the way home, something about her own destructiveness in ripping the photo to shreds having disturbed her deep inside, until suddenly all her sour jealous rage blew away in an instant. She braked to a harsh stop on Greenwood, right in front of her geraniums. The front door stood wide open with the living room light pouring out unnaturally and every bug on earth heading for it. And his pickup was gone. She left her car running and sprinted for the door, yanking out her service pistol on instinct.

'Maeve! Jack!' She paused a second on the porch. 'This is LAPD, Sergeant Ramirez! If you're a burglar, you got two seconds to get on your face or you're dead where you stand!'

She came in slowly, her eyes scanning the front room with care. Nothing. She knew she should call for backup, but this was different, and she rushed the kitchen with the pistol thrust ahead of her, some of her training evaporating in the face of this violation of her personal space and the alarm over her vulnerable loved ones.

She checked the pantry before moving on, starting to get a grip and shutting doors behind her now. She would hear anything come open. She found the old house landline phone with its receiver smashed – something Jack might do in frustration. Loco glanced up at her curiously from the back porch, but the screen door was hooked and no one had come in or out that way. The dog wasn't alerting on anything, if he still had it in him, but he did look uneasy. In another few minutes of rampaging through the convoluted old two-story house, she'd satisfied herself that there were no home invaders in any closet, or under a bed, or behind the shower curtain. At least no one over a foot tall. And she knew for a fact that neither Maeve nor Jack was at home either. Not good news – not in Jack's case especially – unless maybe he and Maeve had left together. But it would have been a real struggle for Maeve to move Jack by herself. And where was Jack's car? Gloria finally stuffed her Glock .40 back into the holster clipped against her skirt.

She hated herself for it, but she went straight to the fridge and opened a beer. She'd had a twelve-hour police shift and a four-hour shift of her own and she was beat. *Corona, don't fail me now.*

After sucking down half of it, she called Jack's ex-wife Kathy in Redondo and discreetly found out that neither Jack nor Maeve was down there. OK, when it's the end of the world, who do you call? Everybody has someone. Someone you never wanted nor expected to see failure in their face.

She speed-dialed three. It was the cell of Paula Green, her best friend from the Academy, who'd offended somebody upstairs and been stuck in the Foothill station in Pacoima in the north San Fernando Valley for three years – for a black woman it was like being assigned as liaison to Guadalajara.

'Green.'

'Paula, thank god. This is Glor. I really need a friend.'

'Don't hyperventilate, girl. You know you got one.'

Chopper laid out a thick bedding of newspapers on the far side of his small cardboard home, for insulation and padding, and then offered Jack Liffey a fraying blanket he'd borrowed from the tent next door. He had a thin old foam pad for himself and a comforter that was leaking stuffing.

'Well, Richard, we best beat a retreat indoors. They more rain on the way. Lot of skipskaps push theyselves into the missions on the rain nights, but we got a nice dry home out here. And safe from all them steal-me-Elmos. Can't trust nobody indoors.'

He dragged Jack Liffey foot-by-foot into the shelter and on to the newspaper padding, and then settled the blanket over him. Almost immediately a patter started up on the plastic over the top of the fridge boxes, then steadied, curiously like the sound of fire. 'Stay warm, man. Better to stay than fight to get there.'

Jack Liffey made a gesture of writing on his palm.

'I get you. We a little short a' pens and pencils in here, Richard. And I ain't so good with readin' neither. Got some a' that dis-lexus thing with words I been tole.' He lit an old olive-colored kerosene lantern with a cracked glass chimney and set it in the doorway, though once Jack Liffey's eyes had adjusted, he could see a faint glow of the city still reflected off the clouds over the buildings. The rosy warmth of the lantern felt good and the local light was immensely reassuring. Jack Liffey had never in his life felt quite so helpless. He almost laughed at himself, at how, some time back, how dependent he had once *thought* he'd been, when he was still in a comfortable wheelchair, and still had shoes and a wallet, and a writing pad, and a world of loved ones around him. Now he had none of that, but he'd certainly become well-traveled in misfortune.

'Hey dere, perfessors,' Chopper called out to a pair of cops walking past, the nearest one a black woman. They wore long transparent raincoats and plastic shower caps over their hats.

The woman squatted down to peer inside.

'Good evening, Mr Tyrus. S'up witchou?'

'Nothin' pricey. I be shelterin' a new frien' and he cain' hardly talk. He a real moot. Man want to write to me. Either of you got a ol' pencil stub to borrow me?'

The male cop remained disdainfully back from the boxes, on his guard, while the woman patted her shirt through the transparent plastic. She dug out an old Bic and handed it to Chopper. 'Who you got back there? You didn't go and mug Mr Richie Rich, did you, Chopper? That's not like you. Are you OK, sir?'

She pushed the lantern aside and crawled half into the shelter, shining her flashlight on Jack Liffey's face. A kind of stubbornness made him nod, rather than put himself into the care of the police.

'Why don't you write me your name, sir? And your last address.'

Just as she was digging for a notebook, a powerful car accelerated past them, and Jack Liffey caught sight of the tail end of a police car. Both of their chest-pack radios started squawking orders. Then a siren whooped from the fleeing car.

'Gotta go, Diana,' the male cop announced. 'Ten-thirty-two. Gun – it's just two blocks away.'

'You take care of yourself, sir,' the woman said, as she patted Jack Liffey's leg. 'Chopper's a little schizy but he's harmless, and I happen to know he got a great big heart.' She patted Chopper's leg and backed out of the shelter. The two cops hurried off.

'Why she gotta say that?' Chopper complained. 'I as rationalistic as a sober judge. Here, Richard. Write your name on some a' that paper under you.'

IM JACK. THANK YOU, CHOPPER. He wrote big and slowly in the wide margin of a display ad from the *Times*, then showed it to Chopper, who laboriously sounded out the message, let it sink in and seemed to comprehend it as part of a slow process of absorption.

'You *Jack*, not Richard. OK, Jack. Give me pounds.'

He held out a fist and Jack Liffey returned the old greeting as best he could, a couple of fist-bumps and then a finger-clasp up and down and a pull-away. They both smiled, knowing its Nam roots.

'Knowledge is power,' Chopper said. 'Good Conduct.'

Jack Liffey had a tattoo on his upper arm that proclaimed those very two words – acquired on Tu Do Street during a night of drunken revelry, under the superstitious urge to stay out of trouble long enough to get home unkilled. He was tempted to show the forlorn message to Chopper, but the air was just too cold for any disrobing. He'd read recently that they'd renamed Tu Do Street these days. It was Dong Khoi now – which was supposed to mean *uprising*. Why not – it was their country. They could call it Death to Americans, if they wanted.

MY WHEELCHAIR WAS STOLEN.

This one was much harder for Chopper to decipher, but it seemed only a matter of time and false-starts, because eventually the man nodded with great gravity and repeated it aloud.

'That's so low. They's hitters out dere gonna steal yo' dirty underpants wit' you in 'em.'

I WILL PAY YOU TO CALL MY WIFE TO COME GET ME.
TOMORROW. Somehow, Jack Liffey just couldn't bear any more
humiliation tonight, and he didn't want to move any of his aches
and pains. He was relatively comfortable in his exhaustion where
he lay, and he felt a kind of loyalty to Chopper's hospitality. It
might do him some good in the general humility sweepstakes to
spend a night on The Nickel, especially with this gentleman that
he'd been assured by the cops was trustworthy – if a little off his
rocker.

Chopper finally mouthed out the message and took it in without
a hint of questioning Jack Liffey's motives for waiting until the
next day. 'OK, Richard . . . Jack. Tonight I beat you at chess.'

Oh, *shit*, Jack Liffey thought. He hated chess, a game that required
insane concentration. He'd played seriously for a while in high
school, until his friends had started reading books on it, and then
he'd walked away from the game until forced to play it again by
his buddies in the radar outpost in Thailand, where there was virtually nothing else to do. As far as he was concerned, chess was a
dark angel that thrived on OCD. Too much eyeball-to-eyeball, too
much descent into some as-yet-to-be mapped intensity center of the
brain that he had little access to.

One of his missing-child cases had carried him into a strange
cultish circle that had worshipped Jack Parsons, the Jet Propulsion
Lab scientist (and devotee of the black magician Aleister Crowley)
who had blown himself up in his home in Pasadena in the 1950s.
Parsons had left a note before the blast: 'I saw those guys playing
chess and suddenly decided that I did not want to end up like them.'
Yes.

But Jack Liffey reclined on his elbow like a Roman feaster and
resignedly watched Chopper Tyrus set up a tiny traveling peg-seated
chess set between them. What the hell. One night.

Chopper took white, and Jack Liffey knew within a few moves
that he'd be OK for the night. Chopper played jailbird chess, speed
chess – every fervent move chosen within a few seconds, never
thinking more than one move ahead. It was like playing with
Tweetybird on crack. '*Ooooh, look! A move!*'

Jailbird chess was so subversive of the choking intensity of the
game as he'd known it that he wouldn't be challenged at all. For
one evening he could be a good sport.

                            *   *   *

Paula came immediately, as Gloria knew she would, toting a little
overnight bag that said OJB on the side. That was for Oscar Joel
Bryant, the name of a black L.A. cop who'd died arresting three
gunmen in the 1960s. The LAPD's African-American officers association was named for him.

'Thanks a bunch for coming, Paula. Your Captain up there in the
far valley still calling you a *nee*gress?'

'I think somebody got him wise. I'm black now. Not African-
American, mind you, but you can't expect some of these guys to
get too sensitive all at once.'

'No, it would probably signal the end of the world. President or
not. Thanks again.'

'You don't send out a distress signal because there's a little leak
under your sink.'

'Maeve and Jack are both missing.' She handed Paula a beer and
the woman took it and sat heavily. 'Either separately or together. I
don't even know. Her car's gone. His car's gone. The front door
was standing open when I came home. That's not a good sign.'

'Jack's still . . . the same?'

'Same old same old. Maeve is playing PI a bit again, looking
for a missing boy. Supposedly she was just making the first moves
in order to crank Jack's motor a bit. The boy is the son of an old
friend of his.'

'So do we go after this boy or Maeve or Jack?'

'As far as I can tell, it's mostly taking place on Skid Row so
maybe we can do it all.'

'Oh, OK. Only thirty or forty square blocks of missions and
flops and dead old buildings. And more cardboard tents than you
can peek inside in a week. In the rain. That ought to be a snap.'

'And flesh-eating bacteria if you touch the wrong skell. Or triple-
TB – the nasty one that meds can't stop.'

'Shit, we could all end up in *Magic Mountain*.'

'The amusement park?'

Paula swigged down some more beer and smiled. 'The book.
It's about a TB asylum. Never mind. Should we do it now?'

'All I needed was your moral support to get me back there. I've
been around the block a few times with no luck, but I didn't look
under every leaf. I'm sorry to drag you out, but I just can't leave
Jack out in that hard rain, not in his condition. I talked to the locals
down there but those boneless cops were no use. Rookies.'

Paula nodded. 'Don't I know them. Last week I got called to a banging in east Pacoima. The kid who was shot was still lying on the porch, very dead, waiting for the coroner, and three cops were interviewing his pals. This was all taking place in Spanish, of course.

'Then I heard a shriek – "*El mismo carro!*" – from one of the kids. I recognized the sound of a throaty old 1950s' muscle car rolling up the street behind me.

'When I turned, I saw an Impala low-rider with faces and head-bands in all the windows, and I just went into some deep instinct. I walked across the yard and pointed straight at the car like an old witch. The car took off fast without even anybody waving a *pistolo* or throwing sign. When I looked back at the porch, that whole crowd of macho men had emptied itself inside the house. Forget backing me up.'

She drank off the beer. 'I admit I was scared to death, and it was a fairly dumb move, but, you know, it wasn't the kids in that car that got me – I hate to say, but even to save my damn life I wasn't gonna be seen backing off by a bunch of guys on the job. Maybe I'll leave Foothill Station a legend.'

'You're a legend right now, girl.'

'Fuck me, Eddie – you give to that bitch and her Home For All?' Moses Vartabedian exclaimed. 'That's just one loud-mouth nun.'

Vartabedian fussed with a black stogie, then reamed the end with his gold cigar tool.

'Shit, yeah,' Wolverton said. 'Give the do-goods a little public help. It sends a signal when the feature writers come around.' Indeed, he thought. He still remembered the woman from *L.A. Loft Living* who'd talked amazingly dirty for three solid minutes while she was stripping for him and then had done a few tricks on the carpet he'd only really heard about.

'You don't mean that.'

'Actually, I do, V. I'm not that cynical. I really do believe in helping the homeless. We're gonna coexist down here, like it or not.'

'What do you guys think?' Vartabedian exhaled smoke from the stogie and glared at his two hirelings, McCall and Thibodeaux, who seemed content to stand either side of his door like mismatched stone lions.

'Nobody remembers givers for shit,' McCall said. 'Just look at

the world's greatest taker.' He flicked his head at Thibodeaux, who
was running a finger along his unopened switchblade as if petting
the head of a snake. 'Nobody ever forgets Rice.'

Thibodeaux snicked the blade out, as if on signal, then walked
the open knife end-to-end along his fingers in a showy way, like
George Raft with a quarter on his knuckles. Having their full attention, he concluded his act by pretending to saw his own dick off.

No, Wolverton thought, flapping away Vartabedian's smoke. Even
if he had fifty more years of the architectural redesign of these
insipid beaux-arts buildings in Downtown and all the other half-
assed gentrifying, and having to chum up with other slippery
shmucks like Vartabedian who had the money to finance it all, he'd
probably never forget this one job and this one little loon who'd
turned up somehow on it. It was a pretty big job, worth a million
and change for his studio, or he'd've checked out already, maybe
start on the hill house that Madonna had wrecked above the reservoir that was waiting now for a fresh look, or hunt up that magazine chick for a second interview, though he couldn't even remember
her name or what it was exactly that she'd been howling there at
the end when she was down on all fours.

'I'm about to miss the ballet,' Wolverton said. 'Can we get on
with this?'

'Ballet?' the big Armenian said.

'It's a joke, V.'

'You got a funny sense of humor, Eddie. The problem is real
easy. We got a couple days to clear out the Fortnum and get started
or our permits expire. There won't be no extensions. That HFA nun
and her ilk have been to the *Times* and the permits people and
complained that we're bidding up the prices so much that the goody-
two-shoes can't set up no more flophouses. Just what Downtown
fucking needs – a bunch more flops for winos. These jerkoffs want
to see some kind of *Blade Runner* out there.'

'I liked *Blade Runner*,' Wolverton mused.

Vartabedian winced. 'I liked *Godzilla*, too, but I don't want to
live with him.'

'Godzilla!' Rice Thibodeaux cried out, as if activated by a magic
word. He swung his arm blindly and slammed the knife into the
lovely rosewood door, an inch from McCall's ear, who stirred his
golden ringlet curls by pulling slowly away. Steve McCall rotated
his neck glacially toward his partner.

'Don't even nick me, mouse. I got a .50-caliber Desert Eagle I could stick in your ear any damn time.'

Thibodeaux gave a lopsided smile. 'Face-to-face, ten feet apart. Quick draw on your pathetic gun and my knife. Any time you say.'

'Gentlemen, *please*,' Vartabedian said. 'You already have a job on your plate. And a plan.'

This idea of a settled plan was what worried Eddie Wolverton. His reputation would be ruined if one of his remodels was caught up in some kind of wildcat thuggery. 'What's the plan, Stan?'

'We'll get the bitter-enders out of the hotel real soon.' McCall raised his palms to calm the others. 'No one will be hurt. The Fortnum got no elevators now, no heat, no water. And they know we're threatening two of their buddies. The message is clear. Living there is asshole deep in the shit, and they got them a generous offer from Mr V. to move on.'

Wolverton glanced once at Thibodeaux who was waggling his switchblade to pry it out of the once-perfect door, then he glanced at Vartabedian. 'This is terrific, Vart,' Wolverton said. 'My firm is lead architect of record. We're mostly done with the plans. But I don't need any . . . what you say, bad press.'

'You take your commission, *hombre*,' Vartabedian snorted. 'Reality is always a hardship for you prissy guys. We're both whores for the bucks, and you know it.'

'Maeve?'

'I'm so exhausted.' It wasn't quite her own voice. She opened one eye and everything around her was dark. No movement. The animal, whatever it was, had apparently gone some time ago, and she'd almost fallen asleep. Maybe she had.

'Me, too. I need you to help me remember a lyric.'

Her anger flared for an instant. How narcissistic could this guy be? They were handcuffed to pipes, prisoners of dangerous loonies, and he wanted help with his career.

'I know it's stupid,' he went on. 'But I've got to remember it. I've been working in my head so long it's going to get lost.'

'Go on,' Maeve said dejectedly. 'We'll both memorize it line by line.'

'Oh, Maeve. You're a princess.'

They went through it one line at time, repeating each back and forth until they were sure they had it:

'Well I been to L.A. and to the lights of San Diego,
And I been up to Frisco, and to the frontera de Mexico
But I can't see no godhead, wherever I go.

My junior high woman, she said she loved me, but I know it was a
*   lie.*
My high school woman, she said the same, and I know she told a
*   lie.*
It's all dark now, and I lay here and cry.'

There were two more verses with the same chorus, plus a catchy
drumbeat that he rapped out on the floor, and Maeve found she
actually liked the song.

He opened with his king pawn once again. Chopper countered
with a wacky knight opening that Jack Liffey hadn't seen since
high school. His eyes were beginning to sag with fatigue in the
lantern light, and he decided to play this one out and then insist
on sleep. The speed games didn't take all that long. Big rain-
drops pattered like fingertips, almost countable, on the plastic
over the boxes, and small gusts flickered the lantern and rustled
up the newspapers under him. Now and again people hurried
past.

   'This your rent, Jack. Obliging me so kind.' He pronounced it
o-bul-idg-ing, which probably meant that at some time he'd sounded
the word out slowly and had never heard it in daily conversation.
'I can see you pretty tired. You got to enjoy the moment you in,
friend. Who know how many fine games you gonna get wit' a friend
like Chopper?' He chuckled.

   Jack Liffey brought out a bishop recklessly and drew an appre-
ciative nod from his opponent, who snapped a tiny pawn down hard
into its peghole like a Jamaican playing dominoes.

   'Whoa,' Jack Liffey said.

   The other man didn't react for a moment, nor did Jack Liffey.
Though the universe seemed to have shifted on its axis. He felt
there was another presence there, watching him. Was he still alone
in his life?

   Chopper's eyes came up. 'Man, you just done *spoke*. Do it again.'

   'Whoa. Whoa.' Jack Liffey grinned in amazement, even laughed silently. He moved his lips into position for something more complex. 'Ack. Ack.'

Damn. Quickly, he tried to get back to *Whoa*, but he couldn't find his place, like a book he'd dropped and it had fallen shut. He seemed to have lost the knack of connecting words and sounds. He shrugged and sighed. 'Ack,' he said sadly. Another sound had come out only a moment ago. Maybe it would come again, then a third.

'Don't get down on yo'self. Maybe some mornin' you wake up, be recitin' the Gets-a-bird *ad*-dress.'

Fourscore and seven years ago, he thought with eloquent precision. *Our forefathers brought forth on this continent* . . . His mouth muscles would not make any of the adjustments necessary for those words. 'Ack.' *It's all in your head, Jack. It's all trauma, irrational clutching fear.* The tingle was in his legs again and he imagined a toe moving. These tics were like promises from a mischievous god.

'*Ack!*' he bit off one more angry attempt.

'Don't go there right now, man.'

OK, this is just the peewee league of bad, Jack Liffey thought. There's cancer and third-degree burns and being gnawed to death by wolverines. He laughed aloud at his own thoughts, but all that came out were puffs of air.

'Let it be, Richard. You take one night at a time.'

They climbed back into Gloria's RAV-4, both pretty well done in by exhaustion. It was 4:30 a.m. and even the night-owls of The Nickel had run out of hoots and perched somewhere. Here and there in the corner of her eye a shadow disappeared down an alley, but no one stirred openly in all that gloom. Gloria knew it had not been possible to stick their heads into every flop and tent and cardboard condo to hunt down Jack or Maeve or the boy.

'We done our best, I think,' Gloria said. 'For one night. Let's say nobody gonna die in one night.'

'I'm game for another block, if you are.'

Paula and Gloria looked at one another, sliding in and out of focus, then both laughed at the presumption that they were alert.

'Jack's a big boy, even if he is lame and mute,' Gloria said. 'We ain' gonna do him no good like this, we draggin' ass. I'm a walkin' zombie, girl.'

'I don't know how to have these conversations,' Paula said.

'Normally I got no give-up. But, I will say I'm sinking into the plant kingdom.'

Gloria smiled. 'I've been up twenty-four hours a hundred times on the job, but tonight I'm starting to get those waking dreams. Ever have that?'

'Maybe so. You know what I see when it come? I see the night back in the day that I answered a radio call to that ol' Chippendale's club on Overland. I badge in the door to a thousand screaming women. They all be jumping up and down watching men strippers dressed like cops and cowboys an' shit. It's like the sight of those women burned theyselves on my retina to stay forever. Jeez, girl. They was such heat in that room, but it wasn't no normal pussy heat. I think it was some kind of sex-kill they wanted – kill all men forever.'

'Crap,' Gloria said. 'Men ain' the real problem.' They both sat in silence for a while. 'I really get the vision thing sometimes. Last week in the early morning, I saw a plains Indian in all that feather headdress and buckskin shit stand right there in front of the car and point at me like he wanted me. I think he wanted to warn me about something. I even got out of the car, but, course, he wasn't there.'

'You know, girl,' Paula said. 'Neither of us done give birth to no babies. Maybe something trying to get out of us late at night.'

Gloria reached out and squeezed Paula's hand. 'Sweetie, it's too dark and rainy for talk like that. We'll end up saying we in love just 'cause we know how the other one feel inside. Let's direct ourselves out of this bad place to a warm house with beds.'

'I could sleep on your sofa fine,' Paula said.

'Girl, I could sleep on a atom bomb tonight,' Gloria said.

Across Los Angeles County, there are roughly thirteen persons with severe mental disorders for every shelter space available.

ELEVEN
The House of Pain

Jack Liffey was awake well before the sun, the oblong of sky he could see, over the brickwork opposite, grown just perceptibly brighter than the ambient black. He was conscious of the pungent smells of urine and human shit, then rotting food, and something else that was a bit fishy – maybe the body odor of his chess-partner snoring away across the cardboard shelter.

Slowly he began to realize what had woken him so early in the still-dark. A raspy sound was drawing near, unpleasantly, like an army of devils grinding away the surface of the world. Just as the sound reached crescendo, headlights lit the gutter and a street sweeper burst into view in his small frame of reference and lumbered wetly past. He wondered if they'd chosen to sweep Skid Row so early on purpose, to annoy and awaken all these non-taxpayers. He knew that many building owners on The Nickel hosed down the sidewalks for just that purpose. He could sense that he still had his wristwatch – it was only a Timex and had either been overlooked or hadn't been worth stealing. It was still too dark inside the box to read the time.

He dozed off again, awoke to see unlaced tennis shoes hurrying past, then dozed again. Finally, day was unmistakably arriving, then gloriously. The rain was over. Sun flooded down with its promise of renewal. Hallelujah. The worst had not happened. He felt a strange excitement, almost elation. He was truly out among the masses of the most wretched of his country's poor, and he was all right. Someone had come out of nowhere to help him. Chopper Tyrus. Wonderful name. Bless him; bless all humanity.

His arms were doing fine this morning and he managed to sit up and shunt himself gradually into the entrance of the boxes, keeping the blanket over his shoulders. Chopper Tyrus apparently had the knack of sleeping soundly well past dawn. A sign of depression? The activity outside slowly picked up, individuals and then groups walking past, presumably migrating toward breakfast, or propelled by other needs. A few greeted him graciously and he nodded. Cars and trucks shished past on the slick wet. He had a desperate need to pee. He'd have worried about Maeve, but for some reason, after listening to golden-curls, he had never taken the threat against her seriously.

The damp road was just beginning to lose its sheen when his companion had a coughing fit to mark his awakening.

'Ack-ack,' Jack Liffey said. *Good Morning*.

The man blinked a few times and glanced over.

'Why, Richard! You still right here.'

Chopper Tyrus crawled past him and then stumbled out to pee for an inordinately long time through the hurricane fence beside their house. Then he came back and got Jack Liffey and propped him on his knees against the fence a few feet along, and let him handle the rest. Such a relief! His knees wobbled, but the legs seemed to be adding a little strength to his posture – until he finished and let go of the chain-link with his hands and crumpled like a sack of doorknobs. Damn.

'You, *Jack* – I disremember.' Chopper helped him back to the tent. 'Every man due his real name in truth. I's supposed to call home for you this morning. I know a place wid a heart, lets us make a 'mergency call. Right after morning coffee. That be OK with you?'

Jack Liffey nodded happily, and the man began scaring up what he would need from the corners of his gracious home.

Maeve, too, woke in an agony of needing to pee. Her bowels were telegraphing spasms, and her mouth was sticky, her lips glued together. Light diffused through the awful room, showing what it was – a series of half collapsed grey cubicles. Dozens of wire conduits dangled from the ceiling, an upside-down forest.

She saw no evidence of the animal life that had worried her so, not even droppings.

'Conor!'

'Yes, Maeve. Good morning to you.'

'How are we going to pee?'

'I'm afraid I've already gone in my pants. It's a humiliation.'

'Oh, crud. At least I read that pee is sterile.'

'Hey, that's reassuring.'

'No snark, pal, don't start,' she said. 'Did you get some sleep?'

'A little. Thanks. I'm pretty sore and stiff. How about you?'

'I've been worse, but not in this life.' She felt a strange kinship to her father's impairments, but she also realized how lost and alone his disabilities had been making her feel. No self-pity today, please. 'Any songs this morning?'

'Don't be mean, Maeve.'

'Any ideas about escape?'

'Most of my thoughts in that direction deal with superpowers that I don't seem to possess,' he said. 'I'm the wrong generation. Mostly I missed comic books for music. My dad talks about his dad reading him Tom Swift books. You know those?'

'No. I did read a Nancy Drew once. It was pretty sappy and her boyfriend showed up to save her. Not going to happen, is it?' Her last boyfriend had been a girlfriend in any case – a lovely, brilliant girl who'd taught her how to drink absinthe, and had been hustled off to a private school called Le Rosey in Switzerland as soon as her parents found out what was going on.

'Conor, can you try to saw your handcuffs on the pipe or something? We've got to get out of here.'

'It's not that easy,' he said glumly. 'My feet are attached to a chain that only lets me move a couple of inches. There's nothing at all in my little orbit. Nothing.'

'Do what you can.' She started sawing away with her own handcuffs against the pipe.

Chopper Tyrus had thoughtfully propped him up against a building before writing the number down and going off to telephone. The boiled coffee was pretty dreadful but – not to seem ungrateful – Jack Liffey went on sipping it from a small tin can from time to time. He nodded to passersby, once bumped fists with a young black man who had paused and spoken to him, and he managed to make it understood with gesture and gulps that he couldn't talk. He felt like a goldfish who'd splashed to the floor, taking big hopeless breaths. Mostly he just watched the passing parade of the homeless, having no real game plan, alone in his life. Gloria would come before too long, and he knew this was the last hour or so of his edgy detachment as a non-speaking non-person, in a universe that did not generally value that option very highly.

He was still Other for now, he thought. He was pure object, pure outsider, the done-to. Metaphysics didn't really interest him, but as an immobile mute he seemed to have become nothing but metaphysics. There weren't even many distractions to escape the whirling of his thoughts.

And isn't everyone driven to try to kill the Other in some way? That primeval fear of the unknown. But maybe what everyone really wanted was to undo the terrible distance between them and the Other – to undo the Human Condition. Fat chance, he thought. He tried to laugh at himself for the rank sentimentality of that idea, but no sound would come out. That was the kind of idea that would always get sand kicked in its face by a bully on the beach – or get its wallet and shoes and wheelchair stolen. Soon Gloria would come, and he'd need to be quite hard-headed and sensible again. He tested one leg after another, then his voice. Nothing worked, but it all had a different feel this morning, a hopefulness.

He watched a one-legged pigeon fight other pigeons for a paper plate of soggy food that had been abandoned along the fence. The lame pigeon kept being muscled out, and every fiber of his being wanted to help. *That's how hard-headed you are*, he thought. But wasn't it a deep human responsibility to help the weak? How did we keep children alive through the age of the saber-toothed tiger? How long would Einstein or Joyce have lasted, thrown into a pit of gladiators? Why should the strong and ruthless always win?

When he glanced up, his mind went into a kind of overdrive of shock. It was amazing how immediately he recognized her after ten years – Eleanor Ong, ex-nun, his first great love after leaving his wife, a relationship that had been supremely intense for a fleeting time that might as well have been forever. She smiled enigmatically at him from only a few feet away, holding the handles of some sort of transport chair – four little wobble-wheels and a canvas seat on a light frame.

Too much remembrance flooded back at once, and too many emotions. His brain was a mood-light spinning madly through its colors. He remembered he'd been her first lover. Along the banks of the Sespe River. The power of that dewy innocence taking off her sweater for the first time for a man while well into her forties. How impossibly tight her portal had been after years in the convent. Then, later, he'd almost got her killed – that was the overriding memory – dumped into a storm drain by thugs during a rainstorm, and the jeopardy of his own life frightening her back into her convent of renunciation and silence.

'Oh, Jack, it's so good to see you,' she said. His mind whirled into another reality.

So much for her silence, he thought. If only *he* had permission to speak, too. There was so much to say. He felt tears running down his cheeks.

Beside her, Chopper Tyrus stared curiously at Jack Liffey. 'She seem to know your name.'

'I met Gloria looking for you yesterday, Jack,' Eleanor said. 'And I knew you were around here. A white man with bright blue eyes, this friend of yours tells me this morning. Name of Jack.'

'Ack-ack!'

'Don't, please. I know you're in trouble. I offer both of you a healthy breakfast at our shelter, and then we'll make your call and get Gloria over here.'

'Whoa!' Was that his voice? His elusive second sound was back.

'Moms was a gentle woman,' Paula said in the car that was awash in a hopeful morning light. 'Of course, she was also a schizophrenic who couldn't find it in her strength to take her meds regularly, so eventually I was taken away from her and put in a home. The less said. But I got to *say*.'

'I was fostered out, too,' Gloria said. 'You know that. That's probably how we recognized each other.'

Paula nodded as Gloria drove west toward The Nickel. She was not to be denied the rest of the story that she'd held back for years. They hadn't had much sleep, but it was going to have to do. 'My new home was a kind of school of violence, with the fosters turning their thumbs down like Caesars as they pitted the rough girls against theyselves. They didn't know nothing but to put their anger out there. Sometimes it was yelling, sometimes a weird passive burn and yell thing, but mostly it was hitting and biting and scratching. Every Thursday was rope-a-dope night. Two of us was picked to fight it out.'

'That's awful!' Gloria stopped at a light and watched an old man on a bicycle cross their path. His bicycle was adorned with a big plywood airplane tail and he hauled a wire trailer containing recyclables. The old man stood on the pedals to get his contraption going, eying the gutters and sidewalks for ready money. The light changed and Gloria waited for the whole rigamarole to inch past before starting up.

'After I been beaten to a pulp enough, I learned what I had to.' Paula wiggled her broad nose for a moment like a rabbit remembering a nose punch, then rubbed it with the back of her hand. 'I learned to use my own anger. I learned to live with a bit of pain, and mostly I learned to take me some satisfaction from the pain that I could inflict. Moms and her schizo gentleness was long gone. She came to seem nothing but a dream of a lost world.'

Gloria was about to say something about her own mom – who'd tumbled into a fog of alcoholism – but decided it would be insensitive just then. 'What lousy fosters you was dealt. Is your mom alive?'

'No. She kept her meds in a secret place for weeks and then took them all at once. She's in a happier place, if there is one.'

'You believe in heaven?'

'No. Six-foot pine box a happier place than Geneva was ever at.'

'Aww.' Gloria reached over and gripped her friend's hand a moment. 'Girl, don't go thinking that way. Not never. You got good friends here on earth.'

'I know it. Neither of us gonna copy our mommas, don't you know. But I miss that gentle kingdom Moms lived in. I did once live in it, too. I don't know why I picked to be a cop. I shoulda hid in the basement of a liberry, stamping numbers on books.'

'You got a lot to give, girl,' Gloria said. 'Jack used to always say pain was a hell of a university, and struggle was a law of the world that taught you the best stuff – whether you like it or not.'

Paula nodded. 'Struggle was highly regarded at Sixty-fourth Place.' Abruptly Paula seemed to notice something outside the car. 'There's the spot we left off at.'

'Yeah,' Gloria said. 'No more moms right now, girl.'

'Fo' shizzle. So we got to put off the good death till it permitted and come down the chute on its own.'

'Don't be that way, honey. No, no. Them thoughts take you down the wrong track.'

'Sure, hon. I happy with the House of Pain we be in now. We best find your Jack and Maeve real quick.'

Chopper wheeled the chair with difficulty along the obstacle course of The Nickel sidewalk toward the shelter, avoiding the mushy piles that were best not studied too closely. The little wheels made it a chore, but Chopper was strong and lifted him and the chair bodily over the worst obstacles. Jack Liffey could hear Eleanor's voice, now and again, familiar, reassuring, but could not see her at all where she walked behind him, and it gave him time to prepare himself. The simple idea of her had stirred too much, and his awareness had developed a pristine intensity that worried him. He saw the day's weather building in the sky above, and some of him wanted her to walk right back into his life.

On the fence that guarded the lawn there was a small plaque saying Catholic Liberation House beside an intercom, and she unlocked the gate with a key she kept on a chain around her neck.

'Chopper, I'm sorry but men aren't allowed inside the shelter. I'm going to make an exception for Jack in his condition, but I ask you to wait on one of those chairs on the lawn and I'll have a nice breakfast sent out.'

'Don't trouble yourself, ma'am. I thank you kindly.'

'You're very welcome.' She took over and pushed the chair up the zig and zag of a ramp that doubled back to the front porch. 'I'll get you some writing paper, Jack. I want to talk a little before I call Gloria.'

He nodded his concurrence. This woman's body had once driven him mad with desire – an actual virgin in her late forties who had been so rattled by noticing her new sexual desires that she'd had one foot on the gas and the other on the brake at all times. With a pang he remembered her stripping off a dance top and saying something like, 'Of all these fruits you may partake,' which utterly bushwhacked an unexpected vein of innocence that he'd found buried deep inside himself, too. More prosaically, he remembered that it had been several worrying days before he could actually penetrate the object of desire, testing every non-toxic lubricant known to science.

'Let's go in my private office. I'll have some food and coffee sent in. Black and strong, as I remember. Jack, I do remember a lot.'

He nodded and made a desperate writing gesture in the air, glad she couldn't see his face. He felt fiery tears welling up and would have to brush them away discreetly when she wasn't looking.

'Yes, paper and pen. Sorry.'

He heard a phone being picked up. 'Jenny, would you send Kenisha Duncan out front with a really big breakfast for a friend of the house. His name is Chopper. And send about half that much to my office with two black coffees.'

The phone hung up. 'Oh, my gosh, I'm sorry.' She'd parked him facing a wall, only inches away, in fact facing a classy Cuban poster for a play called *Madre* that had plucked out of the Guernica mural Picasso's image of the screaming head-thrown-back woman with a dead infant in her arms. Isolated, it was a stunning image, but it seemed pretty much out of place around here. She turned his chair around and he tried to keep his eyes away from the unbearable radiance of her face. It was a tiny office, full of filing cabinets and a few of her paintings, plus a small battered desk. The paintings weren't any of the old ones he remembered, but he did remember her bold heavy-outline style. She handed him a yellow pad and a pencil.

'I'll bet there are things you need to tell me, or want to,' she said. 'Curse me if you want for absconding and hiding away. Take your time. It's good for me to just look at you a little. Pretend I didn't say that.'

I HAVE NO CURSES. SO THEY SPRUNG YOU. TOO GOOD A WORKER ON THE OUTSIDE TO WASTE.

'It doesn't work that way, Jack, but that's not important. How have you and Maeve been?'

SHES SUPER. SHE HAD SOME BOY PROBLEMS BUT ITS OK NOW. He didn't mention the gangbanger or the pregnancy or the *girl* problems. It was all too complicated for notes on a yellow pad. WE LIVE IN BOYLE HEIGHTS WITH GLORIA. Part of him wanted to write that it was a struggle keeping Gloria happy, but *no*. No hint of that.

'I liked Gloria a lot,' Sister Mary Rose said. 'Obviously a strong woman. I gave her a copy I kept of that old painting of you. Remember?'

PLEASE DONT ASK ME TO REMEMBER. HOW DID YOU GET OUT OF THE CONVENT?

'Oh, it's a long story, Jack. It took a bishop to decide I was better suited for service than adoration, and he had to overcome my deep-seated reticence.'

Reticence. He laughed, and a little sound came out. She had virtually fled full speed back to the convent after a taste of the violent world, his violent world. He remembered clearly the last words she had spoken to him, from her hospital bed after his job had got them both badly hurt, but he wasn't about to remind her in his present state. *I don't think you're going to make it, Jack.* That was her way of dismissing him and his world in order to re-enter hers.

'But tell me how you come to be mute and – you know – your legs.'

He wrote as briefly as he could about being buried alive in a massive landslide after a dynamite blast, and the fact that the experience had re-triggered his lifelong claustrophobia, something she would remember from their own ordeal down the storm drain. He didn't think his condition was permanent, but it annoyed him when various shrinks said the same. He had no idea what would unlock his body.

'That's so sad. I'll pray for you.'

WAVE A DEAD CHICKEN OVER MY HEAD TOO.

'Don't be mean, Jack.'

I WONT PRETEND TO BELIEVE IN GOD, EL. AND YOU WONT PRETEND TO LOVE THE STORMS OF FREEDOM.

'Wow, that's full of beans.' Her idiom always had been dated. 'Are you quoting?'

He nodded, but she didn't push it, and he didn't have to admit he couldn't remember whom.

'I know you're not fond of religiosity – that was your word – but would you give me permission to pray over your affliction?'

NOT RIGHT NOW. TALK TO ME OF YOUR LIFE – THESE 10 LOST YEARS.

'Not lost. I don't know if the details matter so much. I was cloistered in Mount Grace Convent in St Louis. It's not a vow of utter silence as you think of it; it's a *rule* of silence. We speak when we have to for reasons of health or urgency. "You're burning the vegetables." But not very often. It *is* very quiet and peaceful. And we do leave the walls for some purposes. We wear gray robes outside instead of the rose ones that we wear within, in order to be less . . . showy. Here's something for you to scorn if you wish, Jack. We have Adoration Periods before the image of Jesus. It's crepuscular – I read that word about the activity period of domestic cats. Generally for about forty-five minutes early in the day and an hour in the evening. Maybe you'd like them better if I called them meditation periods. Contemplation is our only real outlet. I'll demon-strate.'

She lowered herself to her knees beside the wheelchair, which made him extremely uncomfortable, but she closed her eyes, and there was no way to protest her prayer other than whacking her on the head.

'Blessed Mother, our Lady of the most Blessed Sacrament, be with me at this time which I am spending in the presence of your divine Son and another good man. I ask you to be my companion and to help me and to help this man. Reveal your divine Son to me, O Mary. Make me love Him as you did and inspire me to live for Him and for others. And do what you can for Jack Liffey, please. Amen.'

'Ack-ack.'

ENOUGH PRAYING PLEASE.

'Almost. Blessed Mother, may this man regain his speech and the power of his legs so he may do God's will in the world. I know God desires the return of missing children. This is a good man here, even if he does not believe. I know this for certain, as you do. Amen.'

ENOUGH ELEANOR! TELL ME NOW ABOUT YOUR ESCAPE.

'You shock me twice. I haven't been called Eleanor in ten years. Oh, once or twice. And that's a cruel word – "escape!"' She touched the word on his page as if to lessen its power in some way. 'The Mother Superior decided I wasn't happy at Mount Grace – well, not *suited* to the contemplative life, though I thought I was doing my best. She had the bishop speak to me at length, over many months. He decided it was either Catholic Worker or Catholic Liberation that would suit me better. Direct service to the poorest of the poor, and a little sense of social struggle thrown in. I think you can approve that. My old Liberation House down in Cahuenga had been closed down, so he sent me here. A shelter for battered women, if you haven't divined it.'

OF COURSE. JUST REMEMBER, EL. THE MASSES OF POOR WEREN'T CREATED JUST FOR YOUR OWN SPIRI-TUAL ADVANCEMENT.

She puffed out a breath of shock. 'Oh, you can be such a hard case still. But you're so right, Jack.' She stood up and squeezed his hand. 'It's why I loved you so. You made me think. I'm sorry. I know I mustn't say love.'

I LOVED YOU TOO. WE MET EACH OTHER AT A NEEDY TIME FOR BOTH OF US. IT WAS AN AMOROUS COLLISION. THE HEAT MAY NEVER BE REPRODUCED. CALL IT AN EVIL FRUIT IF YOU LIKE.

'Never. I *never* will, Jack. You opened me up in so many ways. Oh!' She covered her mouth like a bashful Japanese girl, realizing the literal content of her words.

DONT BE EMBARRASSED. WERE ALL WILD BEASTS TOO. IM SURE EVEN MOTHER MARY KNOWS THAT. Sleeping with God must have been quite a trip, he thought.

'Oh, I do miss being beside someone wise.' She moved toward him, glacially, as if drawn by a great magnet through some immensely resistant medium.

Eleanor Ong reached out and rested a hand on his shoulder. 'As smart as nuns can be, there's something always a little spoiled and childish in our protected state. All that moral earnestness and caring for others without any real personal connection to them. That's one reason I took myself back into the domain of silence.'

DIDNT YOU FIND YOURSELF SHRIVELING INSIDE?

'I don't really want to answer that. The bishop and I talked for so long. The official answer has to do with the abiding love of Jesus, the company of the saints, and the richness of the world of the spirit. But, honestly, I missed *you* terribly, Jack. For years and years. I missed your company and your skeptical goading and your jokes and your good heart. Did you miss me at all?'

It took him a while before he nodded, ever so slightly. He tried to write but his hand shook, and he pressed so hard on the pad to still his fingers that he snapped the pencil lead, and then he had to wipe tears against his shoulder. She'd taken her hand away, and soon he noticed she was locking the office door and he nearly panicked. *No, please.*

She touched him in many places, cheek, neck, shoulder, ear, mostly innocent, like a sculptor working the final shapes into a clay maquette, and then she was sitting in an impossible position over the chair arm, kissing him and shuddering and bawling with too many emotions flooding out at once, her hands grasping the back of his head. 'I'm sorry, I'm sorry, I'm so sorry.' He remembered: her feet pressing down hard on accelerator and brake at the same time.

His own arms went around her and he seemed to have lost control of them in a new way. This is what they used to call a swoon, he thought. And today they only call it lust. Their mouths found one another, and when his tongue wouldn't probe her mouth in return, physically wouldn't, despite his willing it, he became self-conscious of his disabilities. Move, legs, dammit. But they only tingled.

As gently as she could, she lowered him to a hooked rug that provided minimal padding, and her hands worked at his clothing. At some point she stopped what she was doing and stared into his eyes, resting on all fours above him, half undressed herself. 'Nod if you want me to stop.' She was gasping for air. 'I've got to be fair.'

'Ack-ack.' It was no struggle now: he shook his head.

Several times there were knocks at the door, and they both stayed as silent as they could each time. He assumed her sense of guilt was tremendous – what she was doing locked away in her private office in a women's shelter where men were not allowed at all, and certainly not male lovers, but a sense of release overwhelmed him. He hoped this wasn't going to interfere with his feelings for Gloria, but he had no power to stop now. He noticed how he had swollen uncontrollably. Zen master of the penis. That mystic still worked.

'Jack, oh!' Over and over she cried out. He remembered the surprisingly sharp-voiced bark, and how he had once loved it and watched for it and triumphed in her surrender to passion. She was just about as tight and closed off as he remembered. Surprisingly his tongue began to work.

Later, covered with sweat, she rolled off him and lay beside him holding his hand, catching her breath softly.

'I don't care what I've done,' she announced. 'It's wrong, but we're not monsters. We'll both survive this.'

He had no energy to write a note, but he nodded, hoping she saw it. Sexual heat inevitably creates such confusion, he thought. And such purpose. The body had taken over, with far too much to do to think about what the mind was getting itself up to. Sweat and other secretions – the whole world had been about nothing but moistness for a long while.

He did not look closely at the fleeting guilt-tinged thought that this event had been more powerful than it had ever been with Gloria or anyone else, even Eleanor herself, in the before. It was circumstances, that was all. But he remembered the ancient feeling that he and Eleanor were burning each other down to ashes with their combined fire. Deep inside, he had a sense that nobody believed they had a right to something like this.

He forced himself to breathe more slowly and deeply, and he began to notice thoughts gathering like alibis. Maeve. Gloria. *I couldn't help it. Forgive me. Oh, yes, I will certainly lie about this down the road a little.*

'Jack, I have to think of this as the will of God. I can't fully know His will. I realize I didn't pass unmarked through my first love of you. And I was clearly ambushed by my passions today. But I make no claim on you. In ten minutes, when I can speak calmly, I'm going to dress you and put you back up in your chair and then call Gloria to get you. Here, write. Do you hate me?'

She handed him the pad and pen and then rolled away from him and wept uncontrollably.

Jack Liffey set the pad aside and rose to his knees. His knees worked. He grinned. 'You wouldn't happen to have any chewing gum, would you?' he said aloud.

Homelessness does not constitute the entire picture of economic deprivation in L.A. The true rate of those living in dire poverty in the county now hovers at over 20 per cent of the population — well over a million and a half people. For the average family of four it is said to take at least $70,000 a year just to have a roof, a car, health care, new shoes, and to eat regularly in Los Angeles County. This is three-and-a-half times the ludicrous Federal poverty standard of $19,300 for a family of four.

TWELVE
Central to All Attractions

'Chewing gum?' Eleanor wrenched herself erect, startled.

'Bad joke. Sorry.' After uttering those few words, his throat already felt raspy. *Whoa*, he thought. *If this is recovery, it truly is beyond amazing. Take it in while you can, all sensation, all wonder, and all awe. You won't have something like this again.*

'Jack, talk to me.'

Bad joke indeed. Maybe later he'd tell her about the Indian Chief in *One Flew Over the Cuckoo's Nest* and his first words after an interminable period of feigning being mute – thanking McMurphy for a piece of Juicy Fruit. He had no real excuse for the joke, only a kind of ecstatic leap, giving the momentary jest its sway.

'Wait.'

In a more urgent context he had to focus now on what it was that had released him to speak aloud, unlocked that precious gift. She had prayed over him, of course, but, more significantly as far as he was concerned, she had offered the shock of their all-consuming lust. Omigod, he thought. Could that have been the catalyst?

Legs, now. One more test. He used his hands to help lift himself alongside the wheelchair, grasping its black plastic arm for support and almost toppling himself as the chair came off balance to his weight. His legs were shaky with disuse, but they had unmistakably helped lever him erect, and he sat down heavily on the floor, truly stunned. *Oh, yes*, he thought, *I staggered, I am staggered.*

'I don't know I want this to be happening right here,' she said.

Eleanor fell on her knees beside him, and started thanking God privately. At least she was offering up the prayer in silence, he thought with relief. He'd probably rather thank some Greek goddess of intense sensual emotion – who was that? Aphrodite? – though that explanation had its own problems. Who could doubt that intense pleasure brought about many life-transforming shocks? And there had been hints of the return for days. Whoa.

He wondered if surprises like this – anomalies, sudden visions, seeming cures – would go on being spiritual prostheses for true believers forever. The pilgrims to Lourdes, to the Ganges, the Madonna of Guadalupe at Tepeyac. He wanted nothing to do with what Eleanor would undoubtedly insist was heavenly intervention. No thank you and move on. No secret had torn free from the realm of angels.

God, listen now, neither you nor the psychologists did this for me. I claim that passion like a fiery sword was driven through my mind by my own ecstasy, by the beast we loosed. Anyone who denies this has forgotten that terrible jolt of a moment of emotion from just beyond the mundane either/or. And it wasn't just sexual orgasm. It was that intense and overpowering shock wave that comes unpredictably in our daily orbit around the commonplace.

'Jack, God bless, can you walk now, too?'

'Of course. Can't everyone?'

'Oh, don't deny the miracle, *please*.'

'I'm becoming myself . . . once again, that's all. My muscles are a little anemic from lack of use. Yes, you helped do it for me – by fucking me like crazy. Sorry, but God didn't fuck me. We always knew how to burn each other to the ground. Emotion like that unlocks everything. You know that. Just hold me close . . . and keep God to yourself.'

She braced herself and helped lift him to his feet to hug him, weeping in spasms against him. He sensed the relief and joy in her and something else, too. Mortification?

Inside himself, he felt a kind of amnesty. Deep down, nobody really believed they had a right to this kind of sudden reprieve, he thought. Small changes hid away beneath daily living, working their transformation in the dark, and then suddenly made themselves manifest. A butterfly bursting the chrysalis. Whatever had happened, he accepted it gladly, but he would not let it suggest magical worlds.

'God's love . . .' she started.

'Don't. Don't make this . . . supernatural.' He coughed from the rawness of speaking with his unused throat, but he knew it was urgent to talk now. 'Assign it to your own love. I do. You gave me what

I needed. I love Gloria, too – but for whatever reason, she couldn't give it these days in the way I required. Maybe she was too needy on her own hook. Or she was too angry at me for everything. For abandoning her to silence. Maybe you were free of all human encumbrances for that half-hour, maybe that's just what it took.'

'Jack, don't make it all pedestrian.'

'I love you and I love Gloria.'

'I know you do. No matter what happened, I'm not going to turn my life upside-down again, I can't. I want you to go back to Gloria, but don't you dare forget what happened today. Some day it may bring you to God.'

That chopped him down to size. 'You didn't hear me, did you? I don't believe in meaning – most especially religious meaning. I'll never forget what you've done for me, Eleanor, how could I? But I won't let it build a fantasy palace.'

She said nothing more as she helped him dress where he had sat hard on the chair, then grasped him with both hands without kissing him, her head two feet above his own, and she lifted. He wrapped his arms around her waist. Then she pulled free and stood up and went to unlock the door, leaving him balancing with one hand against the chair. She held the door for a moment as if against an onrush of the hostile world, and then she went to sit at her desk, like someone exhausted.

'When you can, please call Gloria,' he requested. 'I have enough trouble trying to come up with some neutral explanation for my great cure. Lies get complicated.'

'I wish you didn't have to lie, Jack.'

'What is the truth? Should I tell Gloria that I can walk and talk again because you fucked my brains out? Oh yeah, with a little help from Mother Mary?'

She turned her face away. 'I understand, Jack. Please. You mustn't make fun of idle wishes. Or religious impulses.'

But she had only the home number on Greenwood and that didn't answer. He realized he should know Gloria's cell number by heart, but for too long he'd relied on the note on the fridge, or the one in his missing wallet, or the one on the all-purpose writing pad that had buggered off with his wheelchair.

By dint of immense physical efforts that had hurt her quite a lot, Maeve had licked and spit on her right wrist for lubrication and finally wrenched her small hand out of its steel hoop, scuffing the widest points raw and leaving a long red abrasion below her thumb. But she was free now, rubbing her sore hand against her hip and dangling the cuffs as she walked cautiously in and around the collapsed cubicles to find Conor. He was lying full length, with cuffs on his ankles through a loop of heavy chain over a substantial pipe.

'I got loose. Oh, owwie! How're you doing, bluesman?'

'You're a miracle,' Conor said.

'That's why I'm here,' Maeve said, but when his sheeplike eyes fixed on her, she added, 'Kidding, guy. There aren't any miracles. Look at that sore on my hand. If I could work miracles, I'd snap my fingers and turn you loose, too.'

'I gotta get loose. I'm gonna go crazy.'

'I suppose I can stand here tugging on that chain for months, or I can abandon you for an hour and go get some help.'

'Being here alone is pretty scary.'

'Gotta be, mister. I'm sorry.'

He took a deep breath. 'Don't stand there explaining. Get out of here.'

She patted his shoulder once and headed for what looked like a fire exit door. As she hurried, she grabbed the embarrassing handcuff swinging from her left wrist, and tried to make it seem like no more than a counter-culture bauble.

She pushed open a crash bar into blinding daylight. Luckily no alarm went off. She tried to orient herself immediately to this particular door in this particular building to be able to find Conor again. An abandoned-looking brick building directly across the street displayed a newish sign saying Good Lucky Toys, Jung Park, over the number 528. But what street was it? Was it east–west or north–south? The sun was overhead but for all the camping and orienteering she'd done with her father, she was too jangled to work out directions by the sun. She would have to reach a corner street sign to find out.

And then, to her astonishment, only two blocks to her left she saw a vertical sign for the Fortnum Hotel, the neon tubes mostly broken away and dangling. Painted on the sidewall of the building were the fading words Air Cooled, with cartoon ice congealed on the drop-shadow letters, probably sixty or seventy years old, and beneath that, Central to all Attractions. Almost without conscious decision, Maeve ran toward the Fortnum.

*   *   *

Samuel Greengelb and his neighbor Morty Lipman were doing their best down in the sub-basement to inspect the piping with flashlights and see what had been done to sabotage the big boiler that provided steam heat to their radiators four floors up. The damage looked obvious – maybe twenty feet of vertical one-inch pipe had simply been removed and the lower end capped off with a shiny new iron cap.

'Sammy, this is illegal. They can't *do* this. Who do we talk to?'

Greengelb led the way to the one working pay phone in the neighborhood, at the mini-market, and dialed 911.

'Help, already!'

'What is your emergency, sir?' He could tell it was a colored woman responding.

'They cut off our heat.'

'Is someone hurt at your location?'

'We're freezing to death at night, *nu*. Isn't that enough hurt?'

'Where are you, sir?'

'We live in the Fortnum Hotel on San Julian Street. We got proof here that the owners are cutting off heat to drive us out. Pipes are missing.'

'What is your name and address?'

'Samuel Greengelb, Room 322. So . . . I'm not ashamed or afraid, not a bit, to report a crime.'

'What is the crime, sir?'

'Cutting off the heat in the middle of winter so some *farshtinkener* owner can drive away his long-term tenants and make the rooms into fancy lofts for yuppies.'

'I think I agree with you, sir, but I don't know the crime, *exactly*. In fact, if you're not in immediate danger of harm, I'm going to have to hang up to free this line. I can advise you to call another number.' She gave him the number, but he didn't even bother to copy it down. Why take all the trouble with some city agency that would put him on hold for an hour and then take months to send someone out? From that game, he was well acquainted. 'Sir? Did you get the number I told you?' He was amazed that she had enough sympathy to stay on the line a little longer. Coloreds were often such kindly people.

'So, what if I said I have ice growing on my face?' Greengelb said. 'Cold is cold, madam. It can kill.'

'Sir, it's fifty-eight degrees outside right now. The ice on your

face will melt pretty fast. God bless you and a good morning.' The
line went dead.

Greengelb's expression must have shown that she had hung up
on him.

'We could try the rebbe at Anshe Emes Shul,' Morty said, as
they left the mini-mart and headed back toward the hotel.

'Feh, and we could read Torah and *davnen* with a bunch of
Chasids for the rest of our life. There's got to be a city department
that forbids this. But you know what it's like *kvetching* to a civil
servant who all he's thinking is where to eat lunch.'

'I know. The under government is a bunch of Kafka rats in
tunnels. But the Jewish rats are still searching for justice, always.'

'I think we can fix the pipe ourselves and then put our own lock
on the boiler room door,' Greengelb said.

'*Now* you're talking.' Morty almost cackled.

'I know a plumber owes me a favor.'

'Uh-oh. I know a carpenter owes me lots of favors. You don't
never want to breathe the air around this guy if it's after three or
you get second-hand drunk . . .' Morty slapped himself on the cheek
and grinned. A little joke, perhaps.

'No, no, this Fishkin is sober as a judge, believe me. Stop
kvetching. I even wrote down his important number – the number
reserved for his Jewish mother in the event of being late for lunch.'

Morty laughed. 'I had one of those, too. I made sure it went to
the city zoo.'

Samuel Greengelb sighed. 'I saved my special number for if the
Messiah ever called.' They had got back to the hotel. The desk clerk
had gone missing for some reason. They went down to survey the
damage to the boiler again.

'Hey, guys!'

They both glanced back up in surprise and Greengelb brought
their flashlight around to see a girl at the top of the stairs. He
seemed to remember her, but he wasn't sure. Short term, he was
having his troubles.

'The guy at the desk told me you went down here, but he sure
didn't look like he wanted to tell me anything and then he split.
Your friend Conor Lewis needs your help. Pretty quick. He's not
far away and he's stuck in handcuffs.' She showed off her own set
of handcuffs by dangling the free one.

'Bad *mazel*,' Morty said.

'Is this about that boy with the guitar?'

'Yes,' Maeve said. 'Hurry, please, Conor's really scared. And he's all alone.' She changed her tone. 'Musketeers, he needs you.'

'Listen, you fucker. Either you tell us where the girl has gone, or I'll let my friend here loose to carve you into a party decoration,' the big golden-blond one threatened. The shorter one was playing with his knife, sending it from hand to hand with intricate flips and leaps.

'I don't know, I don't *know*, I don't know. I swear. Honest to God, I swear. She won't be coming back. Please don't hurt me.'

McCall pressed a large thumb against Conor's nose. 'Can I give you some advice, tweak? Don't be such a pussy. Nobody likes a pussy. But *nobody*. So is this girl your girlfriend?'

'I don't even know her name. I don't know why she was there when you guys grabbed us.'

'Whatta you think, Rice? You think he's being loyal to his cooze? This nose would make a nice hood ornament, wouldn't it?'

'Let me play with him a little. What is done out of love always takes place beyond good and evil. Mr Nietzsche said that.' Rice Thibodeaux held the switchblade vertically in front of Conor's face with a ghastly grin.

'You hear that, tweak? I think the best way we can impress your Jew pals is we start sending them some small pieces of you. Don't worry; we'll start with the expendable ones. What would you like to lose for starters? An earlobe? A pinkie?'

'*Please!*'

'An ear's the thing. Very *Reservoir Dogs*. I know it'll be good for me. It'll be good for Rice here. You may be of another opinion.'

Now Rice was using the index fingers of both hands like a juggler, flipping his open switchblade back and forth in space like a baton-twirler's trick.

'Jesus Christ,' the big one said. 'You got an endless line of bull-shit tricks, don't you, Rice? You oughta try out for the circus.'

The little man suddenly tossed the knife at McCall's feet, so it stuck in the floor, vibrating, between his black Doc Marten boots. 'In heaven all the interesting people are missing. You got a lot of empty talk, Stevie-boy, until somebody some day puts a knife straight into your ear,' Thibodeaux said. 'You wanna get old in this lousy world?'

'It's a lot better than the other thing.' McCall glanced at Conor. 'I hope you're getting a vibe of evil here? I sure am.'

Conor was silently weeping.

There was a crash nearby, and Rice quickly retrieved his knife from the floor.

'Conor, you OK? I brought help!' It was the girl's voice, bleating from along the corridor with all kinds of false confidence.

The big one pointed right at Conor. 'Shut the fuck up, tweak.' Then he shouted, 'Your pal's got a knife into his neck. Come on over if you want to see a lot of blood.'

'Same to you, *gonif*! If you got a soul, run away now. We're coming to get our boy.' *Weird* – the voice of one of those Yids, he thought.

'Oh, terrific, I can work with *that*. A coupla old kikes and a girl come to the rescue. Go on, cut his head off, dude.'

McCall waved off his command frantically, as Thibodeaux was just stepping up to do it.

No, no, no no, he mouthed, shaking his head hard.

'Don't touch that boy!' Greengelb shouted. 'The police are on their way.'

'And Batman, too, right? You went and put up the big search-light. Look, you Yids go and get lost and we'll talk about this later!'

But McCall could hear footsteps coming along the hallway.

'Don't do a bad thing, *golem*!'

A siren approached in the street, and McCall tensed for a moment, but by careful discrimination, he could tell it was a fire engine, which went on past.

'That your cops, Greengold? Bring 'em on.'

'I've got a gun,' another male voice put in.

'Aw, Jeez, I'm quaking in my booties. Maybe you better come over then and shoot me.'

'Good idea, *chozzer*. I'm coming for you. Just you.'

McCall was starting to get a little worried. Sometimes it seemed that everybody in L.A. was strapped except him. Maybe it was time to back off here. If they really were coming armed, it would put a serious crimp in things.

'You want a grenade in the face, come on.' McCall picked up an old broken pencil sharpener and hurled it down the hallway, where it clattered hard. The footsteps broke off for a moment but then came on.

'Let's book,' McCall said softly to his friend, nodding to the fire exit across the room. The tempo of things was going wrong, and he was unarmed. 'This is lose-lose.'

'Aw, cuz.'

Just then a tiny old man spilled out the doorway, tripping forward in his agitation. He waved a square little .25 automatic, a girl's purse pistol, and then fired it wildly in their direction, three times, almost as panicked as they were and tripping over a tangle of cords.

'Oww!' Conor cried out.

McCall couldn't see any wounds. Thiboideaux grinned, and he could tell his partner had given the boy a love poke with the tip of his flick-knife. He was now wiping the blade on the boy's shirt, carefully keeping the boy between him and the toppled gunman. Then the two enforcers took off running, and McCall glanced back once to see the old man getting up on his knees, preparing to fire with two hands like a TV cop, and he loosed off another shot in their direction.

'Faster, Ricey. Don't get in my fucking way!'

'What's your weakness?' Gloria said, halting long enough on her way in to talk to the happy-looking black man who was eating a sumptuous tray of breakfast in a lawn chair, attended by a large black woman.

'I gave up crank a long time ago, ma'am. My weaknesses are chess and fine food and taking care of strays. I got a deep personal esteem for strays. Would you believe, the men so mean here they even steal dogs?'

'You the one they say adopted my man last night, didn't you?'

'You say Richard? I mean Jack? Uh-huh. He play a crap chess.'

'I owe you one, old man. Who are you?'

'Chopper Tyrus my name. Money is always accepted here.'

She turned back. 'Got anything, Paula? I'm good for it.'

Paula gave him a twenty, and they went up the steps into the musty feminine smells of Catholic Liberation Shelter just as Sister Mary Rose was coming along the hall toward them with a determined stride. There was something newly fretful about her manner that interested Gloria. She also noticed the political posters along the hall for the first time, and wondered what had become of her powers of observation the other night.

'Prepare yourself for a shock,' the nun announced.

'I don't think I'm shockable, Sister.' There was something about this woman that pissed Gloria off down deep, especially since she knew she'd once been Jack's girlfriend.

'I'm talking about a shock you're going to like.'

What mattered, Gloria thought – caught up in a series of images of terrible cruelty that she carried around with her day-to-day from years of police work – what really mattered was knowing the relationship minute by minute between what was bearable in your daily life and what was not, and avoiding letting your mind sink into the what-was-not.

'Jack seems to be getting better. A lot better.'

'Bull.'

'Go see him. He's your man. You'll know.' The nun stepped aside and gestured for Gloria to pass.

Gloria stared hard at her for a moment and then went by. She was so used to Jack being a dead nerve in a dead tooth that any news of a change for the better had to make her suspicious. She found herself tuning her radar up to its highest sensitivity, not quite knowing what was worrying her about all this.

In the tiny office, Jack Liffey was supporting himself on his arms against the rim of a small desk and trying to sidestep around it, apparently for practice. Yes, this was new all right.

'He is risen,' Gloria said, and she did not know why she'd allowed a mocking note to creep into her voice.

'Gloria! Wonderful. To see you. I love you.'

His croak of a voice stopped her in her tracks. 'And he talks!'

'I can't. Believe it. I was beaten. Kidnapped. My chair was taken, my wallet. A black man sheltered me. We played chess.'

'And you met a nun you used to fuck.' Or still do, she thought.

'This morning Chopper brought me. We used her phone.'

He turned and settled on the edge of the desk with a sigh of near exhaustion.

Gloria hit one of those unexpected air bumps that rearrange your feelings without you knowing it. Sometimes it wasn't garment-rending wails. Just recalling something within reach. She decided all at once not to be so cross and mistrustful. *Jesus, woman, this man you love has been yanked back from the very edge of the precipice. Don't be so Grinch.* She went across the few feet and hugged Jack to nearly break his ribcage.

'I'm sorry if I take a while here, Jack. I'm stuck in the bad old world. I should remember the eight-story hotel.'

'Don't know that,' he said.

'I'll tell you later. How are you doing, *querido*? Tell me about your legs and your voice.' She felt Paula's presence behind her, but the woman sensibly kept her mouth shut.

'I don't understand. Last night my faculties started. To come back. Just a little. I said "whoa" not "ack" to Chopper. May never know how. I was beat on the head. Maybe that. I don't know. I love you, Glor.'

Something wasn't quite right here. 'Answer me one question,' she insisted.

'Course.'

'I mean it. Promise solemn to tell me the truth, Jack.'

'Yes. I will. Total.'

'Why am I feeling that there's something about your recovery that you know but you won't tell me?'

'I don't know.'

'Does it have anything to do with the little Miss Nun?'

His head sank into a deep nod, chin to chest, as if his neck had lost all muscular support, and Gloria's heart dropped like a stone through all her fears.

'Gloria. Sister Mary Rose prayed. Over me. On her knees. To Mother Mary and all the saints. Do you think I want to admit. A religious miracle? *Me*?'

Gloria laughed aloud, feeling inordinately relieved.

One consequence of the 'Safer Cities' policy of ticketing so many of the homeless over and over for petty crimes like jaywalking or sleeping on the sidewalk was ultimately to send them to state prisons, which are already under Federal court supervision for failing to provide the most basic health and mental care to prisoners. On their release – after up to two to four years of true hard time – these poor souls are now 'felons' and ineligible for federally subsidized housing programs, drug rehabilitation, or even food stamps.

THIRTEEN
Circling the Wagons

R ice Thibodeaux thrust his splayed palm against the dashboard of McCall's Dodge RAM-3500 and played mumbledy-
peg thereupon, chivying his switch blade in between his
fingers and leaving tiny slits everywhere it struck down on the
leatherette. McCall sighed and gave up any attempt to keep the man
under control. Used cars could always be sold, no matter how weirdly
abused, but partners like Rice were irreplaceable when you needed
a bit of evil-eye fear-provoking aggression. Anyway, they were
yoked together now like an ox and an ass in some twisted folktale.
No question that the game they were playing with the tenants was
good psycho, bad psycho, and it was always fun to watch every
single victim keep a weather eye fixed on the crazy little Louisiana
bugger.

'Say, babe, could you dial it back a little. I know that trick's
piquant and all, but you're puncturing the leatherette.'

Rice closed the knife with a slap and a frown of displeasure.
'Piquant, you say? Shit-ass. When do we get to fuck up the Hebes?'

'How would you feel about fucking the tenants up if they were
blond and Norwegian?'

Rice looked at him as if he'd just spoken in Urdu. McCall doffed
his cap and shook out his golden tresses that were beginning to
turn into coiled dreadlocks.

'Anglos got poor people in SROs, too, babe,' McCall said. 'Ain't
all colored guys and others.'

'Bring some around. I'd like to meet them.'

McCall laughed. The guy wasn't as stupid or slow-witted as he
sometimes pretended. He claimed to be a big fan of Nietzsche, for
chrissake. McCall wasn't even 100 per cent sure who Nietzsche
was, though he might have read about him in JC. Whoever – when
the chips were down, Thibodeaux was every bit as malicious as he
showed out and that could be useful.

'I got the plan, Stan,' Thibodeaux said. 'In that shithook Fortnum we string razor wire across the stairs at neck level and then set off a fire alarm.'

'Great plan, babe. And doing all this work – measuring, like, neck height for these dwarves, drilling the holes, screwing in the wire – it's all real good exercise, just like coyote setting up his Acme booby-trap to get the roadrunner. It's all real life affirming.'

'What the fuck you talking about?'

'We don't need these violent fantasies right this minute, *compadre*. It's tough, but embrace the suck, OK. We fucked up. Right now we got to report to our fat money-dispensing boss, tell him the kid we picked up got away. Remember that? Everybody got away. And the asshole Yids at the Fortnum are armed now and probably already repairing the heater, maybe even the elevator. And nobody seems to want no money. You want to tell him all that yourself? I'll go have a drink while you do.'

'Eat me, Steven.'

Vartabedian had insisted on meeting them again in the derelict Japanese Garden, obviously his way of keeping them at arm's length, and McCall gave the guard at the main door the finger when the old Japanese man asked where they thought they were going. 'Japan, asshole, where do you think?'

The old man shrugged. They took the elevator down and swaggered through the far glass doors to the decaying garden that was even rattier than it had been a week earlier. A line of bamboo had overgrown itself and its spindly second-growth branches bowed across the pathway, some fronds actually touching down.

Thibodeaux began hacking bamboo away with his switchblade like Bogart going ape-shit on the sedge blocking the *African Queen*.

'Why does the fuckhead put us through this?'

'If you're determined to be the straight man, babe, he's the guy that pays. The guy that pays puts you through whatever he fuckin' wants. Until we can pay, we get to follow his rules.'

'You got *your* idea of rules,' Thibodeaux said, flailing crazily for a moment at the overgrown bamboo with his oversharpened knife. 'But I got natural law. That's my thing. Natural law says they only do shit to you until you carve them a new eating hole in their neck. Save your wisdom for somebody of your own mental weakness.'

They got past the bamboo and stepped over coils of black plastic gardening borders that somebody was presumably going to bury alongside the path one of these days.

'We don't want to kill no golden goose. Ricey, we get three bills a day retainer. That's my natural fucking law.'

'That's ten minutes on stage to a rock star, Steve-o. I know what money is worth.'

'Get back to me with your demo tape, Mr Rockstar,' McCall said contemptuously. 'V's pay is just fine for now, and it lets me do what I'm good at. I'm good at diddling people.'

'I'm good at hurting people bad. When do I get to do *that*? This whole program is fucked up.'

McCall sighed. 'Maybe soon, Rice. But we follow orders now. I absolutely require it. There's the greaseball now.'

Vartabedian sat on a rock bench at the far end of the disused garden, smoking a cigar as if he didn't have a care in the world.

'Any of you know your hat size?' the big man said as they approached.

'Huh?'

'Fuck no.'

He tsked and shook his head. 'The world's changing. When I was a kid, every swingin' dick used to know hats.' He held out his smoldering cigar. 'They knew Cohibas from Coronas, too. Now nobody knows shit from Shinola.'

'Hey, I know Shinola,' McCall said. 'I used to carry a shine rag in my back pocket in high school in Banning.'

'Good for you. So, when are the tenants gonna be out?'

Rice Thibodeaux emitted a manifestly phony laugh. 'Ha-there, yeah. Steve-o, whyn't you tell him how they're all packing up to grab the next plane for Israel?'

McCall glared at Thibodeaux for a moment before answering. 'It was a real shock, believe me, Mr V. Those old Yids went and got themselves guns. They broke the fuckin' kid we was holding loose, and then shot at us like they was at Coney Island. No shit, man. They near greased us. I was pretty sure you didn't want us to kill them back.'

Vartabedian had sat straight up at first, but as an apparent act of self-control, he blew two smoke rings off into space before speaking.

'For God's sake, man. Did you two . . . just re-up in the space patrol? No, let's be clear – I do *not* want anybody "killed back." I got a perfectly legal city permit to convert the Fortnum Hotel into loft apartments. What do you think happens to that permit if you start whacking old men in there? Don't answer me. I don't have

any use for your propositions. I mean, even morally, I don't want
anybody killed, OK? It's against my principals. I got to worry this
out.'

'Fuck them guys, man,' McCall offered. 'It's all in the degree
of fear . . .'

'Shut up, man. You two want any more paydays, you follow the
letter of my orders down to the dot over the T. I'm a tenderhearted
soul but there's limits. OK, here's the deal. You two go home, have
some beers. Watch some crap on TV tonight, play cribbage, buy a hat
– I don't give a shit. Call me in twenty-four hours at the office. Don't
go anywhere near the Fortnum. You do, you're fired. Now, fuck off.'

McCall did his best to strut away. His mind immediately flashed
back to Baghdad and other chewing outs he'd endured from junior
officers with less time in than him. All those daily patrols into the
nightmare, the taunts and blind alleys, the little kids trying to piss
on you from windows. After a really bad patrol, and there were plenty
of them, the only way to redeem yourself with the L.T., no matter
what he said to you, was to make the next patrol a big win. You had
to come home with the bacon – some real intel on the Ali Babas or
maybe whack one of the *hajis* with his picture up in the mess.
Whatever. You had to do something that would really light up the
report to the guys who lived up above reality, up in the Green Zone.

Maeve was still jangled and upset by the gunfire. It wasn't that
she'd never experienced guns fired in anger before – and sometimes just in bravado. L.A. was the world capital of urban gunfire,
and no one avoided it entirely. The worst time had been the South
Central uprising when she'd witnessed her father shot down by a
thug standing over him. Some people she knew took it all in their
stride, like trash talk or a couple of punches in the playground. But
guns were a whole stage worse. She didn't like the cocky strut of
them. It was so masculine and brutal, a stir of that disorderly Y
chromosome. Morty Lipman had put his little pistol back into his
pocket and managed to look a bit shamefaced.

'Come on, kids,' Samuel Greengelb urged them up the stairs.
Not a soul had been in the lobby, nor behind the wire grille at
reception. 'You best stick with the old *pishers* right now. It looks
like the Indians are restless. Probably our worst enemy – Sitting
Bagel himself.'

Maeve laughed in surprise at his unexpected joke. But her laugh collapsed when she noticed that the smell on the staircase was foul enough to choke a horse. Pee and mildew and something like fruit that had gone rotten a long time ago.

'You have to walk up this all the time?' she asked, wrinkling her nose.

'Since those *shmucks* busted the elevator. You get used to it. What's your name, daughter?'

'Maeve Liffey.' She'd told him once, but you made allowances. 'And yours, sir?' Conor trudged up glumly beside her.

'Samuel Greengelb. Call me Sam, please. I think they picked up . . . this boy here . . . to get our goat. He's a new neighbor.'

'My dad is a detective, and normally he'd help us, but at the moment he's kind of physically disabled.'

'We can always use another *kalike*.'

'What's that?'

The old man grimaced. 'A guy who's a bit inconvenienced. Sorry.'

'The word means cripple, doesn't it?'

'Strictly speaking.' They went toward his room

'We gotta fix the heat,' Morty said.

'We gotta circle the wagons,' Greengelb said. 'The Indians are coming. Tonight, for sure.'

'The elevator is completely dead?' Maeve asked.

'Yes.'

'OK, let's block the stairs.' She was getting into it. 'My stepmom will be looking for us before long, I'm sure. She's an L.A. cop.' The lack of an actual marriage to her father made wordings awkward. 'My cell is gone but maybe we can contact her. Any of you have a phone?'

'We should afford a cellphone on Social Security? Feh. The pay phone downstairs was killed first. Most of the rooms are empty now.'

'*Fraynd*,' Morty Lipman insisted. 'I want some heat tonight. An ice cube I'm not planning to be.'

'OK, first we fix the heater. There's only a pipe missing. Then we have fun with booby traps.'

'I can help with that,' Conor Lewis put in.

'Wouldn't it be safer to go someplace else?' Maeve said.

'Then the *schmucks* have won, little lady,' Morty said. 'They'll padlock our doors and we're all included out forever.'

Gloria and Paula had taken Jack home and supported his shaky walk to an old comfy chair on the back screen porch beside the ailing

Loco, to console one another, and left him with strict orders to stay put. Then they'd headed back downtown to look for Maeve at the address Jack Liffey had been given, but that was utterly empty.

'What is going on in The Nickel?' Paula asked. 'The real estate is, like, utterly worthless and people are fighting over it? What Yuppie wants to live with a hundred per cent vandalism, a hundred per cent homelessness, a hundred per cent graffiti? The old hotels are like sewers.'

'Cities are doing it all over the country, at least before the collapse. People seem to want to be urban now – as long as they don't have to be bothered by urban people.'

'Ah, crap,' Paula said. 'You know – whites are always so sure they can get the upper hand.'

Something about Paula's attitude annoyed her. 'Yeah, maybe all caucasians need to be held down and raped by a couple of mokes of color. That'll let them know how the world really works.'

Paula seemed a bit startled. 'Jeez, that's pretty intense. Where you going with shit like that?'

Gloria locked the car doors and stared at her friend over the roof. 'No farther than you talking about the "good death," girl. Sorry. We probably both need a mood adjuster to mellow down. I don't know why I'm so angry.' She had faint memories of a nasty pit bull at one of her foster homes. She'd made a sign for him: *Don't even THINK of trying to pet this dog*, and then she'd tied him outside McCowan's market, doing her assigned chores, and she came back to find the beast methodically chewing and destroying the sign. 'Am I getting worse, Paula?'

'Yeah, recent-like. Maybe it's having to take care of your man when he's such a basket case.'

'It's before that,' she said with distaste. 'It's in my head. But you know what happens if I go to a shrink. It gets back to the brass in five seconds flat. That unstable bitch. Put her in traffic.'

A terrifying image came back for a moment – a dream from her childhood that had recurred again – so intense for that moment that it took her breath away: her nine-year-old self standing and screaming defiance into a dark open doorway and knowing utterly that her insolence would set something lethal to flying out of the darkness at her – but screaming anyway. *Girl, you need something. All this crazy rage down in there.*

They walked through The Nickel, past a number of men reclining

amongst dubious possessions. Gloria and Paula were both silent for
a while, awed by the actual presence of so much human misery –
and their own.

'Shit,' Gloria said. 'I keep thinking there should be labels posted
over those guys back there, you know – common name, habitat,
Latin name. That really sucks, doesn't it?'

'Yeah, c'mon, honey. Ain't no zoo. And we're not on duty. Let's
get you a minor mood adjustment.' She took Gloria's arm and tugged
her into a bar with the unlikely name of Ed's Bang-Up.

'This is a bad road to start down,' Gloria objected ineffectually.
A grizzled old drunk lifted his head from a round table as they
came in, meeting her eyes with hollow red-rimmed false hopefulness, and she looked away. Too much pain everywhere. *OK, we're
all out here together in this shit*, she thought.

Fortunately Samuel Greengelb had the right tool: a pipe-wrench
he'd borrowed from the super once, when they'd had a super, and
never given back. He scavenged five feet of half-inch pipe from
where it ran through the fourth floor basins, and then he capped
off the stub that he'd left using the pipe-cap the thugs had used
on the heater down below. It was hardly worth capping off. The
water was shut off. Two of the five original Musketeers had fled
the building for good, and the third old-timer, Joel Wineglass, had
moved two doors down from Greengelb, but he'd been losing his
resolve for days, and Greengelb wasn't even sure he was still in
the building.

It was lucky Greengelb had a few other tools in the kitbox his
nephew had left him, despairing whether his uncle could or would
ever use them. But Greengelb had always seen himself as handy.
An *arbeiter* of sorts. Hammer a bit, saw, paint, screw and unscrew.

He stuck the pipe-wrench in his pocket like a six gun and carried
the long pipe he'd swiped down the staircase by himself, an ungainly
spear, grazing and scarring the walls from time to time, accidentally ramming hard at the landings.

'Sam, that you *zhlubbing* down like a flock of elephants?'

'Who else? The Messiah come to fix our plumbing? I got pipe.
Heat you're going to get, my friend.'

'*Lang lebn zolstu!* The boy and girl are off collecting junk from
the empty rooms to make a barricade. I'm on guard. I'm Jeff
Chandler, the Jewish cowboy.'

Greengelb came out onto their floor and saw his friend clasping the pistol with determination.

'Enough with the gun, Morty. The *shmucks* can get plenty of guns, I'm sure. So help me with this pipe.'

'OK.'

The pipe was about a foot too long to fit between the heater outlet in the lobby and the pipe coupler that had been left dangling empty behind an access door on the next floor up. They had no tools for rethreading the pipe, but by trading off the hacksaw and working arduously for twenty minutes, they managed to cut a foot off the iron pipe. They screwed it in below and jammed about a quarter inch of the sawn end of the pipe into the coupler. They wrapped and tied it in place with duct tape and all the rags they could find, finished off with old stiff wire.

'A plumber I'm not, but a pure genius. A *genius*, I admit it.'

'You keep thinking that when we light up the boiler and all fly to the moon. But even poor old men can have *mazel*. It could work.'

'Of course it'll work. Let's light it up.'

As soon as the women had left him to his own devices, Jack Liffey had stood up shakily from the comfy chair and forced himself to start walking around the house, lurching at first, then stabilizing himself by holding on to doorframes and the old darkened oak chair rails, enjoying this new tentative state of being. He could tell it would be a while before he was steady on his feet without support, but there was a strange elation in moving around on his own legs now. *Damn*, he thought, *I should get myself something outrageous to celebrate, something that would shock Maeve and Gloria both – a big pirate earring, maybe, or a Yakuza tattoo on my neck.*

Loco followed him around the house curiously, mewling now and again in complaint or anxiety at his stumbles. Some areas of the house newly terrified him, the wide open spaces without handholds. But this euphoria at his new freedom of movement was almost as if he were drunk.

'It's OK, boy. Walking was once my normal state of being, remember? I can talk, too. La la la. Good boy. Love you, Loco.' His voicebox deep in his throat hurt when he spoke aloud, but he tried to ignore the rasp, and he was amazed that his vocal cords seemed to work fine. Goodbye, Mr Ack-ack. Life was so delicate and so robust at once, he thought.

Thank God I'm not abandoned over there in The Nickel, stuck on the flypaper of an abused childhood or a traumatized military deployment or the slow collapse of my hopes or just plain bad luck – and a jobless and homeless future. So many of those men had been robbed of their kindness, too – he'd seen their eyes turn toward him with calculation, revealing neither compassion nor pity. It was remarkable that a few with so little of their own could still reach out and help. He decided to track down Chopper Tyrus and do something generous for him. Not just money. He would try to find something the man needed to right himself in life.

He thought of Gloria and Paula over there right now – looking for Maeve! The notion hit him like a giant slap across the face. Guilt sent him sprawling awkwardly into Gloria's easy chair. Christ, Maeve was still in danger!

Somehow he'd resigned himself to letting Gloria take over the watchdog role. But he was no longer helpless. Somebody had brought his pickup back to the house, Gloria or Paula, but had kept the keys, probably to keep him out of trouble. But it didn't matter. There was a spare key in a tiny magnetic box.

But first he went to the stash of books where he kept his .45 in a hollowed-out *Oxford Companion to American Literature,* and he remembered instantly – the book sitting open on the desk – that he'd taken that away with him and had it ripped out of his hands some time ago by the little psycho. OK, he knew where Gloria kept her old backup .38 Smith & Wesson Police Special, more or less abandoned when the Department had gone over to .40 Glocks.

The big fat revolver tugged uncomfortably in his waistband, making him a bit more unsteady, but he couldn't do anything about that until his leg muscles healed.

He got into the pickup and fought the spare key into the ignition.

Maeve and Conor had scavenged what they could from the abandoned flophouse rooms that were full of ratty clothing, old magazines, crusty eating bowls and unmatched single shoes. None of which was very useful for the proposed barricade – between the second floor, wholly empty now, and the third floor, where everyone was living. What she and Conor had finally settled on using were the unpadded box springs on almost all the bed frames, and a few light dressers and cabinets, which they'd shoved into the hall.

Maeve was still worried about barricading rather than escaping the building for help, but it seemed to have become a matter of principle to the old men, and she was willing to do what she could for them. She decided there was something really noble in their resistance.

Once the furnace had been lighted and was up to pressure, and the new pipe joint was declared imperfect but serviceable – leaking a steady jet of superheated steam on to the second floor landing – they could build the barricade. They all helped in carrying the bedframes down the staircase one by one, then they shoved the rubbish they had collected down the stairs and stacked it all together into a massive tangle tied rigid with some old stiff wire and duct tape from Samuel Greengelb's tool kit. It made an almost impassible barrier, but Maeve noted that it was equally difficult to breach the barrier *either* way, and she secretly left a weakly linked tunnel on the handrail side that could be yanked apart in an emergency so they could crawl out fast if they had to. She didn't even tell Conor about her secret passage, but she made the last downside layer of her secret tunnel as strong as she could so it would look impenetrable from below.

She hoped somebody had some food up here, and, as usual, she felt she had to think of everything for them all. They wouldn't be able to live up here forever. It was hard enough to imagine what would happen the next day – but she wasn't that worried somehow. The whole city would hardly sit back and ignore an assault on three old men and a couple of teenagers.

They gathered in Greengelb's room to appraise what they'd done and pat each other on the back. Maeve's purse was long gone so she had nothing to contribute, and Conor had only a Honer 532/20 blues harmonica – an instrument he called a 'harp.' No one had a cell phone. They would have to signal by yoo-hooing out the windows or flashing lights dot-dot-dot after dark, if anyone would be looking and if anyone knew Morse code any more. But who would be watching for Morse code from Skid Row? Lipman still had his little pistol, and luckily Joel Wineglass's room revealed a formidable stash of food, though a lot of it ran to bottles of gefilte fish, canned herring, chicken broth, and several jugs of deep purple concord grape wine – none of which struck the teenagers as particularly palatable or even edible.

*   *   *

'Man, didn't you hear Mr V? We're supposed to disengage and leave the world painless for tonight.' Rice Thibeaudeaux had given up fussing with his flick knife, but he was too restless to give up all perseveration – a very high-functioning autistic, McCall finally decided – as the midget drummed erratically on the dashboard with two fingers.

'It's my worry, sweetie.' McCall knew that things got dangerous when you disobeyed orders, but there was no way he was going to walk away now. No way. Only assholes walked away. It was an ocean-to-ocean freak show in America these days, and you couldn't let down on your hard edge or they'd put you in the cage with the geeks and glass-eaters.

'Let's do it to the old goofs,' McCall said.

'Fuck them up?' Thibodeaux's face lit up.

'That's what you said you're good at, sweetie.'

NOTES FOR A NEW MUSIC

Day 7

Miss M, I'm waiting here
For you to reach out to me.
We're both homeless without love
And loveless without home.

Miss M, I'm terrified
That you'll tell me
My feelings are a big mistake
And I have no shelter in the storm.

O, Miss M, is this the end
Or just one more day of waiting?
I need somebody to help me hang on
But I swear I won't burden you longer.

The average income of the top one per cent of taxpayers in California more than doubled between 1995 and 2005. The typical hourly wage worker's wage declined by 4.4 per cent, while that of the lowest-wage workers declined by even more. Even before the crash. Almost five million full-time workers in California have wages beneath the Federal poverty line. This is all well known. Why is it allowed to happen?

FOURTEEN
My Yiddish Mama

'Remember those airstrips out in the boonies that were nothing but sheets of perf steel over the sand?' McCall said.

Thibodeaux snorted derision. 'They brought us in on big 747s. Right to Baghdad SDA, man. All the best for Blackwood. We had *stewardesses*, f'chrissake. No Spam-in-the-can shit for us. Then straight down the twelve klicks of the Irish Run in armored rhinos to the Green Zone and the Intercontinental Hotel, drinking cold beer all the way. We only had one bump the whole trip.'

McCall wondered why the little psycho was being so voluble tonight. 'I only asked because the way the damn wind is kicking up.' Loose newspaper sheets, wisps of dirt and old Styrofoam cups were gusting past the windshield. 'Choppers on those boonie fields always blew a storm of crap in your eyes.'

'Goodie for you, Mr. G.I., with the blue cord on his shoulder. I hope you waxed some towelhead for every annoying minute you spent over there.'

'We did try to rack them up,' McCall said. 'Staying even is good for the soul.'

'Whatever. It was a pretty strange war,' Rice Thibodeaux said.

'The whole sandbox was strange, babe, not just the four-star hotels with the hookers where you mercs lived. Glad to be home, I tell you, out of the evilness.' McCall cracked the truck window; he could tell immediately it was a cold wind out of the west, the big pineapple wind that would bring more rain.

He cranked the window closed and looked over to find Thibodeaux glaring unnervingly straight at him. The little man didn't often meet your eyes, a strange-o most days, but he was doing it now.

'I didn't know you were that way,' Thibodeaux announced.

'What way is that, friend?'

'Poison toad – scared of biting yourself.'

'Bullshit, little man.' He was riled, it was true, edgy, worried a little and maybe angry, but he wasn't scared. 'OK, when it's dark tonight, we go in and mess with them.'

'Can I do some hurt?'

In his imagining, McCall saw the L.T. on his last patrol in country, bringing his knee hard up into the balls of an Iraqi father whose whole family was spaced along the wall of his home, watching. An RPG had flamed into their firebase from this guy's house or maybe nearby. Mortaritaville. 'OK, let's change levels. We go off the grid tonight. Our enemies are gonna cry. Happy?'

Thibodeaux put up a fist and McCall sighed and popped it. Let smiles cease, McCall thought. He'd made his choice. This is where we all go to hell.

Gloria showed her badge to the beat cops that the LAPD had out walking The Nickel these days, a Dick-and-Jane pair not long out of the Academy. The woman was brown skinned and fine featured. A Brahmin East Indian, Gloria guessed. Pretty odd cop. Paula hung back talking to a group of young black men sitting on the curb as the sun sank into a dark cloud bank behind the skyscrapers off to the west.

'Strange assignment down here,' Gloria said. 'How long you two been up?'

Gloria could see the woman intentionally defer to her partner. 'Since the chief decided the best thing to do about the homeless was bust the shit out of them every time they jaywalk.' He was a cocky young man with a mustache so blond you could hardly see it. 'I'm no Monday-morning quarterback. Maybe it was the thing to do then. We've run off a lot of dirtbags that were living off the poor winos. Selling dime bags to them, for shit's sake. Stealing a man's only pants. That's the honor of Afro gentlemen for you.'

The comment set off a lot of alarms for Gloria. She'd thought the Academy worked a little harder on racial tact these days.

The woman cop gestured to the man's chestpak radio. 'That's an open carrier, Denny.' She made a mute gesture of caution.

Apparently they had a way of leaving their radios on during the foot patrol. That was new to Gloria. Maybe it was only local, or maybe their training officer was babysitting.

'Look, I need to find these kids. You seen 'em?'

She showed the pictures of Maeve and Conor.

'Sergeant, these kids look like they just stepped out of the Wide

World of Disney,' the male cop said. 'We don't get a lot of that around here.'

He probably just meant they were white, Gloria thought.

The woman cop took Maeve's photo from her and looked closer. 'Yeah, we did see this one. She drive a little white Toyota?'

Gloria perked up and nodded.

'Two nights ago we saw her doing just what you're doing – canvassing the neighborhood.'

The male cop made a scornful sound. '*Neighborhood.* That's a nice one, Bina. Maybe they got a Thirty-one Flavors around the corner.'

'What they got is plenty of kids in school,' Gloria snapped. 'And life is all uphill for these poor kids. Try to imagine it, Biff. And, meantime, just shut up.' She turned to the woman. 'Anything more recent you remember?'

She handed the photograph back. 'Sorry. We'll keep our eye out. How do we reach you?'

Gloria gave her a card with her cell number. 'Were you born here, sis'?'

'Gujarat. That's just north of what you know as Bombay. Lots of high-tech. But my parents came over when I was two. All I really know is Palo Alto.'

'You got a strange job for a dot-on-the-forehead Indian,' Gloria said. 'I'm a feather-on-the-head Indian, if you don't take offense.'

'Ethnicity can be a funny moral area.'

'If you got a sense of humor,' Gloria said, and turned away before the obnoxious male partner could put in his two cents.

Somewhere Morty had found a big can of baked beans, and they warmed it on a can of Sterno so the kids didn't have to eat gefilte fish and chicken soup, but not much ambient heat was making it uphill past the steam leak that they could see billowing out into the staircase when they took turns as scouts with the one flashlight, and it was going to be a chilly night. A jet of steam, probably very hot at first, shot out of the wall enclosure and eventually billowed part way up the stairs but was pretty much defeated by their barricade. The radiator in the room was slightly warm.

They all sat in sweaters and overshirts, scattered around Sam Greengelb's room after Conor had given up the hunt for his missing guitar and reverted to the harp. Greengelb and Morty Lipman were teaching him, syllable-by-syllable, an old Yiddish folk song, one they told him that Billie Holiday had once recorded. He was game, but he insisted on knowing the chorus in English.

Maeve watched out the window, which had a pretty good view of Main Street and a bit of Fifth, and no one out there looked like the thugs, not unless they were hiding in old refrigerator boxes. But there *was* a big navy blue SUV that didn't look like it belonged there. She began to wonder how they were going to get through this weird night unscathed. But she liked all these people and would never have run out on them.

'*Men koyft dos nisht far keyn shum gelt,*
Dos krigt men nor umzist.'

Conor wrinkled his forehead and memorized phonetically.

Maeve saw a police car with a big 179 painted on its white roof and a 1 on its trunk. It cruised along Fifth and she wished she could flag it down. She was chagrined to think they were just as imprisoned on the third floor now as the bad guys were locked out.

'*A yidishe mame,*
Es gibt kayn besers oyf der velt.
A yidishe mame, oy vey,
Vi biter ven zi felt.'

She had no idea what they were singing, and even less interest, given their situation. She decided to be the responsible party and, while there was still a little daylight, she went upstairs with the flashlight, to make sure nobody else was hiding out there and to check exits. Mostly the room doors stood open to cheerless barren cells, the way she and Conor had left them, with stained mattresses askew and nothing personal on the walls or dressers. A few rooms had a rickety chair and a table the size of a hanky. Nobody answered her hollers. This had to be one of the most anonymous and forlorn habitations on the planet, she thought.

But something inside her objected to the thought, as if she had just affronted the homeless and impoverished. *Every place people live is as valid as every other place*, she decided. *So much of life is just luck.* The days in Skid Row had affected her deeply. *When this is all over, I will do special exercises, or special penance, or just special charity, to feel normal again.*

The sounds of the folksinging drifted up the steps as she started back down. For just an instant she felt terribly lonely – maybe more than she'd ever felt – but she knew that she had loyal allies down there, if not close friends.

Later, when she was back and pretending to take part, the old men taught Conor the chorus of their song in English, swaying back and forth beside one another where they sat on the edge of the bed.

> 'My yiddishe mama,
> I'd like to kiss that wrinkled brow.
> I long to hold her hands once more
> As in days gone by
> And ask her to forgive me
> For things I did that made her cry.'

Maeve couldn't help thinking of her own mother, and various things she had done to make *her* cry, and her eyes burned a little as she let herself settle into the burden of the song.

Jack Liffey parked his pickup half a block from the Catholic Liberation shelter and took a really deep breath. He'd already returned to the horrible warehouse and found it utterly empty, and now he had only two possible starting points for searching The Nickel – here and Chopper Tyrus's cardboard condo. This one was harder, at least emotionally, but he had a feeling it would probably be more helpful. He was still pretty shaky on his feet and had to grasp the brickwork and chain-link from time to time as he approached

'Hi, ma'am, remember me?'

The big black woman sat on her folding chair in front of the center. She set down a paper plate of beans and franks and frowned hard into the dusk to try to make him out.

'You the man come here wid Chopper. You the miracle man.'

'Absolutely correct. Could you tell the sister I'm here?'

'Which sister you mean?' Cagy – for some reason – as if there were lots of nuns in residence.

'The skinny nun.'

'Ah, Miz Mary Rose.'

It was hard for him to think of her as anything but Eleanor Ong – or a couple of pet names he'd once used – but he nodded. Sister Mary Rose it was. Even if the memory of her straddling his lap and muffling her cries of pleasure was fresh enough to start arousing him again.

'Where I'm at right now, I like you-all to do me a favor, sir.'

'But of course.'

She directed him to the paper bag behind the dumpster just outside the fence, and he could tell from the feel of the sloshing bottle that it was probably a half-drained pint of some twist-cap fortified wine. He'd once known their names but had forgotten them all except Thunderbird and Night Train. Gallo made most of them but didn't put its name on the labels.

'How do I get . . . this package in to you?' He was afraid to toss the bottle over.

'They's a cut in the fence.' She showed him a short slit in the wire and she held it open hard, just enough to pass the bag through. She took a good head-back slug of whatever it was and then gave a grateful smile to Jack Liffey.

'You ever need a good time, mister, you come find me.' He decided it was positive news: she didn't seem to know what had gone on between him and Eleanor. The woman hid the bag behind a bush and went inside.

It was still early evening but starting to become chilly and windy out, like the rainy night before, and he felt a new sympathy for all those caught out on the streets in the winter, homeless and destitute, even in L.A. He'd had his share and didn't want another.

Then *she* stepped out the door, dazzling and confident, and came to a dead stop on the porch when she saw Jack Liffey. 'We can't do this.'

'It's not what you think. I'm looking for my daughter. You told me you saw her. *Please* – let it be the thing that you do for me.'

'Yes, I did see Maeve. She's sure grown up. But it was two days ago.' She set her arms akimbo. 'I have no idea where she is now.' She waited a while, then sighed. 'All right, there's a woman staying here that Maeve helped. She'd do just about anything for her. Let me ask.' The sun was declining beneath a black cloud bank far to the west, and a last gleam of light lashed out, between the skyscrapers of downtown, and caught her like a Kleig light, in a thoughtful pose, watching him. 'You're a sore temptation, Jack.'

'You, too.'

She turned and went inside without another word. He'd have understood if she'd just sent him away immediately.

She'd once told him – her very last words to him way back when – that she didn't think he was going to make it. She and Gloria were a pair. He wondered why he was drawn to such strong women – if it was a vanity of some kind.

Then a skinny woman with the caved-in face of the dustbowl and limp blond hair came out the door. She wore a thin dress, a pink sweater, and weird rubber shoes. A smaller edition of the woman peeked around the door, her expression as ferocious as a guardian angel.

'Sister said Maeve was in trouble,' the woman offered.

'I'm her father, Jack. Who are you?'

'Felice Stone. I been looking for my old man Clarence, from San Antone. You know him?'

Hope really was eternal, he thought. It was starting to get cold out, and he saw how thin their clothes were. 'Sorry, no. Do you know where Maeve might be tonight?'

'What's her trouble?' the little girl snapped out.

'She has too much sympathy for her own good, I'd say,' Jack Liffey replied.

That seemed to make the little girl even angrier.

'I'm sorry, what's your name?'

'Millie,' the girl said. 'Can you help us find my father?'

'Probably not, Millie. This is a pretty big city that tends to swallow people up. But if you tell me what you know about Maeve, I'll ask a police officer I know to help with your father.'

Sister Mary Rose came out behind them, carrying a folded blanket. She threw the blanket to the black woman eating the last of her dinner. 'Don't leave now,' she said. 'The rule is you can't come back in after sunset.'

'Eleanor – shame on you,' Jack Liffey said. He had a strange intuition that these two could just possibly help him find Maeve. 'If we all followed the rules, the bullies would win every time. These women love Maeve, I can tell. If they want to help, I'll protect them.'

'Can you even protect yourself right now?'

'Ooh. You hit low. I'm still here, you see.' He was tempted to add, 'And I'm armed,' but he didn't. It wouldn't have carried the right weight with Eleanor. 'Millie, do you know anything about where Maeve might be?' he asked.

'No, siree.' She seemed genuinely apologetic.

'I made the decision to let them hear your story, Jack. You can see they can't help you. Let them stay in the shelter where it's warm and safe.'

He was about to agree.

'We all know they ain't no safe, not nohow, Sister ma'am,' Felice said with her beleaguered intensity. 'Not in this here world. Even good union men from strong companies get laid off now. Even schoolteachers get just junked out with the junk.'

Eleanor let her head nod to one side, as if she'd been chastised by her Mother Superior. 'Thank you, Felice. That tells me where I live. Go with God and Jack, if you wish, and help him. He's a good man. Jack, God help you if you let any harm come to these innocents.'

Strangely, though still unsteady on his feet and clinging to the fence, he felt that he had been waiting years and years for just such a responsibility. He wondered if he might still be trying to prove himself to Eleanor, whom he had once failed spectacularly. 'This one isn't about you,' Jack Liffey said softly to Eleanor.

No, it was his task – the one he would ride until the wheels fell off.

'Are you so sure?'

'I'm not sure the sun will come up tomorrow. Please get them coats,' he requested.

She nodded once and went inside. Quickly she came back with the requisites.

'Come on, ladies,' Jack Liffey said. 'Our job, should we accept it, is to find Maeve *tonight*. She's out here somewhere. And it's a cold and dangerous night.'

Eleanor let the girl and her mother out the gate with her key, and she followed them to his pickup. 'Lend a willing ear, Lord God, to our prayers, and bless this truck with Your holy right hand. Direct Your holy angels to accompany it tonight, that they may keep those who ride in it from all dangers, and always guard them.'

'That's impressive,' Jack Liffey said. 'Do you have a blessing for skateboards, too?'

'Shut up, Jack.' But he saw her suppressing a smile as she turned away. He did his best not to look in the rearview mirror.

The bench seat of the little Toyota pickup wasn't really roomy enough for all their hips, even skinny as the women were, and the little girl had to sit forward in the middle, her legs on her mom's side of the hump. 'OK,' Jack Liffey said. 'Ideas? Anything? Places you saw her.'

'Kin you git me a cigarette first?' Felice asked. 'I think I going to die if I go another night without smokes.'

So *that* was part of her motive. 'Easiest thing in the world. But think about Maeve, please, while I drive. Where would she go?'

'She was looking for a boy.'

He nodded. He wished he had a photo of Conor. If there had been any extras in thc house, Gloria had grabbed them. He'd seen

one of Maeve's copies briefly, but he hadn't seen Conor in the flesh
since he was about two years old.

'Please. I need a ciggie.'

In a few blocks he pulled up on a hand-lettered sign for Mike's
Market and parked in front. 'What's your brand?' Jack Liffey asked.

'Cheap is good. American Eagles is good.'

He'd never heard of it. Some brand they'd come out with since
he'd quit so many years ago, he thought. 'How about I get you
something nice? Virginia Slims or Marlboros.'

'Oooh, Slims. Please.'

That was good because it sealed him off from temptation. Gloria
had always said that if a man even touched one of those skinny
pastel cigarettes, his balls would fall off.

As a big black security guard loomed in the shadows watchfully,
an Asian clerk peered out a small hatch. 'Have you got any single-
malt whiskeys from Islay?' Jack Liffey asked.

The clerk frowned. 'You want walk with the king? In this store?
No got.'

It'd just been a tease. 'I'd like a pack of Virginia Slims, and . . .
here.' He plucked a Milky Way out of a display and set it in the
metal declivity that passed under the bulletproof glass.

The price he rang up on the cigarettes made Jack Liffey lift his
eyebrows a bit since he hadn't bought smokes in two decades –
$6.67 a pack – but he knew the real problem was still coming, what
he called his people's credit card, the $100 bill he always kept in
his glove box. His wallet was long gone. 'Look, this is the only
cash I have right now. Can you accept it?'

'No take. Too big.' The clerk shook his head firmly at the bill
and held up two palms.

'How much would I have to buy in here for you to take it? How
about fifty dollars of stuff?'

'Sixty dollah.' Life was a haggle.

'Fifty-five.'

'Sixty. Gotta be more half.'

He decided not to argue the math, and he wandered the two
cramped aisles in the little mart picking up treats at random for the
women, candy, potato chips, mac-and-cheese boxes. There weren't
a lot of luxury goods. And nothing much appealed to him.

'What would you buy?' he asked the black sphinx who was
eyeing him neutrally.

'I go for the beef jerky, man.'

Jack Liffey grabbed a handful of cello packs of some mini-mart brand of over-processed flaked-and-formed beef jerky. Back at the clerk window, he told the man to throw in a full carton of Slims.

It was well over $60, and the clerk took Jack Liffey's Ben Franklin. On the way out with the paper bag, he stopped and tossed the beef jerky packets to the guard.

'On me, friend.'

'Jesus be with you tonight.'

That was twice in a half-hour Jesus had been enjoined to watch over him. He wished he could trade those blessings in for ordinary luck. He had more faith in that.

He handed the bag in the truck window to Felice. Millie had crawled across her mother's lap, her face was outside, hung over the truck window and her finger jabbing urgently at something out there over his shoulder. Whirling around, Jack Liffey felt a chill, as if a man with a three-foot machete was about to attack him.

What he saw was an empty sidewalk and the window of Mike's Market, if you could call it a window any longer, every inch blocked by cardboard cartons, a fading 'Special' sign for milk, posters for fortified wine, and dozens of promotional notices that had seen better days, some for products like Colgate Dental Cream with Gardol that no longer even existed – or maybe they did. Down in the lower right corner someone had managed to slide in a 'Missing Person' notice, with a boy's photograph and a request to call what he recognized instantly as Maeve's cell number. He walked over and squatted down to it and quickly noticed the resemblance to Mike Lewis, almost impish, dark wavy hair and wise eyes.

'Hello, Conor,' Jack Liffey said to the photo. 'Haven't seen you in donkey's years.'

He went straight back into the store to ask about the notice.

In California, service sector jobs increased from 79 per cent of all jobs in 1990 to 84 per cent in 2006, many of these making or serving fast food. A full 43 per cent of the newest jobs were in the lowest fifth of the earnings distribution. The typical Latino worker's hourly wage declined by 8 per cent, and African-Americans fared even worse.

FIFTEEN
To Get out of the Box Canyon Alive

'How soon from the last tenant out on the street to the stripping crew coming in the door?'

Eddie Wolverton shrugged. 'I don't really handle that end, Mose. Danny's your structural engineer, but I bet he could put a contractor on alert. Probably six a.m. the day after, and they could be hanging the waste chutes by seven. But it's not like there's a lot of folks standing on line to take your place. You know, some guy with shiny Manolos just waiting to relaunch the Fortnum as the ritzy new Fortnum-Sheraton Skid Row.'

'Don't kid yourself,' Vartabedian said. He held out a box of his second-best Corona Canelas, and Eddie waved them off. He didn't keep his best ones here in his local office. 'There's three public housing agencies who'd love to have that building to rent out to lots more bums. I bid high to drive them off in the first place, but it's all contingent on this fucking catch-twenty-two about the place being empty.'

Vartabedian plucked a cigar out himself, rolled it in his mouth to wet it, and then used the little gold guillotine off his desktop to circumcise it. From where he sat, by turning his head slightly to the right, he could see a big red sun inching down and across the narrow slit between the KPMG tower and the Deloitte & Touche. He nodded to suggest the interesting view to Eddie, but he didn't notice whether Eddie bothered to look. It really was a glorious sight, he thought as he puffed hard. He watched the tail end of the sun creep across the opening, an incandescent red gasbag sinking at a shallow angle into the Pacific. His father had burned out one of his foveas watching a solar eclipse in Turkey when he was twelve, but there was little danger of that here with the sun so low and all the smoked glass on his retrofitted windows.

'Making something good, man,' Vartabedian mused. 'Remaking something better. The whole motherfucking creative process. It just floats there inside you.' He puffed hard and blew a ring, then blew a smaller ring that passed through it. 'Sometimes it's better than sex.'

'Speak for yourself.'

Moses Vartabedian had to admit he was letting himself get carried away just a little at that moment, but he had four more buildings on hold, set for after the Fortnum. 'You're the rehab artist, dude. Don't lose that feeling. You should go with it.'

'I'll take a good blow job over a rehab, V.'

'Sometimes a blow job is just a blow job,' he said, eyeing his cigar and smiling. Freud was dead. 'You know, they're doing amazing things with the old Cecil two blocks from the Fortnum. Actually promoting it as a European-style hotel, whatever the fuck that is.'

'Roaches, you think?' Eddie said slyly.

'Nah, the place itself isn't so bad. Intimate and quaint, I bet. It's the location.'

'Yeah, these classy Euro tourists, I bet they get a kick out of stepping over winos to get to their taxis. I bet the owner doesn't advertise the Cecil had an Australian serial killer staying there.'

'Jesus, I wouldn't even advertise we had Bukowsi, and I know for a fact he stayed at the Fortnum for six months.'

'No shit? I loved Buk. He leave anything behind?'

'You mean that would grow in a Petri dish?'

Wolverton smiled, then laughed. 'Nice one, Mose. I meant a poem in his Gideon's or some scribbling on the wall. It'd be worth a pretty penny.'

'Cokehounds stole everything in that room years ago. Amazing what they think has street value. I had a smelly guy try to sell me a clapped out Bic pen for ten cents once. Jesus, it was plastic see-through and clearly had no ink in it. Right out front of the Fortnum, as a matter of fact.'

Wolverton shrugged. 'I'd like to do a study of the scribblings in the bathrooms there. I could probably get a Ph.D. in folklore. But you're the guy insists we scrape the plaster back to brick, expose all the ducts and pipes the way those loftheads love it.'

'I should put out a rumor the Fortnum is haunted. I swear, these mix 'n' match spiritual kids today, they'd do tours.'

They waited in silence for a moment, as Vartabedian puffed away and watched the last of the deep red ball winking out on the north side of the Deloitte & Touche, leaving everything in the western sky banded scarlet. He relished the puzzled thoughts he seemed to be drawing out of Eddie Wolverton, whizzing around in the air around them. Something was making the man edgy, and finally the architect came out with what it was.

'You got the Katzenjammer Kids out of the picture, right, V? I mean that big guy that looks like Custer and his sidekick, the little knife-man. They're a loose-cannon sandwich. I don't want any association with those nutcases. If the gutter press finds out, it's like you been raping some high school boy. Reputation is delicate, Moses.'

'True, true. I admit – they were a bad idea from the git-go, but they came highly recommended as fixers. So McClatchy got it wrong. I already yanked them off the case totally, today, and told them to stay home or else. I'll go talk to the old tenants myself in the morning. Everybody's got a price, in a very civilized world. Maybe I got to give some big bucks to their favorite Jewish cause. No problemo.'

'There!' the girl said excitedly, pointing.

It was a lot closer than he'd expected. A vertical neon sign hadn't yet flickered on, if it ever would, but it was just readable in the reddish dusk. **T– –   – – –num.** The dangly part of it, clearly **he Fort**, had swung free from one neon tube and was hanging upside down. It would probably never light up again.

Jack Liffey had dived back into Mike's Market to ask about the missing-boy poster in the window, and the clerk had immediately suggested either St Michael's or the Fortnum down the block. He didn't bother asking why. It hardly mattered. His first impression of the Fortnum, with Millie almost snarling out the car window as he parked, was an expanse of cracked wired glass where the lobby should be, one window covered with raw plywood, which may have gone back to the Reagan administration.

'I'm just a little slip of a thing,' Felice said, 'but I'll help you all the way with this, mister. But only if you help us find Clarence.'

'I promised I would,' Jack Liffey said. 'I keep my word.' Most of his attention was focused on a big black high-boosted Dodge truck down the street, on the far side of the road, with what might have been two faces inside the murky windshield. The dusk denied him a good look at the men inside, but something about the look of them, the way they held themselves, and the damn truck itself, teased a few neurons that hinted at the thugs who'd kicked him around. He was here and he was still there, feeling it in his ribs, all at the same time. He wondered if everybody lived in overlapping realities.

'My dad was a Polack,' Felice announced to him, apropos of nothing. 'He was always teaching me to sing the Polish national anthem, but I only remember the first line.'

'Lord, what's that?' Jack Liffey said, hardly listening. He was waiting for a giveaway movement from the truck, but nothing came.

'It's *Jeszcze Polska nie* and something something. He always told me in English it means, "All is not *yet* lost." He was that kind of man for his family. You could count on him to help you, you know?'

'Good for him. It's a wonderful human trait.' Not so great for a national anthem, though, Jack Liffey thought. He tried, but he had trouble bringing a sense of irony to bear. He was too worried about the men he might be seeing in the truck. *OK, stay alive, Jack. All is not yet lost.*

'Let's look inside this place,' he said, and he touched the pistol in the small of his back for a little reassurance. 'I have a hunch this is the place.' He wasn't sure how strong the inclination was, but what he really wanted to do was walk straight over to that boosted truck and blast them both with his pistol, on general principles – guys who would throw a wheelchair-bound man around like a sack of potatoes.

This impulse to shoot them wasn't like remembering. It was happening now, in his head. Long ago, he'd killed a man, pretty much in cold blood, when he'd been left no other way to save Eleanor Ong and himself from a world of thugs, but that killing still invaded his dreams off-and-on like a rogue fact disguising itself as other things.

He knew he wasn't a samurai, or anything even close, but he'd known one, of sorts, an American Nisei incensed by what had been done to his family. And from him he'd learned that even samurai – men of supposedly pure and ferocious honor – weren't allowed to exterminate people just like that. They needed a validation. He'd heard of things past guilt, but he'd never found anything past guilt himself except a lot more guilt. How come you never got over things like that? It mattered on a night as iffy as this one.

*   *   *

'Cripes, this is got to be a smack dream,' Steve McCall said. 'But I don't *do* smack.' A man who could only have been their wheelchair guy, the big old guy who'd pounded on their roll-up door – Liffey, he remembered the name. He got out of the little white pickup followed by a skinny bedraggled woman, and then a wraith of a girl-child and they trotted right into the Fortnum, with the wheelchair guy stalling a bit at the door to look around like a Secret Service ace, scouting the President's line of march. And doing his best not to look straight at their Dodge. Which was pretty weird, too, when you figured their shiny new hi-rider was the only other vehicle on the block and, basically, downright peculiar on Skid Row.

'That's that guy that braced us,' Rice Thibodeaux said. 'Cha cha cha.'

'Sure looks like him, only he must have been to the Holy Rollers since we saw him. He's got his legs back. Man, this really weirds me out.'

'Nothing weirds me out,' Thibodeaux said impassively. 'Not if I can stick it with a knife.'

'Well, tonight might just be the fucking night, my friend.' McCall was losing patience with the whole assignment, with Vartabedian, and with a world that had never even come close to giving him his due. 'I have a feeling that funny little fuckers like that old guy are going to get their just deserts tonight. I feel it deep in my pancreas. And those asshole old Jews in the Fortnum, too.'

'Now you're talking, man. I had dealings with Jews down in Carolina, and it was always best to take them out right away.'

McCall sighed. 'Can we not go to massacre mode right off the bat?' he suggested. 'I'm not really comfortable with mass-murder. Maybe we can *hurt* somebody and still make some money here.'

'Oh, yeah, *money*. That's always a kick. But, you know, Steverino, in the end Nietzsche and I don't give a shit what you citizens think.'

The expression 'citizens' put his back up; it caught out his vanity in some way. McCall was mildly sorry he'd ever gotten stuck with this feckless little psycho, but war taught you that when push came to shove, in a violent universe, that's who you wanted on your side in the end. Keep your sob-sisters and your sensitive souls, your poets and religious junkies. When it was wartime, you wanted a stone realist who'd kill everything in sight and get you out of the box canyon alive.

Jack Liffey hit the little brass ring-a-ling bell on the hotel counter
one more time, but it was becoming obvious that on this night the
hotel crew had all abandoned ship. And that probably meant a ferocious monsoon was imminent.

Felice cupped her mouth and hollered up the staircase in a surprisingly penetrating halloo, 'Maeve, is you up there, girl? This here's
Felice!'

He wondered if there was any logic to thinking Maeve and Conor
were in the same place this night.

Only a Steinbeck logic. *Wherever people are in trouble, there I
will be*, he thought. Or whatever it was Tom Joad had said at the
end.[4]

He held up his hand to keep Felice from yelling again so he
could listen. Faint harmonica music wafted down the staircase and
singing. It sounded live. And there was a separate hiss, like a big
deflating balloon.

'Maeve!' he bellowed. 'Conor!' It set his throat on fire to yell.

The music stopped abruptly, so maybe his restored voice had got
through. He stared upward into nothing. Into more darkness, inky,
sinister. It was like his nightmares, maybe everyone's nightmares.
Maybe we were all just a long trail of ants, bearing the same insights
off into the unknown.

'Hello?' a man's voice called down faintly. Somebody wanting
to sound like he was in charge. 'Who's there?'

For some reason Jack Liffey's eyeballs ached, staring so hard
into that formless darkness. He began to make out the suggestion
of a landing half a flight up.

'Jack Liffey. And friends.'

'Wait,' another male voice said, and then, '*Dad!*'

'Maeve!'

'You can talk!'

He almost laughed. 'Just like any parrot! Only not as smart. Can
we come up?'

'Uh, that's a bit tough.'

'Explain tough!'

'We got a blockade!' the man's voice called. 'We made it

---

[4] But only in Woody Guthrie's song and Nunnally Johnson's movie script,
both of which were vast improvements on the embarrassingly sentimental
breast-feeding scene at the end of the original book.

impenetrable. *Nu*, so maybe you could come back tomorrow, Mr Maeve.'

'Dad,' Maeve overruled, 'who are these friends, please? The guys up here are expecting real gangsters. They're afraid.'

Jack Liffey looked at the skinny woman and child. 'I don't think there's any danger right now. This is the woman and girl you dropped off at the shelter.'

'Felice! Millie!'

'Hi, Maeve,' Felice called. 'Your daddy said you were missing.'

Jack Liffey could hear people disputing upstairs for a while. It was becoming absurd, like hearing drunks carrying on in a locked men's room when you needed it badly. Finally Maeve called down, 'Dad, come up a floor and a half and I'll get you in. Watch out for the hot steam. It's one floor up.'

Jack Liffey went ahead of their party, and the world started to get even darker, and damper. No lights were on anywhere. At the top of the second flight, he kept to the right, feeling the wet heat off to his left and hearing the ugly hiss grow insistent. He tested the blowing spout of steam with an outstretched hand and yanked away when he found it grew scalding fast. The source had to be superheated vapor, like from a boiler. There was a little outside light from the end of the hallway, and as his eyes adjusted he could see that the enraged fizz seemed to be erupting from an open rectangle on the wall.

'Stay all the way to the right, folks,' Jack Liffey called behind him. 'On the left, the steam gets hot enough to burn.'

For some reason, nothing was really worrying him. The vitriol of weeks of bondage to the wheelchair seemed to have drained out of him, and he was freewheeling now on a kind of recovery euphoria. He'd been intimate with drugs and drink long ago, and this was as good as that, he thought – a buzz like a couple of serious drinks.

Up another half flight of regathering darkness, he came up against a wire barrier that was almost invisible. Wires, hard edges. A flickery lantern light began to move around on the upward side to help a little. He made out a tangle of innersprings and random chairs that had all been taped and wired together.

'Jack here!' he called. 'How the hell did you folks figure on getting out of here for food?'

A small balding man in a brown wooly suit stepped into the

lantern light. He was doing his best to look fierce, arms akimbo, but really only managed to look like a constipated Leprechaun.

'We don't anticipate the standoff lasting forever, Mr Liffey. We just have to make it known we're still here. If we slow the whole process down, maybe Vartabedian Enterprises can't strip everything out of the hotel and go forward with the loft conversion.'

He could sense the worry underlying the man's voice. How simple and true, he thought. 'This is going to be yuppie lofts? *This?*'

'I know, man. *Feh!*'

'Maeve, come out and talk please,' Jack Liffey called.

Then a door slammed well below them and they all turned abruptly. Probably the street door since a faint purr of the ambience of the outside world abruptly ceased. Uh-oh, he thought. Incoming.

'Tell me you didn't know they were right behind you,' the little man challenged.

'Man, look, I'm your best friend. Believe me. My daughter's up there. But we're stuck on the wrong side of your barrier.' He touched his .38 momentarily. 'Does one of the guys you're expecting have golden dreadlocks?'

McCall and Thibodeaux stared up the linoleum staircase, listening to the faint voices under the insistent fizzing sound and feeling something like a condensation on the air, vaguely warm.

'What the hell?' McCall said softly. 'The boiler's fail-safe. I worked on this shit in Chicago. You can't fire it up if there's no back pressure in the steam line.'

'Only bitches got teats,' Thibodeaux said. 'But then you and me got teats.'

The big man's evil eye came around on him. 'Why are we talking about this? Is this more of your Nietzsche shit?' McCall said.

'And here we are.' The little man took out a big ugly K-bar Special Forces killing knife that he'd picked up somewhere. 'Yo, fuckers. This has all been unacceptable from the beginning.'

Thibodeaux turned and charged up the steps, well ahead of McCall, who sighed and then plodded after him in his long-suffering way, heading into the unintelligible howl of the world and in no particular hurry to run himelf into another hornets' nest. Then Thibodeaux screamed up ahead of him, and McCall heard the knife drop to thunk into the linoleum.

*   *   *

Maeve was wriggling her way down the outside of the barricade like a caterpillar, forcing her way underneath, ripping tape free and shoving aside corners of bare bedsprings, pushing under and through the tangled mass of junk. The lantern up above showed her progress.

The two short old men beside the lantern were not very pleased to see how easily she was getting through, evidently suspecting a kind of treason.

'You gotta crawl under stuff the way I'm doing,' Maeve announced to those below.

'You left a path for the *shaygets* to get at us!'

Maeve ignored the complaint from above as her head emerged at the bottom, pushing aside a big oblong of torn plywood. 'Quick! Everybody.' She beckoned them to follow her back up. 'Stay in the corner over here. Push stuff up or away really hard and tuck under.'

They heard running footsteps down below and then a terrible scream. Jack Liffey decided not to argue about anything. Maeve lifted the plywood for the little girl first and then Felice, and then she wriggled ahead to hold the bedsprings open at the next level. Jack Liffey went last, holding up his own barriers.

'Gentlemen, give us a hand!' Jack Liffey called. Reluctantly the men began to tug at the upper reaches of the barricade.

Maeve seemed a bit jittery. 'I better seal it back! Dad, go past me.'

It was a lot harder than it looked, since he was bigger than any of them and sapped by his weeks of immobility. He went over on his back and wormed himself up the stairs, pushing with his legs, the bare bedsprings riding painfully across his face and scraping down his body. Maeve wriggled behind him, carrying a roll of silver duct tape, waiting for him to clear a little space for her.

Thibodeaux came running blindly down the steps, his hands clapped to his eyes, and McCall tried to catch him, nearly bowling them both over in near darkness. McCall lifted him up bodily and held his still running feet above the steps as the man whimpered and cried.

'Jaysus, man, suck it up! Be frosty now!'

'They blinded me!'

'Shit, stay right here.' McCall set him down hard at the foot of the steps, against a wall, and hurried upward, drawing the huge .50-

caliber Desert Eagle from his shoulder holster. The old Jews could wave their little .25 purse-gun all they wanted now.

Maeve was scrunched up, fixing the oblong of plywood back in place with her tape on the uphill side as Jack Liffey kept forcing his way under the box springs, urging Felice and Millie on ahead.

Time is all that matters, he thought; it's the only narrative we've got. Hurry or die. 'This is all bullshit!' It was a man's deep and resonant voice, yelling from well below them. The voice was vaguely familiar to Jack Liffey – Goldilocks. 'Just fall in where you are! OK. Ow, you got live steam blowin' loose, don't you? Did you plan that? I can get past this shit!'

'Go away, *golem!*' one of the old men called from above.

'You're outgunned, man! Don't think you can make war on an old warrior!'

Jack Liffey knew that he and Maeve were still sitting ducks – trapped in a maze of wire bedsprings if a shooting war broke out. By the lantern light, he could just see Maeve working rapidly and clumsily with the roll of duct tape, tying things back together below himself.

Reluctantly Jack Liffey reached into the back of his waistband and drew out the .revolver – a terrible lump between his hip and the floor that had bruised him at every step. He aimed it high, well over Maeve, but still held his fire. *OK, kiddo, this is where we all find out who we are*, he thought.

'Listen to me, my blond friend!' Jack Liffey called out. He knew who the voice belonged to now. 'Whoever you are, whoever you're working for. I don't know you and you don't know me – other than dumping me on Skid Row in a wheelchair. Not very brotherly, I must say.'

'Who the fuck are you, man? Are you Liffey? I've still got your wallet and gun.'

'I have a better pistol. I've been through Tet in the big Nam, and I'm guessing you've seen your own share of hell in Iraq. Am I right?'

'Well, I think you're an asshole, Liffey. You're just a guy of nothing, less-and-less as you turn into a senior citizen.'

'So what was *your* MOS? 44C?' Jack Liffey suggested. That was the military occupational specialty for accountant – a challenge that was well over the edge of insulting.

Maeve continued wrapping the duct tape around wire frames at his feet, and he wormed up and up through the convoluted barricade to stay ahead.

'Screw you, gimp! MOS 11B and proud. What about you, friend? What was your stupid MOS?'

Eleven B was plain rifle infantryman. This guy had never even made NCO, or made it and got busted back down. He himself had been a 350G – imagery intelligence technician, a radar watcher who'd tracked the B-52 runs from Thailand, but he wasn't going to cop to that, nor was he going to falsely claim eighteen something-or-other for Special Forces. No lies when you were this close to death. 'That's for you to worry about, creampuff!' Jack Liffey shouted. 'Maybe I was in a sniper team! These people up here are under my protection tonight, son. Like *Have Gun, Will Travel*. Wire Palladin, San Francisco. Or were you too young to remember all that?'

'What the fuck you on about?'

So he *was* too young to remember even the reruns of that wonderful old Richard Boone TV show. Basically, Jack Liffey was just trying to keep him occupied while he gestured frantically for Maeve to do a less thorough job of sealing the barricade and step it up a notch. She nodded when she felt him pluck at her back.

Chills ran up and down his spine whenever he realized they were trapped like insects in amber. He had no doubt his 11B infantryman opponent downstairs was well armed. There was something in this terrible moment that he knew he would remember in his nightmares.

'What's your name, soldier?' Jack Liffey called.

'Maybe you could just tell me who the fuck you really are, Mr Big Nam.'

'I'm a specialist in protection now,' Jack Liffey said. 'Like all those trigger-happy jerkoffs Blackwood sends to guard the Baghdad embassy and shoot up civilians.'

There was a sharp bark of a laugh below. 'Then you'll love my partner. That was him for two years. Blew away whole families of towel-heads just for getting too close.'

From the progress of the voice, Jack Liffey sensed the man was working his way slowly up the stairwell, and he strained to see into the darkness below. Unfortunately, the kerosene lantern threw most of its light on him and Maeve. They were only two-thirds of the

way through the entrapping barricade, but there was no way he was
going to hurry on and leave Maeve behind, methodically wrapping
her duct tape.

'Be very careful about entering my line of fire, Private Eleven-
B,' Jack Liffey called. 'The minute I can make you out, you're part
of my business.'

'Why you protecting these folks? We ought to get together on
this. There's big money in clearing out this building.'

'What're they promising you, soldier – a thousand a head?'

Suddenly, he thought he saw a blur of movement down below,
then a point-source flash, and a powerful gunshot *pazinged* past
them, a kind of chime at one of the box springs. The deep boom
a half-instant later echoed deafeningly up the staircase and raised
the hackles on Jack Liffey's neck. It was the loudest pistol shot
he'd ever heard, probably some oversized magnum. There was
little chance the man was still standing where he'd seen the
muzzle flash. Whereas, if he fired back now, he'd show his
own muzzle flash, and he couldn't dive quickly away from it.

'Don't do that again, son,' Jack Liffey called, with all the authority
and calm he could muster. 'I don't want to hurt an army brother.'

Then Jack Liffey heard two men down below, speaking in that
voiceless voice that was often quieter than a whisper. He guessed
his opponent had retreated one landing at least.

'Who's your pal, Eleven-B?' Jack Liffey called out. 'Mr
Blackwood finally show up? In a world of bad things, mercenaries
are about as bad as you get!'

'Fuck you, asshat!'

It *was* the other one he remembered. The shrill voice he recognized, the knife man who'd grabbed his gun. He'd hoped to provoke
him, get a kind of read on him, and he had already: a voice that
was off-center, carrying some peculiar undertow of impassive
madness. Jack Liffey knew he'd been a small man. He guessed he'd
been something of a loser all his life.

He grabbed Maeve's collar with his free hand and bodily dragged
her away from the taping chore that she was intent upon. The barricade would just have to do as it was. '*Up,*' he said very softly but
urgently a few inches from her ear. '*Now.*'

She knew better than to resist. She crawled over him and wriggled under the last of the barricading box springs. It would do fine
as a barrier as long as they watched it.

'Hey, Liff,' the knife-man's voice called scornfully from down below. 'One good trainee from Blackwood could wax ten of you bearded doper draftees from Nam. What you got – a peace sign tattooed on your forehead?'

Keep him talking, Jack Liffey thought as he wormed his way out beneath the last springset, pinning his own arms dangerously for a few moments. 'Why not the regular army for you, Shorty? I bet they wouldn't take you. You a Section Eight? You one of those dingbats who eats his own shit?'

'You're mine, Liffey! I'm a knife man. Whatever else goes down here tonight, whatever iron you're carrying, I'm going to git behind you some time and carve you like a jack-o-lantern.'

Jack Liffey's legs came free and he jumped to his feet too soon and then toppled forward into the barricade – he'd forgotten how weak and dizzy he was on his feet. He waved several people nearby to get around the corner of the stairwell and pointed urgently at the lantern until Maeve got the idea and took that away as well.

Now the payback, if they came up to the landing. He wished he had a reload for Gloria's .38.

'Come on up, pals. Let's talk. I have a weakness for dingbats.'

There was only silence and he figured they were ascending silently.

He aimed to the right side of the stairwell, timed it out as best he could to what he heard and fired twice. Not as loud as theirs, but loud enough. Then he fired once quickly to the left, just for the hell of it.

'Work with that, *pendejos*!' Jack Liffey shouted, 'I'm Palladin tonight. There's plenty more to come!'

Recently immigrated Latino teens are, remarkably, the highest paid of all teenage workers, largely because they work a whole lot more than anyone else. Second-generation Latino teens are paid much less, experience higher unemployment, and have much lower rates of job-holding than the recently arrived immigrants.

SIXTEEN
The Laughing Buddha

'Oh, man, did you hear that?' Paula said quickly to Gloria. 'That wasn't no firecrackers.' The gunshots had been blocks away, muffled by the walls of a building, but they both knew the difference between a gunshot and black powder tamped into a small cardboard tube for a festival. They knew it intimately and from far too much experience.

'Makes my day,' Gloria said, settling into a kind of job-related assurance. 'Damn big handgun. Drug-dealer's piece maybe. A.forty-five or a mag, I'm sure.' She realized this guessing the caliber of a gunshot was like other L.A. residents speculating on the Richter level of an earthquake, an endless local sport. *Probably only a four-point-two, unless it was far away.*

'But I bet there's a lot of that night shit out here. I spent my first New Year's Eve on the job in Seventy-Seventh Street Division, and it was like, you know, Baghdad on steroids. There was automatic weapon fire solid from eleven-thirty to twelve-thirty, I swear to the God of guns, whoever he is. Some of us went out onto Broadway and followed our ears and caught a big Latino family in their own back yard walking a circle around two card tables with a dozen weapons, guys grabbing the next and the next and firing in the air, while the women sat on folding chairs reloading like the Alamo. I guess it's a tradition in Sonora or wherever. The next morning the janitor showed me what he'd swept off the division's flat roof – two big buckets of fallen blunts and copper jackets.'

They stood beside Gloria's car in the dark and listened intently to the thrum of downtown noise – a crackling transformer on a power pole, the faraway freeways, maybe something deep in the earth turning over slowly.

'Made me want to wear a metal hat next year, but Ken got me down to Harbor, and Harbor Division wasn't half so bad.'

'I say it came from there,' Paula pointed. 'I got radar ears.' Her finger pointed off through a vacant lot. Not far from where her pointing finger ended up she was startled to discover the head of a leather-skinned man with long straight black hair under a head-band standing stock still only three feet away, as if catatonic, eyes wide open.

'Sorry, man,' Paula offered, but he didn't so much as budge.

He looked like a true burned-out case, Gloria thought. A Native American – she guessed that much; her own people. Gloria waved a hand in front of the man's eyes but he didn't come around.

'Shit. It is the Nature Channel,' Paula said.

Crystal meth could leave people frozen like that for hours, Gloria thought. 'Let's go on foot and listen for more shots. The car's too loud.'

'Go, girl,' Paula said. 'I love this and I hate it.'

'Really? What part?'

'The hunt for trouble. Isn't it what we're trained for?'

'I don't know,' Gloria said. She'd never heard this note of edgy melancholy in Paula's voice. 'I always think the best part of the job is *un*tangling things. People all choked up in their problems and their relatives. Trying to bring peace to them.' The momentary upset began to melt back into her bloodstream, her nerve fibers.

'Sure, all that, too. But hunting them out. First you find them, then you whack them a few times upside the head to get their attention – then you bring the peace.'

Gloria tried to take it as a joke, but the tone was pretty grim. Something was demoralizing Paula.

'And maybe the only peace you bring them is a hellhole like Corcoran for twenty-to-life. So be it,' Paula said.

'What's this about?' Gloria said. 'I'm always here for you, Paula.'

'Welcome to L.A., girl.' Paula laughed, without much humor, as they reached the far side of the vacant lot. 'What you perceive here is the curse of being an emotional human being. No, a *woman*, a vuln-able pussy under all this damn gear. Sorry, sister. Dieter dropped me hard last week.'

'Oh, shit. I'm so sorry. You didn't say.'

She shrugged. 'He was 'sperimenting, I guess to tell. White boys and that ol' brown sugar, you know how it go.'

'I can't barely see, man. I'm a cutter, but I got to see good to carve. We got to wait a while for my eyes to bogue it out.'

'Go for it, Mr Rice. Keep your eyes tight shut. Ain't got no eyedrops but the water'll help.'

'That steam was awful bad.'

'Are you gonna be OK?'

'Outstanding,' Thibodeaux said. 'A few minutes or so here.'

'Take your time, little brah,' Steve McCall offered from where they sat side-by-side on the staircase. *A sad little song*, was what he really thought. *This psycho is going to go down hard one day, maybe very soon.*

'He's got iron balls, whoever this Liffey is,' McCall said. 'Palladin, shit. That fuckstick.'

'Maybe we got to burn them all out. I got the gas.'

'Vartabedian wouldn't like *that*,' McCall said warily. 'You can send that scheme back to your idea fairy.'

'Burn the fat Armenian out, too. Fuck him.'

'Man, this is so far beyond right and wrong. Shit belongs to the guy who stays in control.'

Thibodeaux tried to open his eyes, which watered and burned. He knew his partner wouldn't recognize the source of the quotation that was coming. 'It's nobler to declare yourself wrong than insist on being right – especially when you're wrong.' He cackled, but the pain made him grimace, and he had to press the heels of his palms to his eyes.

McCall stared hard at the little man while he seemed to be blinded. This is just more of his adolescent crap, he thought. 'That some of your Nietzsche shit?'

'Get ready to ratfuck the weak,' Thibodeaux fluted. 'I had my ass on the line in the sandbox over there just like you, man. You know damn well the bold always fuck over the slaves.'

Things became primitive so quickly, McCall thought. He watched the little man with something like pity. The compulsion to be a loser was always there in losers. For all his bravado, Rice Thibodeaux embodied it like a genuine retard. Petulance was the only real emotion Rice seemed to know.

But then McCall started to recognize a tiny mirror of himself. He, too, had lost everything he'd once owned – a passable marriage to his high school sweetheart with really big tits, a pretty nice cabin behind his in-laws, a job he liked in a hobby-and-comics shop – a whole sense of self back then as a guy for whom things were starting to come out right. Little by little his assets had fled, without him ever making a genuine outcry against the gradual decline of expectations. Betty picked up a librarian lover, moved out, the folks asked him to go, his boss insulted him, and then walking in impulsively and enlisting in the strip-mall Army Center beside the Ralphs. Maybe after that his brain had been devoured by the parasites of the Eyeraq syndrome that they all laughed about. He'd read somewhere that you always decay from the inside out.

So, maybe the little psycho was on the right track after all: they were both just lying there as speedbumps in life when they ought to stand tall.

'Is there another way to get up here?' Jack Liffey asked.

'The fire escape is rusted out at the bottom, frozen. Won't move an inch – that ladder thing.'

He'd learned this man's name was Samuel Greengelb, and he acted like the one in charge. They all sat on the hall floor now, around the corner from the barricaded staircase, the boy with his harmonica and notebook and Maeve carrying an aluminum baseball bat for some weird sense of protection. The other small man was wearing a yarmulke and tweeds and cradled his little purse .25. There had apparently been a third tenant standing with them, but he was gone, whisked away by the winds of looming threat. Jack Liffey rested his .38 on his lap, the barrel still vaguely warm from his warning shots. Sitting around the lantern, he guessed they looked like some demented campfire party at a pretty haphazard scout jamboree. The boy was scribbling away like mad, as if taking notes from memory.

'So, Morty, you're wearing the yarmulke. For religious I never figured you.'

Morty shrugged. 'I had other things on my mind. Everybody's marginal something. Maybe at heart I'm a Jewish commando.' He grinned. 'The Lehi Group, Avraham Stern, and all that.'

'Calm down,' Jack Liffey said. 'Gentlemen, please concentrate. Any other ways up here? Service stairs? Elevator? Over the roof from another building?'

'My blessings on you all anyway,' Morty said.

'There aren't any other stairs, Mr Liffey. The elevator's broken. If they fix it and try it, we hear it groan and gasp maybe ten minutes on its way up.'

'I don't trust the fire escape,' Maeve put in. 'The bottom may be broken, but what if they go up to the second floor and go out a window?' She gave them a moment to consider her logic. 'It comes out in that room. I saw it.' Their eyes all went to a doorway standing open nearby.

Greengelb clapped his forehead: the What-an-ignoramus gesture. 'The young woman is perfectly genius. I never thought. What a *shmuck*! That's the old Rubio room, the cookroom. A little hibachi Miguel kept out on the fire escape so we could all cook some meat. About his *carnitas* he always warned us was pig.' He shuddered a little.

'You're Morty?' Jack Liffey asked the man with the .25.

The man nodded. 'Morton Lipman. Retired working-class Jew. I'm a proud cobbler. Yes, Jews without money, we exist.'

'Mr Lipman, you're armed. Would you go into that room and keep watch for now? You can fire a couple of wild shots if somebody starts to come up. Please try not to hit anybody.'

'Take my light,' Greengelb said magnanimously, holding out a red plastic flashlight wound with tape.

Morty Lipman seemed to give everything he did some extra thought. 'I'm leaving the door open, OK, so I can run away from any *golems*. Man makes plans but . . .' He poked his thumb toward the ceiling to indicate The Man Upstairs. '*He* laughs. Anyway, the darkness I don't like. I admit.'

'The Lord will provide,' Greengelb said.

Lipman winced. 'I only wish He would provide until He provides.'

'Go,' Jack Liffey urged. 'We don't have time for a theological dispute.'

'It's *cultural*,' Lipman said earnestly, and he walked stoically toward the open doorway.

'Anything else?' Jack Liffey asked. 'Air shafts? Trash drops?'

'Nothing, sir. You think our slumlords offered all the fancy amenities like Mr Hilton? Swimming pools? Gym? We're lucky to have glass windows.'

The man laughed for a moment, his belly snapping open two buttons of the tight white shirt, his legs still tucked under him stiffly. He looked like an outlandish update on the Laughing Buddha, Jack Liffey thought. And why not? Children were surrounding him – Maeve and Conor. If he remembered right, the Laughing Buddha was the one who would bring abundance – patron of the weak, poor, and children. Maybe one day he'd become a Buddhist. His goofy mental state hadn't completely left him, despite the danger.

'How long have you lived here?' Jack Liffey asked Greengelb.

The man seemed a bit chagrined. 'Seventeen years, Mr Liffey. When I came – staying here so long as that, I had no intention at all. But they fail you badly sometimes, families. Am I not right? And I was a bigger asshole then, too. To divulge this is not so easy with my mind slowly failing.'

'Yes, families fail,' Jack Liffey agreed.

'Dad!'

He held up a palm. 'People all do their best. Sometimes more, but it's up to the children to do better.' He meant Maeve.

'The children . . .' Greengelb gave an elaborate shrug. 'Mine moved away. They forgot this old embarrassment, their father. The *putz*. Their mother remarried. Slowly I got forced out of the jewelry business. And they never answered my cards. For many years. It eats the soul, all that being ignored – if there is a soul. But, you know, after a while being ignored is just another kind of under-pants you wear.'

He was indeed a Buddha, Jack Liffey thought. Reconciled to loss. Desire extinguished.

'Hey, retards!' An angry shout up the staircase burst over their little campfire chat. It was the man with the golden curls. 'We got guns tonight, too. And we got matches and lotsa gasoline. Think it over if you got some big yen to burn up alive. Every one of you.'

Jack Liffey stood up and waited near the staircase, with his back to the wall. He had a strange sense of being inside the moment, on top of things. 'Your boss wouldn't like that!' he shouted. 'You'd burn the hotel down to save it?'

'Fuck my boss, all the way up and down his asshole! We got a failure to connect here, Mr Palladin. Don't go and disengage. Here it is: you're all going out on the street *tonight* or you're crispy crit-ters! End of story.'

Jack Liffey thought of loosing another shot, just for the hell of it, but what good would that do? The threats sounded serious.

'Let's get your man Vartabedian down here and negotiate!' Jack Liffey called. 'It's all doable. I promise.'

'I don't think so, Mr Palladin. This is just you and us –. tidy as shit, no capitalism involved. Just our egos.'

'I'll have to consult,' Jack Liffey said. 'We got armed men out on guard. Give me an hour.'

'Don't bullshit a bullshitter. You got fifteen minutes to live, and
then I torch the whole place. There won't be no more warning.'
    A chill went up Jack Liffey's spine, extinguishing the last of his
strange euphoria. Burning alive was one of the routes to death that
terrified him. Right up there with all the others.

NOTES FOR A NEW MUSIC

Day 7 later

I feel bad about this. It's such a crazy idea of mine – all this
trying to learn about life by dipping your toes into poverty for
ten whole minutes.

> All I want is something to believe in.
> But the street is dark and vile.
> Some say the beautiful things in life are the best.
> But that's just a pose I know.
> When you're down you fight the most for.
> Food and shelter and let the rest go.
> Oh won't you help me now.
> Just enough for a meal.
> Spare a dollar, spare some change.
> Just meet my eyes, man, that's the deal.

These are real people with real problems and I doubt if I've
learned very much about them. Maybe Dad could figure it all out.
Of course the system has failed them, but there's so much more.

The two female cops came warily around a corner that reeked of
rot and human piss, Paula almost chipper again to be on the job,
but then Paula raised the back of her hand, like a soldier walking
point on patrol. She nodded at the high-lift Dodge Ram, black and
shiny and expensive, parked down from the Fortnum Hotel.
    'I see it,' Gloria acknowledged. No one around here, certainly
not the residents, the mission ministers or the psychologists, even
the bleeding-heart welfare workers, would drive that beast. Then
she remembered there was a fire station only three blocks away.

'Maybe a fireman,' Gloria said. 'They love that macho shit.'

Paula shook her head. 'They have their own fenced lot. You don't leave a money-trap like that out on the street at night, not around here. It's just screaming "I got a big fat stereo."'

'Yeah. I feel like ripping it off myself, on general principles. Bust any cocksucker who'd drive that thing.'

Paula grinned. 'Editorials later, sis. Look there.' She pointed.

Two blocks farther away, in murky dusk-light, there was an old white pickup truck. It was amazing, Gloria thought, how little profile you really needed on a vehicle to recognize it. 'Jesus Christ. It's *got* to be a coincidence.'

'I don't believe in coincidence. Wasn't that the first lesson at the Academy?'

'I had a friend drive that to my house and I left Jack so fucked up and weak he looked like he was going to sleep for a month.'

'Look at me,' Paula said.

Gloria did, surprised. The urgency in the woman's voice had been stunning.

'I'm right at the rock bottom of literalness here – girl.' There was something desperate and furious in her tone. 'Don't confuse me with long explanations. My cop soul is not going to take its clothes off for a long, long time for nobody. Is that Jack's truck? Simple yes or no.'

'Ninety per cent.'

'Do you know the black one?' Paula asked.

She was a little hurt that Paula didn't quite trust her. 'No. Zero. Except it reminds me of half the asshole cops I know. Why do you want to drive a truck that'll tip over at the first pothole?'

'Op-eds later, as I say. OK. We got your husband on the job here – on his own job – and we got at least one Buford in the mix. And we know Buford doesn't live here, because nobody leaves a car worth anything like that down here overnight. You think he's that guy you heard was the enforcer?'

'Logical. He had a pal, too.'

'Nearby somewhere I bet they all come together, friend and foe.'

'I talked to an old Jewish gentleman at the Fortnum right there. That's the next target of the loft builders and he told me they were getting jammed up.'

'Backup?' Gloria said.

'On what basis? We're not even officially here, girl. This

is do-it-yourself night. You picked it. Girls' bowling night.'

'Oh, the world is so full of bad news. Hold that thought.' Gloria was already walking toward the over-tall black truck to check it out. The bed had a steel tool chest, bolted down and locked. The thick plastic bed liner wasn't even scratched, as if the truck had never been used for any trucklike purpose.

The cab was almost as anonymous under her flashlight, with an empty CD case discarded on the dash, and a few gum wrappers on the floor. A red-striped rag lay on the far seat.

She felt Paula come up behind her. 'Ever watched your laundry going around in the dryer?' Gloria asked.

'Not so much.'

'Check that stripy thing on the seat.' Gloria yielded her some room.

'I don't know.'

'It's a man's boxer underpants. Look at it,' Gloria said.

'If you say so. So there's a guy out there who can get his dick caught in his zipper. Or maybe it's just a rag. I know I'm off my feed, but what's got you by the short hairs tonight?'

'I check out everything. I'm an Indian, hon. We're the original folks on this continent that figured out that nothing ever works out for us.'

'Oh, let's not get into a pissing match about who's more beat down. Your people walked happily over the land bridge from Asia. They weren't downstairs on the slave ships.'

'True dat. But watch this.' Gloria knelt at the front wheel of the truck, unscrewed the rubber cap from the air valve of the giant tire and used the refill of her ballpoint pen to let the air hiss out of the knobby tire so the truck sank slowly like a big shot elk coming down on one knee. 'Just another evening in paradise,' she said.

'You on the warpath, girl.'

Gloria smiled. 'Real warpath woulda been taking out my Swiss Army knife and stabbing that sidewall like some *pendejo* juvie. This is just a little stick-around message.'

Paula's eyes went to the Fortnum. 'Let's go round up the mokes.'

Rice was still whining about his eyes so McCall led him down the first floor hallway until they found a bathroom. It was filthy and strewn with ribbons of unspeakable toilet paper and broken porcelain basins. Some of the piping had even been stripped from the walls, leaving tracks ripped out of the plaster. Must have been copper. One sink still worked and there was a rubber stopper with a broken chain waiting patiently on a little glass shelf. McCall stuffed in the stopper and ran the water. Both taps ran cold.

'You gotta soothe a burn,' McCall said. 'It hydrates the metapringles and all that shit.'

'The what?'

'Don't worry about it.' When the basin was full, McCall pushed the tiny man's face down into the water.

'Hey! Shit!'

'Suck it up, man. It's honest pain. We got work to do tonight.'

'Owie. *Owie*, man!'

McCall was actually enjoying inflicting a little hurt on the asshole. Why not? Thibodeaux had been a crimp in his tailbone ever since the evening he'd run into him in the Porthole Bar on Wilshire playing with his knife and talking about all his secret missions in Eye-raq. Bullshit *in extremis*, for sure.

'The next time your eyes hurt, just remind yourself that the only thing you see is light. You don't really see the shit you're looking at; you just see the photons that bounce off the shit, and photon's got no weight at all. Therefore no way to cause pain.'

Rice Thibodeaux started to object but McCall pushed his face back down into the basin. He knew he was making it hard to breathe, but the little fuckster ought to get a taste of that – having bragged so much about waterboarding towelhead *jihadis* for Blackwood. *How do you like it your ownself, you pissant?*

Lipman had come back from his post, freaked by various noises from outside and some shifting shadows. The old men had begun deferring to Jack Liffey as they discussed their predicament, and he could see they now expected miracles from him. Why not? His pistol was bigger than theirs, he thought, with the last outpouring of his strange mood. He could see they were pretty scared – and that anyone could respect; that was simple and true.

They were all back around the lantern in the hall, five minutes of their fatal deadline elapsed. There were tiny sounds in a bedroom nearby, maybe rats and maybe not, but he couldn't worry about that now.

'Basically we've trapped ourselves in a box canyon,' Jack Liffey said. 'I understand the theory – you gentlemen circled the wagons on your home turf, but if the hostiles are serious about torching this place, it's a whole new ballgame. They don't seem to be operating on the same wavelength as – what's your landlord's name? – Moses Vartabedian? Presumably, this guy's chief wish is to keep the building in good shape for the future. But he's hired exactly the wrong leg-men.'

It was so nice to be able to form words out loud that he could sense himself going overboard, yakking away at the obvious, but he couldn't stop himself. An immense wheel had turned inside him and opened the floodgates. 'They're different from each other, these two, from what I've been able to observe, but they have one thing in common. I think they're the kind of army vets who've been through some nasty traumas, and they find it hard to sit still now. I knew them from Nam. You're in a frigid room with one of these guys, and they get up and open the window to make it colder. They need movement, any movement, to tell them who they are. They cope with surprises by grabbing control, and if they can't control, they lash out. They'd probably destroy the world, if they could. The job, the hotel, us – it's all nothing to them. That's my guess, and just so there's no illusions here, I'm betting Vartabedian hasn't figured it out yet.'

'So?' Greengelb interjected.

'I think we better promise to leave the hotel tonight but stall as much as we can and see what happens. Listen. It's not the end of things if we leave tonight. Safety first. I'll get us back in if they board it up, I promise.'

He was highly tuned to the logic of their aggressors and of these two old men now. He could see both sides had worked one another up to a fever pitch, and he didn't want either to do something irrevocable, hurl some challenge that would set off the other. He understood at once that this was the way the world would blow up one day, lonely rage against lonely rage.

He tried to take responsibility. The boy scribbling in his notebook beside Maeve was still an unknown quantity – Mike's son and maybe a handful in his own way – but that situation looked to him like it could wait.

'I wish to thank you, sir, for putting yourself in danger for our sake,' Morty Lipman said. It sounded like the preface to a dismissal. 'It is what we would all wish to do if we had the chance, to be one of the just men in the world, but I doubt if many of us could do it. As for me, leaving the building is not an option.'

Jack Liffey's eye drifted past Lipman to the women, and a Dorothea Lange photograph came to life right there, materializing silently, a forlorn-looking woman in a cotton dress so threadbare it looked like its own insubstantial weight might tear it off her shoulders, and nestled beside her, a much younger, but exact, edition of herself. Both of them not so much blond as bleached out by adversity. The daughter leaned into her mother and clung fiercely. More to protect than for her own comfort, he guessed.

'I reck' you OK, mister,' Felice said when she caught his eye.

'He's my dad,' Maeve put in quickly. 'He *is* OK.'

Jesus Christ, Jack Liffey thought, *this is all too much*. The moment took on an eerie calm – surrounded by all these refugees from the violent and unaccommodating world outside.

'Dad, you know Felice and Millie now. This is Conor. I should have introduced him immediately.' She smiled with a kind of embarrassment. Conor lifted his eyes from his notebook, in one of his rare acknowledgements of his present surroundings. 'Since you know his father and he's kind of your case.'

'Hello, Conor,' Jack Liffey said. 'I know Mike well.'

'I know you do, sir. He speaks highly of you.' The boy met his eyes for a moment, obviously reluctant to give up his scribbling.

'I'll get you all out safe,' Jack Liffey said, though he wondered what compelled him to make a rash promise like that. He guessed it was going to be a rough night. He checked his watch and saw he had three minutes left on golden-curl's ultimatum.

Overconfident Palladin confronts the sociopaths, he thought. The jerks downstairs were like the damaged Viet Nam vets of his own generation, who'd mostly been abandoned to their own devices. More than a few of them had fallen as far as The Nickel out there, or worse. *Stop thinking, man. It's time to act.*

He was about to call out to the thugs – trying desperately to think of a delaying tactic – when a door clapped open and a familiar woman's voice skirled up the staircase, distantly, as if hollered across a wide canyon, rather than directly up the stairwell.

'Hello, in there! This is the LAPD. We're looking for any of the Liffeys or Conor Lewis!'

'We're looking for any of the Liffeys or Conor Lewis!'

McCall heard it clearly. He immediately let Thibodeaux yank his head out of the basin of water and sputter. He reached for his big Desert Eagle in its shoulder holster. If they really were LAPD, though, that was not a very good idea at all, he thought, and he left the pistol snug where it was.

'Shit.'

Thibodeaux stood straight and shook himself, throwing water like a dog coming out of a lake, and then he rubbed his eyes.

'Shhh. You OK?' McCall said softly in the bathroom.

'OK by me, jackoff,' Thibodeaux whispered. 'But fuck you. You're a mutant.'

'Shh, there's cops out there.'

McCall pulled the big pistol out anyway, since its heft gave him comfort. 'We need cops tonight like your guy Nietzsche needs a smiley magnet.'

'Huh?'

'Forget it.'

'Don't hold out.'

'I'll tell you later.' Jesus, how did he get saddled with this goofball?

'*Also Sprach* McCall,' Thibodeaux murmured, which meant nothing at all to McCall.

The following is an accounting of the actual number of flophouse rooms available on The Nickel on a given night, nowhere near enough. Special needs means for the handicapped, physical or mental.

<u>Single Room Occupancy</u>
The Carlton, 45 units.
The Courtland, 97 units, 4 for special needs.
The Ellis, 56 units, 14 for special needs.
The Eugene, 44 units, all for special needs.
The Florence, 61 units, all for special needs.
The Harold, 58 units, 43 for special needs.
The Haskell, 38 units.
The La Jolla, 51 units, 33 for special needs.
The Leo, 38 units, 33 for special needs, all
for recovering substance abusers.
The Leonide, 66 units.

The New Terminal, 40 units.
The Palmer House, 67 permanent units.
The Prentice, 46 units.
The Regal, 69 units, 20 for special needs.
The Rivers, 76 units, 35 for special needs.
10 artist live/work lofts.
The Southern, 55 units, all Veterans.
The Ward, 72 units, 16 for special needs.
The Yankee, 80 units, 56 for special needs,
22 at market rate.

Transitional housing:
The Golden West, 61 units, all special
needs.
The Marshall, 74 units, all for recovering
substance abusers.

Emergency Housing
The Panama, 221 units.
The Russ, 198 units.

SEVENTEEN
Camels and Lions

'Gloria!' Jack Liffey hollered down the staircase. He ducked out of the way, awaiting the gunshot, but nothing came, and he peered out again. 'You're exposed!'

'Jack! I hear you.'

'Take care! There's a hot steam leak one landing up, right at face level on your left. And there's two thugs down there somewhere. I'm sure they're armed. One is a big guy with gold ringlets like Shirley Temple on acid, and the other is a crazy midget with a knife.' He intended the descriptions to enrage and draw them out.

'We've got so many badges here there's nothing to worry about,' Gloria called. 'We brought a whole tac unit. If these guys want to die quick, all they got to do is step into plain sight and wave a weapon.'

'Let's see if we can keep everybody alive!'

'Good to hear your voice, Jack! I mean it.'

'Yeah. At this end, too. We don't have a working phone up here. We were about to . . .' Oh, Jesus, *no*, he thought – not send smoke signals. 'I don't know, throw out bottles with messages.'

He heard her talking much softer, as if to a partner. 'Stay where you are, Jack!' she called. 'We'll take care of the police business.'

'Yes, please.' He could feel the relief in his voice. It wouldn't be the first time she'd saved his bacon. If only he could work out the hidden wrinkles in their relationship, the spleen that reared up so unexpectedly. He really loved her, but he was frightened that she was gradually drifting away from him. It couldn't have been easy tending a mute paraplegic, he knew. And the duty of that had probably covered up a lot for a while.

McCall slid a barrel bolt across the basement door as quietly as he could. *Shirley Temple on acid*, he thought to himself. 'Fuck you, wise guy.' Luckily Thibodeaux had been down at the bottom of the wooden staircase, playing with his huge K-Bar knife and hadn't heard himself described as – what? – a crazy midget with a knife. Not so far off, really.

'We got to hang down here a bit,' McCall said as he descended quietly. 'There's cops in the lobby like shit in the cowhouse.'

Thibodeaux snorted lightly and went on flipping and spinning the big killing knife with his index fingers, emulating a cheer-leader's baton. The weird serrated knife must have been eighteen inches long, some kind of fetishistic nonsense. The boilers were leaking down here, too, jetting hot steam into the room with a hissing damp in several places. The sizzle was like a cheap short-order grill frying a number of eggs.

'Which one you becoming?' Thibodeaux asked lightly, as he went on performing with the knife.

'Say what?'

'You still a camel?'

'I don't smoke no more.'

The small man looked up with great scorn, but somehow he kept the knife laddering up and down his fingers without watching it.

'Nietzsche's camel, you mutant. You're the one told me you once read the master.'

'I don't remember no camel. Jesus H. Christ, Rice. We got a situation here.'

They both froze as the door up the staircase rattled, then really gave a *whoomp*, as if taking a shoulder. McCall raised his Desert Eagle. The bolt on the door was nothing mighty, and it might have busted wide open, but it didn't.

The shadowy, hissy room taunted them for a minute or two before Rice said, 'The camel is the stage of evolution where you take on big heavy tasks and really get into enjoying your strength and how you can persist. Maybe we're both camels right now, huh?'

'Sure, why not?' This guy was going to get them in trouble for sure, McCall could see that. 'Maybe we can persist forever, just you and me. Let's see if we can get past the cops.' He hoped to nudge the man back to some kind of reality.

'The next stage is the lion,' Thibodeaux said with a maddening serenity. 'That's a whole lot better. The lion goes against all conven-tion and morality. It kills whenever it wants. It does what it wants. Nietzsche says this is the secret wish that our dreams protect.'

Abruptly Thibodeaux snatched the long knife out of the air.

McCall could see, for all his bravado, he'd caught the blade wrong-side round in his fist. He gave no indication of pain. There were shadows everywhere in the maddening hissy basement, almost like a third presence, and Thibodeaux tried to hide his blunder in the shadows, but McCall could see the dark fluid begin to drip down the man's fingers and off his wrist. His own blood. Oh, Jesus Christ.

'I'm already like the lion, mutant,' Thibodeaux went on, unfazed. 'Lion goes for the kill.'

'Where you getting this shit?'

'*Also Sprach Z.* I thought you read it, man.'

'Well, it was a long time ago. I sort of got with the *idea* and shit.'

'We ain't even got near the *idea* yet. So what you think the idea *is*?' The short man gave a private smirk.

McCall had backed accidentally into a small plume of steam off the noisy boiler and quickly moved aside. He wriggled his shoulder. Even through his jacket, the scalding heat smarted. 'We got us a kind of cop predicament out there right now, Rice-aroni. Can we hold off the fucking camels and armadillos for later?'

'Relax, we ain't going nowhere for a while.' Slowly, without emotion, Rice extracted the big knife from his fist, and he pressed his hand tight against his hip to try to stop the bleeding. 'How come you said you liked my Nietzsche so much?'

'He ain't *your* Nietzsche, man. I had a philosophy course in JC and I loved him. The guy threw out all the sentimental crap. He was hard as nails. Them that can, takes what they want. We walk right over the pussies with our size elevens.' The brute edge in his own voice surprised him. He knew perfectly well that Thibodeaux's foot probably didn't even come to a size five. Cruelly, he thought the man had to buy boys' shoes.

'OK, you say you're on the case,' the small man said. 'So what's the third stage, after the camel and the lion?'

'Jesus, I don't know, man. The psycho-killer?' He wanted to go back to worrying about the cops, but Rice was like a mockingbird who wouldn't stop worrying a hawk, whirring around him and squawking and pecking.

'After the strength of the camel and the ruthlessness of the lion, you become a child again,' Thibodeaux said with satisfaction. 'The infant who's going to grow up to be the superman. The first self-propelled man.'

'OK, great. We're supermen – red tights and all.'

'Mutant, you're the one said tonight was the night. I say we make all these people dead.'

They both looked at the gallon cans of gasoline they'd cached at the top of the basement steps. Three of them.

'Pain way or easy way?' Thibodeaux said.

'Man, how can you say that so casually? Are you some kind of evil emanation?' McCall said. He realized that Thibodeuax was sliding out of control.

'I thought we were *way* past that.'

'Jack, for Chrissake!' Gloria called. 'Clear this shit off the stairs. We can't help you with this in the way.'

Paula had her flashlight and pistol aimed together, over-and-under, as they'd been taught, and the two women stared in utter surprise at the complex barricade. They'd just done a thorough search of the street level and then floor two for any thugs, and Gloria's only worry had been the locked door behind the counter, with an old enamel plaque saying *Boilers*. She was also concerned that she hadn't made up some plausible story and called for backup. A team from down-town would have had the standard Blackhawk Thunderbolt Entry Tool – really just a heavy ram with handgrips. When they couldn't open the door – the only hiding place they'd bypassed – Paula had piled half a dozen wooden chairs precariously against it, set to topple on anyone who pulled it open from within.

'We'll clear the barricade!' Jack Liffey called down. 'You're sure the bad guys are gone?'

'No, we're not. Their truck is still outside. But they're not on floor one or two unless they can hide inside a toilet tank. We've blocked the basement. Please stop chattering, Jack, and clear this junk.'

'I miss you, too, Glor.'

'Utter nonsense.'

'Give me a minute to organize.'

'Don't take long. I have a bad feeling.'

Gloria and Paula conferred, and Paula agreed to wait down on the ground floor, beside that one questionable basement door.

Vartabedian parked at the valet stand at the head of the driveway. He could hear a live jazz band riffing softly inside the amazing cantilevered house that jutted out over the Hollywood Hills. The whole of the evening city, spread to the horizon, was beginning to light up in the rain-sparkly air, a million pinpricks through some dark surface to a fiery underworld. He had reluctantly decided to come to Eddie Wolverton's housewarming party. He had a feeling he'd be better off watching over his new loft building downtown, sweetening his last offer to the rump residents and waiting with a board-up crew to rush in. Warily he handed the valet the keys to his AMG-tuned Mercedes, the big SL-65 coupe with twin turbos.

'Careful with that, *Señor*, it's got almost seven hundred horses.'

'*Que? Caballos?*' The valet tossed the keys in the air once and grinned. 'Relax, Granddad. It's safe with the ace.'

He listened for over-revs that didn't come as the car moved away, and Vartabedian went on toward the wooden bridge to the open doorway. After coveting it for years, Wolverton had just bought one of the great post-war Case Study houses, the Lautner-Domus, all glass and angled wood beams suspended far out over Hollywood. A dark moat cut it off on the hill side, and city lore claimed that the first owner, director Joseph van Sternberg, had electrified the water, and his staff had had to fish the bodies of would-be movie stars out every morning and incinerate them. None of that was true, of course, but the house was still a delicious part of the Golden Era, photographed by Julius Shulman, and you could imagine stumbling on starlets down on their knees in every room.[5]

'Moses, man, good to see you!' Wolverton gave him a hug and a cheek-buss. The jazz band sounded pretty good, not too hectic.

'Congrats on the pad.'

Wolverton made a face. 'It's not as austere as one of those Frankie Wrights where the mandatory chairs are so square you have to sit with a pole up your ass.'

---

[5] In the interest of historical accuracy, it was the Pierre Koenig House, Case Study House No. 22, at 1636 Woods Drive, that Julius Shulman famously photographed for one of the most iconic L.A. images of all time. The von Sternberg legend of the deadly moat refers to a very similar house built by Richard Neutra in Northridge across the San Fernando Valley. As usual for L.A., this second one was demolished in 1971 to make way for a commonplace and forgettable housing tract.

'But you know better, my man. You know it all. Soon we'll get started on the Fortnum. Want a cigar?'

'Not inside, Mose. Too many vegans this night.'

Wolverton wagged his head toward the reflecting pool outside that was the logical and practical end of the moat, the water lapping right up against the glass wall. 'Out there. Throw your butts over the edge. It's all New Hollywood down there, drug dealers and feeb heavy metal headbangers from Florida.'

Vartabedian took one look around the beautiful people crammed into the open-plan house, men grasping cocktail glasses and chatting to women with too much of their breasts hanging out, and then he slid open a glass door and stepped out into the faint breath of city noise that rose off the startling panorama of lights.

A severe-looking woman in glasses was talking to a fat man nearby and it reminded him of a well-known tale about the house that he did believe – Ayn Rand with her whole retinue had shown up at an early party here and descended on the wrong man, an unassuming structural engineer named Marx Ayers, who looked a bit like the grand old architect Lautner, and she had brayed how much she loved rebel architects and wanted to fuck him right there and then. Supposedly Lautner had been watching from nearby and had taken his own retinue and fled the party.[6]

Moses Vartabedian stopped near the edge of the unrailed dropoff beside the pool, where it was perhaps 300 feet straight down a chaparral cliff to some lesser houses, and he clipped and lit up a *Romeo y Julietta*. He let himself savor that velvety fist-in-the-chest taste of that very best Cuban tobacco. Whatever came now, he could survive it. Fuck 'em all. The sense of hovering above the whole city out there emboldened him immeasurably.

He heard another sliding door come open and he watched Wolverton circle grimly toward him. Something was up.

'Mose, please tell me about those two loose cannons you got working for you. I had a run-in with them today. I don't want my props in this town going to hell because of some goofballs you picked up in a bar.'

'Just glance out there, Eddie.' Vartabedian swept his arm across the basin, a sight that he felt should impress even the gods. 'Man,

---

[6] All true, but about Richard Neutra, not Lautner.

you're the guy who's gone and acquired this narcissist's house. What could matter beside that view?'

'My reputation could matter. My bank account.'

'A weakling concept. Look at the lights, man. Where's your Nietzsche instinct?' He indicated the southerly horizon again with a nod. 'It's so awesome it makes one's own loneliness trivial.' He found himself blowing smoke in Wolverton's direction, not sure how intentionally.

'Christ, that's a strong stogie.' Wolverton waggled a hand in front of his face. 'Do you smoke like that expressly to piss me off, Mose?'

'Don't run any of your shit on me, Eddie. We got our universes. When we die, we'll both start to be forgotten in less than a New York minute. I promise you it's all going to be OK at the Fortnum. I have a feeling you're never going to appreciate it, but truly letting yourself enjoy Cuban cigars and the best cognac and really fine shoes like Manolos or John Lobbs is a big part of what it's all about.'

Eleanor Ong, formerly and once again Sister Mary Rose, by special dispensation, was wedged behind her desk in the cramped office, tapping away on a tiny giveaway calculator from a long-gone local bank to find a way to stretch out the subsistence allotment the shelter got from the diocese – actually from what she called the child abuse slush fund, she occasionally joked a bit too pointedly, on the rare occasions the archbishop deigned to see her. Abruptly Kenisha Duncan opened the office door and led Chopper Tyrus into the doorway behind her. They'd have had trouble fitting in the free space if they'd actually come all the way in.

'Sister, I'm sorry to bother you, but he swear it real real important.'

Tyrus yanked off a threadbare Dodgers cap. 'I ain' sure you remember me, Sister ma'am. . .'

'Chopper, I surely do remember you. You're a good man. You protected a mute and ailing human being, just as Jesus would have done, and then you brought him here for help.'

He smiled broadly. 'Thank you, ma'am. Praise Jesus and all that.' Then his face wrinkled with disquiet. 'But there more trouble tonight about this man Richard – I mean Jack. You know the Fortnum Hotel?'

'Of course. The developers are in the process of grabbing it before the housing charities can put a claim to it.'

'Well, your Jack – he done go in that place tonight,' Chopper

Tyrus said. 'On his own feet along with two of your womens from
here. And now they's lady polices inside, too, and some pretty bad
men.' He shook his head as if to disavow all of it. 'A guy on the
street, he say, Jesus, he absent from the Fortnum tonight. He say
men belong with the devil camp, they at work in there.'

Everything was tiptoeing along on the very edge of Sister Mary
Rose's comprehension – but that was really all she ever expected
on The Nickel.

'Kenisha, have you seen Millie and Felice come back?'

'No, ma'am. Not so's I saw, and I been out front.'

Reluctantly, Eleanor Ong stood up. She didn't want to get
involved with Jack Liffey again. It had nearly cost her her life the
first time, and, worse, it had cost a significant part of her faith –
which it had taken her a decade of renunciation and worship in
the convent to repair. And, of course, this most recent visit of his,
added so opportunely to her own weaknesses, had snatched away
a lot of the soul-repair that had cost her so dearly. In pure human
terms, it had kicked the traces right out from under what she had
come to think of as her peace of mind. He could do that to you,
Jack.

'Would you come with me, Chopper? I may need to send you
to the fire station for help.' The firefighters were the only reliable
assistance on The Nickel, as everyone down here knew – with Fire
Station No. 9 proud of having the most arduous EMT assignment
in the city. Cops came to The Nickel when it was fashionable, or
on somebody's political agenda. Then, for a time, officers fresh out
of the Academy would flood Skid Row and do their best, but the
agenda at the top always shifted and the cops always went somewhere else, slapping their hands clean and lining up for their gamma
globulin shots.

Eleanor knew she was no Mother Theresa, but she shared the
firefighters' compassion for the very worst off in the city. Only in
her case, she suspected the feeling had its roots in pride, which was
not something that she or God would treasure. It had been so simple
in the convent, and it was so complex out here. *Oh, Jack, I missed
you so. Oh, God, I miss Jack.*

Conor hung back in the corner of the small squalid room, scribbling away as the others argued. He felt he was living in a strange
kind of time that was basically unoccurring – waiting on pause so

he could observe all around him and absorb it all. The newest arrival, Maeve's dad, was going around to the others demanding that they help him clear the barrier off the stairs. Basically, the man seemed to want to let the normal world reassert itself, and he didn't know how he felt about that.

'I live with one of these policewomen,' he insisted. 'She's my wife, really. They'll be fair to us and protect us, I promise. But we have to let them come up.'

'Cops've evicted people before,' Morty Lipman insisted. 'They're forced to do the dirty work for the landlords, I know. It's the law. Maybe you think you know a cop, but that's like taking an old video out of a box. You never know if it's been rewound.'

Jack Liffey just stared, struck wordless for a moment by the peculiar comparison.

'Man, are you out of date,' Maeve objected. 'The world's digital now. Tapes are gone. Anyway, my dad is right, we can't fight the police *and* fight these dangerous guys, too. What was your wonderful word for them? *Putzes.*'

Morty almost smiled. 'I don't know digital, but I know *putzes*, and I never trusted the police,' he said.

'Yeah,' Felice said sourly. 'I ast them over and over to help me find my old man, and they treat me like a shoo-bug.'

'That policewoman downstairs is my stepmother,' Maeve insisted. 'I love her, and I know we can trust her. Look, I can tell you what's going to happen. We either let her up to help us or we're gonna get SWAT. You want a bunch of shouting Nazis in black helmets to blow up our barricade and run up the steps waving machine guns?'

Conor looked up from his scribbling to see where things had gotten, but nobody seemed on top of it – which to him meant Samuel Greengelb appeared undecided. The man had been good to him and had been the brains at the hotel so far, but now he sat on his rickety chair looking sad, looking defeated and confused.

'Why are we always victims?' Greengelb said. 'We just want a place to live. That's asking too much already?'

Something about the depth of feeling within the man's voice hit Conor like an electric shock. He knew a little of what had happened to the Jews over centuries – pogroms, hatred, the Holocaust. And still his friends at school, none of whom had ever even met a Jew, cracked terrible anti-Jew jokes all the time. The children of the deeply Protestant outer suburbs of San Diego County – morally asleep, he thought – knew almost nothing of what had gone on in America to the Indians or the poor, let alone what had happened in Latin America or faraway Europe. And if he happened to repeat a Jew joke at home, his father would always patiently explain the tragic history – and he, Conor, would be overwhelmed with guilt, feeling a thousand times a fool, unfairly caught between two worlds or two incompatible moral bubbles, or whatever labored phrase you used to name this impossibile contradiction.

'We're legal tenants,' Greengelb insisted. 'I've been here seventeen years. A man's home is his castle! You're all in my castle right now talking to me about leaving as if it's nothing at all. Don't tell me how to feel, sir! Don't anybody tell me how to feel about my home!'

'I'm truly sorry, sir,' Jack Liffey said, touching the man's shoulder. 'In my limited experience, if justice ever comes at all, it comes in by the back door, very quietly, while you're waiting for it at the front.'

Conor looked down at his lyrics, and quickly added a line:

> Housing the poor they say
> It's just an issue to solve
> And I've never learned
> The secret of moving on
> I tried to root here but
> I have nothing left now
> That I can call a home
> I have nothing left . . . nothing
> Don't tell me how to feel!

Rice Thibodeaux walked his big knife up and down his fingers again like a tiny nonchalant George Raft. The basement grew danker and hissier as they waited.

'Man, do you have to do that?'

'Who's asking?'

'Who? The guy who brought you on board, dickhead,' McCall said.

'The guy who can't make a fuckin' decision? I see three big cans of gasoline. I see two legal proxies for the owner of this building hiding down here for no reason, when they should be acting. I *don't* see no supermen, ready to become or not. I don't even see no lions. Jeez, I don't even see no *camels*, mutant.'

'Listen, Mr Densehead. Those are cops up there, *real* cops. It changes everything. Rule one in life is never ever antagonize the fuzz when you can get away clean.'

Thibodeaux screwed up his face in thought, without even slowing down the knife-walk that was whirling up and down his fingers. 'I thought rule one was never back down.'

'Even cats know you got to save your attack for when you're strong.'

'Cats? You shitting me? Housecats? I *hate* housecats.'

'The rules of guerilla war, man. You back off when you're over-powered and you wait for your chance. I'm sure Sun Tzu learned it all from watching his own cat.'

'Uh-huh, loser – let's all learn our big life lessons from animals that clean their own assholes with their tongues. I'm getting tired of you, yellowhead.'

'Well, I'm getting tired of you, too, dwarf. When this job is over, let's be splits.'

'Get tired of this.' Rice Thibodeaux took one step and drove the large serrated knife hard up into Steve McCall's abdomen, just above the turquoise belt-buckle.

McCall's mouth dropped open wide, but no sound came out, and Thibodeaux twisted the big knife around and then changed the angle and yanked it upward, the way he'd read true believers were supposed to perform hara-kiri – or, more properly, *seppuku*. McCall hardly deserved the honor, but he'd had to be shut up.

Only a little blood came out, no sound issued, but Steve McCall, eyes and mouth wide open, began to list to his right, and Rice Thibodeaux yanked out the knife with a flourish, the way he imagined a true samurai would.

'Not just yet,' McCall squeaked as he leaned farther and farther and then crumpled to the concrete floor of the basement.

'Happy now, mutant?'

EIGHTEEN
Rust Never Sleeps

'What were you people thinking?' Gloria Ramirez stood down below with her hands on her hips as the motley crew yanked at their barricade. It came away faster than Jack Liffey had expected.

'They couldn't get to sleep up here knowing the bad-doers could get at them,' he explained.

'Uh-huh,' she agreed. 'So you were all going to nest up here forever like a band of Robertson Crusoes.'

He and Maeve caught one another's eye, but said nothing. Was there ever a right time for pedantry?

'Don't even try to explain where you were going to get your food,' she went on.

She really had her dudgeon on, Jack Liffey thought, but he was happy not to be the prime focus.

The two old men fought the sticky duct tape off the final bedsprings and pushed, and the denuded box spring swung outward like a cell door.

'Welcome to our fortress, young woman,' Samuel Greengelb said kindly. 'There was a kind of powerful logic residing inside our logic, but I admit the *seykhl* appears to be lacking. "Common sense" to you.'

For just an instant, Gloria smiled benignly back at him, probably at the 'young woman.'

'Paula!' she called. 'Come on up here and meet the whole sideshow.'

'I thought I heard something,' Paula called back, her voice cold and hard, on the job. 'I'll stay on point a few more minutes.'

Gloria noted her tone with a raised eyebrow and then stepped through the big gap in the barricade. 'Any other ambushes waiting? Big falling weights? Trap doors?'

Greengelb blushed, and Jack Liffey was pleased to see that Morty Lipman had hidden away his little .25 auto. Gloria's old Police Special

.38 was snug in his pants, but he could tell that Gloria's X-ray vision had spotted it. She just wasn't going to make an issue of it right then. Later, he'd pay. He had no concealed weapon permit, and there wasn't a prayer L.A. County would ever give him one. Only a handful were ever given out and mainly to celebrities ducking stalkers.

Gloria glanced along the hallway at the litter that their hasty scavenging had left and sniffed a bit at the aroma on the air, not as bad as the lower floors – a suggestion of urine, a little unwashed body, and a little decline of human expectations. 'You were preparing the Armageddon to save this garbage dump?' she asked.

'Home is where you find it,' Greengelb suggested. His face seemed gray and exhausted. 'It's like this, young lady. My family is dispersed from this place and that. *Nu*, to be honest, none of them are anxious to have a curmudgeon old *shmo* in their home eating their bread. I've been living here seventeen years and more. It may be a dump but it's my dump.'

'In the Fortnum twelve years for me,' Morty Lipman snapped, as if she'd called for a count-off. In his voice, there was no hint of the possibility of self-deprecating humor, only a kind of simmering of wrath. 'These *golem* who come to drive us out of our home for the master-builder – curse the *chozzer* – they give us no respect at all. Nothing I have touched will ever be touched by them, I assure you. Before I let them drag me out of my home I will kill myself.'

'Whoa, let's just talk about tonight, sir, please,' Gloria said quickly, and Jack Liffey watched her better nature come alive in an instant, like a kindly old guru who'd been distracted for a while. 'I'm on your side, sir. I represent the full legal authority of the City of Los Angeles, and I offer you my respect and my protection tonight. Could you make me some coffee or tea, please? We can sit down and have a talk.'

He bowed slightly. 'A table is not blessed if it has fed no friends.'

Jack Liffey marveled at how quickly Gloria had calmed him to civility. In his experience Lipman had a tendency to fly off the handle with little provocation.

They all trailed toward Lipman's room. 'Do you like English breakfast tea, ma'am? Typhoo. Our electricity is off, but I can boil some water on a Sterno.'

'That will be perfect,' Gloria said.

'I love it, too,' Maeve added, more or less on behalf of everyone.

*   *   *

Rice Thibodeaux looked at the big sprawled thing lying there on the concrete floor with a frown of curiosity. Deep inside, he felt a bit lost now. He moved around the thing, as if he might make more sense of it from a different angle. He kicked once. It was both soft and hard, big boned and angular. He kicked again. The thing didn't budge at all.

'Fuck you, clown,' Rice said tentatively.

The thing shuddered once and Rice hopped back. A wash of golden curls had come free, the baseball cap lying apart, and there was a pool of dark blood at the belly now, purplish in the dim hissing light. A soul patch grew beneath the man's lip, so blond it was almost invisible.

He reached out with his toe and nudged a hand that was splayed open on the ground.

'OK, come on back now . . . mutant.'

The thing made no move, and he kicked the hand hard so the arm swung around to a ridiculous angle, making the thing look funny. Rice giggled once softly. The skin of the belly showed a little and a dark ooze was still flowing, barely. In the leather shoulder-holster, Rice saw the handgrip of the man's huge Desert Eagle pistol. Rice wasn't much of a gun man, but he'd used his share in Iraq, and just about everyone knew how to fire one.

He bent over and tapped the pistol gingerly, as if expecting it to be electrified. Nothing happened.

You get somewhere at first by standing out, he thought, and after that you have to try to fit in or you make enemies. It made no sense. He thought of New Orleans and how much easier it had all been, at least before Katrina. Upper Ward Five. People you could trust. All the way up to the Ponchartrain. Royal Street. The can factory across the bayou. L.A. was just not the same. Things weren't solid.

He plucked the pistol quickly out of the funny thing lying there. It was unwieldy, top heavy and far too heavy. Strange thing it was. Not elegant and simple like a knife.

They sat around the floor and the bed in the cramped room clutching mugs, tin cans, juice glasses and two proper teacups, each with a paper tag dangling over the side as the water pot on the Sterno can whisped a little vapor trying to boil.

There didn't appear to be any sugar and Jack Liffey knew he

was not going to be able to drink much of it raw, but he figured
they were all just being polite anyway, like some dreadful first
campfire at a Scout Jamboree. He tried to make out the books in
a blocks-and-board bookcase next to the bed where his back had
come to rest, but the titles were mostly in angular Hebrew characters, and a few seemed to be in German. The only thing on the wall
was a magazine photo that he took to be the massive hilly sugar-
cubes and domes of old Jerusalem.

'Don't get excited, please, but why didn't you report the harassment?' Gloria asked, sitting near the door for her own purposes.
'For instance, I protected some women down in San Pedro when
their landlord demanded sexual favors. But they had to *tell* me about
it.'

Morty Lipman raised both eyebrows like a TV host with an
awkward guest. '*Oy*, "for instance" is not a proof, Officer. It's not
even an argument. You think the police here mobilize their big
squads to protect poor single-room renters in The Nickel? Begging
your pardon, for your police colleagues and their own problems,
ma'am, but we really don't count.'

She opened a palm. 'I'm here now. In everybody's defense, there
probably weren't any obvious acts to report, were there?'

'Sabotage of the elevator,' Greengelb took over with a sigh.
'Sabotage of the heating system. Sabotage of our door locks.
Pounding on our doors and yelling "Wake up, Kikes!" in the middle
of the night. The manager disappears. Even human *kak* left in front
of our doors.'

'I understand, sir. But nobody saw who did any of this, did they?
Don't tell me the owner you talk about came down here in his fancy
suit and personally did this.'

Greengelb's head dropped a little. 'Who is the witness to this?
I call a man, and isn't that *exactly* what he says to me, word for
word? The *shmo* in a police uniform actually asks me this *mishegoss*.
Is the whole world populated with stupids? How is it so hard to
figure out who goes home rich and who has to wash his hands?'

'The law requires witnesses,' Gloria said. 'I'm sorry. There's a
reason it works that way, and I'll bet you can appreciate it.'

'I understand. But isn't there some intermediate path between
blindness and total observation?'

'*I'm* the intermediate path,' Gloria said, tapping her chest. 'I can
nail all this down. Is this harassment happening now?'

'Did you see a manager downstairs? Did you see a working elevator? Morty and I had to fix the heater today, though very poorly, I'm sorry to say.' He touched the radiator with his fingertips and made a disappointed face. 'This mysterious somebody removed a connecting pipe. I tell you, those *golems* are down there *somewhere* right now.'

Gloria glanced out at the hallway, listening hard. Her hand went to the radio-pack police mike pinned to her breast pocket. But it didn't respond to her touch, and she dug for her cellphone as her attention was yanked back by the shrilling of the teapot.

Thibodeaux had a hard time deciding which hand to use to hold the knife and which the pistol as he slowly climbed the wooden basement steps. He didn't feel right without the knife in his good right hand, but he wasn't a fool, and he knew the big pistol was a much more effective weapon. In the end he went for comfort and kept the big Special Forces knife in his capable right hand. Any idiot could probably shoot with the left.

He heard a scurrying behind him and spun around and nearly fired, but there was no chance of seeing anything in that gloom of conflicting shadows, and he remembered that something, another sentient being, had already fired this pistol three or four times and so he had little ammunition to waste on ghosts. Or brother rats, he thought. *Be with me. Evolve with me. Have I somehow contributed to a world in which all is doomed?* He felt that there was something wrong and froze halfway up the steps *I can feel my distrust of the life current,* he thought.

Not at all, a voice told him.

Yes, I feel uncertainty.

No, not a bit. The world is dry and clear, with a steady wind pushing you forward. Go on about your business. But don't forget the gasoline.

'I've already put the cans on the top landing,' he said aloud, but softly. 'Why don't you know this?'

Your petty situation doesn't interest me very much.

'I think it does.'

No, not really. Just don't do things half way, the way you often have in the past. Do things so they're definitive. Be a man, be a lion. And I'll watch you become a babe of the new order. That might just appeal to me.

Thibodeaux turned away from the basement and deliberately took the last few steps to the top landing. Very slowly, almost silently, he used his knife hand to turn the key that had been left on the inside of the old deadbolt. An oversight? Haste? Who had locked it? Who could tell the intentions of anyone at all? Ordinary minds were so disordered. Then he turned the knob and felt its catch release, and as he did he sensed a strong pressure against the door, a great weight leaning into it, and quickly he twisted the key to latch it shut again. What could be out there? A camel, leaning into it?

He moved the sloshing gas cans to the side to clear his path, then took a deep breath and readied the knife, his most reliable friend, though he kept Mr Pistol ready, too. He knelt slowly and gripped the head of the doorkey with his teeth, feeling like a pirate. *OK, whoever you are*, he thought. *I make you this promise. I'm reliably on the side of human evolution. I'm a fool in many ways but not in this one. I'm ready. Can you deal with it?*

Go for it, the voice insinuated. Mr Nietzsche is in favor of first-strike. Always. He has nothing but contempt for the reasonable and the dutiful man.

He kept a shoulder against the door and bit down on the key. He twisted his head to rotate the key until he felt the beginning of give, and the pressure was just starting to overwhelm the furious push of his shoulder. One-two-three, he counted off for whatever sentient presence was watching over him and speaking back. Then he hurled himself to the side and let the door fly open. The opening brought bedlam, but a little light. He used the knife in his right hand to stab and fling a toppling chair down the staircase, as other chairs followed.

'Freeze, police!' he heard. A woman's voice.

He'd braved the unpredictable clout and slap of falling chairs and then he was out the open door and flat against the wall. In the faint hall light he saw a silhouette, almost certainly going for a gun. *I'm prepared, O Future!* He flung the knife hard and then fired once at the silhouette.

'Paula!' Gloria cried out. 'I'm coming!' She was on her feet at the first cry of her voice and then the shot, and something that had been in her hand, a can of hot water, went flying aside, causing voices to yelp. Gloria rounded the staircase and then yanked herself backward on instinct as a small shadowy figure appeared below and fired twice at her with the biggest pistol she'd ever seen.

'I am bringer of death!'

She darted around the corner low with her own pistol out but she didn't shoot, holding her fire-discipline because she lacked a definite target, as she'd been taught. The short figure was gone. She heard a deep *whoomp* and immediately a lick of near-transparent flame gestured around the corner in a tease, then yanked back.

She patted the radio-pack mike on instinct but it was still on the fritz for some reason. She pulled out her cell and hit the 911 button that she'd programmed.

'Officer down! Officer needs assistance! Shots fired! Building on fire! Ten-99!' She glanced around. Jack Liffey was right behind her. 'What the fuck's the address? I can't think!'

'Fortnum Hotel,' he leaned forward to yell into her phone. He gave the cross streets. 'We're taking gunfire. We're *on* fire. Send a bus, send a ladder truck, send backup for LAPD Officers Ramirez and Green. Officer Paula Green is *down!*'

Gloria made a face. She wasn't even supposed to be working in this division, but it was done now and there was no avoiding the consequences. She left the phone on and shoved it into his hand.

'Paula!' she hollered down the staircase. All she could see was a throbbing orange glow on the walls that was definitely not good news. 'Talk to me, Paula!'

The only answer was a high-pitched male giggle.

She grabbed hard to stop Jack Liffey descending with his stupid pistol – it looked like her old .38 – but at the turning they both surrendered to a flare of intense heat which drove them back up. 'Up, everyone!' he shouted. 'Fire!'

She grabbed his arm. 'Jack, don't be a jerk and get people hurt. This is under control, dammit.'

She could see him take a deep breath to calm himself and cede her the authority with a nod. 'No it's not,' he said softly. 'Take control.'

'Up one floor, now!' Gloria ordered. 'Everybody! Come out in the hall now! Don't stop to grab a thing! The lobby's on fire.'

She heard one more shot below and prayed the small shape she'd seen wasn't finishing Paula off. 'If he shot Paula, that fucker is on his way to hell.'

'I get you,' Jack Liffey agreed.

The motley company began straggling out of Morty's room and then allowed themselves to be herded ahead of Gloria toward the staircase.

'Hurry along, folks. No sightseeing.'

One doorway on the next floor up still had a lit EXIT sign above it, and they headed that way. Incongruously, it led into a filthy wrecked bathroom with pipe torn from the plaster walls, and the basins and toilets smashed for no rational reason other than to make them unusable.

Maeve found herself shoved out in front of the whole crew, and she hurried to a window under a second EXIT sign and pushed hard. She couldn't budge it and started thinking about breaking the glass when Conor and Morty joined her and managed to tear loose a generation of paint and force the sash up. The window opened to a slatted iron fire-escape platform. They all sucked down a cool draught of city air. Conor stepped over the waist-high sill first and hurried across the iron grid to grasp the metal stairrails.

'*Yaaaaa!*' His torso disappeared abruptly.

Maeve's heart skipped a beat as she saw the boy plummet out of sight. She hurried to the edge and gasped to see him just below her, clinging furiously to the handrails and one stub of metal step. Several rusty steps in a row had crumbled away to nothing under his weight.

'Rust never sleeps,' he announced a little shakily, looking up at her. She was probably the only other one there who knew that was the title of a Neil Young song and album. She grasped the upper hand rails for extra support as her dad lay down on his chest across the iron platform that seemed to be holding, in order to reach down to grab, first, her ankle, and then Conor's wrist.

'I've got arm strength, kid.'

He hoisted the boy slowly toward the landing, Conor's feet scrabbling for purchase. The platform itself looked none too secure to Maeve, with big scabs of rust coming away wherever she wriggled.

'Stay inside, people,' Jack Liffey called. 'It won't hold.'

'We need a ladder truck,' Gloria said at the window. Maeve backed very slowly toward the brickwork of the building, feeling the iron straps flexing a little under her weight. She looked down and could see a flickery glow emanating from the windows two floors down. Glancing up on a whim, she counted three more floors to the roof. Iron fire escapes were probably fine if you painted them with Rustoleum once a decade or so, she thought angrily – damning all slumlords.

Gloria was on her cell, explaining their predicament angrily to someone.

Maeve stayed outside with her father, helping boost a shaken Conor in though the window. When they got inside, Gloria shooing them all out ahead of her into the hall. Taking up the rear, Maeve was struck suddenly by the amazing surplus of vulnerability in their little group – a skinny girl from half a country away, a lost woman hunting for her husband, two very old unhappy men, one probably with first-stage Alzheimer's, a boy who seemed permanently a little bemused, then herself – she wouldn't judge herself – and a recent paraplegic who was none too steady on his feet if you watched close. The whole straggling crew emerged from the bathroom just as a burst of flame found its way up some flue in the hallway and belched out behind them, lighting everything in sight with a flare.

'*Oy!*'

'Now!' Gloria shouted, pushing one of the old men toward the stairway. 'Folks, let's go! Up is the way! We're gonna be fine! I promise.'

They hurried up the steps, feeling the heat rising ominously up the stairwell. Jack Liffey stayed back to guard the rear. Maeve took the crook of Sam Greengelb's arm, helping him climb. Ahead of her, Conor and Millie had their hands through Morty's elbows like bookends, boosting his stiff legs up the steps in a rather drunken gait, like a three-legged race at a picnic.

Taking up the rear with Jack, Gloria was on her cell again, shouting repeatedly at someone. 'You get *everything* here fast, Miss Oh! Absolutely everything. You heard me, officer down! Officer needs assistance! Code three! Fuck the codes. I don't care about any basketball riots you got at Dorsey High or any drive-bys in the Shoestring Strip. Get your choppers. Get your SWAT. Get medevac for Sergeant Paula Green, LAPD, and get the fire boys to bring one of their firesuits. They may have to send somebody straight into a real fire inside the Fortnum to get our Paula out. I'm badge 21-437, Harbor Division, honey. If I don't see that ladder truck the minute we get to the roof, I'll come over there tomorrow and kick your ass all the way across town.'

Maeve realized with a chill that Gloria's friend, Paula Green, whom she had met and liked a whole lot, must be caught down there somewhere in the inferno. But hopefully below it or protected from it.

Rice Thibodeaux slipped out of the Fortnum, after pouring the cans of gasoline everywhere, with flames brewing up nicely one floor up and licking down into the lobby. He crossed toward McCall's big truck and glanced back at a crashing sound to see a ball of fire punch out a second-floor window and flames begin to caress up the brick walls above the window. The other windows on the second floor were already aglow with fire. Bless the fury of gasoline, he thought. It couldn't have been burning more than a few minutes since he'd run along the linoleum hallway emptying the cans. He heard sirens in the distance and climbed the Dodge's footstep to pull confidently at the door. *Shock!* The shitty thing didn't give! That asshole McCall had locked up by habit and taken the keys, instead of leaving them in the ashtray as they'd always arranged. Fuck him. Where was McCall? Oh, yeah. He was in the basement, a crispy critter before long. And then his heart sank after he realized the front tire was dead flat.

A number of old black men along the sidewalk were watching him curiously. He was really pissed off suddenly to be watched, but held it in. What business was this of theirs? Spades always thought the world owed them something. Why *was* that? What was it about niggers? They had some peculiar idea of justice wedged up their ass, and none of them – none – knew a thing about Nietzsche and making your own future.

'You got a fucking problem!' he yelled at all of them.

He jumped down from the Dodge and walked to the curb to confront the old men. Thibodeaux had left the useless empty pistol back in the cleansing fire, but he yanked his big new killer knife out of his waist. He'd yanked it out of McCall and now he felt the incredible momentum as its big blade waved around in his hand. He'd found the outlandish eighteen-inch copy of the Marine knife in a Tijuana tourist shop. It was his sop on a trip down there so McCall could see a stupid donkey show he'd heard about, which never even happened. The tourist shop had been full of onyx birds, onyx Mexicans in *sombreros* sleeping against cacti and strings of firecrackers and cherry-bombs. The knife was probably only meant to be window décor, he realized. The shopkeeper had snickered, setting an inflated price, but he'd ignored the old fool's game and paid what he wanted, $50.

'Calm down, mister,' one of the spades against the fence called out to him. 'We all cool here.'

'All you coons stay back on the sidewalk!'

'There's no need for that kind of talk, mister.' That had come from the biggest colored man of them all, a brawny man twice his height and width, and Thibodeaux had half a mind to knife him down immediately, set an example to the others.

But he heard a noise and whirled to guard his back, brandishing the big knife from a crouch. No one was there. He could see the Fortnum clearly in the dusk, and it was extremely satisfying, cooking up just like the two-story farmhouse his Blackwood team had barbecued near Falluja with the kids screaming upstairs, *If you don't want to die, fuckers,* somebody on his fire team had shouted, *don't let the* hajis *shoot at us from your house!*

'Some bad shit's going down,' a man still sitting on the sidewalk said.

Thibodeaux whirled again. 'I'm not gonna negotiate with you sambos! I mean it. Just shut the fuck up. I got to think.'

'This is a free country, man. We shall overcome.'

Sirens were howling nearby, a block or two away. And a chopper was scooting overhead, sweeping its bright sunbeam across the buildings of The Nickel, tapping at them like the probing cane of a blind man.

'You want to fuck with *me*? I know a place all you Zulus can go to die! Learn about Fred Nietzsche, Niggers.' Thibodeaux started edging away from them, into the middle of the street, but the biggest Negro stepped off the curb with his eyes narrowing.

'Hold on, man. Why you got to go racist on us?'

'Back off, nig.'

'Why you got to be *doin'* this? Did some black man hurt you? We don't mean you no harm at all, son.'

Thibodeaux ended his retreat. He planted his feet and poked his knife toward the big menacing Negro. 'Stay back, heavy-duty! You think I'm deaf and dumb?'

'Not at all, not at all. I think you're a sad man who's worried about something that's coming down on him. Look, we all know how mean the world can be. Just look at us. We got nothing. Why would I want to hurt you?'

'Well, here's some nothing!'

Just as the first fire engine came around the corner, Thibodeaux ran toward the big black man with the long knife thrust out in front, like a knight with a lance.

Moses Vartabedian hadn't felt like going to an empty home, with a stack of pizza boxes on his fancy granite counter, so he'd returned to his local downtown office from the unpleasant party at Wolverton's where even the gold-diggers were too young for him. Coming in the door, he knew he needed a new ream of paper for the buzzing fax, and he was fussing through the racks of office supplies he kept in a small back room, with spiffy orange metal racks from some pricey Italian company. There was a wired window at the back of the supply room, an original sash from the sweatshop it had once been. No point in fixing it up because it looked out over Skid Row, then the L.A. River, and then the heart of Mexican L.A.

It was only chance that led him to glance out. He saw the column of black smoke first, then a flicker of flame.

'Grandmother of God!' He backed away and saw his own reflection in the glass. Who was this – the bland pasty look of a prey animal? No more than a mile away a helicopter was weaving its bright light in figure-eights over what was unmistakably his Fortnum building, and unmistakably on fire.

I was happy once, Vartabedian thought. *I was on top of things, confident, rebuilding wrecks, honored for it. Is it all gone?*

For every emergency shelter-bed or transitional shelter-bed in Los Angeles, there are approximately twenty-five homeless souls every single night. The Ninth Circuit Court of Appeals determined that the amount of beds for the homeless was so ridiculously inadequate that they suspended the city's anti-street-camping ordinance within the official boundaries of The Nickel.

NINETEEN
You Can't Save the World By Yourself

The up staircase ended abruptly in a dark vestibule with a pitched roof and a locked door that led to the roof, and Jack Liffey's whole retinue started piling up behind him. The heat and now the growling animal noises of fire were gathering below them. Almost by instinct he yanked out the clumsy .38 Police Special and put his last three slugs straight into the doorframe where the latch-tongue would be, alarming everyone behind him to a frazzle and causing one of them to scream, but then he kicked the door open on fresh cool air. The doorframe was so rotten the shots had probably been unnecessary. But he was on the edge of panic himself, feeling responsible for so many lives.

The approach of fire pressed a sadistic thumb on one of his rawer nerves – not three years ago he'd been chased in a long scramble down through brush and gully by the wind-driven Malibu wildfire that they had taken to calling the Cold Canyon Fire. Cold Canyon, set by an arsonist at the height of the Santa Ana Winds, plus the arsonist himself had killed a Jamaican he'd come to like a lot, right beside him, along with several other hapless people, and it had burned out seventy-three 'structures,' as the fire department put it, many of them multi-million dollar homes.

The last of the Fortnum residents pushed out on to a tarpaper roof so dry that it crunched a bit underfoot, but it seemed to hold their weight well. Gloria hung back at the vestibule a moment, yelling into her cell phone. Jack Liffey walked cautiously to the knee-high parapet above Fifth Street, hearing a fire siren dying away below, and sure enough, six or seven stories down, a big ladder truck was deploying, with its men in yellow slickers hurrying this way and that. But they weren't raising the ladder yet, and that was absolutely all he had a mind to see.

'Dad!' Maeve was pointing.

A police helicopter approached like a killer Apache run from

Nam, coming in just above the roofs and blinding him for a moment with its big Nite-Sun beam that swept over him.

'Yeah, I see it.'

Gloria was done with her rant on the cell phone and started toward them.

'Close the door!' Jack Liffey shouted. All they needed was a heat flue to suck the fire upward.

Gloria went back and shouldered it shut. Several of their group began waving frantically to the approaching helicopter, as if it might miss them and fly straight past. He glanced down again and the firemen still hadn't begun to raise their ladder.

Conor squatted against the parapet, writing fast in his notebook, amazed that he'd found so much focus and intensity. He knew it was a way of trying to control his gathering dread, but it was better than letting fear take hold.

Day 7 later still

How does memory work? Last semester we read a book about it in Social Studies. It said memory was like cubby holes where images you've seen are stored away. You can get it all back, if you have to, with hypnosis or just superior recall – like one of those autistic savants, human telephone books. I don't think so. I argued with Mr LaRue that memory isn't like that at all. I'd seen too much self-deception. And Dad had just written a weird article on the chemistry of memory that was pretty hard to follow, but it convinced me that memory was really an active thing.

When I think back, sometimes, I get things pretty bad wrong. But the memory always <u>seems</u> right, no matter. I think what you really do is grab a few fragments, a few images, and your brain fills in the rest from what it <u>wants</u> to believe. The reality of this hotel fire will never be secure from my own fear of burning. Not for me. I will see Mr Liffey taking charge, Maeve standing by me, relive my own fears.

'Conor! Wake up! They need us to get off this side of the roof!'

Strange. Without meaning to, he had apparently drifted to the opposite side of the roof from everyone else, and Maeve was tugging him to his feet. A noisy helicopter was hovering directly over his head as if it wanted to come down. Lord! He was so intent on blocking things out that he hadn't even noticed.

She took his hand and they sprinted across the roof, driven into a crouch by the noise and beating of the aircraft descending, flailing their hair and clothing.

Omigod, he thought. Watching his feet on the black tarpaper as they ran past the vestibule in the exact center of the roof, he could see big bubbles swelling in the tar.

He did his best as he ran to call Maeve's attention to the boiling tar in the center of the roof, but she was too busy rescuing him and watching her father at work on the far side of the roof organizing others and pushing them across toward the chopper.

'They can only take three this time!' Jack Liffey said. 'No arguments! Women first!'

Jack Liffey coralled Felice and Millie and then grabbed Maeve and pushed them all into the blast of wind where the police helicopter hovered, only a foot above the roof, its overworked engine straining and groaning. A policeman in a black helmet leaned out the wide open doors to haul the women in. The skids tilted and touched down lightly from time to time as the big machine bobbed in its fierce struggle against gravity.

'They'll be back, and the ladder truck's sending up its ladder, too!'

'Dad, I won't leave you!' Maeve objected from beside the beast.

'I said no arguments! Go!'

Maeve wailed some complaint into the overwhelming noise as she was tugged aboard last by the officer at the same time she was pushed by her father.

'Don't you dare get hurt!' she shouted through cupped hands at her father as the machine rose straight up.

Jack Liffey flapped both arms upward in a needless shooing gesture as the chopper doors slid shut and the machine tilted forward and shot away, carrying Felice, Millie and Maeve. Next would be the old men and the boy, he thought. He and Gloria would go last.

Conor grabbed his shoulder and stabbed a finger wordlessly at the roof near the vestibule. *The tar, the tar*, he kept saying wordlessly. And the roof was clearly forming and popping big tarpit bubbles.

Oh, Christ, Jack Liffey thought, *leave me to worry about one thing at a time.*

Why was that damn ladder truck shilly-shallying?

He stared down off the edge of the roof to see a plume of fire shoot straight out of the hotel where the firetruck had once been parked. The truck had already backed away for some reason and was repositioning around the corner on San Julian where firemen were pouring streams of water over the building. *Take your time, guys,* he thought. *We've got all night up here.*

'Jack, Jack!' He knew Gloria needed his attention, but he'd heard the roof door flap open and on instinct he raced across to the vestibule and slammed the door shut with his back, feeling the escaping air like a blast-furnace. With his foot he scraped hot tar and torn crescents of tarpaper against the outside of the door. Then he took out his Swiss Army knife and shoved the blade into the door crack, pounding it home with the heel of his hand. None of this would hold for long.

'Jack!'

He looked at last and saw Gloria leaning hard on the parapet, pointed off to his right. In just that instant, he could tell that she had been injured and could barely stand up, and he wondered how it had happened. What turnabout! He wanted to go to her, but where she stared with such intensity drew his own gaze to the top of the fire-escape, arcing over the parapet, where the two old men were fighting over who would get on the fire-escape first.

'Stop! Stop!' Jack Liffey shouted. 'Don't even think about it! It's rusted out!' Why was this like herding squirrels? He hurried toward them.

'Listen, Mr Liffey, you got exactly what miracle to offer?' Greengelb insisted. 'You got to go *down* in fire! I shit on fire!'

'Fire is my *shtendik* enemy!' Morty began to titter and chatter in almost simian fashion, trying to force his way past Greengelb.

'Stop it! Look here!' They were so light; Jack Liffey tugged them both toward the corner of the roof above San Julian. 'The fire department is raising their ladder right now. We'll all be climbing down to have a beer in two minutes.'

'*Nu,* I'm already completely incinerated!' Morty Lipman announced, wavering where he stood.

Jack Liffey shoved them both to the ground. He'd pictured some kind of panic dragging all three of them over. The world was asking too much of him.

'You were both fighters!' Jack Liffey shouted. 'Wait for the pros!'

He turned back and saw that Gloria had crumpled on to the roof herself. 'Aw, *shit!*' Jack Liffey forgot the men, forgot everyone else and ran to her.

'I'm OK, Jack. I just twisted my ankle rounding up those women. It was stupid.'

'Can you stand up?'

'I think so.'

He offered an arm and felt the burden of too much of her weight as she hauled herself erect against him.

'Just set me on the ledge. You're damn good at taking charge, bless your heart.'

'Fire's coming up the stairwell, very soon,' he explained softly, because she deserved to know. And like invoking the name of the devil, the door of the vestibule blew open, and a fireball billowed out into the night air like a frightened being escaping something far worse below, followed in half a second by the deep *crump* of an explosion below. He reached out to hold her shoulder, some kind of superstition. 'We've got time,' he said, though he had no particular reason to think so. 'The firetruck is here.'

There was a roar and they all looked back – against their instincts – to see the entire vestibule blown upward thirty feet in a firestorm like the insistent flame of a blowtorch. The whole inferno below was apparently venting through this one chimney.

Jack Liffey had read somewhere of thirty-minute walls and sixty-minute walls, built into condos as a matter of county fire code to slow a fire and allow escape, but he bet nobody had heard of that when the Fortnum was built. They probably had two-minute walls at best.

'How you doing?'

'The ankle smarts – but hurting is just life. Don't let go of me yet.'

'Not *ever*, Gloria Ramirez. I swear to God, not ever.'

He could tell she wouldn't welcome any further emotion just then.

'Gentlemen! Gather over here,' Jack Liffey called and beckoned. 'You, too, Conor. Stop daydreaming. This is all real life.'

Greengelb gave Lipman a boost up and the two of them argued for a moment before starting toward Jack Liffey. Where was that fucking helicopter? He scanned the sky but saw nothing at all, which was strange. Usually the TV news choppers were on to any event like flies on shit. But, of course, this was only Skid Row, he thought. Only the homeless dying. Just the sparrows falling.

He steadied Gloria at the edge and then allowed himself to look over. With a sinking heart he saw they hadn't even budged the ladder yet. He had a burning urge to hurl an explosive down on the firetruck, see it burst into an orange fireball, and if he'd had a grenade handy he probably would have done it. OK, he told himself, there was a rational reason for the delay – they weren't idiots.

'They've got some kind of hitch,' he whispered to Gloria. 'But they'll come. Don't look down. Not where you're sitting.'

He heard a rending crash and glanced behind him to see a chunk of roof sailing away from a widened urgent flame that was howling straight upward like the flame out of a rocket engine. That would pretty much discourage the choppers, he thought.

'Let's think about this,' he said softly to Gloria. 'You've got the experience. We need to keep everybody calm.'

'Judging by your face, don't let them look over the edge.'

He sighed. 'I'm sure the ladder's coming, but there's some hangup.'

'Liffey!'

It was too late. Greengelb was stabbing his finger urgently over the parapet. Jack Liffey looked down to see the ladder truck pulling away from the building.

'What the fuck! Let me have the cell,' he said to Gloria.

She didn't even want to look, as if a light had gone out within her. He could see by her ashen skin and clenched teeth that she was in intense pain. He punched in 911.

'Please state your emergency—'

'Shut up and listen! I'm on the roof of the building that's burning down on The Nickel, the Fortnum Hotel, and your ladder truck is driving away. I have five people up here who need help. What the *hell* is going on? I want to know *now*!'

'Sir, I'm sure that—'

'Don't you fucking reassure me! Put me in touch with someone who knows what's happening.'

'Sir, I'm sure they're—'

'Stop now! One of the people up here is a cop who's hurt – and I swear to God, the way she's looking right now she's going to come down there and shoot you dead if I tell her you're saying one more meaningless word to me.'

All he heard at the other end was a kind of electronic wind. He looked over to see Gloria suppressing a grin. 'Great, Jack. Maybe they'll all just drive away now.'

The noise of the venting flame had become almost intolerable – a jet airliner fifty feet overhead – and the flame had eaten a big rude shape in the roof.

The others had gathered around him, but he heard a squawk coming back from Gloria's cell in his hand. He could see she was almost unconscious with the hurt and he supported her back, on the parapet.

'Hello, are you on the roof?'

'Yes, I am. Who is this?'

'This is Fire Captain David McConnell. We're doing our very best with mechanical problematics here, sir. We'll get you down, we will.'

'Define the crap you just said.'

'Please don't be angry. This never happens, but it did. The ladder mechanism on one of our trucks locked up. They test it every week. But you don't care about that. Another truck will be here in minutes. In the meantime we're going to be spraying you with water to keep you cool. We can do that. Is that all right?'

'Man, is a bear Catholic? Look, if your folks can get inside the hotel, there's a black policewoman in the lobby who's injured. Possibly shot.'

'Do you know where she is in the lobby, sir?'

He noticed that the man's voice didn't even betray a hitch at the word 'shot.' How could you become that inured to catastrophe? He shook Gloria's shoulder to call her to full consciousness. 'Where do you think Paula is?'

She came around, barely, and he felt the weight against him lessen. 'Near the basement door, behind the counter.'

He repeated it.

'Stay on the line, sir. I'm going to hand you over to firefighter Willie Stone while I attend to things. You're in good hands. Is that OK with you?'

'Go, go!'

'Hello, sir.'

'Hello, Willie. How come you're expendable?'

The man laughed once. 'I'm a rookie, but my dad was a big fire hero so they keep me close to the captain. And I know what I'm doing. Who are you?'

'My name is Jack, and I've got four other people up here that I'm responsible for: a teenage boy, two very old men and a police officer who's my wife and who's nearly unconscious with injury. Tell me the truth about the chopper.'

There was the tiniest of hesitations. 'Aerial won't be back, sir. Not with a twenty-meter plume of flame shooting out of the roof. Sorry, Jack, the Fortnum looks like a birthday cake from hell. But it's all defined procedure now. We've got you. It's a toss-up whether Westlake Number Eleven from Seventh and Union, or Chinatown Number Four from North Main will get there first to replace the defective truck. They're both less than a mile away and coming like hell on their sirens. They'll be there damn fast, I promise you.'

He could hear the wails approaching. 'Have you got guys inside yet?'

'Yes, just now. Tommy Smiley from Station Number Nine with a full silver firesuit and oxygen.'

A mist began wafting across the roof and then a steadier patter, plopping down on them. 'Whoa, we got water here.'

'Good. You'll get more, sir.'

And as he said it, the artificial rain redoubled.

'I suppose that's reassuring,' Jack Liffey said dubiously.

'Yes, sir.' The man didn't add, 'That's probably all it's good for,' but Jack Liffey could sense that's what he was thinking.

The water streams arcing down at several points couldn't do anything about the superhot flare in the middle of the roof, steaming away to nothing as they approached it, but he noticed that where water pattered down on the tarpaper nearby it was starting to boil off to a fog, and he felt the roof getting tacky under his shoes.

Then the water began to splash heavily on to them and became a little unpleasant.

'You got an ETA for those ladder trucks?' Jack Liffey asked.

But Willie Stone was apparently otherwise occupied, though the phone crackled as if the line was still open.

'I'm a narc!' Thibodeaux shouted, as they surrounded him. 'You're all in real trouble now!'

'Man, you're so fulla shit your eyes are brown.'

'I'm going to set off a grenade and take you all to hell with me!'

A man named G-dog tripped him from behind and several of them pinned the minuscule white man down to the street against his desperate thrashing.

'Listen up, assclown, you nothing at all!' G-Dog shouted in his face. 'Stay the fuck still.'

Two police officers were striding their way toward them – Smarty and Pantsy, as they were known locally, but not to their faces. Chopper Tyrus was sitting on the curb, holding his stomach and arm where he'd been stabbed, and he was moaning a little, but he didn't appear to be bleeding badly. A middle-aged woman held out with two fingers the large knife someone had grabbed from Thibodeaux – as if it were a dead rodent.

'Officers! That there's the cutter who attacked us. You gots to take him.'

Is there more vanity in holding on to your miserable scribblings or in throwing them carelessly into a fire to suggest that you just don't care about your own ego and its outpourings?

'Stop writing now, Conor! You have to pay attention to what's happening right here!' He wasn't actually writing. Jack Liffey grabbed the small black notebook out of his hand as he seemed to be contemplating tossing it toward the pillar of flame.

Ironically, he came near doing the same thing out of pique. But he hesitated, with a glance at the boy, as if to check whether he was worthy. The whole world around them was transforming into a miasma of hot fog.

'I'm sorry, sir. I'm a bad accident, I think. Go on and throw it in the fire. It's valueless.'

He tucked the notebook into his pocket with a grimace. 'Maybe everybody deserves to try to be known.'

Moses Vartabedian had finally managed to get the smeary little sash window in his supply room to stutter up eighteen inches, and his chin rested on the sill, his eyes fixed on the scene outside – a single towering flame rising off the roof and more fire down at street level. The blaze was obviously well on its way to consuming any hope for a Fortnum Luxury Lofts, the heart of the new arts downtown. The rear of a big firetruck was visible peeking around the building from San Julian and fire hoses seemed to be having little effect.

He watched the tiny moving figures on the roof of his dying hotel with the water streams playing over them. The instant he'd first seen those human apostrophes in obvious danger, he knew he was utterly ruined. Every dark alley of his thought process yawned open. His building as good as gone. Journalists would be after him. Detectives at his door. Maybe even off to prison for hiring those two sad sacks.

He had no doubts, really, no rationales to struggle with any more. McCall and Thibodeaux had gone apeshit over there for some reason – predictably, he supposed, but expressly against orders. Yet who in the press or the D.A's office was going to take the side of an Armenian slumlord? A man with far more money in the bank than any of them had. *Look here, people, a prime example of immigrant greed.* And he'd contributed to them all, too – election years, public record – so they'd be forced to make an example of him to exonerate themselves.

All he'd ever wanted to do was his part to make the city better and more habitable, more beautiful, one or two buildings at a time. It did no favor to the homeless to bottle them all up in that one sewer of neglect, and certainly did no favor to the city. The Nickel. Skid Row. He hated those expressions. The New Arts District was what it would be. It was just starting to happen and would come to fruition one day, but without him now, he knew that.

'They're here!' Jack Liffey yelled.

As fate would have it, both the replacement ladder trucks arrived at the same moment and began to defer like mad to one another – Alphonse and Gaston – but finally one conceded the game and the other one backed up to another flank of the building. None too soon. The blowtorch flame had been carving the roof outward minute by minute despite all the water pouring onto it. One section of roof toward the far edge had caved in and was leaking ugly black smoke. They hugged one another in the artificial rain and fog, their immediate world getting very warm and humid.

'Willie! Willie Stone!' Jack Liffey called into the cell phone.

'I'm here, Jack. Sorry – had to check in.'

'Look, I've got two very old men up here and a woman with a broken ankle.' Gloria opened one eye to his statement and he waved her quiet. 'What can you do for me?'

'I can't send you a chopper now, no shit, man. That's in the protocol. I can send you some gorillas strong enough to carry anyone down a ladder.'

Jack Liffey thought of trying to carry Gloria himself, and he knew damn well he couldn't. You can't save the world by yourself, and sometimes you can't even save a small part of it.

'Send the gorillas,' he said.

In the first decade of the twenty-first century, despite endless political posturing about 'doing something about homelessness,' the net change in affordable housing in Los Angeles was a decrease of 11,000 units. And over this time about 7 per cent of the homeless – the invisible homeless out in the suburbs – had become divorced middle-class women who were sleeping in their aging SUVs and spending their days in libraries and malls.

EPILOGUE
Walls

T he next time he looked down, both ladder trucks had outriggers planted, and one ladder was already on its way up toward him like an arm reaching slowly for something on the top shelf. Several other firetrucks were parked anyhow and they still emitted scurrying men in yellow overcoats who were carrying big sacks and cases of unidentifiable apparatus. Jack Liffey took a few steps and felt the tar underfoot suck and grab at his feet.

'I feel like this all happened before,' the boy said, staring down at the ladder trucks.

'It did,' Jack Liffey said. 'Just not to us.' Something made him think, *I need to calculate time differently now, or the night will be made horrible with our cries*. 'Gloria goes first, carried down,' he announced.

He could tell she was about to demur.

'You're hurt. We've got to get you out of our way. Go with it now, there's too many people to argue!'

She seemed to give up and withdraw into herself again. It was as if she drew in all slack, all softness, gathered it into a hardened unresponsive core. He was not even sure whether it was something she was actually doing or some warp of his own consciousness under the influence of his fear.

He did his best not to look at the biblical pillar of fire that was so loud now it made them shout to be heard. Look or not, it warmed their backs and sides unpleasantly and filled the air with the tang of asphalt and char. The last time he'd had a peek, the flame had gnawed itself a dramatically larger vent and was apparently spreading through something stored in the attic or whatever lay directly beneath them. And now the roof trembled underfoot like an endless subway train.

Abruptly the top of the first fire ladder appeared, bristling with hose attachments, lamps and strange sockets. It poked up over the parapet and then stopped at eye level, swaying in mid-air, the periscope-weapon of a movie alien come to visit.

He glanced down quickly and two big men were scrambling up the ladder fast, tugging themselves along by the handrails. The lead guy was black, still a bit unusual in the fire department as far as he'd seen. The second ladder was about halfway up and coming. At last, at last.

Heat welled around them, plus unendurable bellowy noise. He could barely rip his feet out of the tar. Jack Liffey held on hard to whatever composure he could muster, but he was starting to lose his focus.

'So, *nu*, I suppose we trust this *shtarker*?'

Jack Liffey looked at the two old men, who had touchingly linked their arms, obviously very frightened, waiting trustingly in front of him. 'Stand right here. You're number two, and you're third, after Gloria.'

'*Oy*, you're right but you're wrong.'

'No arguments.'

'No but yes.'

Chopper Tyrus sat straight up, holding his gut and wondering if he'd been forgotten. It wouldn't have surprised him. Luckily the bleeding seemed to have slowed to a slow seep. Nearby, the cops had taken over wrestling with the strange little white man, who was bucking and screaming about his inalienable rights, and most everybody else was watching with more fret than satisfaction. MaryLou was still trying to interest the police in the knife, like a vendor with a day-late fish.

'Today is my birthday,' Chopper said, bemused, to the dark empty air.

'Birthdays ain't what they used to be,' a man he didn't know commented with a wry twist of his lips.

'Yes, friend, I believe that a true statement.' He heard a siren, and his practiced ear could tell that this one was an ambulance. He felt a sense of relief. A night or two in a real bed up in County, real food, attended by kindly women.

'Hey, could one o' you gents look after my stuffs? I think I go away for a time. It right back there in the blue condo.'

'Chopper, man, I look after it for you. You know me, Jonas. But you been saved by the blood of the lamb?'

He could see that Gloria was doing her best to tolerate the classic fireman's carry, lying head forward across the big black man's shoulder, one of his arms bunching up her skirt across the inside of her right knee as his hand came around front to hold her right wrist. So encumbered, he backed expertly down the ladder, sliding his free hand in fits and grabs. Before giving in to her pain, she had glanced up for an instant at Jack Liffey. It only took that instant to read: *You will never mention this to any of my colleagues, under the very worst of penalties.*

A second big fireman had snapped, 'I'm Don, come closer.' He stabbed a control box into one of the receptacles at the top end of the ladder as if he were angry at it.

'We're only allowed five hundred pounds on the ladder at a time and were almost there now,' Don explained, mostly to Jack Liffey. 'But we can't wait.' Nobody needed to mention that the fire had noisily engulfed more than half the roof. The fireman had spun off his big yellow coat and was letting the others shelter from the heat behind it. As he used his controls to manipulate the ladder to angle down to rest against the masonry, he shouted to Jack Liffey, 'I'll brace it and take a chance. Bring me one now.'

The second ladder was just appearing, rearing its own movie alien face a few yards away.

Jack Liffey shoved Morty Lipman at the fireman.

Lipman's eyes went wide as the big man swung him bodily through the air and deposited him on the ladder. 'Go down as fast as you can, man! If you hang us up, I'll kick you off!'

They all knew he wouldn't, but Lipman started down as if bee-stung, clamping his eyes shut against panic. It wasn't the way Jack Liffey had envisioned it at all, but it was working.

A section of roof right behind them gave way with a howl and a wave of sparks washed over the coat and then over them. They all ducked down to protect themselves from the new heat.

'We all go now,' the firefighter said. 'Don't wait for the other ladder. You!' He grabbed Samuel Greengelb, and swung him on to the ladder. 'Go!'

Conor Lewis shielded himself in front of Jack Liffey leaning into him. 'I'm burning up.'

'The boy next!' Jack Liffey shouted.

'But where's my dad? I want to know about my dad!'

'Honey, calm down. I'm sure he's OK.' A woman in a blue uniform – fire? police? – was trying to give Maeve Liffey a

Styrofoam cup of coffee that smelled rancid, but she didn't like coffee of any kind.

Maeve pushed the cup way. She felt tight and angry. 'Do you know how annoying that is when I know for a fact you don't have a clue about my dad?'

'Sorry, hon. I'll go find out.'

One ambulance had already howled off carrying Paula Green. She was in bad shape, but might make it. Jack Liffey sat tenderly on the curb beside the fire engine, resting his hands on his knees. He was careful to hold as still as he could and not disturb the burns on his back and shoulders. They'd given him something like codeine, and the pain was tolerable, but just.

He'd gone next to last, right after the fire had virtually engulfed them on the roof, but the firefighter Don, going last an instant later, had reclaimed his fire coat and seemed pretty much OK now. Most of the back of Jack Liffey's favorite linen and wool jacket had charred away, and some of his shirt beneath it, too. An EMT with a weird flat-top had slathered his burned back with some sticky white ointment and then hurried off to check the others.

Jack Liffey's attention was caught by a movement across the street. He glanced over and saw what was unmistakably Eleanor Ong – or Sister Mary Rose, watching him from behind a car without much emotion. He beckoned, and she shook her head. He had a feeling this might be the last time he would ever see her, and he tried to beckon, more urgently. She smiled and shook her head. Then she gave him a big thumbs-up. OK, sister. This is the best you can do. You're negating the last goodbye message you offered me: I don't think you're going to make it.

After a few minutes of contemplation, Conor came and sat down next to him. The boy appeared unhurt, though maybe a little sunburned. What a difference a few moments of escape could make.

'Hi, Mr Liffey.'

'Are you ready to go home?' Jack Liffey asked him, not unkindly.

'I guess. Nothing like a big scare. I miss Mom and Dad.'

'Did you learn anything important out here?'

The boy smiled, then glanced around himself, as if for dangerous beasts. Jack handed him his notebook and he took it with a glum smile. 'The poor manage to stay so upbeat. It's incredible to me. They're much more kind than the people I grew up with.'

'Yes, I think so, too.'

'Liffey!' The EMT with the flat-top strode their way and reached down to tug Jack Liffey to his feet. 'Your daughter has been moving heaven and hell to find out how you are.'

'I'm going to live, right?'

The man stepped around and plucked at some torn cloth on Jack Liffey's back, each pluck a twinge of pain. 'You won't live forever, but a while yet. If you're virtuous.'

'What does virtue have to do with it?'

'It's always a good idea.'

'Fuck you. Get me a stronger painkiller.'

'Tell his daughter he's got a big mouth but he's OK,' he barked into a radio.

The man sat him on the edge of a gurney near an untended ambulance and left him there.

Jack Liffey looked around him and realized that the Fortnum was right at the cutting edge of gentrification. A fancy refurbished building just across the street had a doorman standing just inside the thick glass doors, wearing an implausible red sash, like some factotum out of Graham Greene.

And what had he himself learned through this mess – through the weeks trapped in the wheelchair, the immobility and loss of speech, the days on Skid Row, and now the preposterous trial by fire?

He stared across the street again to see the windowless bottom floor of the gentrified building that had been artfully disguised as pattern but was really a blank windowless concrete wall. A wall to keep out even the curiosity of the poor. This new model for society was taking on an overwhelming power: the blank wall. The wall between us and discomfort, us and the poor, us and *them*, with all their grief and rage.

There were fresh walls everywhere in America now, so many since he'd grown up. Separating the needy homeless and the new Downtowners. Walls and gates around the fancy suburbs. Walls at the *frontera* between so many desperate workers and the jobs in *El Norte*. Walls, he thought, between genuine deprivation and the lies that denied the existence of deprivation.

It seemed to him the essential activity of the rich and powerful these days was to build these walls. Of concrete, of disguised foliage, of electronics, of military power, of spy satellites – plus an opaque media that ignored it all. The time of the walled-out and defeated and homeless seemed to stretch on forever now, but it couldn't.

How can anyone go on living their lives, he thought, without an impulse toward tearing down walls? But in his heart he knew his daughter would have that impulse, and so would the Lewis boy.

ENDNOTES

All statistics and other information on homelessness in Los Angeles come from the following sources:

Anderson, Troy, 'Homeless Plan Stirs Debate Among Board [of Supervisors],' *Los Angeles Daily News*, March 28, 2006.

Bartholomew, Dana, 'Transients Hope to Get Back into Stable Life,' *Los Angeles Daily News*, April 7, 2006.

Blasi, Gary, Michael Dear and Jennifer Wolch, '5 Steps to Get Out of Skid Row,'*LA Times*, December 31, 2006.

Blasi, Gary, 'Policing Our Way Out of Homelessness? The First Year of the Safer Cities Initiative on Skid Row,' *The UCLA School of Law Fact Investigation Clinic*, September 24, 2007.

California Budget Project, *A Generation of Widening Inequality*, Sacramento, CA, August 2007.

Cousineau, Michael R., 'Dumping the Homeless on Hospitals,' *LA Times*, December 31, 2006.

DiMassa, Cara Mia, 'L.A. County OKs "Historic" Homeless Plan,' *LA Times*, April 5, 2006.

DiMassa, Cara Mia and Richard Winton, 'Possible Homeless Centers Identified,' *LA Times*, April 6, 2006.

Fry, Richard, 'Labor Market Outcomes of Hispanics by Generation,' *ERIC Clearinghouse on Urban Education, Institute for Urban and Minority Education*, October 10, 2003.

Geis, Sonya, 'L.A. Police Initiative Thins Out Skid Row,' *Washington Post*, March 15, 2007.

George, Evan, 'Teaching Junkies to Save Each Other's Lives,' *Los Angeles Daily Journal*, January 17, 2008.

Hoag, Christina, 'L.A. Seeing More People Living Out of Their Cars,' *TIME* Magazine, June 23, 2008.

Inter-University Consortium Against Homelessness, *2008 Report Card On Homelessness In Los Angeles*, University of Southern California, June 2008.

Jordan, Miriam, 'Blacks vs. Latinos at Work,' *The Wall Street Journal*, January 24, 2006.

Los Angeles Homeless Services Authority, '2007 Greater Los Angeles Homeless Count,' Los Angeles, CA 90013.

Tong, Eugene, 'Homeless Plan Raises Optimism: New County Step Watched,' *Los Angeles Daily News*, April 6. 2006.

Valle, Ramón, 'Los Angeles: City of the Stars Becomes US Homeless Capital,' *World Socialist Web Site*, October 17, 2005.

Villaraigosa, Antonio (Mayor) and Jan Perry (Councilwoman), 'Appraising the County's Homeless Plan,' (Op-Ed) *LA Times*, April 6, 2006.